MORDOR, CALIFORNIA

NICK BASCOM

switchboard
PUBLISHING

For my sons, who are just starting their quests. My heart goes with you, always and everywhere.

And for Uncle Harry, who is waiting for all of us in Middle-earth.

"There is more in you of good than you know, child of the kindly West. Some courage and some wisdom, blended in measure. If more of us valued food and cheer and song above hoarded gold, it would be a merrier world."

— Thorin Oakenshield

1

REBEL FRED

The mutants were close. He could practically taste the radiation in the air. The attack could come any second now, and with everyone expecting assaults on the White House, the Pentagon, and the giant Dippin' Donuts just down the street, no one was protecting the school! He had tried to warn everybody that the school was the real target, but his "superior" officers had laughed at him. They didn't think aliens would care about a grade school in a small southern Oregon town, but he knew better. These weren't your average evil mutants from Jupiter's plasma moon—these guys were smarter. And if he didn't stop them, they'd wipe out the whole fourth grade and blow up the school!

On second thought, he decided if something had to go, it might as well be the school. Fighting a mutant army was not a turn on the tire swing, after all. There was no way he could save everything. But if these mutants thought he would lay down his ray guns and let them take the kickball field, they had another thing coming. He was Commander Fred T. Hawkhammer, and he would not be defeated!

His troops were another story, though, and he sighed heavily as he looked them over. Some of the poor souls were nothing but boys—chubby-cheeked and wide-eyed—and he had been forced to use them in countless battles already. They were still recovering from the Massacre at the Monkey Bars, and they hadn't eaten anything but gruel for months. Even Fred was starting to think he'd rather take a mutant laser bolt to the gut than endure another 'Meatloaf Monday' or 'Fish-stick Friday.'

For a moment he thought he might rally his tired troops with the totally brilliant speech he had just made up on the spot, but there was no time. With a sudden, sharp crackle and thunderous boom, the alarm rang out. Soon all sorts of nasty looking creatures were lurching across the kickball field on their crooked mutant limbs. Some of them had pointy jaws like insects, while others had no mouths at all. Still the mutants managed a terrifying battle cry. For a moment, Fred thought it sounded almost like a hopscotch song, and his intestines started playing double-dutch with his heart.

The mutants must have outnumbered them a hundred to one, but Fred wasn't going to let that stop him. Giving a shout of his own, he finally burst from cover, leading his troops into the fray. He dodged laser beams and flying shrapnel as he searched for a better attack position. His ray guns took out mutants by the millions. A glowing heap of neon bodies filled the mulch bed between the tire swing and basketball hoop.

Dashing across the blacktop, he came up below the mutant flagship. Through the shifting smoke, he caught a quick glimpse of the strange letters painted on its side. It had been years since he'd spoken Jupiterian, but this was one name known to everyone this side of the Milky Way.

"*The Golden Dragon*," he said aloud, the little hairs on the back of his neck standing up like frozen tetherball poles. The most feared starship in twelve galaxies was speeding right for him. And every one of its thousand cannons was shooting giant bolts of fire!

He didn't know what to do! *The Golden Dragon* was invincible, or at least that's what everyone said. There were rumors of a single weak spot in the ship's armor, but, unfortunately for Fred, no one had ever gotten close enough, or lived long enough, to spot it. If he wanted to bring the dreaded ship down, he'd have to find the chink in its armor on his own. It would put him in the worst kind of danger to keep searching for it—laser bolts were zipping by close enough to burn the hair on his bulging, muscle-bound arms—but Fred knew he had to find the weak spot if he wanted to save his troops.

Though he could barely see the sky now through all the smoke and laser fire, he ran deeper into enemy territory and kept searching. A gust of wind blew the smoke clear for an instant, and a volley of blaster fire lit up the underside of the gargantuan ship. That's when he saw it: the tiny hole hidden just behind one of the ship's giant warp engines. Fred had been lucky to get this close, and he knew he would only get one shot to take the ship down. He ripped a grenade from his belt and bit off the clip. Taking careful aim, he chucked the bomb towards *The Golden Dragon*. He had to dive to avoid a giant laser blast, but he managed to get back up in time to see the grenade disappear into the hole. A second later, the ship was rocked by a huge explosion—one of its giant engines tearing away in a flash of fiery metal. *The Golden Dragon* started spinning wildly, dropping mutants and metal all over the kickball field.

With a final burst of flame and a deafening thud, it crashed to the earth.

His troops shouted in triumph, and Fred pumped his fist in the air. It looked like they just might send the mutants back to Jupiter's plasma moon with their tentacles tucked between their... other tentacles. With their flagship destroyed, the mutants were fully on the retreat.

Fred was preparing to tell his troops to mop up the scattered mutants when an excruciating screech erupted from the wreckage of *The Golden Dragon*. Searing pain sizzled through Fred's entire skull. He fell to his knees, grabbing his ears because he was worried the sheer agony might cause them to drop straight from his head.

The vast, horrible noise that was all around him suddenly sharpened into a single blade. "Fred!" it bellowed, slicing at his mind. He doubled over in pain, still clutching at his head.

How do the mutants know my name? They must already have spies in my ranks, he thought. *Was there anything these mutants wouldn't do?*

"Fred!" the mysterious creature shrieked yet again, and radio waves drilled into Fred's mind even worse than before, rattling his brain like a jackhammer. "What did I tell you about throwing rocks?"

Fred tried to rise to his feet but couldn't. The pain in his head was too intense. He had to concentrate just to keep breathing as the agonizing sound grew closer. Just when Fred thought he couldn't bear the pain any longer, the smoke parted. Fred gasped at what he saw striding out of the smoke. It was a thing of pure horror. A Titanium Encased Android Capable of Hypnotic Electrolyzing Radiowaves—the dreaded **T.E.A.C.H.E.R** model of robotic warrior!

Fred's tart was officially toasted.

He gathered every ounce of courage he had left to answer the robot. "Umm...that I should warm up first or else I'll throw out my arm," he taunted, trying to sound unafraid. If his men saw him take any lip from the **T.E.A.C.H.E.R**, they'd crumple like empty soda cans.

The android raised a plasma-cannon-sized arm and pointed it at him. "Sass me back one more time, and you'll have inside recess for the rest of the year," it screamed. "And I'm not going to say it again—when the bell rings, recess is over. Now get in line."

Fred fought against the hypnotic waves the **T.E.A.C.H.E.R** was shooting at him, but he was powerless to resist. It was as if the android had put invisible handcuffs on his wrists. He was forced to obey the android's order and watched his platoon do the same and fall in line behind him. The **T.E.A.C.H.E.R** was leading them back towards the school, and Fred guessed that the mutants had already taken the school and turned the classrooms into dungeons to hold his troops. They were surely leading him to a torture chamber, but he was not afraid. Let them try to torture him. He would show them a thing or two about cour—

"Yo, Fred," someone called out from behind him. This time it was a human voice interrupting his thoughts. Fred turned and watched his best friend Stan skip ahead in line to talk to him. Stan's smile was so big, Fred's imagined battle scene flickered and faded. The giant spaceships and smoking fires slowly disappeared, until he and Stan were walking across a regular playground with slides and swing sets and snot-nosed kids swarming everywhere.

"What's up?" replied Fred. Without his imaginary eye-patch, armor, and ray guns, he was now just a lanky, brown-haired boy disappointed that recess was already over.

What is a boy? No doubt these strange creatures need some description nowadays, since it seems they are growing up faster than ever before. In fact, some babies have been known to turn directly into businessmen. Soon boys might fade entirely into myth, so it is best to describe them now while they are still among us.

For the most part, they are a little people, boys, but, unlike the dwarves, they have no beards. Some of the older ones have ugly little mustaches but nothing more than that. Though smallish in nature, boys have hearty appetites. They tend to eat seven or eight meals a day, if you consider chocolate milk and cookies a meal, that is, and some boys have been known to grow to trollish proportions. Boys chatter constantly, and they have mischievous little laughs, which can be heard most clearly when they are playing tricks on teachers or girls. Unlike some other creatures, boys don't typically have hair on their feet. But they do go barefoot in the summer months, and sometimes their feet get so dirty it *looks* as if they're covered in hair. That's why boys wear sneakers most of the time—to hide how dirty their feet are. Generally, they are not tidy creatures. Some of the messier ones even put goblins to shame. Boys also enjoy horseplay, video games, comic books, and adventure, and there is more than a little magic about them —especially the boys at the heart of this particular adventure.

"I just wanted to know who we're going to fight on Monday," Stan asked Fred, "the dinosaur biker army from Rexxog 4 or the cyborg zombie horde from Nocttoon 7?"

"Um… I'm not sure," said Fred. "Why?"

"I was just trying to decide which tennis shoes I should wear," said Stan.

"I see," said Fred, rubbing his chin. "It's always good to be prepared, and I wish I could tell you, but it all depends on who attacks us. Unfortunately, we don't get to choose our enemies. If we did, it would be a whole lot easier."

Stan shrugged. "I'll just wear my Heelys, then," he said. "That way I'm ready for anything."

Fred gave him a thumbs up.

"Are you riding the bus back home today?" Stan asked him

"No, my mom is picking me up," Fred said, smiling. He hadn't seen his mother in a while and was looking forward to the ride, even if she was only ferrying him back to his father's house, where he stayed most of the time. "But you should come by the tree house later because she says she's got some new comics for me."

"Good for you," said Stan, smirking. "Just don't think that's going to get you out of taking a beating in Magic."

Fred sighed. He was not nearly as excited to play Stan in Magic as he was to see his mother, but this was only because Stan had just added one of the best creatures in the game to his deck. Stan had pulled off a ridiculous trade with the most gullible student in their class to get the card (Stan had only given away three marbles, two of which had been promptly swallowed). Even though Fred knew he could never beat Stan as long as his best friend had this card, he had no choice but to play. Losing at Magic was still a lot better than the alternative.

Later that afternoon, Joanne, the woman who had been dating Fred's dad for the past six months, was throwing a birthday party for her own father—a large, surly bald man named Leo. Of course, she had decided to throw her party on Fred's front lawn. So even though Fred and Stan spent most afternoons in Fred's tree house, today they had even more reason to do so. Fred absolutely hated Joanne, Leo, and all their friends and would do anything to avoid speaking to them, even let Stan crush him at Magic cards.

"Just don't rub it in too much when you win," Fred said as they entered the classroom, "because then we'll have to play Mario Kart, and you don't want any part of that."

"Bring it on," said Stan. "You couldn't hit a Chomp Chain if it were chewing your fender."

"Cut the chatter!" said their teacher, Mrs. Bonneville, before Fred could respond. "I'm this close to splitting you up for the afternoon." She raised her hand high above her head. "I mean I've had it up to here with you today," she corrected, this time pinching the air with her thumb and index finger. "Oh, it's only lunchtime and you've already done it to me," she said over the class's laughter. Out of frustration, she kicked the last remaining box of brightly colored decorations that had belonged to the class's beloved former teacher, Mr. Louis, who had departed suddenly and under mysterious circumstances. The wife of a wealthy, local businessman, Mrs. Bonneville had been the only one available on short notice to take over for Mr. Louis, and Fred shared his mother's suspicion that Mrs. Bonneville had been partly responsible for Mr. Louis's sudden disappearance.

Lydia Bonneville, whose students called her "Mrs. B" not because they liked her but because they had trouble pronouncing her name, was a tall, broad-shouldered woman with a booming voice. Today, the unseasonal heat was causing rivulets of sweat to mess with her makeup so that Fred thought it looked as if her face was slowly melting, or as if she was wearing a mask that didn't quite fit....

Fred smacked himself in the head. He couldn't believe he hadn't realized what was going on sooner. "Stan!" he whispered out of the corner of his mouth as they took their seats. "The mutants have upgraded their **T.E.A.C.H.E.R.s** with human suits!"

Stan didn't look over at him. He watched Mrs. B nervously as he raised his finger to his lips to silently signal to Fred to keep quiet. Fred couldn't tell if Stan believed him or not, but it didn't matter—he was convinced. None of the other teachers wore such fancy dresses, high heels, or sparkling jewelry to school. It was as if she and the other mutants had tried to figure out how humans dress by looking at magazine covers.

When Mrs. B turned her back to write something on the board, Fred leaned over and whispered to Stan again: "I think she's been stealing our comics to brew a potion that will keep her human suit from falling apart! But it's starting to melt. See?" Fred pulled his cheeks down and rolled his eyes up into his skull, but Stan wasn't looking at him. He was still watching Mrs. B closely to make sure she hadn't heard them talking.

When Stan finally responded it was in such a quiet whisper Fred almost had to slide into Stan's seat to hear him. "You know she just hates comics because she thinks they're filth that only lazy people read," he said. Fred wasn't buying that for a second. There was no way Bruce Wayne, who worked all day running an enterprise and then fought crime all night, could be called lazy. Fred knew what was really going on. And he wasn't going to lose any more of his Batman comics just so Mrs. Bonneville, or whoever she was, could keep tricking everyone into believing she was human.

He also hadn't forgotten that the last time Mrs.

Bonneville snatched a comic from him she told him his imagination was "overactive," which is just what the doctors had said about his great Aunt Tess' thyroid gland right before they had taken it out. Fred thought if Mrs. Bonneville ever managed to drag him to her underground lair, she'd try to remove his imagination in just the same way—without giving him any of that giggle gas he got at the dentist's office. Well, there was no way in Helm's Deep he was going to let that happen.

"We've got to get the comics back and drain her energy source," Fred said to Stan. "We'll need some grappling hooks and ninja stars and probably a canister of glowing green oo—"

"Would you shut it!" Stan whispered through his teeth. "I don't want to get held back from art class again."

Excited as he was to plan a heist, Fred had to admit that Stan made a good point—art class was the one subject he never wanted to miss either. "You're right," he said. "That will be the perfect time to draw up some diagrams of Mrs. B's underground lair." Fred winked at Stan and then sat forward in his seat, pretending to pay attention as his teacher turned to address the class.

"You can keep your art notebooks in your desks today, children," she said, smirking, it seemed, almost directly at Fred. "In fact, you can take them home with you today. You won't be wasting any more time in that little farts and crafts class for the rest of the year."

Fred felt like an action figure that had just had its arms and legs torn off. He stared in anger and amazement back at Mrs. B. *She's on to us, and she's striking first,* he thought. *Smart move, mutant.*

"We'll be taking advantage of all that time spent butchering hot cross buns in music class, too," she continued, ignoring the gasps of surprise from the twin violinists in the front row. "The school board has finally given me permission to start my *Win the Work* program, so for the rest of the week we'll be taking a series of aptitude tests and then placing you on appropriate career tracks." She was clearly hoping for cheers and applause, but the class stared back at her, stunned into silence. Mrs. B's smile wilted, and her eyes scanned the room like a terminator searching for a target. Unfortunately for Fred, her lifeless eyes locked onto him.

"First, we're going to go around the room and have everyone tell the class what it is that your parents do." Jenny Mitchell was begging to go first—bouncing in her seat and flapping her hand like a jittery flipper in the air—but Mrs. B's gaze didn't waver. "Mr. Oglesburg, why don't you go first? You are the perfect one to show the class how important it is to choose a solid career path."

"What do you mean?" growled Fred.

Mrs. B smiled so big then she accidentally exposed some of the titanium teeth at the back of her mouth. "Well for starters, your stepmother tells me your grandfather has gone directly from magician to mental institution."

"She's not my stepmother!" Fred shouted. "And she's the one who put him in that rotten place."

"Watch your tone, Mr.," said Mrs. Bonneville. "That's no way to talk about someone who sacrifices her own career just so she can take care of you."

Fred nearly melted through his seat in shock. This was a boldfaced lie. Joanne had never sacrificed anything in her life. She didn't work because she was lazier than a blanket. Joanne didn't even clean her own martini glasses, and she'd never lifted a finger to help Fred with anything.

Mrs. B never gave Fred a chance to protest. "But it's

your parents I want you to tell the class about, anyway," she said.

"Fine," said Fred. "My *real* mom is an amazing writer. She writes fantasy novels, and she even does the illustrations. She's written *The Ghost Sword of Tol'tha'nor* and *The Nymphe Queen of Mystia* and..."

"But is there anything you'd like to add about her...situation, Fred?" Mrs. Bonneville interjected.

"Just that her books make the *Hunger Games* read like a happy meal wrapper and you should all buy them," said Fred.

"If that's what will get her out of the trailer park, I'll buy one myself," said Mrs. B with a little sneer.

Fred nearly pulled a muscle trying to get his eyes to shoot lasers at Mrs. Bonneville, but her human suit must have been creating some kind of force-field that suppressed his super powers. He eventually gave it up and sank back down in his seat.

"Tsk, tsk, Fred," said Mrs. B. "I didn't say you were finished. Tell us what your father does for a living. We need some *positive* examples, too."

Fred was sick of this exercise. "Nothing important," he said.

"Now, Fred, we both know that's not true," said Mrs. Bonneville. "Your father is very successful. He and my wonderful husband do business together all the time. Tell the class what he does."

"My dad's a lawyer—he just spends time in court and on the phone and in meetings," he said in a rush.

"And he works with some of the most important businessmen and politicians in the process," his teacher added. "Thank you, Fred. That will be all. Stan, why don't you go next?"

Mrs. B had infuriated Fred so much, he hadn't thought this stupid little exercise could get any worse. But he'd been wrong. This was Stan's first year at the school, and Stan hated speaking before the class even more than Fred did. Stan especially hated to talk about his parents. When it was just Fred and Stan hanging out, Stan almost never shut up, but right now he was leaning into his desk as if he were a crocodile trying to hide just beneath the surface of the water. Unfortunately, this did not camouflage him from Mrs. Bonneville. She continued to order him out of his seat.

Fred watched helplessly as his best friend slipped from behind his desk to stand fidgeting before the classroom. Stan's face was turning redder every second, and Fred thought the dark curls in his friend's hair might suddenly go straight. Fred would have done anything to take the attention away from Stan at that moment, but nothing came to mind.

"My mother is, well, she works for a doctor," stammered Stan.

"What does she do, Stan?" asked Mrs. Bonneville.

"She just answers phones and hands out suckers, I guess," Stan said and quickly sank back into his seat.

"Well, I can see why you two make such good friends," said Mrs. Bonneville. "You do everything the same. Stand back up and tell us what your father does, Stan."

Stan buried his head in his hands. This was exactly what Fred had been afraid of—he was the only one in class who knew that Stan's dad was in prison. Stan was too ashamed to even mention his father's name, and he and Fred had only talked about it once. To make matters worse, Stan's mom's new boyfriend wasn't making things any easier for Stan at home. Fred figured the guy was a big reason why Stan spent so much time over at his tree house, though Fred had never dared to ask.

"Stan, we still need to hear about your father," sang Mrs. Bonneville. "We're not moving on until you tell us." She wasn't letting up, even though Stan was now near tears. Mrs. Bonneville's arms were crossed, but she wore that same smug smile that made Fred wonder if she knew all about Stan's father and was just trying to embarrass him or make another example. Mutant android or not, Fred wasn't going to let her crush his best friend. It was up to him to stop her.

But he didn't have a plan! What he would have given for a magic wand! Ah, her force field probably could have stopped that, too. He'd have to do this without magic. His eyes quickly scanned the room. Jenny Mitchell's braided pony tail swung before his desk. Should he cut it with scissors or glue it to the desk? No—that'd been done before. Plus, he needed a bigger disruption. He would have cooked up a spitwad, but his mouth was still bone dry after speaking himself. That left him only one option. He tried to remember what he had for lunch. Hopefully it had been nachos, for he would need the power of cheese for his plan to work. He took a full breath, and then, with incredible concentration and just the slightest lift of his left leg, he let rip a thunderous gas bomb that caused the whole class to erupt in laughter.

And then, for the second time in as many weeks, Fred Oglesburg was ordered to the principal's office.

2

TROUBLE ON THE HOMEFRONT

Mrs. Bonneville must have assumed Stan had been in on the plan too because she sent him to the principal's office as well. "You will complete these tests while you wait!" she added, slapping the heavy packets into their hands.

The class was still giggling as Mrs. Bonneville ushered Fred and Stan to the door. Fred couldn't resist winking at them when Mrs. Bonneville turned her back to open the door.

"I'm going to stand here and make sure you head straight there," she said, crossing her arms and flicking her eyes down the hallway.

Fred smiled. "Okay by me," he said, starting to walk in slow motion. He pretended as if he were bounding across Jupiter's plasma moon, letting his legs float in the air.

"Move faster!" shouted Mrs. Bonneville.

This was what Fred had been hoping she'd say. He broke into a sprint, tearing straight down the halls so fast the kindergarteners' drawings tacked to the walls ruffled like leaves in a storm.

"No running!" Mrs. Bonneville yelled. Fred slowed to a crawl again, walking like a robot that hadn't been greased in years. But when Mrs. Bonneville started stomping down the hall in a furor, Stan grabbed Fred's arm and pulled him along at a normal pace.

Stan didn't speak until Mrs. B had made it back to the classroom and shut the door. "I know she said she canceled music class," he said finally, letting go of Fred's arm, "yet I could have sworn I heard some kind of rusty, battered tuba go off just now."

"She did call it *farts* and crafts," said Fred. "Besides, everyone knows you can't cancel the musical fruits."

"Yeah, well, don't get cocky, kid," said Stan. "I give it a 7.3 at best."

Fred was hurt. "You give that heroic butt trumpet solo a measly 7.3?" he said.

"Don't get me wrong," said Stan, "you get points for timing, and it started off well—good bass tone—but it didn't have that nice wheezing sound at the end. It's the little things that get you on the medal stand."

"You just couldn't hear the big finish because everyone was laughing," said Fred.

"There were a few chuckles," Stan said, smirking. "But I've heard more laughter in a goblin torture chamber."

Fred just smiled. He knew this was Stan's way of saying thank you, and he couldn't have been happier to have helped his friend.

Neither one of them had any particular interest in talking to Principal Goodman, so they decided to make the trip to his office take as long as possible. The boys stopped to make funny faces in a couple classroom windows and fashioned paper airplanes out of the surveys, which they sent soaring down the empty hall. When the airplanes were too crinkled and smashed to fly any more, they pretended as if the hallways were shifting, moved by the elementary school's resident ghosts, who never wanted them to leave the building. Fred got really excited for a moment when he thought he spotted a phoenix near the trophy cabinet, but it was only a (mostly) dead ficus. Such a shame. Fred thought that he actually might like to go the principal's office if he got to whisper a password to a living gargoyle. But, alas, he had no such luck.

Still, for the most part, he felt the afternoon was starting to turn around. Goofing off with Stan certainly beat taking a bunch of dumb tests. And, just as they had hoped, the final bell rang before they had even made it anywhere close to the principal's office. They chucked what remained of their surveys in the garbage and headed towards their lockers.

"I'll just come by your place as soon as I stop home to get my deck," Stan said, splitting off towards his locker.

"You can use one of my decks..." said Fred hopefully.

"I'd rather play house with my sister than do battle with one of your noob decks," Stan hollered back.

Even though he knew he was doomed to lose all afternoon, Fred couldn't help laughing a little. "Alright, see you then," he said, waving to Stan as he took off down the hall.

Fred paused for a moment to examine his locker. There was something gooey growing on the underside of his cubby hole—*probably a pop-tart left too long*, he thought—and he had to reach around the dripping globs to snatch his book bag. Fred wasn't too worried about it. The mess didn't look like it was becoming sentient any time soon, so he figured he had a few more weeks before he had to clean it up.

He didn't have time to take care of it today, anyway. His

mother was picking him up, and he wanted to get to the curb as soon as possible. Since his parents had divorced, Fred stayed primarily with his father, which meant he only got to see his mom on weekends, holidays, and special occasions. He never wanted to be late on the days she gave him a ride home.

Slinging the bag over his shoulder, he ran all the way to the curb in front of the school and eagerly searched for his mother's car. He smiled when her rusty old station wagon came sputtering up to the curb. It looked out of place among the other larger, shinier cars, but he didn't mind. His mother's car may have been painted an ugly shade of brown, but Fred loved it, probably in large part because the two bumper stickers stuck to the rear fender read "Elves Go Green" and "I Brake for Hobbits."

Fred was grinning from ear to ear as he started for her car, but his happiness didn't last long. As he darted through the crowd, he heard someone hiss the words "dirty hippie," and his smile disappeared faster than a skittish hobbit. Fred turned in time to see Jenny Mitchell's mother look at his mom's brown hatchback as if she'd just smelled the worst tauntaun fart and then usher Jenny away. Fred instantly regretted not chopping off those pigtails, but he stopped short of shouting anything back at Jenny or her mother. For one, he wasn't quite sure what the word "hippie" actually meant. He gave the two of them a hateful stare instead, and then he walked quickly towards his mother's car.

"Freddy!" said his mother when he opened the creaky door. She leaned across the divide to kiss him on his cheek. Fred instantly wiped the kiss away with the back of his palm.

"What's wrong?" she said.

"Jenny Mitchell's mom just called you a hippie," he said.

"Oh, Fred," she said, laughing as she pulled away from the curb. "That's a compliment coming from someone like her. I've been called a lot worse, trust me. You can't let things like that upset you — you'll go grey before you're twelve."

This didn't cheer Fred up very much. He even passed on the obvious "Gandalf the Grey" joke and continued to stare at the floor, swinging his feet angrily.

"C'mon, don't be such a grump," said his mother playfully.

"What does it even mean?" asked Fred.

"What? Hippie?"

"Yeah — is it some kind of mix between a hippo and a harpy?" asked Fred.

His mother laughed again. "Well, at least I know why the word made you so upset. No, honey, that's not what a hippie is, though you can bet good money that the 'harpopotamus' is going to feature in my next book."

"So, what is it?" asked Fred, still too angry to enjoy the fact that he had given his mother an idea for her book.

"Well, the word means different things to different people," said Lucy. "To some, hippies are good-natured, free-spirited, peace-loving people. But to someone like Mrs. Mitchell, hippies are lazy, wasteful, and unrealistic. I guess the important thing to realize is that people will call other people names because that way it's easier to ignore them or belittle their point of view. But they only do it because they're afraid."

"Afraid of what?" he asked.

"Of losing what they have," she said. "Of change."

"Sounds boring," said Fred.

"Some people prefer boring."

"Not me," he said.

"Me either," she said. "What do we always say? There's no such thing as normal..."

"...You're either mental or you're ornamental," finished Fred.

"That's right," said Lucy, "and I know which one I prefer to be." She smiled at Fred.

Fred smiled back, finally letting himself enjoy the ride with his mother, who always knew exactly what to say. Fred's mom, who had published five fantasy novels under her maiden name, Lucy Owen, was a brown-eyed brunette, and if she hadn't started to show just the slightest signs of aging, her son would have pegged her for an elf. Since people always told him he looked more like his mother than his father, he often imagined that he was the last descendant of a line of elf kings who had married with humans to hide from the likes of orc assassins. The fact that his mother had introduced him to fantasy books a few years ago probably had something to do with this theory. He'd read every fantasy series he could get his hands on, but of all the books he read he liked his mother's novels best. Years of fighting to get her books published had given his mother light streaks of silver in her hair — more proof that like the X-man Rogue she had supernatural abilities. She was a great mom, and Fred wished more than anything that other people would start to recognize how smart she was.

"So how was school today?" asked his mother. "What are you reading now?"

"We're reading *The Trumpet of the Swan*," said Fred, "but I read that nearly two years ago, so I'm reading a bunch of other books on my own."

"They can't keep up with you in language arts, can they?" said Lucy. "But you make sure you follow along if they're reading something you haven't read yet."

Fred smiled. "Sure thing, ma."

His mother tousled his hair. "That's my boy," she said in a joking, husky voice. "So, what else did you do today?" she asked.

Fred shifted nervously in his seat. "First, can I see the comics?" he asked, afraid she wouldn't give them to him if she found out he'd been to the principal's office yet again.

"Frederick Dylan Oglesburg," she said, the tone of her voice shifting, "tell me what happened at school this instant."

There was no use lying. His mother had invoked the power of his middle name. Plus, the principal's secretary would have already sent her a note. "I got sent to the principal's office again," he groaned.

"Fred, that's twice this month already!"

"But it wasn't my fault," he said. "Mrs. B was making us fill out these papers to decide what job we'll do from now until forever, and she was making us stand up and tell the class what our parents do, and she wouldn't leave Stan alone about his dad, and I just had to stick up for him," Fred explained in one long breath.

"Wait, what?" said Lucy. "There's no way they're going ahead with that ridiculous idea to put you onto career tracks at age ten!"

Fred shrugged his shoulders and tried to look as outraged as she did, which was tough because he was secretly hopeful that changing the subject would cause her to forget all about his most recent visit to the principal's office.

"Uggh, I can't believe it!" shouted his mother, shaking

her head in disgust. "I just don't have the time to keep that Board in line. But, rest assured, mister, I always have the time to deal with you. So don't think for a second you can distract me from the real issue. Unluckily for you, your father pulled that stunt one too many times."

Fred sighed. His little Jedi mind trick had failed, and he'd only delayed getting scolded for a few seconds.

"Fred, you have to clean up your act," she said. "First you go to the principal's office for pushing a boy you claimed was bullying that Vaughan kid, and now you get sent there again for standing up for Stan."

"But what about—"

"Don't even," she said. "No, I don't want you to just blend into the background. Yes, I want you to always challenge things you disagree with. But we need to find a balance. Is there any way to perform these acts of chivalry without getting into trouble?"

"Not that I see," he answered.

"Well, look harder," she fired back. "I hope you know that just because Hulk and Wolverine always get into fights, it doesn't mean that you have to resort to violence to stand up for what you believe in."

"I know, ma," said Fred. "I'm not stupid."

Lucy took a deep breath. "I know you're not, sweetheart," she said, and her face softened.

Thinking he'd escaped at least a week's grounding, Fred was momentarily relieved. Then he recognized his mother's mood. There was no mistaking the sadness in her eyes. She was only backing off because she had worse news to give him.

"The comics are in the backseat," she said. "I think I got everything you asked for."

"Just tell me what's going on," he said staring straight ahead.

For the first time ever, Fred's mother seemed lost for words. "Okay," she said finally. "As a matter of fact, I do need to talk to you about your father."

"What about him?" said Fred.

"Your father and I, we just wanted to let you know that the living arrangements are going to be changing slightly," she said.

"Am I going to live with you now?" Fred asked excitedly, spinning around his seat and grabbing her arm.

His mother patted his hands. "No, honey," she said quietly. "Your father and I still agree that it's better if you stay there. With him...and Joanne."

"Why do you say Joanne?" asked Fred.

"Well," Lucy paused, taking in a deep breath and glancing over at Fred, "your father told me earlier this week that he's thinking of asking Joanne to marry him, and he wanted me to talk to you first, so that you knew I was okay with it."

"What!" Fred exclaimed, feeling like someone had just stunned him with a phaser blast to the gut. "But, Mom, I can't stand Joanne!" he said. "She's terrible. She doesn't do anything but boss Carlita around and say terrible things about other people. She's just mean, and I hate her. I don't know what Dad sees in her."

"I know that she can be...difficult...sometimes," said Lucy, "but your father loves her, and we both have to respect that."

"Now I really don't want to live there if *she's* going to be there all the time," whined Fred. "She's there too much as it is. I want to stay with you."

"We've already had this discussion, Fred," his mom

said, unable to keep her voice from breaking a little. "You need to be in the best situation for you, and right now that means living with your father. I'm not saying it's going to be like this forever. My agent thinks that my latest book could be a bestseller, she really does. I just need one of these books to make it big, and then people will buy the others. With that money coming in, I'll be able to give you everything you need on my own."

"I don't care about money," said Fred. "I just want to stay with you!"

"I know you say you don't care," said Lucy. "But you need certain things, and your dad works hard to provide them for you, and you should respect him for that."

"So why don't you just get some money from him?" said Fred.

Fred's mom huffed and looked away. Fred was furious, but at the same time it killed him to see his mother this upset. His heart was all twisted up like a Twizzler, and he hated it. He didn't want to make her feel bad, but he couldn't understand why he just couldn't live with her. He was stuck between a bob-omb and a hard place, and he thought he might explode himself if something didn't give.

His mom suddenly pulled the car over to the curb and put it in park. She took a moment to compose herself, and then she turned and looked at Fred. "Fred," she said, "I want you with me more than anything. But I need to be able to support you on my own for the same reason you couldn't let Mrs. Bonneville embarrass Stan today," she said. "It's about doing what's right. It's about honor."

"But it would be so much easier," whined Fred.

"You're right," she said. "It would be easier. But it would teach you the wrong lesson. Honor is something you can't buy, Fred, but it always comes at a price."

Fred had been ready to complain again, but when he saw the tears welling in the corners of his mother's eyes, he nodded and turned away.

"Now I want you to be good for Joanne's party this afternoon," said his mom as she dropped her tinted glasses over her eyes and started driving again.

Fred was too despondent to answer. He kept staring out the window. He was starting to think that no matter what he said or did, he'd never change her mind. But that certainly didn't mean he was going to let this happen without trying to stop it. Living with Joanne was quite possibly the worst fate he could imagine, and he was already thinking of ways to keep her from moving into his house. He could always stay in the tree house every night and stop taking showers altogether. The stink alone might convince his father to dump that pile of harpopotamus dung he called a girlfriend.

Oh, who was he kidding—his father would never be around enough to be disgusted by the smell, anyway. In the end, the stink would just make Carlita's job even tougher, and that was the last thing Fred wanted to do. If there was one person who was going to be more upset to hear that Joanne was moving in, it was the Oglesburg's poor housekeeper. Joanne had made Fred's father hire Carlita, and it seemed to Fred like Joanne hadn't stopped yelling at the housekeeper since she started. Even when Joanne was napping on the couch, she somehow blurted out orders between snores. If Fred chose to stop showering, she'd probably just have Carlita hose him down in the backyard or drive around all day looking for some kind of special air freshener they only make in Iceland every ten years out of baby seal fins or something. No, he'd have to think of another plan to get rid of the wretched witch who was trying to invade his home.

"Can I count on you to behave yourself tonight?" his mother asked again.

"Stan and I are just going to hang out in the tree house," Fred said quietly.

"Make sure you stop in to tell Leo happy birthday, at least," said his mother. "Some of his old football buddies might be there, so it's important to him. He'll be your step-grandfather, so be nice."

Fred couldn't believe that everyone wanted him to be excited about a huge birthday party for a bald bully while his real grandfather, who was actually a good person, sat rotting in a loony bin. No one had even mentioned Alfred, and it made Fred want to barf. At least he'd found a clever way to get some revenge without directly disobeying his mom. "Don't worry about that, Mom — I even bought Leo a gift," said Fred. As angry as he was, he couldn't stop a diabolical smile from creeping up his cheek.

"When you say 'don't worry,' that usually means I should," said his mom as she stopped the car in front of the house. "Just make sure it won't kill him. Explode in his face or something."

Fred nodded. He was ready to get out of the car, but he stopped when he saw Stan suddenly appear over the hill, rocketing towards the car on his Heelys. Stan must have been trying to break his personal record because he wasn't slowing down. Fred was transfixed. Stan was starting to wobble something awful. It looked like his best friend was going to crash right into the car, but at the last second, Stan cut sharply, jumped over the curb, and rolled to a stop in the grass. When he stood up, he held his brand-new Magic card high in the air as if brandishing a sword.

Lucy laughed at him, but Fred was still too angry to be amused.

"You boys are crazy," she said as she stuffed the comics into his book bag. "Okay, I'll see you soon, Freddy." She leaned over and kissed him goodbye. "I love you."

Fred reached for her and hugged her tightly for a moment, and then he turned and kicked the door open so hard he had to reach his hands out to prevent it from swinging back and hitting him in the face.

"Careful!" she said.

Fred didn't answer. He slammed the door shut and then watched as his mother drove away. Her car sputtered and rocked, coughing up puffs of smoke every few feet. He had to fight back tears as he watched her go. But he wasn't going to cry this time—he'd already cried enough. It hadn't done him any good. Things had only gotten worse. He knew it was crazy, but he couldn't shake the feeling that he'd never see his mother again. It was as if Joanne were some kind of changeling that had finally taken his mom's place completely. A Shape Transforming Execution Predator Made Of Metal, a.k.a. a **S.T.E.P.M.O.M.**—the most fiendish cyborg yet.

Stan asked him a question over his shoulder, but Fred barely heard him and didn't answer. He lingered at the curb, staring down the street even after his mother's car had disappeared around a distant corner.

There was no doubt of it now—an evil was spreading over this place, corrupting everything. Fred's epic bowel howl had helped him escape its grasp once, but he would need to do something much more powerful to rid his world of it completely. Yes, something truly extraordinary had to be done, and he had to be the one to do it.

The trouble was, he had absolutely no clue what to do.

3
ARCHERS, RINGS, AND MEAN OL' THINGS

"I said—did you want to get schooled in Magic before or after we read the comics?" repeated Stan, nudging Fred's shoulder.

"I don't care," Fred answered finally, dragging his feet through the gravel as he turned towards the house. His eyes down, he nearly collided with a van he hadn't been expecting to find in the driveway. Looking beyond it, he saw the entire driveway was packed with big vehicles, and strangers were zigzagging in frenzied preparation all across the front yard. In order to get to his house, Fred was going to have to skulk alongside the fence like a burglar. He kicked the nearest tire as hard as he could.

"Ooookay," said Stan. "Someone's grumpy. But that's why we should play Magic—there's nothing like a good butt kicking to cheer you up."

"I guess you'd be the expert," said Fred.

A loud bang from the neighbor's yard drowned out Stan's retort. The boys turned together to check it out. Over the top of the fence, they saw Fred's neighbor, Jimmy Dingleman, perched on the edge of his parents' garage roof, holding a blue NERF crossbow in his hands. He was wearing a neon green and blue track suit, a bicycle helmet, and some sort of harness, which was connected by a long elastic rope to the big oak tree in the Dingleman's front yard. When Fred looked closer, he saw that the rope was really just a bunch of small bungee cords duct-taped together at the hooks.

He and Stan watched his neighbor shuffle up to the gutter. An intense look on his face, Jimmy pumped his legs a couple times and then took off. He hung in the air for a second and then plummeted straight to the earth like a little duckling trying to fly for the first time. Fred and Stan gasped, expecting to hear a loud splat when Jimmy hit the pavement, but then, like a phoenix in swishy pants, Jimmy came springing back up into the air. Limbs flailing, he crashed straight into the leaves of the oak. For a moment he tried to struggle free, but he got himself so tangled in the rope and the branches that he eventually had to give it up. He collapsed on a big branch like a sleeping leopard.

Fred was so amazed, he forgot how upset he was for a moment. "Wicked, Jimmy!" he shouted.

"Thanks, Fred," Jimmy replied, trying to keep his helmet from slipping over his eyes.

"What the flip is that?" Stan asked.

"It's the aerial bridge, of course!" said Jimmy.

"But of course it is," said Stan sarcastically.

"Well, it looks like you've got the aerial part alright, Jimmy," joked Fred.

"Yeah, still have a few kinks to work out, though," said Jimmy. "Say, you guys wouldn't happen to have a ladder, would you?"

"Sure thing, Jimmy—we'll get one from the garage," said Fred, as he and Stan bolted down the driveway.

"What the heck is the aerial bridge?" Stan asked him as they ran. "And is your neighbor a mad scientist? Or does he just, you know, wear that helmet all the time, if you know what I mean?"

Fred had forgotten that Stan hadn't ever officially met Jimmy, who seemed to be working all the time these days. "Jimmy's just obsessed with this show called Nickelodeon *GUTS*, which was on television back when he was about our age," he said. "They had all these weird sports events, and they were always bungee jumping around."

Stan shrugged. "Never heard of it," he said.

"Well, don't tell Jimmy that unless you want to know everything there is to know about *GUTS*," Fred warned.

Stan and Fred turned into the garage, where, unfortunately, they ran into Joanne. She was screaming at Carlita and a handful of caterers, who were lugging around trays of drinks and finger foods. Joanne was clicking around in her heels, testing the food with the tiniest of nibbles and ordering it taken back with a disgusted look on her face. As Fred and Stan made for the ladder, they heard Joanne command Carlita to bring out more ice and napkins. The boys covered their ears at the sound. Joanne's screech made the **T.E.A.C.H.E.R**'s supersonic scream sound like a lullaby.

"Carlita, Carlita!" she said, grabbing a handful of shrimp in a well-manicured claw and shoving them in the housekeeper's face. "The shrimp cocktails need to be chilled. Chilled! This isn't some Cuban dockside shrimp shack, do you understand? This is an important party for important people. Food poisoning may be a foregone conclusion where you come from, but here it's a sign of a poor taste."

"Sí, si, Mrs. Jo," said Carlita quietly, scooting off to grab more ice.

When Joanne turned to inspect more food platters, she finally noticed Fred and Stan. "Fred, what are you doing here?" she asked, putting her hands on her hips. "Can't you see that I'm terribly busy?"

"Don't work too hard," Fred said with as much sarcasm as he could muster. "I just came to grab the ladder."

"Well, hurry up. I can't be wasting time dealing with you." She patted the sides of her large, frozen hair and sighed irritably. "As you can see, I've got a catastrophe on my hands. The whole party is likely to fall apart if I don't mind these *people* every second, and I want things to be perfect for daddy."

All of the caterers threw her a cold look but kept pulling platters of food from the van. They were clearly done dealing with Joanne, and so was Fred. As he moved away towards the ladder, a little boy, who was no more than four years old, marched by, intently following his parents. Fred watched him with curiosity because, unlike everyone else, the boy was smiling. The kid wasn't doing much (there were only three strange-looking rolls on the little tray he was carrying), but he certainly looked happy to be helping out.

Joanne must not have seen the little boy because when she turned to yell at someone setting up decorations across the lawn, she bowled over him, knocking him down and causing him to spill his tray. The boy immediately started crying, but, to Fred's horror and amazement, Joanne did nothing to help him. Instead, she scrambled away, looking down at her dress in disgust. "Can't you at least keep your filthy kids out of the way long enough for me to enjoy the party I've been planning for six months!" she shouted. "Carlita! Carlita, I need something to clean this dress. Do we have anything that will get out piccata sauce and toddler tears?"

A terrified Carlita sprinted forth with a bag of ice in each hand, shook her head and said, "I don't know, Mrs. Jo."

"You're worse than useless!" Joanne spat and brushed by her.

"Someone forgot to take her princess pills," Stan whispered, but Fred had already started towards the fallen boy, who was still crying. He grabbed an old action figure from the depths of his bag and offered it to the kid. Fred made blaster noises and turned the jet into a robot warrior, which finally got the boy to stop crying. Turning to the boy's parents, Fred tried hard to remember the Spanish Carlita had taught him so that he could apologize. "Lo siento," he said slowly. "Ella es una gringa tan loca."

Most of the catering crew laughed, and the boy's mother said, "Gracias, niño." Fred heard another woman say to Carlita that he was a good boy and lucky to have someone like the maid around to teach him manners (he didn't understand every word, but he thought he got most of it). Carlita kissed him on the head and told him to hurry up before Joanne got any madder, because the maid might lose her "nalgitas" if she did.

Stan helped Fred pick up the ladder, and they carried it around the fence into the Dinglemans' yard. They leaned it against the trunk of the oak, and Fred climbed up and helped Jimmy to untangle himself from the rope and branches. Jimmy then followed him back down the ladder, carrying the rope and his bow with him.

"Thanks, guys," said Jimmy as he set his feet on the ground and examined his bow. "Dang, my string broke. I'll have to fix it again."

"Hey, Jim, Stan didn't know about *GUTS*," said Fred, throwing a private wink at Stan.

"No way!" Jimmy exclaimed. "Well, they stopped airing them years ago, so I don't blame you. They show the occasional rerun, but I've got them all recorded if you want to borrow them. Hey, why don't you guys come check out my shop," he said, pointing to his parents' garage.

Once Jimmy had turned his back, Stan made fun of the older boy by pushing up a pair of invisible eyeglasses and popping his front teeth out over his lower lip. Fred smiled and rolled his eyes, and then he pulled Stan with him into his neighbor's garage.

"That's *GUTS* right there," said Jimmy, nodding at the little television set propped on his workbench. "The 1993 semifinals, I'm pretty sure."

On the screen, kids in red, blue and purple shirts bounded high into the air using much better bungee cords than the one Jimmy had stuck together with tape. When the buzzer sounded, signaling the end of the game, a man appeared and shouted that the contestants would be racing around a track and paddling through the whitewater of a pool when the show returned from commercial. When an ad for batteries flashed on screen, Fred turned away and examined the rest of Jimmy's workshop. There were tools scattered all across Jimmy's workbench and the floor of the garage. Some of the clutter looked like half-finished projects. Missing a hind wheel and leaning to one side was something that resembled the strange recumbent tricycle Fred had seen on the television. There was also a pair of homemade moon-shoes, which were really nothing more than some stolen bowling shoes tied to storage crates by large rubber bands.

Clearing a space for himself on his workbench, Jimmy

gently laid his bow down and pulled another length of bowstring from a tool drawer brimming with all kinds of bizarre objects. "I've modified the bow with higher tensile wire," he explained as he began restringing the worn toy. "I've also hollowed out the compression chamber and fitted the arrows with real eagle feathers I collected in the park. Legolas himself would envy this bow."

Jimmy stopped fussing with the wire long enough to gaze dreamily upon his weapon. It made Fred a little nervous to realize that Jimmy clearly believed everything he was saying. Turning back to the table, Jimmy finished restringing his bow, looping the wire through the horn of the plastic bow stave and drawing it down to the yellow handle. He threaded the string through the hole in the plastic, tied it off and then tested the tension by pulling on the handle several times. Looking satisfied, he put the bow down.

That's when Fred saw the bulletin board propped against the garage wall. There were sketches of people tacked to the board that looked like wanted posters or pictures of missing persons he had seen printed on milk cartons.

"Who are the people in those drawings?" Stan asked Jimmy.

"Oh, those," said Jimmy. "Those are sketches of former *GUTS'* contestants, updated, of course, to show what they would look like today."

"Um, why do you have them?" Stan asked. He sounded nervous. Fred caught Stan checking to see how many steps it would take to dive back out of the garage.

"Well, when they bring back the show for the *Super All-Star Classic Reunion*, I want to be ready," said Jimmy. "It's only smart to know who you'll be going up against. Sure, I was only an alternate, but you have to think that at least one of the original contestants won't be able to compete."

"Yeah, Jimmy," Fred said as he and Stan turned to look at each other, raising their eyebrows in disbelief. "Well, we should be getting to the party."

"Thanks again for helping me," said Jimmy. "You guys will be the first to try the aerial bridge when it's completed."

Fred waved goodbye to Jimmy, and then he and Stan started walking back to Fred's house, stopping to pick up the ladder where it was still leaning against the trunk of the Dingleman's oak tree.

"Did you hear that, Fred?" Stan said once they were out of earshot. "We get to be the crash test dummies for your neighbor's death leash. Not in a million years, pal. What is with that space cadet? It's like Arkham Asylum is having a garage sale."

"C'mon," said Fred. "He's a little...strange, but he can be really cool."

"I bet," said Stan sarcastically. "And not that I didn't think that bow was totally awesome, but isn't he a little old for it?"

"I don't exactly know how old he is, but I think he's like twenty something, because Joanne is always talking about what a disappointment he is still living at home," said Fred. "Besides being obsessed with *GUTS*, I know he does taek-wondo and works at the local grocery store. He's just a nice dude, though. He even gave me discs of some the cartoons that were on TV when he was our age: the original Teenage Mutant Ninja Turtles, Inspector Gadget, and the X-men even."

Stan didn't look very impressed. "Who uses discs anymore?" he said.

"I'm telling you," said Fred, "The original Thundercats makes Pokémon seem like your sister's dance recital."

"Really?" Stan asked. "Why am I imagining Charizard wearing a tutu right now?"

The boys laughed.

"I keep forgetting to show them to you," said Fred as they dropped the ladder off in the garage. "The discs are in the tree house any time you want to watch them." As they started for the tree house, Fred poked his head around the corner of the garage to check the path to the kitchen door. "You can take the comics on up," he said to Stan, handing over his bag. "I'm going to go grab us some snacks before all Joanne's friends get here."

"Did your dad's girlfriend order cupcakes?" Stan asked, his hands moving to his growling belly.

"Yeah, I think I saw some," Fred replied.

"Grab a few with Oreo frosting if you can," shouted Stan.

Fred moved carefully through the maze of caterers, keeping his eyes peeled for any sign of Joanne. Luckily, he made it to the kitchen without being stopped. The counters were absolutely overflowing with food. "Redwall Abbey eat your heart out," Fred said as he searched for the cupcakes.

He finally found a few with marbled frosting and grabbed as many as he could fit in his hands. Just as he was about to turn to leave, someone shouted at him from across the room to put the food down. Fred snapped his head around in fright. A woman in a white chef's jacket was waddling towards him, shaking her finger. "Yes, you!" she said again.

Fred was about to defend himself, but someone tall suddenly stepped between him and the approaching woman. "It's alright, Cindy, he can have them."

Fred was stunned. He couldn't remember the last time his dad had been home this early.

"But, Miss Joanne said..." the woman stammered.

"If she asks, tell her I said it was okay," said Fred's dad, flashing an easy smile.

The chef's eyes softened. "Okay, but make sure he leaves the edible diamonds on the cake alone," she said. "I've had to shine them up twice already."

This knocked Fred out of his trance. "Edible diamonds! You're joking right?" he asked, but Joanne screamed in the next room, and the woman took off like a cartoon coyote.

"That was a close call, eh, Fred-O," said Solomon, patting his son on the shoulder. "Thought she was going to add you to the menu there for a second."

Fred shook his head and huffed. He'd never really gotten his dad's jokes.

"So how was school today?" his father asked, taking a cupcake himself.

"It was okay." Fred kept his answer short. Not only was he hoping to avoid having to admit again that he'd been sent to the principal's office, but he was also still really angry that his father was going to let Joanne live with them.

"Well, was it nice seeing your mom after school?" asked his father.

"Yeah, Dad," Fred said, turning away. He was a subspace anomaly of emotions, and there was no way he'd be able to express them all to his father. He had decided to keep away from his dad for a while. He didn't think that would be too hard, considering how much his father worked. "Look, Stan's waiting for me in the tree house, so I should get back."

"Oh, sure, go ahead, and tell him I said hi," said Mr. Oglesburg. "Just make sure you stop in for a second to get something healthier than cupcakes for dinner—like ice cream." Fred's dad winked. Fred kept moving towards the door. "And Leo would love it if you wished him a happy birthday," his dad called over his shoulder.

"Uh-huh," said Fred, still not looking back.

"And Fred-O..."

Fred finally stopped and looked back. "Yeah?" he said.

"I love you, man."

Fred blushed as he cradled the cupcakes to open the door. "Yeah," he said quickly. Fred's dad said that every time they saw each other, but Fred couldn't see how his father could mean it now and still intend to marry that awful woman. If his dad really loved him, he never would have divorced his mom in the first place.

Fred tried to think of something else as he crossed the yard and started scaling the tree house ladder because he didn't want Stan to see him upset. He soon realized this was not something he needed to be worried about. As long as he had cupcakes, he could sprout a second head and Stan wouldn't notice. Stan was so excited to grab the cupcakes from Fred, he nearly forgot to help him up into the tree house.

"We're lucky you nabbed these when you did," said Stan, biting into the cupcake with the largest dollop of frosting. "Check out the goblin horde."

Fred went to the tree house window. Stan wasn't exaggerating; a lot of the partygoers had arrived, and a large line had formed in front of the house. Joanne was greeting them at the front door, smiling hugely at whatever they were saying before waving them inside and rolling her eyes as soon as they were past. Fred grumbled as he saw a group of huge black Cadillac SUVs start filling up the street. The vehicles were so big a few of them had to roll their huge wheels up onto the neighbors' flower beds in order to keep the road clear.

"Is Tony Stark coming or something?" asked Stan through a mouthful of cupcake. "Why all the security?"

"It's not security," said Fred. "One of Leo's old teammates owns a bunch of car lots."

Stan shrugged and finished his cupcake. "They look expensive," he said.

Fred left the window and sat down to play. The more people who came to the party, the less he wanted anything to do with it.

Stan started shuffling his cards. "What if Mrs. B's little survey tells us we should be hawking used cars?" he said with a laugh.

"Who cares?" said Fred.

"Seriously, though, what would you pick to do for work if you had to?" Stan asked as he drew his seven cards.

"Don't tell me you're buying into any of that *Work to Win* crap," Fred said.

"Whoa, take it easy," said Stan. "No need to blow another butt bomb. I was just curious."

Fred slapped down a land card firmly and found himself answering in a growl. "I want to make samurai swords, explore strange new worlds, draw comics, tame lions, and... and I don't know," he said. "I don't even know what color lightsaber I'd pick. There are just too many options, and I want to try them all."

Stan smirked and shook his head again. "I'm sorry I asked."

"Don't act like you're any better," said Fred. "You argue with yourself for ten minutes before every magic game about which deck you're going to use, so I don't see how you could know what you'd want to do for the rest of your life either."

"I didn't say I knew," retorted Stan, playing another land and sending three flying creatures Fred's way. "I guess I don't really care what I do, so long as it pays big."

"Funny," said Fred.

"I'm serious," said Stan.

"That's the stupidest thing I ever heard," said Fred.

"Why?" said Stan. "You think lightsabers are cheap?"

"Yeah, 'cause you don't even buy them," snapped Fred. "First you have to go on a quest to find the kyber crystal, and then you've got to build the power vortex ring and blade energy channel all by yours—"

Stan cut him off. "I'm just going to stop you there before you spend the rest of the day telling me how you could build the best lightsaber ever."

Fred stared sullenly at the worthless cards in his hand. He didn't have the mana to play anything and had to discard.

"Look, the only thing Boba Fett cares about is getting more credits, right?" said Stan. Fred reluctantly admitted that this was true. "I'm just trying to say I'm about that Fett life. I'm good with computers—I bet I could score a lot by doing that."

Fred drew another card he couldn't cast yet and cursed under his breath. "Money's dumb."

"Easy for you to say, your dad is rolling in it," said Stan. "Look at this place. Your tree house is as big as my room. My house looks worse than Yoda's little swamp hut."

Fred didn't know what to say. He knew Stan's family didn't have a lot of money, but Stan had never said anything about it before. The last thing Fred wanted to do was to hurt Stan's feelings. But this was something Fred had thought a lot about, and more than anyone else, he wanted his best friend to understand how he felt. He had watched his parents fight over money too many times; he didn't want his best friend to suffer because of it, too.

"My mom doesn't exactly live on a pleasure skiff, but she's happier than my dad," Fred said finally. "And you know that I'd live with her if I could. My dad's got money, but all he does is work all the time—he doesn't have time for anything else. I just don't get it."

"You will when you can't get all the stuff you want," said Stan, sending in his angels for the kill. "Better luck next time, mon ami."

Fred threw his cards down and avoided making eye contact with a gloating Stan. He stared out the window, watching the partiers clump together like fish in a tank. They seemed totally unaware that there was a shark swimming nearby. And it looked as if she'd found her next target.

"Be quiet for a second," he told Stan, as he put his ear to one of the several Dixie cups that dotted the wall of his tree house. Each cup was connected by a length of string to another cup Fred had strategically placed in different rooms of the house. There was a small label beneath each one telling Fred which room he was listening to. They weren't high-tech microphones invisible to the naked eye, but he wasn't Boba Fett—this was the best he could do. He was lucky, too, that the strings were hidden by the branches and leaves of the tree and that Joanne didn't clean anything herself, otherwise she surely would have spotted them and had Carlita trash them immediately.

The sounds of the party were muffled coming through the Dixie cup, but Joanne's voice rang out as loud as a foghorn. "What are you wearing?" Joanne yelled at a young female caterer.

"Just our regular uniform," the frightened worker said, looking down at her clothes.

"I mean what scent?" Joanne barked again.

"Um...I think it's called Preciou$," said the woman.

"That's a $500 bottle of perfume!" Joanne asked. "How dare you steal some from my bathroom!"

"No, I...I didn't" stammered the woman. "It was a gift from my grandmo—"

"It doesn't matter!" Joanne snapped. "That's my scent, and I need you to go wash it off right now! Right now!" She pushed her away.

The woman ran away bawling as Joanne turned to a nearby group of her "friends." They weren't really what Fred would call actual friends—Joanne just hated them a little less because they were more like she was. "Can you believe the nerve she has to wear *my* scent?" Joanne asked them.

"Ridiculous," said a woman who looked as if she'd had her face stretched out by a couple cave trolls. "The nerve. As if you want to smell like the *help* after all you've done to transform this place. It's bad enough you have to deal with that ghastly tree shanty." The woman gestured towards Fred's tree house. Fred clenched his fists in rage. "Tell me, what on earth do you plan to do with it?" she said.

"I'm going to rip the whole thing up from the roots, of course," said Joanne. "Once it's gone, I want to put in a little water garden with some statues of Italian marble—*if* I can find somebody who knows how to work with it. I'd want the little brat off at military school before I invest in something so nice, though."

"Naturally," said the other woman.

Fred gritted his teeth and forced himself to keep listening. Every one of Joanne's vicious words scraped across his nerves like a rusty goblin blade, but he had to hear her evil plan. That was the only shot he had at stopping her.

"Well, that shouldn't be too hard," said a man who looked as if two invisible ghosts were prying open his eyes. "After all, you managed to get one maniac out of here already."

"Oh, heavens," Joanne exclaimed, "we do our best not to speak of Alfred, but you've got it right—maniac is a better word than magician. From what I've heard he was never able to get any of his tricks right, but people kept hiring him because the kids thought it was funny. *Alfred the Grand*—what a joke!" She attempted a laugh. It sounded to Fred more like a baby Balrog trying to belch.

"It took some doing, but I finally got Solomon to put the old loon in Eisen Gardens, you know, over there in Germantown. His dementia was getting worse and worse, and he was starting to believe he was an actual wizard or some nonsense. The night he shot off fireworks in the backyard was the last straw. Frankly, I'm surprised our crazy neighbors didn't just join right in. A couple fireworks are probably their idea of a gala." She had to pause while her friends attempted to laugh. With their severely puckered faces, they could only manage to hoot like sickly owls.

Joanne waited for them to quiet down before she continued. "So, anyway, after that debacle, we had to send him to an institution because I wasn't going to have him here, although Solomon argued with me for a while, I tell you. But the place is a resort. I don't see what the all the fuss is about. And Dr. White is a fantastic physician. You know, one of those sharply dressed older men, very clean cut. And he doesn't allow any nonsense on his watch, so naturally I took to him right away.

"You know," Joanne continued, "with a father like

Alfred, it's a miracle Solomon became such a successful lawyer. Unfortunately, Fred is more like his grandfather than his father, although that's his mother's fault. She did name him after the old kook. You can be sure our kids will be different..."

Fred couldn't take any more. He took his ear from the cup and punched the tree house wall. His dad had told him Alfred was sick and needed to go to the hospital to get better but that had been a total lie. Joanne just didn't want Alfred living at the house, so they had kicked him out. And Fred was next. Positively boiling, Fred kicked over a stack of comics and stomped around the room.

"What is it?" Stan asked.

Fred could barely speak he was so upset. "It's that... that...rancor's anus Joanne. She's trying to destroy my family. By Jaga, I hate her!"

Stan had replaced Fred in the tree house window, and something in the house caught his attention. He craned his neck for a better view. "You better come look at this," he said to Fred. "I think Leo is going to talk with your dad in the kitchen."

Fred rushed over and peered with Stan out the tree house window. He watched the big, bald Leo lumber from the living room, leaving his other enormous football friends to chat about their glory days. When Leo passed before the living room window, the sunlight reflected brightly off the NCAA championship ring the burly old man always wore, causing Fred to shield his eyes.

Nothing about Leo annoyed Fred as much as that ring. The chrome dome never stopped asking Fred if he wanted to look at the golden finger tire. Apparently, most people were way more impressed with the ring than Fred had ever been, because Leo always acted super butt-hurt when Fred told him he'd rather scoop rancor poop with a popsicle stick than sit on the old fart's lap and stare at those space slugs he called fingers. Now Fred was starting to realize why Leo was really so mad about it. Leo controlled people with the ring. In fact, that was probably how he had gotten so rich and powerful. Suddenly, the sight of the retired football team, in their black suits and with their huge golden rings, chilled Fred to the bones. He looked to the street and saw the wheels of their huge black cars withering grass like Nazgul talons. He knew then that they were Dark Riders and that his father was in mortal peril.

To hear what Leo was saying to his dad, Fred dashed over and put his ear to the Dixie cup that had the word "kitchen" scrawled on it.

"Solomon, there you are," said Leo as he burst into the kitchen.

"Hi, Leo," answered his father. "Are you enjoying the p—?"

Leo spoke right over him. "As you know, I've been talking to the Board, and I think they're ready to start sending all the acquisitions contracts to your firm."

"That's great," said Fred's father, taking a sip of his drink.

"I'm going to ask them to suggest to your partners that you personally handle all our major transactions," said Leo.

"Wow, that'd be fantastic," said Solomon, who didn't sound all that excited to Fred. "You guys deal in some major contracts."

"I'm glad you see it that way," said Leo.

"Of course," said Solomon. "It'd be a wonderful opportunity."

Leo shifted his feet and tickled his bulbous nose. "There's just one more thing to discuss then," he said.

"What's that?" asked Solomon.

"Well, you know the boys can be somewhat old fashioned over there," said Leo.

"How so?" asked Solomon.

Leo shoved both hefty hands in his pockets. *He's hiding his ring so my dad doesn't know what he's doing!* thought Fred.

"Let's just say I think they'd be much more receptive to the idea of you handling so much of our business if you were to make my daughter an honest woman," said Leo. "They love her nearly as much as I do, and if you were to be married that would be an assurance to them and to me that you're truly...invested. This is your future, Solomon. You're being offered to sit at the table with the big boys now. This contract alone could make you millions. Make the right choice, Solomon. We all stand to gain by it."

At this point someone from the other room must have called Leo because he turned his head and yelled that he was on his way. Turning back to Solomon, he said, "Think about it. It's good business." He patted Solomon on the shoulder and then turned to leave.

Fred pulled his ear from the Dixie cup and watched Leo clonk back into the living room. Then he turned back to watch his dad. Now alone in the kitchen, Solomon pulled a small black box from his pocket and opened it.

Shattering the afternoon sunlight and throwing a dozen miniature rainbows on the white kitchen tile was the largest arkenstone Fred had ever seen.

4
THE PARTY POOPER

Fred was horrified. Joanne had already convinced Solomon to imprison his own father, and now, with the ring of power in her control, she was going to take Fred out of the picture, too. "Oh, no!" he exclaimed. "I've got to do something."

"Do what?" Stan asked nervously.

"That ring could destroy my very world," Fred said.

"No, no, no," said Stan, shaking his head. "Whatever it is you're planning, stop right now."

"But don't you see?" Fred exclaimed. "It is the *one* ring. We've got to take it to Mordor and throw it into the fires of Mount Doom!"

"Forget it!" said Stan. "You're out of your gourd. It's just a story—Mordor isn't real."

"It is real!" said Fred. "In...in...California somewhere. I think. C'mon, we have to do this!"

"Sounds like a fun little vacation for you," said Stan. "But it's not exactly safe for a Black kid to be wandering around the streets these days."

"Yeah, but your dad's white," said Fred. "So, you're really more like a Halfling when you think about it."

Stan lifted his eyebrows. "Well, that's a new one," he said. "I'm going to let it slide because you're clearly not in your right mind right now. But you can bet Black Twitter will be hearing about it."

"So, you'll help me save my family?" said Fred.

"No way," said Stan. "My mom would kill me for starters. Plus, in case you forgot, all the Black characters in *Lord of the Rings* are drooling goons dying by the millions."

"Yeah, but—" Fred started.

"Call me a Halfling again, and I'll tell your dad what you're up to myself," said Stan.

"You wouldn't," said Fred.

"I should," said Stan. "It will probably save your life. I mean how many stupid fans of the books have already tried this?"

"None, or we would have heard about it," said Fred.

"If you believe that, you've got delusions of grandeur, pal," said Stan. "There are a million obsessed fans, and each one of them has probably dragged his friends on a stupid quest to the ice cream store or to take back the one comic book to rule them all or whatever, trying to get the hottest girl in school or some crap. We're just going to look like idiots and get into bigger trouble. I'm not going." Stan settled into a bean-bag chair and picked up a comic.

Fred was white hot with anger now—he hadn't expected this from his best friend, his only friend. He had finally come up with a foolproof plan for saving his family, and Stan just wanted to shoot it down. "You're just scared," he snapped. "Just like you're scared to go visit your father in prison."

Silence crept into the tree house like a team of angry

ninjas. It was without question the meanest thing Fred could have said to his best friend, and he instantly wished he could take it back. He hadn't realized he was going to say it; he had let his anger get the better of him, and the words had simply slipped out. If he had been hoping on some level to guilt Stan into coming along, he could plainly see now that his plan had backfired. Stan looked like he'd rather kill him than help him. Fred had crossed a line that even the best of friends shouldn't cross, and he knew it.

"Shut up!" Stan shouted as he ran past him.

Fred watched helplessly as Stan climbed down the ladder as fast as he could and went sprinting from the yard. Fred called after him, desperate for his friend's help, but Stan didn't stop.

Hearing a burst of laughter come from the house, Fred reluctantly turned away from Stan to see what was going on. In order for his plan to work, he needed the ring, and he still didn't have a plan for stealing it away from his dad. Scanning the kitchen first, he saw that his father was still alone. Solomon was leaning against the counter, looking at the ring pensively.

Turning to the living room, Fred saw that Leo had started opening his presents. After setting aside a gigantic golf club, Leo accepted the next package from one of his teammates. Fred recognized his own terrible wrapping job and played a riff on his air guitar out of excitement, hardly believing his luck. Somehow, he had created his own diversion even before he knew he needed one. Now was his chance, but he had to act fast.

He scrambled down the ladder and leapt onto the grass, performing a totally unnecessary combat roll before dropping into a crouch and sidling up to the living room windowsill. He peeked over the ledge just as Leo was reaching his hands into the packing paper. Just as Fred had hoped, the bald linebacker held up the hair dryer with a look of total confusion that quickly melted into rage. Sweat started to bead on Leo's shiny bare head, and his face turned red. The room went silent for a moment and then erupted in laughter and gasps of surprise. Joanne screamed in anger.

Fred stood on his toes and looked over the windowsill, desperately hoping his dad would come into the living room to see what had caused the commotion. When he saw his father burst through the door and begin pushing his way through the crowd, Fred took off. He shuffled to the kitchen door, keeping his back flush against the house as if on the edge of a great cliff. *Please let it be there*, he begged silently.

He slipped inside and immediately looked to the counter. He almost shouted with joy. The ruse had worked to perfection! In his haste, his father had left the ring behind. Fred dashed across the room, snatched the ring and shut the box, hoping that when his father returned, he would pocket it quickly and forget to check for the ring. Fred needed a head start if he was going to make it all the way to California, and if his father immediately noticed the ring was gone, he'd come straight for Fred.

Clutching the ring close, Fred sprinted out of the kitchen, across the backyard and up the tree house ladder so fast that he made it there in time to see Joanne turn from her enraged father and confront Solomon. Joanne was yelling at his father so loudly, Fred didn't need the Dixie cups to hear her. She knew exactly who had given Leo the hair dryer and was demanding that Solomon punish Fred swiftly and mercilessly. Fred didn't really care. The diversion had allowed him to grab the ring, and that was the only important thing. Soon he'd be rid of her for good.

His dad was trying to calm down Joanne, but Fred knew Solomon had a better chance of turning the blow dryer into a boggart than he did getting her to relax. Sure enough, a second later his dad turned on his heel and walked back into the kitchen. Fred held his breath as his dad reached the counter and picked up the box. If his dad immediately noticed the ring was missing—he was toast. Solomon was just about ready to crack open the little box when Joanne came bursting through the door, forcing him to hide it quickly into his pocket. Fred exhaled sharply. With any luck, his dad would hide the box and not open it for a couple of days, providing him with enough time to make it to Mordor.

After another short, ear-shattering exchange with Joanne, Solomon slammed open the side door and hurried across the lawn to the tree house. Fred knew that his dad was sure to give it to him, but seeing Leo's face alone was worth that, and getting the ring was way beyond anything he could have hoped for.

His dad starting yelling before he was even halfway up the ladder, but the threats were nothing new. Fred nodded several times during his dad's angry rant and said he was sorry once or twice with as much sincerity as he could muster. He wasn't really listening. He was too busy thinking about what he would need to get to Mordor, California and how his life would be so different once he completed his quest. His recent fight with Stan was the only thing bringing him down to Middle-earth. But, as much as he wanted to make up with his best friend, he had bigger problems to tackle first. He had to get rid of Joanne and get his parents back together, and he needed to destroy the ring to do that.

In the end, his father grounded him indefinitely and ordered him to stay in the tree house for the rest of the party, which Fred was happy to do. He had a trip to plan, and he always did his best thinking in his tree house. Before his dad had even made it all the way down the ladder, Fred was making a list of things he'd need on the trail. When he finally fell asleep later that night, he did so wishing that morning would come quickly. For at dawn began the start of a truly epic quest.

5
THE START OF A TRULY EPIC QUEST

The following morning, Fred woke early to pack. Well, at least he intended to get up early. It was almost 10 a.m. when he finally clambered down the treehouse ladder and crept up to the house. He didn't want his dad or Joanne to catch him poking around, so he moved quietly and double-checked to make sure his dad's car wasn't in the driveway, even though he knew it wouldn't be there.

Once in the house, he tiptoed from room to room, though he doubted even a krayt dragon in labor could wake Joanne in the morning. Carlita was awake, of course, carefully preparing Joanne's favorite brunch (a grapefruit and a mimosa), and Fred told her he'd be spending the weekend at Stan's house. It was a flimsy excuse—he'd only been to Stan's house once or twice—and would fall apart if anyone actually checked, but he hoped the lie would buy him a little extra time, at least.

With his book bag now stuffed with comics and crackers, the next order of business was figuring out the best way to secure the ring. Back in the tree house, he spotted a cheap cereal box necklace on top of a storage crate and after testing its strength decided it would work. It was simple enough getting the shamrock pendant off, but tying the leather cord was like trying to wrestle a greased mynock. He was still fumbling with the ends of the necklace when Stan appeared in the door of the tree house.

"Stan!" he said excitedly before he remembered they were fighting. He forced a scowl onto his face. "I mean, what do you want?"

Stan kept looking at the floor of the treehouse. "I'm going with you," he said, rubbing his arm. He winced slightly as he did, and Fred guessed the rest. The bruises had been there as long as Stan's mom's boyfriend had been there. But he didn't ask Stan any more. He didn't want to let on that he was sorry for him—that was the quickest way to upset Stan again and send him running away.

"Oh, really?" said Fred. "I thought you said it was a stupid idea?"

"I know what I said," blurted Stan. "But I also know that if I let you do this by yourself, you'll end up in a madhouse, and I'll never get to see you again. So, in order to save our friendship, and not because I think it will work, I've decided to come along."

Fred finally gave up the act. He was too excited to hide it. "Great, I already packed the sandwiches!" he said. "Do you think four sandwiches each will get us to Mordor?"

"That depends," said Stan, taking the ends of the neck-lace from Fred. "What kind of sandwiches are they?"

"Bologna," Fred answered.

"With cheese?" Stan asked.

"Double," said Fred.

"That should be more than enough," said Stan, "especially if we have any of that special lemnas bread that fills you up with just one bite?"

"Stan, if we had that, don't you think we'd both be ripped like Thranduil by now?" said Fred. "You think just because we live in a tree that I've got some elves working overtime for me or something?"

"Good point," said Stan. "Chips will be fine."

"C'mon, Stan, they didn't have Doritos in Middle-earth," said Fred. "We're going do this right and use only the stuff they had in the books, or else it won't work." Fred leapt onto a chair, placed a fist over his heart, and bellowed, "I will take the ring to Mordor, though I do not know the way."

"Yeah, but you've still got a good wireless connection out here," said Stan, "so I can just look it up on Google maps and find out exactly where Mordor is."

Fred dropped from the chair and slammed the computer shut before Stan could boot up. "I'm pretty sure they didn't have computers in the Shire and that it's called Google Earth, not Google Middle-earth," he said.

"Right," said Stan. "No computers, no DO-REE-TOEs. I'm not going to have any fun on the trip, am I?"

"Probably not," said Fred. "But it'll be good for you to get out of that trash compactor you call a room. You'll get some fresh air and some sun."

"How many times do I have to tell you that I don't 'need sun' like you do?"

"Then you'll like these then!" With a flourish, Fred pulled out the green hobbit cloaks they had worn last Halloween from a wooden chest in the corner of the tree house.

"Nice try," said Stan. "But there's no way I'm wearing that again. I didn't even like it when you made me wear it last Halloween. Alex Lassiter and all his goons were dressed up like Batman, with the muscles and the rubber nipples. And you saw Katie just falling all over them. Not that she cares that Alex can barely even read, let alone finish a book."

Fred laughed. "He is a total goon," he said, "but you need to let that go already. It's not like you've ever spoken more than a word to Katie, anyway. And it was only just a year ago you hated her guts, now you're all hot and bothered about some rubber nipples?" Stan opened his mouth to protest, but Fred spoke over him. "Look," he said. "We're going to wear the costumes, and we're going to Mordor, and we're going to cast that bleepin' ring into the fires of Mount Doom. And then my dad will realize he loves my mom and not that horrible woman, and they'll get back together. And once they're seeing straight, they'll make sure that I don't have to worry about work but can just be a regular kid with a happy family."

"Hey, where did you say you're going?" asked Jimmy Dingleman, peering over the edge of the fence.

Realizing Jimmy could clearly see him in the window, Fred jumped to the side and slapped himself in the head, cursing himself for being so loud. "Uh, nowhere, Jimmy," he lied. He liked his neighbor, but he didn't want Jimmy tagging along all the way to Mordor.

"You're going to Mordor, aren't you?" Jimmy asked. "Well, I'm coming, too."

"No, Jimmy, we're not going to Mordor, we're going to the uh... the uh... video store," said Fred. "Mordor...video store. Easily confused, so don't worry about it."

Jimmy wasn't going away that easy. "Fred, I still live with my parents, I've been doing taekwondo three days a week for fifteen years and I still haven't gotten my black belt, and my greatest regret in life is that I never got to go on Nickelodeon *GUTS*. What makes you think I would let you go to Mordor without me? Besides, you're going to need someone like me. Someone older. Someone who knows how to get things. I'll just let them know at the super-market that I'll be gone for a week or two. It shouldn't be a problem."

Jimmy let go of the fence to grab the NERF bow he had strapped to his back. "You have my boOOOOOW," he shouted as he toppled backwards from the fence and crashed to the ground. Fred winced and hushed him. Jimmy did an awkward backwards roll as he struggled to keep hold of his bow and quiver and then popped up in a fighting pose and threw a wild front kick. "I can show you guys that move on the way," he said.

"Great," said Stan sarcastically. "I wonder what color belt they give you for looking like a total nincompoop when you fall on your keester?"

Before Fred could answer, Jimmy yelled up at them again: "I'll make some sandwiches and get my ears," he said. "You guys like bologna?" Without waiting for an answer, Jimmy disappeared into his garage.

"This is a bad idea, Fred," Stan warned. "I'm guessing the only thing he knows how to get is the mayonnaise off the top shelf for all the old ladies who shuffle around bent over like goblins. Are you sure you want to take him?" he asked.

"I don't think we have a choice," sighed Fred. "Plus, he's right. He can rent a room at the inn and buy us ale."

"Since when did you start drinking anything other than Chocolate Milk and Mountain Dew?" Stan asked.

"MISTY Mountain Dew," Fred insisted, but Stan just rolled his eyes. "Plus, a pint of hearty ale never did a hobbit any harm," added Fred.

"I wonder how many times I'm going to have to remind you that you're not a real hobbit before this thing is over," Stan said, shaking his head. "Triple digits. At least."

Jimmy reappeared from the garage and came dashing across the grass. In addition to his NERF bow and quiver, he had a gym bag strung over his shoulder. He had already stuck on one pointed ear and was trying to attach the other one when he tripped on a stone and crashed into the fence. His head made a loud crack as it broke through the planks. Jimmy shook the wood shavings from his hair and looked up to the tree house. "You guys think four sandwiches will be enough to get us to Mordor?" he said. "Hey, where is Mordor anyway? Is it by the laser tag place? Because if it is, we should stop there after we, um, save the world or whatever."

"It's in California, Jimmy," Fred answered. "And could you be a little quieter. My dad is at work, but he'll come back here if Joanne calls him shouting about all the noise we're making, and then the whole jig is up."

"California, huh," Jimmy cocked his head to the side as he pondered the distance. "Yeah, four should be okay," he said. "I used double cheese. When do we leave?"

"Right now," said Fred. "With any luck we'll have my grandpa busted out of that fortress at Eisen Gardens by nightfall."

"Wait, what?" Stan asked. "Why would we do that? He's mental!"

"Hey, you're either mental..." started Fred.

"...or you're ornamental," finished Stan. "I've heard that before, but I'm not sure your mom had the smoke bomb bandit in mind when she made it up."

"He's not crazy," said Fred. "He's just been really sad since my grandmother died, and he gets confused sometimes, but he can still help us."

"Help us with what?" said Stan. "Our cholesterol medication?"

"C'mon, he's not just some regular old codger," said Fred. "He's a flippin' magician, Stan! Besides, I'm not going to leave him in that horrible place. You should have heard Joanne talk about it. He's miserable in there."

Stan sighed. "Alright, Fred, this is your show," he said. "Let's get your kooky grandpa and go to Mordor."

Stan and Fred packed up the last few things together. They rolled up their tauntaun sleeping bags, pulled on the hobbit cloaks over their t-shirts, and made sure to stuff several more comics into their backpacks beside the bologna sandwiches. Then they climbed down from the oak and met Jimmy at the end of the drive. Hoisting his gym bag over one shoulder and shifting his quiver into a comfortable position, Jimmy joined the two younger boys as they set out along the road.

Other than the jeans and sneakers, Fred and Stan looked just the part of travelling hobbits, but Jimmy looked more like an elf who had fallen into a music video. In order to keep his pointy ears up, he was wearing a headband, and his tracksuit made high whishing sounds as he walked. Fred shook his head. He didn't really know what to expect from his neighbor, but he supposed things could always be worse. He could be stuck in school taking a boring test or at home listening to Joanne guzzle mimosas and snore like a Gorax. Instead, he was setting off on an adventure, just like in his favorite books. For the first time in a long while he felt genuine happiness, and he couldn't help but smile as they trooped down Main Street towards Eisen Gardens and his grandfather.

6

BULLIES AND BOLOGNA

The boys had only made it to the local park, which was less than a mile from Fred's house, when they decided to stop for an early lunch (hobbits indeed!). Occupying a park bench to eat, they became so engrossed in their comics that they finished all of their bologna sandwiches in one sitting. Once they realized they were already completely out of food, Jimmy tried to nail a squirrel with his NERF bow, but the little creatures always seemed to know just when he was about to shoot and would dart away at the last moment. A big fan of the *Redwall* books, Fred didn't really want to kill a squirrel, anyway. So, he decided they needed to make a quick stop at the Bithbon supermarket to pick up some more supplies for the trip. Luckily, the grocery store was just across the street.

As soon as they entered the grocery store, they were greeted by Jimmy's boss, a portly man whose curly hair jutted wildly from his head at all angles. He shouted an enthusiastic good morning to Jimmy and then followed the boys over to the deli. He stood awkwardly close while Jimmy ordered a dozen more bologna sandwiches, made this time with double cheese *and* double meat, of course. The longer the manager stood nearby the more Fred started to worry the man was growing suspicious of them. Fred crossed his hairy toes and hoped Jimmy wouldn't give them away.

"So, Jimmy, who are your friends?" the supermarket manager finally asked.

"Oh, this is Fred and Stan," said Jimmy.

"I never knew you led a Boy Scout troupe," his manager said. "I'm an eagle scout myself, you know."

"What?" said Jimmy. Fred nudged him in the back, and Jimmy recovered clumsily. "Oh, yeah," he said, "children are the future I always say. That reminds me, I'm taking these kids on a nature expedition to, um, Redwood Forest, yeah, in California, and um, I'm going to need the week off."

"Sure thing, Jim," said his manager excitedly. "I've been trying to get you to take a vacation for months. I'll tell you what, the sandwiches are on me. Have fun on your trip guys. Scout's honor." Jimmy's manager raised his hand and held up three fingers. The boys tried to do the same, but Stan could only get his fingers to make a peace sign and Fred split his fingers into the Vulcan hand signal for "live long and prosper." The manager looked extremely confused, so Fred quickly thanked him for the sandwiches and said goodbye.

Feeling lucky to have so much food for the trip, Fred pushed Jimmy and Stan to the exit. He was hoping they could get out of there without running into anyone else Jimmy would need to lie to because his neighbor was clearly not very good at it. They were almost to the door when Stan suddenly whirled around.

"What is it?" asked Fred. "What's wrong?"

"Nothing," said Stan. "I just figured since we're here I

might as well grab some Gogurt and a few Twizzlers." Fred shot him a sour look. "That's it, I promise," said Stan. Before Fred could say no, Stan was shuffling down the nearest aisle, scanning both sides.

"Curse your bottomless hobbit belly," Fred yelled as Stan turned down another aisle. Fred crept over to the corner by the entrance so that he wouldn't run into anyone he recognized. Then he waited. And waited. After ten minutes passed, Fred was fed up. "I know he knows exactly where the candy is," he said to Jimmy. "What could be taking him so long?"

Jimmy shrugged his shoulders and waved to one of the cashiers. Fred was about to start looking for his best friend when Stan finally came creaking around the corner, struggling to push a shopping cart absolutely overflowing with food.

"Stan!" Fred yelled. Stan's head popped up over the hill of food, grinning hugely. "Stan, we can't take this," said Fred. "There's no way we could afford it, let alone carry it."

Stan's smile quickly disappeared. "Alright, just a couple snack-packs then," he said. "And some bubble-yum, you know, to control the cravings."

"Would you forget it and just come on," Fred said dragging him away from the cart. "Sorry," he told the manager, who just smiled and wished them luck.

"Look, *Evil Overlord of the Trail*," Stan said before they'd even made it out of the store. "I'm looking out for the good of the quest here. I mean, Twizzlers are an essential camping food. Not only are they delicious, but they can also be used to, you know, tie things."

"The only thing they can do is tie your tummy in knots when you eat the whole bag at once," said Fred. "And I don't want to hear your bellyaching before we even get out of Bithbon."

"If that's how you want to lead, you go ahead," said Stan. "I'm just saying some of the troops have been talking impeach—" Stan went silent and stopped dead in his tracks, looking as if someone had just chunked in his Cheerios.

"What's wrong?" Fred asked. "If it means that much to you, we can get the bubble gum."

Stan just pointed across the parking lot.

On the other side of the strip mall, a group of sixth graders was loitering in the alley between Pippin's Pets and Bofur's Books. Fred recognized them right away and let out a little groan. They were Alex Lassiter's gang, the Firebirds. Dressed in their black t-shirts with a red bird stitched on the back, they were unmistakable. Katie Greene, Stan's secret crush, was with them.

Fred loathed the Firebirds. When the gang wasn't making fun of nerds or soccer players like him, they were lighting things on fire behind the bleachers. Fred wondered with a chill what the *Firebirds* would do to him and Stan if they ever found out that they played Muggle Quidditch (a game which mostly saw them running around with brooms stuck between their legs, throwing kickballs at hula-hoops duct-taped to lawn chairs).

"C'mon," Stan said, "let's go the other way. We're wearing hobbit costumes in the middle of April, and I don't want to give Alex Lassiter any more reason to pick on us."

Because he didn't care what jerks like the Firebirds thought or said about him, Fred was going to suggest that they walk right past them instead. But he knew that Stan was sweet on Katie Greene, so he agreed. They turned to cut through an alley, but Alex Lassiter's maniacal laughter caused them to pause. Afraid the gang leader had spotted them, they cautiously peered over their shoulders. Fortunately, none of the Firebirds were looking their way. Fred was momentary relieved. Then he saw what Alex was carrying in his hand. It was a bag full of goldfish. Fred groaned. There was no way the gang leader was planning anything good.

Alex and the rest of the Firebirds started cackling at the tiny fish and frightening the animals by flicking the outside of the bag with their fingers. Then, without warning, Alex dumped the fish onto the sidewalk. Fred reflexively cried out. The fish were thrashing frantically on the pavement, and their orange scales glistened in the sunlight. Alex started stomping on them, while his Firebirds held their sides in amusement.

Fred was sprinting towards the gang in an instant, but Stan still got there first. Stan tackled Alex with such force, Fred heard the Firebird's joints pop. Stan completely lifted Alex off his feet and drove him so far backwards, the sixth-grader's head crashed into the glass in front of Pippin's Pets, startling some puppies on the other side of the window. The puppies barked wildly as Stan rained punches on the startled older boy, who was struggling to catch his breath.

The sixth-grade gang was just as stunned as Fred, and they watched in disbelief as their leader got pummeled. When Alex finally managed to cry out for help, they moved for Stan. Stan was punching so furiously, though, they struggled to get a hold of him. Fred knew that Stan couldn't take them all on for long, so he rushed forward to aid his friend. With a shout, he crashed into one of the smaller *Firebirds*, sending him stumbling and spinning off to the side. Then Fred turned to take on another member of the gang, but this boy was much larger than he was and easily threw him to the ground. Fred's sleeve ripped and the pavement bit into the skin of his elbows. He landed awkwardly on his shoulder and clutched it in pain as he rolled over. The other Firebirds finally wrestled Stan away from their leader and tossed him over by Fred. Picking themselves up, both Fred and Stan backed away from the gang of larger boys, who were now slowly advancing towards them, boxing them in.

The sixth-grade gang members were grinning and punching their palms as they approached. They taunted Fred and Stan with curses, and a few of them spat on the ground.

Fred's hand moved to the ring where it hung from the leather necklace inside his tunic. He was tempted to slip the ring on his finger and disappear, but he couldn't — he wouldn't — leave Stan to face them alone. He let go of the ring and prepared himself to take on one of the larger boys who was walking directly towards him.

The Firebird swung a meaty fist at Fred, who ducked below the punch and dove for the feet of the sixth grader. He tried to bite the bully's shin, but before he could sink his teeth in, a solid blow from the gang member struck Fred's back, sending a wave of pain to his head. He expected the next blow to knock him out.

But it never came.

The Firebird he was tussling with suddenly backed away. When Fred lifted his head, he couldn't believe what he saw...or, to be more accurate, what he smelt.

The entire gang was retreating, either from the sight of Jimmy Dingleman or from the horrible stench that had suddenly filled the area. The Firebird who had hit Fred was clutching at his chest with one hand where Jimmy's roundhouse kick had landed solidly. Oddly enough, the Firebird's other hand was grabbing at the back of his pants. The gang member's discomfort was matched only by his horrified surprise.

Fred turned to look at Jimmy, who suddenly appeared crazy dangerous. He was standing with knees bent, his hands held flat as fins as if he were ready to throw a karate chop at the slightest flinch from the Firebirds. "That's called the solar plexus," Jimmy said, pointing to where the Firebird was holding his chest. "It's a small target, but if you hit it just right, you can make a soft-bellied little boy soil his whitey tighties."

"Tighty whities," rasped Fred.

"Exactly," said Jimmy. "Except they aren't so whitey anymore, are they?"

Whimpering, the gang member Jimmy had kicked went shuffling awkwardly down the alley away from his friends. Fred hoped this would end the fight for good, but Alex Lassiter wasn't intimidated quite so easily. Wiping blood from his nose, the gang leader shoved his way to the front of his friends.

"Stupid greaseball!" he shouted at Stan. "What, did the Special Olympics have a day off or something?"

Jimmy and Stan glared back at him, but said nothing. Fred was surprised. Normally, Stan would have jumped at the chance to put Alex in his place. But Stan just shook his head and scooped up the only goldfish still moving and rushed it into the store.

"What's your glitch, man?" Fred said, sticking up for his friend. "Did you play near drums of sludge as a kid or something?"

"I'm not the one with hair glued to my shoes, geek," said Alex.

"Sorry I don't get a weekly pedicure like you," said Fred. "Speaking of, don't you and your Lady Birds have a tea party or a *Twilight* marathon to get to?"

"No," said one of the thicker gang members. Alex punched him in the shoulder.

"Well, you best run along now, anyway, Tweety birds," said Fred. "Otherwise, my pal Jimmy might have to ninja kick you in the nuggets. And if you think getting kicked so hard you drop a deuce in your drawers is the worst that can happen, think again. Jimmy here is a twelfth degree black-belt in...Shaq...Koon...Do, which means he can look at you funny and put you in the hospital."

Jimmy puffed out his skinny chest and growled like a bear. "I go hard in the paint," he said.

"Whatever," Alex said. "You nerds look funny all the time."

"Watch your tongue, you hunk of Bantha poodoo," said Jimmy. "You don't want to anger me, or else I'll have to release Admiral Ackbar," he held up his left fist, "and Sala-mandastron," he held up his right fist. "I don't mess around, okay. I play pogs for keeps."

Alex rolled his eyes. "I'm going to go crazy myself if I stay here talking to you retards," he said, starting to turn.

Before he could turn, Jimmy took a lightning-quick step across the small no-man's land that had formed between the two groups. All the Firebirds froze as Jimmy's eyes locked onto Alex Lassiter from only a foot away. Alex stood stock still, almost as if he was hypnotized. Jimmy didn't blink, and his face was red with anger. "Don't you ever say that word again," he said. "Ever."

It was obvious to Fred that Alex Lassiter's guts had turned to gloop. Nobody else dared move. Fred was completely stunned at how intimidating the local green grocer suddenly seemed. It was as if the very winds of Lothlorien bore his every word aloft.

Alex finally managed an audible gulp, and then he took a step back. "Yeah, whatever," he squeaked weakly. "Let's get out of here. I don't want to catch whatever it is they've got." He kept backing away, keeping his eyes on Jimmy until the gang was halfway across the parking lot.

Katie Greene didn't go with them. She stood there, staring at her shoes. Eventually she shuffled over to Fred, a sheepish look on her face. "I didn't know he was going to do that," she said. "I wouldn't have—" she stammered. "Can you just tell Stan that I didn't know, and that I'm sorry?"

"Sure," Fred told her, and then Katie Greene hurried to catch up to Alex, who was now shouting after her. "I didn't even think she knew his name," Fred whispered to Jimmy with a sly grin. Jimmy grinned back and knocked his eyebrows up twice in response.

Fred laughed, which only caused his head to hurt again. The pain reminded him that things could have been a whole lot worse if Jimmy hadn't stepped in and saved him. "Oh, and Jimmy," he added, trying to rub the pain in his head and shoulder away. "Thanks for getting that guy off my back. Literally."

"Don't think anything of it," said Jimmy. "That's why I take the classes."

"Well, they sure paid off big time today," said Fred. Jimmy smiled proudly. "Just one thing, Jim."

"Yeah?"

"What the hutt are pogs?"

Before Jimmy could explain, Stan came bursting out of the pet shop. "I told Mr. Pippin what happened, and he said he'll never sell to Alex or any of those buttheads again," he said. "Well, minus the buttheads part."

"That's good," Fred replied. "Alex is such a jerk. I can't believe anyone would do that. I'm starting to understand why you hate him so much."

"That's not even the worst of it," said Stan. "I've heard he puts firecrackers in cat's butts and hits golf balls into parking lots at night." Stan punched his leg. "I just can't believe Katie hangs around that ogre," he said.

"If it makes you feel any better, she told me to tell you that she didn't know Alex was going to do that, and that she's sorry," said Fred.

"She said that?" Stan asked.

"She even knew your name," Fred told him. "You must have made an impression."

Stan fought to hide a growing smile. "She kind of looks like Halle Berry don't you think?" he said.

Jimmy and Fred both nodded in agreement, even though Fred didn't really agree (Katie's hair was big and curly, not short), and he could tell Jimmy had no idea who Halle Berry was.

"And it did feel good, taking him down I mean," Stan said, still grinning.

"Did you ever think about playing football?" Fred asked him. "That tackle made Leo's old highlight tapes look like pillow fights."

"I knew there was a reason why we never invited him up to the tree house for a sleepover," said Stan with a smile.

"Shut up," Fred said, laughing. "Let's keep moving. It's not like Mordor's just around the corner."

The boys adjusted their packs and set off again away from the supermarket. As they did, Fred took one last look back at the dead goldfish. Their scales were dull now, crushed and lifeless. The fire of their lives snuffed out by Alex's sneakers. Mr. Pippin came out of the store and began sweeping the fish roughly into a plastic scoop with an old broom. The sound of the bristles scraping against the sidewalk hurt Fred's ears and grated against something deeper inside him. He turned away before Mr. Pippin dumped the goldfish into a big black garbage bin.

Each time the scoop banged against the garbage bin, Fred felt it in his pulse and in his aching shoulder. Like the beat of a distant enemy drum.

Boom.

Boom.

Boom.

For the first time, Fred felt the enormous evil power of the ring. It hung like an anvil from his neck. The leather of the cord scratched and pulled at his skin like it had never done before. He couldn't understand how people could value something like the ring so much and at the same time throw away life, even the life of a goldfish, as if it were nothing. *The Dark Lord has tricked so many*, he thought. It made him more determined than ever to destroy the ring. He and his friends had the chance to break the Dark Lord's spell over men and show them all what was truly precious.

There was that word—*precious*. Fred was sure the ring had put it into his mind. *It is already trying to control me*, he thought. He would have to remain vigilant or else the Dark Lord's spell would trap him, too. He could not afford that, because the road ahead was long, and he doubted this was the last time they'd face such awful foes.

It comforted him to know that he traveled with such brave and honorable friends. Together, they could take on anything. Together, they could carry the ring to its doom and rescue the world from this great peril.

7
FRIEND AND FOE

Still revved up after their standoff with the Firebirds, Fred, Stan and Jimmy were moving quickly, following the main road southwards out of Bithbon. Fred dodged in and out of the trees that lined the sidewalk, and Stan was nearly skipping with a newfound confidence. Their elation didn't last long, however. Within minutes, Stan was so bored he did exactly what Fred had warned him not to. He started asking Jimmy about *GUTS*.

"So, Jimmy, what was so great about that old show you watch?" he said. "What was it again, Nickelodeon *NUTS?*"

Jimmy huffed angrily and looked at Stan as if the younger boy had just snapped his favorite video game in half. After the incident with the Firebirds, Fred was a little worried Stan was going to get a roundhouse kick to the raspberries so stepped in. "I think what Stan means is that there were so many other great game shows back then," he said. "He's probably just wondering what made *GUTS,*" he made sure to emphasize the right name, "better than all the rest?"

Jimmy huffed again. "Only because *GUTS* was the

single most electrifying show ever to air on television," he said. "It was a perfect blend of mental toughness and athletic prowess. The events were original, suspenseful and beyond cool. And, as if it couldn't get any better, it was hosted by Mike O'Malley, one of the greatest actors ever to grace stage or screen. That man could make bingo night at Eisen Gardens seem as exciting as a last-minute drive in the Super Bowl. Not that he'd have to, of course, because any episode of *GUTS* was way more exciting than football."

"Was O'Mallory the guy who wore a bandana?" Stan asked.

Jimmy almost fell over in rage. "I should put an arrow straight through your heart for mistaking Mike *O'MALLEY* for Dan Cortese," he said. He took a deep breath to calm himself. "But I know you meant nothing by it—you've probably only seen a couple of reruns. I forget that you poor kids don't have the same standard of programming these days. No, Stan, Mike O'Malley was not just some gussied up pretty-boy. He was a man's man, more like Mike Adamle than Dan Cortese, and he was the perfect complement to Moira."

"Moira?" Stan asked.

"Be careful when you speak the sweetest name ever brought to human lips," Jimmy said. "A modern-day Galadriel she was... except shorter... and a brunette. Still, saying her name is like taking a bite out of chocolate licorice. You've got to savor it. I'm telling you, she was a goddess in umpire stripes, whose dulcet whistle blows would so sweetly echo through the mists of the Aggro Crag. Like a mournful elvish tune every time. She'd have a fanny-pack-full of Emmy awards by now if folks knew what they were doing."

Stan was laughing. "Sure, Jimmy," he said.

"It's true," Jimmy went on. "The chemistry those two had was right up there with classic screen couples. Han and Leia, Mulder and Scully, Quirk and O'Malley." He counted the names off on his fingers and then closed them into a fist. "Man, I was so close to living the dream, so close to being on the show. I still can't listen to the Backstreet Boys without getting angry."

"What?" Fred and Stan exclaimed together, totally confused.

"Who are the Backstreet Boys?" Stan asked.

"They were one of those terrible boy bands from the late '90s," Jimmy answered. "Just be glad you weren't born yet. If you can imagine cloning Justin Bieber four times and dyeing just the tips of his hair blonde, you'd have some idea of the utter horror that was the Backstreet Boys."

Fred and Stan winced, their faces turning a little pale as if they might vomit.

"Anyway," Jimmy went on, "A.J. *Mean* McLean was the *bad boy* of the Backstreet Boys, which basically meant he had earrings and wore goofy hats. But before he was a Backstreet Boy, he was just a pompous child actor. He was scheduled to go on *GUTS*, but he told the producers he had to do some cereal commercial and might not make it. I had been harass—" Jimmy coughed, "—*calling* them for months trying to get on the show and finally they called me back and told me that if he couldn't participate, I'd get to go in his place. I was just about to go on—I had the sticker on my helmet and everything—and then, at the last second, McLean shows up in his limo and dashes my hopes. Can you believe the nerve? He didn't even care about *GUTS*. He just wanted some *exposure*. Well, he got exposed alright. He lost to a girl. I would have taken that championship. Who knows, maybe with the right events and a little luck I would have won the *GUTS* tournament of champions, too. That would have taken me to new heights of fame and fortune. Foiled by a Backstreet Boy," Jimmy said, shaking his head. "You don't know how that keeps me up at night."

"Crap!" exclaimed Fred.

"I know," Jimmy said, "and a lesser-known Backstreet Boy to boot."

"No, not that," said Fred, standing on his tiptoes to get a better look down the street. "I think that's...that's Leo's black Cadillac coming down the road! We've got to get out of here."

"Hey, Salacious Crumb, relax," said Stan. "There's no way he knows about the ring, and, besides, the old fogey is way too blind to spot us from that far away."

"Are you kidding me?" said Fred, tightening the straps of his book bag and looking around for the best place to hide. "I'm sure that knuckle buckle gives him all kinds of powers."

"That ring *is* the size of a WWE championship belt," said Stan.

"And don't underestimate how much he hates kids," said Fred. "They're like his kryptonite. He hands out mints and towelettes at Halloween, which he probably just steals from his office restroom. And he's the one who started building that strip-mall over McGillis Park just because the soccer matches were too *boisterous*."

"That reminds me of the last time you dragged me on one of these crazy little adventures," Stan said. "Did you tell Jimmy how last Halloween you made me help you bury your old soccer trophies at McGillis Park because you wanted to haunt the new buildings?"

Jimmy cocked his head in curiosity. Fred gave him a nervous smile. "First of all, that's a perfect plan," he said.

"It was a full moon on All Hallow's Eve and that tournament was named for a ref who got struck by lightning. If all I got was 1.21 gigawatts up my nuts after getting yelled at by berserker parents, you can bet I'd be ready to get my haunt on."

"Whatever you say," said Stan, shaking his head.

"We don't have time to talk about it right now, anyway," said Fred. "I'm telling you—that's Leo. And he'll have us chained up in a filing room doing Gandalf knows what after school for months if he catches us."

"Look, you don't need to convince me Leo's a total Goblin Goon," said Stan, "I've seen his collection of bowties. But there's no way he'll ever see us from all the way down the ro—"

Just then the engine of Leo's Escalade roared to life, belting out gear-wrenching growls. The huge tires bit into the cement, sending smoke and dust swirling out behind them as they hurtled the mini-tank forward at tremendous speed. "Or maybe I was wrong..." said Stan, already backpedaling.

"I'm going to remember you said that," said Fred. "C'mon, follow me!" he shouted as he broke from the path and started sprinting through backyards.

The boys ducked and weaved around several houses as they made their way deep into a labyrinthine neighborhood. They made sure to somersault, sidestep, and soldier crawl a couple times to throw Leo of their trail. After swinging from a playhouse rope like a Wookiee flying through the jungle, Fred led them through a group of trees and pulled up behind a red-bricked house. The three of them pinned their backs against the house and tried to quiet their breathing so they could listen for Leo.

The Escalade's engine was growling nearby, but Fred

couldn't pinpoint where it was exactly. After a minute, the guttural bubbling of the engine began to fade. Fred relaxed a little, thinking they had gotten lucky and lost Leo. He peeled his back off the wall and took a deep breath.

"That was clo—" he started.

"Shh," said Stan. "Listen."

Fred flung himself back against the house. He strained his ears for any sound of Leo, but the whole neighborhood seemed to have grown completely quiet. Too quiet.

With another loud bang, the black SUV burst the silence. It tore around a bend and burned rubber straight towards them, its tires squealing as they left black rubber tracks on the road. It sounded to Fred just like the shriek of a Fell Beast. He was too terrified to move. He was sure the Beast was going to run right over him, and then Jimmy and Stan were pushing him forward. Before he knew what was happening, his legs were moving all on their own. He sprinted until his legs and lungs burned, following Jimmy and Stan deep into the neighborhood. Growing desperate to lose Leo now, Fred changed direction suddenly, hopping over a short fence. He ran around swing sets and over small inflatable pools, knocking plastic basketball hoops and fake palm trees aside. The obstacles whirred by in a blur, one after another.

Fred had just leapt over a hedge and started across a small yard, when the two black Labradors came out of nowhere.

The hounds came howling after them, flashing vicious teeth. The beasts' eyes rolled wildly. The scent of the bologna sandwiches must have been driving them mad. When one of them snapped inches from Fred's heels, a new surge of fear pushed him to speeds he had never reached before. Jimmy was faster still. The older boy tried to draw the dogs away, but no matter what he tried the dogs wouldn't give up on Fred. Still getting shocked by their collars, the dogs were only growing madder and more ferocious. Knowing he couldn't outrun the mutts for much longer, Fred made a break for the nearest tall fence, hoping Jimmy and Stan would catch on to his plan.

He reached the fence first and leapt up at full speed, grabbing the planks and hauling himself over the top before the dog could latch onto his ankle. His momentum carried him right over, and he fell to the ground on the other side with a thud. The fall hurt every bone in his body and knocked the breath out of him. Fred lay there for a second, checking for injuries and trying to draw in air. Everything seemed to be okay.

Then he looked up.

Fear froze every muscle in his body. His mouth was as dry as the Dune Sea, but he couldn't even swallow. He had escaped the two Labradors only to land within a few feet of the largest dog he had ever seen. From a distance, Fred would have mistaken it for a lion. It had a yellow coat and a head the size of a basketball. Lying down, the beast took up nearly the entire patch of the small lawn that was not filled with vegetables or flowers, and his enormous jowls were dropping thick gobs of drool onto the grass.

Fred held his breath and sat as still as possible, cringing when Stan and Jimmy crashed loudly to the ground behind him. They started to groan in pain, so Fred whispered, "Shhh!" through tight lips. When Stan and Jimmy saw the dog, they started to make a break for it, but Fred grabbed them. "Don't move," he whispered again, not wanting to do anything that might startle the behemoth.

Finally, the dog stood up, and Fred was even more amazed to find that up to the shoulder it was as tall as he was. It took all of Fred's courage to stay still as the dog slowly inched closer to him. He shut his eyes tight when the animal raised its snout towards his face and blew its hot, foul breath all over him. He heard the beast lick its lips, and Fred was sure that his journey was over. In a few moments the dog would bite off his head and swallow it whole. The last thing he'd ever see as his head rolled through the giant's stomach would be the sneakers of all the other little boys the dog had eaten.

The tongue that scrolled out and rubbed across Fred's cheek was as big as a paintbrush, and it slathered his entire face with sticky saliva. *It's tasting me*, Fred thought. It just wants to make sure I'm not going to give it a stomachache when it eats me whole. But when he didn't feel the painful crunch of razor-sharp teeth around his neck, he cracked one eye enough to see that the dog's tail was wagging. Ever so cautiously, Fred reached out a hand to pat behind the dog's ear, which was as big as a garden flag. Much to Fred's relief, the dog continued to lick his face as he patted him, and eventually all three boys were scratching all its favorite spots. For a moment, they completely forgot that they were being chased by a big, black Escalade driven by a very surly former linebacker.

"We should go," Fred said after a minute. "Leo's ears are terrible, but those other stupid mutts could wake the dead."

"Are you trying to jinx us?" said Stan. "The last thing we need is a pack of zombies on our trail, too."

"Good call," said Fred. "Bad choice of words."

As they gave the dog one final pat, they heard a woman's voice call from the back porch of the house.

"Griswold, are you bothering these boys?" said an

elderly woman. She had a deep, raspy voice and was wearing a long dress covered in bright flowers.

The dog shook his head as if to say no to her question and drool went flying everywhere. Wiping a glob of it from his face with a grimace, Fred took a closer look at the woman.

He had to choke back a scream when he finally recognized her. They'd stumbled into the old widow Thompson's yard! Any student at Lewis and Clark Elementary who wanted to survive Halloween avoided her house at all costs. Most kids agreed she was a witch, and not the good kind either. She wouldn't help you finish a scroll on the history of giants or defeat dark wizards. She'd chop you up with a sharpened broomstick handle and use you as fertilizer. How else could you explain how everyone else's lawn had turned brown and bare in the middle of the summer, while her flower beds were always still full of color? Most kids were so scared of her, only the occasional dare could bring anyone within arm's length of her house. Dropping into her lawn like this, Fred and his friends had basically offered themselves up for sacrifice.

"He's been very lonely since Goldie died," said the widow, pointing to a vacant doghouse, where the name Goldberry was slowly flaking off rotten shingles. "I'm thankful to you for keeping him company. I've just baked some chocolate chip cookies if you boys would care to join me?" She smiled warmly and beckoned them to follow.

"It's a trick," Stan whispered, "to lure us into her house so she can use our hearts to grow her rhododendrons."

Part of Fred wanted to bolt right then, but something stopped him. There was something in the widow's voice that seemed so sad and lonely. It reminded him of his grandfather—who was one of the nicest people he knew.

Everybody lied about his grandfather being crazy. What if they were lying about the widow, too?

"The dog's nice enough, maybe she's not all bad either," he whispered back. "Besides, she's seen us now, we can't just leave."

"Said Gretel right before becoming meat pie," said Stan.

"Don't be so grim," said Fred with a wink.

Stan rolled his eyes and looked ready to protest again, but Jimmy was already walking up to the house, thanking the widow for inviting them in. Fred and Stan looked at each other a moment before warily following him inside. Neither one of them wanted to be first through the door, so they kept jostling to hide behind the other.

They finally managed to squeeze through the doorway together, but they made so much noise an irritated cat leapt to his escape from the top of a bookcase. The cat knocked over a stack of papers, which caused a brightly colored bird to squawk loudly and dart across the room. Stan tripped over himself trying to make it back to the door. Fred jumped at the high-pitched noise as well, but gathered his wits in time to help Stan up and prevent him from dashing out the door. "Relax, man," he said to his friend. "It's not a pterodactyl. Just a ball of feathers."

"Well, it about made me drop a ball of something in my pants," said Stan. "The witch is already sending her minions after us."

"Would you calm down," said Fred. "The cat is orange, not black, and that's some kind of parrot or something, not a crow."

Stan relaxed a little. His eyes kept searching the house warily, but he didn't say anything else. Fred looked around as well and was surprised to see that the widow had as many flowers in pots as she did in the backyard garden.

Even the wallpaper was decorated with petals. What's more, the house did not have the musty mothball smell Fred had been expecting. Instead, it was filled with the delicious aroma of baking cookies.

"It's been a long time since Griswold and I have had any visitors," the widow Thompson said, directing them to the large, lace-covered dining room table with a wave of her hand. "It is nice to see some young faces around here. I'm Dr. Thompson, by the way, and you are?" she asked.

"A pleasure to make your acquaintance, my lady," said Jimmy quickly, rising from his seat. When he tried to offer a bow, he caught his quiver on the back of one of her chairs and lost his balance. "My name is...Jimmy...of house... Dingleman," he said as he struggled to free his plastic weapon from the chair.

"Oh, so polite," she said smiling. She turned to Fred and Stan. "And you two?"

Fred wanted to be polite, too, and not lie to her, but he also wanted to keep his last name secret. He still wasn't sure about the widow, and they were still really close to home. One phone-call to his mom or dad, and his quest would be over. "I'm Fred," he said.

"Hello, Fred," she said with a smile.

Stan wasn't going to say anything, so Fred had to nudge him.

"And I'm Stan," his friend said finally, "Of house...Makesabadmulch."

Fred wanted to kick Stan under the table, but he held back. He didn't want to startle Dr. Thompson with any sudden moves. To his relief, the old woman seemed amused by Stan rather than insulted by him. She laughed so hard her thick crest of curly white hair shook.

"It's a pleasure to meet you all," she said when she was

done chuckling. Just then a timer rattled off in another room. Stan jumped at the sound and nearly knocked over the large vase of lilies sitting in the center of the table.

"Oh, don't be scared—that's just the timer for the cookies," said Dr. Thompson, disappearing into the kitchen. "I'll be right back," she called over her shoulder.

"I bet they're poison," Stan whispered.

"Well, it'll be the first time you ever turned down a cookie then," Fred shot back. "I'm thinking she's just a lonely old lady with no one to talk to but her big dog out there. So, I'll risk a cookie, because I can't think of a better place to hide while Leo drives himself around in circles out there. Can you?"

"Just because she's a Black woman baking cookies doesn't mean she's the Oracle, you know?" Stan said. "She's probably not even baking. I wouldn't be surprised if she just had like a dozen cookie air-fresheners blowing to cover up the nasty chemical smell of all her jars full of kid heads."

Fred didn't have time to answer. Just then, the widow Thompson emerged from the kitchen with a plate full of cookies and a pitcher of milk. When she placed the cookies right in front of Stan, Fred gave him an "I-told-you-so" look.

"I was baking these for the school bake sale, but I can always make another batch," she said, taking a seat across from them. "Please, help yourselves."

Jimmy had two cookies in his mouth before Stan could warn him. Even though Fred had just told Stan not to worry, he found himself watching Jimmy closely as the older boy savored the fresh treats. He knew it was a ridiculous notion that the cookies were poisoned, but part of him wondered if Jimmy's face would soon turn purple while his tongue swelled out of his mouth, covered in green and yellow spots, or if he'd transform painfully into a mouse. Of course, nothing of the sort happened. After Jimmy finished with the first two cookies, he smacked his lips in complete delight and reached for another handful. Fred shrugged at Stan and then dug into the pile of sweets himself.

He couldn't believe what he was tasting! The cookies were by far the best he had ever eaten. Fred's lucky streak was holding—he had not expected to eat so well on such a difficult journey.

"So, what are you boys up to today?" Dr. Thompson asked them, taking a sip of milk as she sat down across from them. "By that I mean, what brings you into my yard?"

"We're only playing," Fred replied first, worried that if they told her they were on a quest the widow would call his parents. "Yeah, just playing. Sorry if we disturbed you."

"Sorry?" she said. "Why would you ever apologize for playing?"

Fred shrugged.

"You know, I get so angry when I see grumps of all sorts yelling at kids to stop playing around. I'm willing to bet you do, too," she said, and all three boys nodded in agreement, their mouths raining cookie crumbs onto their placemats. Suddenly Fred was very fond of the widow Thompson and regretted never having stopped in to see her before. "Did you know that I was a biologist, and that I studied plants and animals for a living before I retired?" the doctor asked.

Fred shook his head no, but now he was starting to think that this was the real reason why her garden was always so bright and full in springtime. Just as they'd done to his grandfather, people had told lies about the widow and everyone else had believed them. Fred was ashamed of himself for ever believing the rumors, and he felt truly sorry for Dr. Thompson.

"Well, biologists know that young animals play all the time," she said. "In fact, many animal mothers actually encourage their children to play because it's a great way for young ones to practice the skills that they'll need to survive as adults. Did you know that?"

Again, the boys shook their heads no, but Fred was listening extra carefully now. The next time he got yelled at for "destroying his neighbor's dollhouse" or "making reckless use of piles of leaves" he wanted to have an excellent excuse ready, and he thought Dr. Thompson was just about to give him a foolproof one.

"Oh, it's true!" she said, seeing she had their interest. "Cheetah cubs learn how to hunt by chasing grasshoppers through the shrubs, monkeys learn to swing through the trees by flipping and rolling around on the ground, and penguins learn how to become great swimmers and divers by romping around on ice floes and racing through the water."

"Thaps a goob moobie," Stan said, his mouth full.

Dr. Thompson smiled. "Well, just like those little penguins, it's very important for young kids to play, and especially for them to dream and imagine, because humans, more than any other creature, rely on their big ole brains to get by. And when you use your imagination, you exercise your brain the same way those penguins use their wings and their flippers. So, if you ask me, I think you boys are setting a fine example," she said, beaming at them.

"Well, we play all the time," Fred blurted out, hoping to impress Dr. Thompson.

"Then keep it up," said Dr. Thompson, "and keep your classmates playing, too."

"Freb always geps as many beeple as he can," added Stan, surprising Fred completely. Just a moment ago, Stan had been afraid Dr. Thompson was just plumping them up to improve her fertilizer, now he was acting like the widow was his oldest friend.

"That's great, boys, really great," said the widow. "Now I want you to take the rest of these cookies with you because I have a feeling that you're going to be very hungry on your journey."

Fred and Stan shot each other a worried look.

Dr. Thompson threw up her hands. "Don't worry, your secret is safe with me," she said. "But be careful," she urged. "And, Sir Dingleman, you make sure to look after them. If you get into trouble, you call your parents right away, okay."

"Yes, ma'am," they said together and thanked her for the cookies.

"And, boys," Dr. Thompson added. "Do be sure to stop by here on Halloween. My late husband used to own a comic book store, and I've got a million of them gathering dust in the basement. I don't know how I'll ever get rid of them. I try to give them to trick-or-treaters, but for some reason, I don't get many visitors that time of year."

"Comics for Halloween!" Fred shouted. "Why didn't I think of that? It's ingenious. You can bet we'll be back around, Dr. Thompson." He was sorry he'd ever said a bad word about her. She was practically a saint in his mind. After he finished his quest, he'd have to remember to introduce his mother to the widow Thompson—he was sure they'd become best friends.

She smiled at them. "Good then. Griswold and I will be looking forward to it."

She walked them to the front door.

"Um, you wouldn't be able to tell us how to get to Eisen

Gardens, by any chance would you?" Fred asked as they left. "I'm trying to free...I mean, *see* my grandfather."

"That's nice of you, darling," Dr. Thompson replied. "I hear it can get quite boring over there. I'm sure your grandfather would appreciate a jailbreak...I mean, a *visit*." She winked. Fred and Stan smiled at each other. "Take a left onto Main Street, and then a right on Athcorn Street and follow that road for a little while. Eisen Gardens will be on your right."

"Thanks, Dr. Thompson," said the boys together as they hoisted their bags, which were now heavy with cookies, and waved goodbye. "We'll see you on Halloween!"

Leaving out her front gate, Fred quickly scanned the streets for Leo's Escalade. Seeing no sign of it, he followed the widow's directions out of the neighborhood, careful to keep an eye out for Leo. Fred didn't expect to see him, though. He was sure the old man had long since given up the search and driven to his favorite pub, where he would hopefully drink enough to forget he had ever seen the boys. Still, it was best to be cautious.

It didn't take long to reach their destination. Fred *felt* Eisen Gardens before he saw the medical complex. The laughter and noise of the neighborhoods had quieted and the immense building blotted out the sun, bringing a small bite to the balmy spring air. Fred shivered as they passed by a copse of dense evergreens and caught sight of the tremendous tower. He remembered why he'd been terrified to come back. The dark windows looked like demon eyes and the gray brick looked tougher than troll hide.

Milk and cookie time was officially over. Breaking his grandfather out of this dark fortress was not going to be easy.

8

DEADEYE DINGLEMAN

"Okay," said Stan, "how on Middle-earth do you propose we get into this cuckoo castle?"

"Well, for obvious reasons I only came to visit once," said Fred, searching the area.

"I don't blame you," said Jimmy. "It looks more like a gargoyle graveyard than a garden."

"So, you don't know where we're going at all?" added Stan.

Fred shook his head.

"Well, this should be a cinch then," said Stan.

"Relax," said Fred. "I know the area fairly well. I'm pretty sure that there is a side door for groundskeepers...I mean Uruk-hai just through those bushes. We can get into the building without being seen that way."

"That doesn't sound completely impossible," said Stan, peering across the large field. "But what do we do once we're inside?"

"Well, we've got to get up to the top floor where they're holding him," said Fred. "But the enemy will be swarming everywhere, so we'll have to find some way to distract them." He paused, thinking hard. He could feel Jimmy and Stan watching and waiting for him to come up with something, and he started to grow anxious. "I've got it!" he said finally.

"What?" Stan and Jimmy said in unison.

"Grandpa's chest of tricks!" said Fred. "It's perfect. If we can get to the storage room and find that chest, we'll have plenty of things to cause all sorts of commotion in there."

"So, all we have to do is make it crazy enough that we can sneak Alfred out of there?" said Stan. He smirked, "Shouldn't be too tough in a madhouse."

"Exactly," said Fred, "but we need to find some way to warn Grandpa first, so that he knows what we're doing and is ready to move as soon as the escape begins."

"I'm guessing Alfred the Ancient has never heard of a cell phone," said Stan.

Fred shook his head. "Unfortunately, he still communicates by snail mail and butterfly messenger."

"Of course he does," said Stan. "Maybe one of these days we can get him on cricket wireless and convince him that the Twitter bird is an actual bird."

"Fat chance," said Fred. "And it won't help us now."

"If he had his window open, I could fire an arrow up there," Jimmy suggested. "We could attach a note to it. Use a page from one of the comics."

"Or I could just use my cape and fly up to the top floor," said Stan. "As long as we're talking the impossible, I mean."

"It is foolish to doubt my aim, hobbit," said Jimmy. "I've made more difficult shots in my sleep. I'm the best marksman in my LARP squadron. Last event I took out the Drakkylvanian King all the way from our opposing stronghold. With one shot, too. Jimmy 'Deadeye' Dingleman is what my nickname was going to be on *GUTS*. I can pick the wings off a bee at a hundred paces, give an ant a haircut at fifty paces. I can hit a spider between the eyes, I can—"

"Alright, Jimmy, we get it," Fred said. "Bugs are terrified of you. Just get the arrow through the window, okay."

"As sure as my name is 'Deadeye,' I'll make that shot," Jimmy declared as he plucked an arrow from his plastic quiver.

Stan rolled his eyes and muttered under his breath as Fred pulled one of his least favorite comics from the bag. He tore out a small portion of the advertisement page, keeping the size of the note small because he didn't want to disrupt the flight of the arrow. Next, he searched his backpack for a marker. His fingers scratched the bottom of his bag and found nothing. H*ow in Harad did all his pens and pencils mysteriously disappear*? Lately, he had begun to suspect that the bottom of his book-bag had been magically extended by someone looking to mess with him. It had probably been Mrs. Bonneville who had jinxed it when he wasn't looking just so he wouldn't be able to draw comics in class. Well, he wasn't going to let her get the best of him now. He scraped every nook and cranny of his bag, hoping there was at least one marker buried somewhere in its bottomless depths. He gave a quiet shout when his hand finally closed on a magic marker.

"We're in luck!" he said as he held up the marker. "This magic quill is filled with special elven ink that can only be read by moonlight. Only Alfred the Grand will know how to read it. It will be safe from enemy eyes."

"What a stroke of luck that is," said Stan, rolling his eyes.

Fred quickly scribbled *ESCAPE NOW, BE READY* on the piece of paper and handed it to Jimmy. Jimmy pulled the piece of gum he had been chewing from his mouth and stuck the note to the tip of the NERF arrow with the pink adhesive. Then he notched the arrow on his bow.

"I'm not totally sure, but my guess is that it's that one there," said Fred, pointing to an open window on the top floor.

Jimmy nodded. "Fly swiftly, arrow, fly true," the archer said as he took aim. "Be as deadly as the dark and as silent as the light of the moon."

As the arrow leapt from the bow with a heavy thwang, Fred's breath caught in his throat. Maybe Stan was right, and Jimmy had no chance whatsoever at making this shot. In fact, the arrow could just as likely smack into a window belonging to some old lady, who would raise every alarm, thinking a sparrow had crashed into the glass or something. And if they were spotted before they made it into the building, they would never free Alfred, and, without Alfred, they wouldn't make it far on their quest at all.

He clenched his fists as the arrow zoomed towards the building. For a moment, it looked like the foam missile would fall short and hit the window ledge, but the arrow flew as straight as Jimmy had promised, sailing soundlessly through the open window.

Jimmy jumped up and cheered. "And 'Bull's Eye' goes to 'Deadeye' Dingleman!" he exclaimed. "With three hundred points he takes first place. Here's Mike O'Malley with our leader."

Jimmy deepened his voice to sound like a commentator: "That was a legendary performance, Jimmy—do you have any words for our audience?

"Why, yes I do, Mike," Jimmy said in his normal voice. "A.J. 'Mean' McLean can suck on my fletching!"

Fred yanked him back into the cover of the bushes. "Get down and be quiet!" he whispered. "But great shot," he added once Jimmy had quieted down.

"Yeah, one in a million and all that," Stan said. "Except I don't see Alfred. Wouldn't he come to the window to give us a sign that he got the note? What if someone else saw it?"

"Take it easy," said Fred. "He's probably just not in his room right now."

"So, what do we do next?" asked Stan.

"We don't have time to wait here," said Fred. "Somebody will be coming around. There's probably a squad of orcs gearing up for sentry duty right now. We just have to hope he gets it in time. Follow me to the side-door and stay down," he whispered and then began crawling on his hands and knees towards the building, keeping his eyes alert for any sign of movement.

Scampering on all fours, the three boys could easily have been mistaken for large cats stalking mice in the bushes. No one moved to intercept them and within a few seconds Fred, Stan, and Jimmy had reached the side of the building. Fred stood up cautiously and tested the side door, while Stan and Jimmy served as lookouts. Finding the door unlocked, Fred cracked it just wide enough for them to slip inside, and then he closed it softly behind them.

The room was empty except for a small storage closet and a large stairwell. Fred crept up to the bottom of the stairs and peered up. No one was on the stairwell, so he made a walking motion with two fingers to signal that it was safe to climb. Once Jimmy and Stan nodded that they were ready to go, Fred started up the stairs. He relaxed ever so slightly once they'd cleared the first flight.

"Easy as Jedi pie," he said, turning around to grin at Stan. "We didn't even need to dress up as storm troop—"

He never got to finish the joke. The door at the top of the stairs suddenly crashed open. The boys froze and Fred's grin disappeared like a cheap whiz-bang. Two huge orcs were rushing down the stairs straight for them.

9
CHILDE FRED TO THE DARK TOWER CAME

Fred bumped into Jimmy and Stan as he turned to bust hutt down the stairs. He made a frantic, and entirely unnecessary, scurrying motion with his fingers, and all three of them scrambled to find a hiding place. Pressing his back against the door of storage closet beneath the stairs, Fred held his breath and hoped they had not already been seen.

The thud of heavy boots, tinkle of countless keys, and a clank that Fred could only assume was a variety of stabbing weapons knocking together grew louder and louder. Fred peered around the closet just enough to see two huge shapes linger for a moment in front of the exit. For a second it looked like they might grab something from the closet, but luckily for the boys, the guards crashed out the side door. As soon as the door slammed shut, the boys peeled themselves from the wall and sprinted up the stairs as quickly as they could. They needed to reach the top floor before the guards came back inside or anyone else entered the stairwell.

Jumping over the last stair and sliding across the landing, Fred opened the door ever so slightly and checked the hallway for nurses and orderlies. "It's clear," he whispered back and then waved his friends inside. "Grandpa's room is on the other side of the wing, but I think the storage room is just down this hallway," he said as the three of them padded quietly along the shining tile.

In truth, Fred was having a hard time remembering the layout of the ward. All of the hallways looked exactly the same. He tried to let the Force guide him, but if he was being honest, he was truly just turning corners at random, hoping a team of sentries wasn't waiting for him around the next bend. He didn't let on that he was lost, though. That was a good way to get Stan to bail altogether. Luckily, he found the storage room before they ran afoul of any more guards.

Fred was hoping for a little more luck with the door handle but didn't get it. "Dang, it's locked," he said. "We need to get the key."

"You think?" Stan said.

"You *could* help me figure out how to get the key," said Fred. "The sarcasm is helpful, too, though."

"Well, I guess if we had Alfred here, he could just magic it open," said Stan.

"Shh!" said Jimmy before Fred could retort. "I think I hear those goons coming back up the stairs!"

The sound of voices in the stairwell proved him right.

"Quick, into the break room," Fred whispered, pointing to a door just a short way down the corridor.

They scurried across the hall and slipped inside the break room just before the guards entered the hallway.

"Now what?" said Stan. "What if they come in here?"

The three boys looked at each other, eyes wide with

fear. "Hide!" said Fred, and they all searched frantically for cover.

Jimmy flung open the doors to the bottom cabinets and squeezed himself in beside the coffee filters and bottles of dish soap. The ends of his bow caught against the frame, and he had to quickly bend down the limbs on their handy hinges to completely fit. Stan and Fred tried to follow him inside, but there was no room. They took one last desperate look around the room, but there was nowhere else to hide.

They were out of time, too. Fred could hear the orcs right outside the door now. With no other options, Fred and Stan turned and dove underneath the long rectangular table in the center of the room just as the two men entered.

The orcs were chatting as they sunk into their seats near the head of the table, just a few feet away from Fred and Stan. Fred's heart thumped a little slower, but he wasn't breathing easy yet. The longer the guards lingered in the break room, the more likely they'd all get caught. Fred looked for a way to escape, but the room was too small to slip by the guards unnoticed, and there was nothing in the room to use as a distraction. Fred had almost given up hope for the rescue when he noticed the huge key-ring dangling from one of the orc's belts. The key to the storage room was surely on that loop!

That solved one problem, but he still didn't have a plan for getting out. He pointed to the key-ring, hoping Stan would be able to help him figure out the next step. Stan nodded and then pointed to the orcs' shoelaces. Fred knew exactly what Stan had in mind, and he gave him the thumbs up.

The boys inched towards the orcs, who were still chatting idly.

"That Dr. White is something else, man," said one of

the guards. "The man has supposedly devoted his whole life to curing the sick, and yet he wants us to put poison out for cats he thinks he's seen in the gardens."

"Oh, you didn't know he was like that?" said the other man.

"I knew he was a tough son-of-a-gun, but I didn't think he was a kitten killer."

"You haven't been here long enough then."

"I guess not."

"Yeah, he's a mean old devil. The only people who hate him more than the patients are the employees."

Both men chuckled.

This Dr. White must surely be the dark wizard who wards this evil tower, thought Fred as he crawled. He doubted they would be able to escape without dealing with the doctor first.

At the guard's shoes, Fred steadied his hands. Across the table, Stan slowly tugged on the other guard's shoelaces, and the knot uncoiled. Fred reached to do the same, but the guard stood up suddenly before he could grab the lace. Fred yanked his hand back and froze. Stan tensed up too, and both of them watched the guard with the key ring lurch over to the countertop to fill his coffee mug.

"Gotta be kidding me," said the man at the counter, slamming the empty pot back down. Fred looked over at Stan in fright, sure they'd been seen. "Never enough for a cup, and the daggone filter is filthy again. I must be the only one who replaces them."

"Murphy's law," said the guard still sitting at the table.

They hadn't been spotted yet, but Fred was still petri-fied. Unless there were coffee filters on the counter, or in the higher cabinets, the guard would spot Jimmy when he opened the bottom drawer! The guard tried the top cabinets first, standing on his tiptoes to open them. *Find the dang filters*, Fred thought. *Just find them and sit down!*

"Here we go," said the guard.

Fred relaxed a little when he heard the orc open a box. Then the guard huffed angrily. "Don't you know it," he said, "the daggone box is completely empty."

"Murphy's—" started the other guard.

"Law, I know," said the orc at the counter. "And if Murphy worked here and put empty boxes back in the drawers, I'll tell you what I'd do to him."

Fred heard the sound of cardboard being crunched and then saw the guard's legs flex and balance for a throw. He didn't see the guard toss the box, but he turned his head in time to see the crumpled cardboard bounce off the wall, hit the edge of the pail and skitter to a stop against a chair leg.

"I guess Murphy never played any basketball neither," said the guard who had thrown it.

"I'll get it," said the other orc, rising from his seat. "Wouldn't want you to have to bend over and strain yourself."

"What would I do without you?" said the guard with the keys, rummaging through the upper cabinets again.

Great, now they're both up, thought Fred. *We're in for it now.* If the guard at the counter didn't spot Jimmy, his helpful friend would surely see that Fred and Stan had undone his shoelaces—if he didn't spy the two hobbits curled under the table first, that is.

A flash of movement from the bottom cabinets caught Fred's eye. Jimmy's hand darted out of the cabinet, tossed some filters lightly up onto the counter, and then quickly shot back inside. Fred was worried that the guy at the counter had seen too, but Jimmy had timed his throw perfectly. The guard was still digging through the top cabinets, completely oblivious.

"Well, how do you like that?" the orc said when he finally looked down. "They've been sitting there staring me in the face the whole time."

"I won't even say it," said the other guard, who was now standing above the crumpled box near the trash bin.

Fred curled himself into a tighter ball, trying to make his body as small as possible, hoping that somehow the guard would not see him or Stan or that he would mistake their shapes for something else—a coat someone left behind or something. With a grunt, the orc slowly bent down to grab the box.

"What in tarnation?" Fred heard him say. He closed his eyes even tighter.

"What?" said the other man.

Stan tensed beside him, and Fred prepared to run.

"Ah, nothing," said the guard. "Just looks like something was eating away at the base of the wall over here."

Fred chanced a look up. The orc had grabbed the trash and was standing up, looking down at the wall and away from them. They had gotten lucky again—the guard hadn't spotted them. Now if he would just sit down!

"Not our problem," said the other guard, dumping more coffee beans into the filter.

"You got that right."

With those words both guards turned around and finally headed back to the table. Fred and Stan didn't breathe until both of them had plopped down, and even then Fred waited a moment before he reached out for the guard's shoes. Stan grabbed his arm just as he was about to pick up a lace. Fred looked back at him anxiously. Stan was pointing at the other guard's shoe. The portly man had stepped down right on his untied shoelaces! Stan couldn't get to them!

Now they were really roasted ragamuffins. They needed that key! And he couldn't get the key unless the big lug lifted his dirty boot. But he had no clue how he could get the orc to lift his shoe without getting them all captured.

Just then, something yellow slithered across the floor and settled lightly against Fred's hand. It was one of Jimmy's arrows. Jimmy was gesturing at Fred to use the feathers on the end to tickle the guard's ankle. Fred shook his head no at first—there was no way he had the seeing stones to pull that off. Then Stan prodded him in the ribs and Fred reluctantly picked up the arrow. There was a tiny patch of hairy leg peeking out between the orc's dirty sock and pant hem, and Fred inched the feathered end of the arrow towards it. He didn't even try to touch the skin; he merely tickled the tip of one of the long, scraggly black hairs. He did it once. The orc didn't move. Fred was sweating now, but he reached out to tickle the guard a second time.

Slap! A meaty hand came down where Fred had tickled the guard's leg. "The dang skeeters must be out already," said the orc as he lifted his heel to scratch at his ankle. Fred couldn't tell if the orc was looking down or not, but he risked brushing the lace out from under the boot with the arrow. Then he recoiled back into a ball until the guard stopped scratching his leg.

"Y'all don't even know what a skeeter is up here," said the other orc. "We got MOSquitoes dang near year-round in Texas. Y'all got LESSquitoes for one weekend in July."

As both guards laughed, Fred and Stan went to work under the table. Fred tied the key-holder's left shoelaces to the other guard's right shoelaces while Stan tied the key-holder's right shoe to the left shoe of the other orc. They pulled the knots tight, leaving just enough slack in the laces so that the guards would not notice any tugging until the boys were ready to break.

Fred caught Jimmy's eyes through a crack in the cabinet door and winked at him. Once Jimmy signaled that he was ready, too, Fred counted to three on his fingers.

When he reached three, he and Stan dove out from each side of the table. Rising from the ground in a flash, Fred snatched the key-ring from the belt of the orc in one smooth motion. Jimmy spilled out of the cabinet right behind them, sending bags of napkins and sporks flying as he wriggled from concealment.

Completely surprised, the guards attempted to stand up, but they didn't get very far. The orcs yanked themselves down by their own shoelaces. They toppled backwards clumsily, knocking their heads against their chairs. Still dazed, the guards tried to stand up again only to pull each other down again just as quickly. By the time they figured out what was tripping them up, the boys had reached the storage room.

Fred nervously rifled through the different keys. "I don't know which one it is!" he said.

"Just try one!" Stan urged as he glanced down the hall towards the break room. "We don't have much time."

Fred had no idea which key would work, and he knew he'd have time to test only one. There were dozens of shiny keys, some gold and some silver—any one of them could be the right one. Finally remembering what Indiana Jones would do, Fred settled on the oldest, dirtiest key. The metal was blackened with grime and the ridges were worn down to nubs. It was the key least likely to work, but he tried it in the lock, and the storage room door opened with a sharp click. The boys ducked inside and shut the door just as the shoeless orcs emerged from the lunchroom. The boys sat listening by the doorway, ready to run and hide if the guards had seen them.

The orcs stopped just outside the door. "Where did they go?" one asked the other.

"I don't know—I didn't see them," the other replied.

"We should tell Dr. White."

"No way—he's fired men for less! Let's find those punks ourselves."

Both orcs glided soundlessly down the hallway on their socks.

"Whew," Jimmy said, shutting the door quietly. "Good work, guys."

"C'mon, we don't have that much time," said Fred, scanning the shelves of the storage room. "We've got to find that chest quick. Those oafs are bound to tell someone soon, and Grandpa will have gotten our message by now."

The boys searched the shelves, which were crammed to the ceiling with cardboard boxes full of patients' stuff. Fred knew he had told Stan they weren't going to use anything that didn't appear in the books, but the circumstances called for a little bending of the rules and a whole lot of new magic—just what he was hoping he could get out of his grandfather's old chest of tricks.

They found the large black trunk beneath several other boxes at the end of the aisle. The trunk was heavy enough that it took all three of them to pull it down. Luckily, the lock had already been broken and was hanging uselessly from the latch. As soon as they had the chest on the ground, Fred yanked open the lid and started rifling through the contents. Choosing his items carefully, he pulled a multiplying balls trick, a rope trick, a set of mirrors, and a trick cape from the trunk.

"And these will do nicely," he said, smiling at the items at the bottom of the trunk.

"What?" Stan asked, peering into the chest.

"Fireworks," said Fred with a wicked grin, picking up two Roman candles and handing them over. "Let's light this place up."

10

THE GOOD DOCTOR

As the boys were planning their assault on Eisen Gardens, Alfred Oglesburg was sitting in his small, semi-private room. In fact, he was thinking that there really is no such thing as a *semi*-private room. Privacy was just not one of those things that came in shades of gray. You either had it or you didn't. And in this place, you didn't. He wasn't even allowed to lock the bathroom door, for Merlin's sake. And on the days when the cafeteria served "Stroganoff Surprise" that was borderline criminal.

But that wasn't the worst of it. Not even close.

He looked out the window and tried to forget where he was. A bluebird flew by just as his favorite nurse Denise came in carrying an extra blanket. "Any exotic birds today, Alfred?" she said, dropping the blanket on his bed.

"No, my dear," he replied. "Nothing but toucans and pterodactyls this time of year, I'm afraid."

"What a boring world we live in," said Denise, moving over to the chess board beside him.

"An absolute snore," Alfred said, gesturing to his roommate, who was just starting his excruciating nightly snorathon. Denise laughed as she studied the board. "Finally going to make your move today?" he asked her.

"Don't rush me," she said.

"Please, take your time," said Alfred. "That's about all I've got left these days."

"Apparently, you've got a knack for this blasted game, too," said Denise, "because I can't find a way out."

"That makes two of us, my dear," said Alfred.

"C'mon, Alfred, don't be so dour," she said, putting a hand on his cheek. "You're the only one I can talk to in this place."

"Likewise," said Alfred, covering her hand.

Denise looked back at the board and moved her queen impulsively. "There, does that make you happy?" she said.

"A fine move," he lied. Alfred could have taken the piece, but he castled a rook instead to keep the game going.

Someone hailed Denise from down the hall. "Gotta run," she said. "I'll check in on you before lights out."

Alfred waved goodbye and then turned back to the window, trying to enjoy the last few minutes of daylight. Unfortunately, his roommate Mr. Arbogast was blowing F-5 snorenadoes all around the room. It was so unsufferable, it seemed as if the snores had snores. Alfred tried to train his ear to make out distinct bird calls, but it was impossible. Heck, he could barely hear the dirt bikes climbing the hills in the nearby park.

Alfred was starting to think it was Nurse Reynolds—his least favorite nurse, incidentally—and not Mr. Arbogast who had Alzheimer's disease, because she never could remember to put on the nasal strip that kept his room-mate's horrible snoring in check. Alfred tried his best to ignore the excoriating noise, but the snores kept growing louder and louder until Alfred could stand it no longer. He rose from his chair, brandished the magician's wand that had been resting in his lap, and proceeded to lash out at Mr. Arbogast. Mr. Arbogast awoke with a start and howled in surprise. This new noise, of course, only caused Alfred to cane him even harder.

Alfred was a skinny old man, so he wasn't going to cause any real physical harm, but Mr. Arbogast was still shouting loudly enough to send several orderlies running into the room. Clad in pressed white uniforms, the men quickly pulled Alfred away from his roommate's bedside and wrested away his wand. Following the men into the room, a nurse instructed the orderlies to take Alfred immediately to Dr. White's office. As they escorted him out, Alfred and his roommate were creating such commotion no one in the room, not even Alfred, noticed the arrow that glided soundlessly through the window and landed softly on his pillow.

Alfred's thick nest of unkempt grey hair grew tangled about his face as he fought against the orderlies' grasp, but his efforts to escape their clutch proved futile. The younger men dragged him into Dr. White's office and plopped him roughly in the chair before the doctor's desk. Then they moved to the back of the room, watching Alfred closely.

Alfred slowly lifted his head until he was face to face with the doctor. Dr. White could not have looked any more different from his patient. His hair was as white as his name, and he had it slicked back severely. His three-piece suit was crisp and individually tailored, and he held his shoulders back so that his spine stacked up straight as an ironing board. His coldness cast a shadow over the entire room. Opposite the doctor, Alfred sat slumped in his seat, hair standing on end, his ragged medical robes hanging loosely from his bony frame.

The doctor spoke first. "We've got to learn to control these outbursts, Alfred, or we'll have to start sedating you again. And I know how much you dislike that."

Alfred was still raging. "Let me put a flatulent brachiosaurus in your room, and we'll see how well you sleep," he yelled. "Though I imagine it's bad enough sleeping next to that cave troll of a wife."

Dr. White gazed back calmly across the table. "Does it make you feel better to insult me and my wife, Alfred?" he said, pulling a pen from his breast pocket and scrawling something on his notepad. "To put me down, so to speak?"

"What are you writing?" Alfred asked, leaning over the table. "Probably nothing about the howler monkey my roommate is keeping in his nose, but something about me isn't it? Does it make *you* feel better to scribble your stupid statements?" said Alfred. "Do I get a shiny new condition because my roommate has a pair of overactive olfactory oboes in the middle of his face and you won't do anything about it? I do so look forward to putting a new badge on my sash. Don't you think all the other scouts will be so jealous?"

Alfred's joke was lost on Dr. White, who continued writing in his pad, his thin lips pressed tightly in a straight line. The silence frustrated Alfred. "Or are you already analyzing my alliteration, Aaron?" he shouted when he could stand it no longer.

Dr. White never looked up from his pad. "I've told you repeatedly to refer to me as Dr. White, Alfred—it shows a recognition of your situation. And I'd probably conclude that your unusual speech is a defense mechanism. Communicating in a bizarre and often cryptic manner gives you the illusion of control, which you relish with great zeal, Mr. Oglesburg. You're very clever, but the fact remains that you are not in control. The sooner you admit that fact, the sooner we can begin your rehabilitation."

"Hogswallop!" Alfred exclaimed. "On Merlin's wand, I swear you're wrong. Your black magic will not avail you!"

"Calm yourself, Alfred," said Dr. White. "I thought we had worked past this specific delusion. And this ridiculous accent. It appears you have regressed. Perhaps we should resume our *aggressive* therapy."

The change in Dr. White's tone was almost imperceptible, but Alfred didn't miss it. The memory of Dr. White's therapies made his teeth tremble. He grew very still, his grey eyes burning with a look of wild terror. "No, that won't be necessary," he said quietly.

"That's what I thought," said Dr. White. "You have a very bad habit of confusing fantasy with reality, Alfred, a habit I suggest you try very hard to break. The world is changing outside these walls, and your place in it, which was very small to begin with, is only getting smaller. If you have any hopes of being reintegrated into the real world, I suggest you join me in my efforts to correct these psychotic tendencies of yours."

"The world's not that simple, Aaron," stammered Alfred. "Or it is...but in another way."

Dr. White sighed in annoyance. "Whatever do you mean, Alfred?" he asked.

Alfred's thoughts were racing, and ever since his wife, Vera, had passed, he had felt as if he simply could not catch up to them. It frustrated him to no end! It was more than just grief, though he still felt that deep in his bones. It was an abiding sense of failure—to realize, to respond. To save his wife even though they had no way to pay for her treatments.

But he had figured it all out. He had solved the whole entire mess. He knew he had. He just couldn't get his thoughts out! Every time he went to grasp them, the ideas crumbled, and he ended up looking like a doddering old fool...or worse. He didn't want to endure that shame again, so he concentrated with all his power now, hoping he might finally convince Dr. White of his sanity.

"I mean that it should be easy," said Alfred. "Pursue your passion and care for the people you love. But the spell, Aaron, it infects us and twists our minds until our will is not our own, until we are slaves to a heartless cause, driven to do its bidding even though it pits us against each other and against the very goodness in our hearts. It's a darkness that dwells inside us and only real magic can keep it at bay. Do you see? Do you see?"

"You must hear how paranoid that sounds," said Dr. White. "And still all this talk of magic. You were a *clown*, Alfred—a comedian at best, a fool at worst—merely something for the kids to laugh at during birthday parties. So why don't we dispel this notion once and for all that you were ever, or are still, a real magician."

"And what other magic is there but laughter and love?" Alfred asked him. "I've got my tricks the same as you, Aaron."

"So now you are comparing the work of an amateur magician to that of a psychiatrist?" said Dr. White. "I assume that because I try to help you, I'm somehow one of the blind and desperate fools wasting their lives on useless enterprises? That seems a bit extreme, don't you think?"

Why can I not explain this? Alfred screamed in his mind. Vera would know what to say. Vera always knew what to say. A wave of remorse swept over him, disorienting his thoughts even more. "You wouldn't have to be, not if...not if you could..." Alfred stammered. "I mean, you're in a position to do great things, great things, but you keep letting the system control you, Aaron."

"Alfred, you know perfectly well that conspiracy theories are unhealthy," said Dr. White. "Scientists and physicians work very hard to help people. I know you're smart enough to realize that. Let's not add a new paranoia to your already long list of psychoses."

"You're not listening, Aaron!" Alfred exclaimed. "I'm trying to tell you these are people you're dealing with! Strange, imperfect people! Not broken machines you can reset. We have not all been bred for a singular purpose." Alfred could feel the haze in his mind beginning to clear. "And maybe the people out there are the crazy ones, just another kind of crazy," he said. "Not demented, but bent on profit and destruction, their whole lives subjected to it. I mean, a man who spends millions on glitzy baubles while children starve, or...or die of...of cancer," the word caught in his throat, "well, he is a lunatic if ever there was one. You can't just call us sick and throw us away when we're no longer good for breeding riches. We are so much more than that."

"We're getting off-track here, Alf—" Dr. White started.

"People are dying!" Alfred interjected. He could feel the guards inch towards him and lowered his voice. "What I mean is that money is the illusion," he whispered. "It's not real, you see, and what it hides is tremendous suffering. We are driven by it like a mindless dark army. Like ruthless, raving, rapacious psychopaths we crush real people beneath our heels at its command. Our vicious lieutenants stockpile endless treasures like dragons while people die of poverty, starvation, and disease, and they whip us into a mad frenzy to help them do it. They are deranged if any man ever was, but why don't you put them in here and lock them up?"

"So now you're going to tell me who's crazy and who isn't?" Dr. White scoffed. "I suppose we'll just set you all free and cram everybody else in here. Is that what you'd prefer? And please tell me, how did the fireworks feature into your grand plan?"

"Sometimes people need a wakeup call," said Alfred. "Something to shock them out of their funk."

"Yes, and sometimes disturbing thoughts need to be put to rest," said Dr. White. "Fortunately for you, and for everyone else, those of us with medical degrees get to make that decision."

"Love and laughter, Aaron," said Alfred, shaking his head, unable to muster anything but this simple refrain.

"It's Dr. White!" boomed the doctor, standing up from his leather chair and snatching up his alabaster cane. He pointed the pearl handle, with its frightening engraving of two snakes twining around a staff, straight at Alfred's face. "You're delusional, Mr. Oglesburg, and there is a veritable army of people like me trying to help you get better. How are you going to convince them all? What makes you think they'll listen to a man who believes he is a wizard?"

"Everyone wants to believe in magic," said Alfred. "Especially magic they can practice themselves. I just hope that there is enough good magic left to combat the darkness. I hope there are some still who are ready for a different adventure."

"Just pull the rabbit from the hat and make it all better, I presume," said Dr. White.

"Those are just tricks," said Alfred. "I'm talking about

doing real magic. Something that will help people to truly see."

"Yes, well, that's all very delightful, Alfred," said Dr. White as he eased back into his seat and fingered his tie. "But we can't have you running around frightening people with this talk of magic. You're asking the impossible, anyway."

"Sometimes, asking the impossible is the only reasonable thing to do," whispered Alfred.

Dr. White snorted and wrote something down in his pad. "You know, Alfred, I think your wife would be very disappointed at your lack of progress."

Alfred launched himself from his seat and scrambled over Dr. White's neatly organized desk, reaching for his tie. "How dare you speak of her!" he yelled.

The orderlies rushed across the room and managed to grab him before he got the doctor into a stranglehold.

"Very well," said Dr. White. "You've left me no choice. It's apparent that you have lost all connection to reality. Nurse Reynolds," he beckoned. The squat woman standing in the corner waddled over to his desk. "Would you please escort Mr. Oglesburg back to his room and start him on the maximum dosage of thorazine."

"No!" Alfred yelled, struggling against the grip of the orderlies. "Don't make me like the rest of them! I can't bear it!" But it was no use. He kicked a final time against his restraints before hanging his head in defeat. He let the rest of his body go limp. "I'm sorry, Vera," he whispered to himself. "I failed you again."

As the orderlies pushed him gently down the hall, Alfred's eyes welled with tears. The bright fluorescent lights reflecting off the white walls hurt them terribly. Through his watering eyes and matted curtain of hair, he watched all the other patients slumbering in their small rooms or staring blankly at their walls. They were like figures in a fever dream. All of them lost. All of them waiting for the end. Alfred began resigning himself to the fact that he was going to live out the rest of his days in this pale prison, too.

When he arrived back at his room, Alfred was greeted by a particularly robust series of snores.

"My, he's got a mighty set of pipes on him, doesn't he?" said Nurse Reynolds, smiling stupidly.

All Alfred could do was issue a little flabbergasted laugh. "I hadn't noticed," he said.

Denise entered the room and handed Nurse Reynolds a pillbox containing Alfred's medicine. Turning around, she threw Alfred a desperate look, and he could see she was holding back tears of her own.

"Check mate, my dear," he said, patting her softly on the shoulder.

Unable to hold back her sobs any longer, she ducked out of the room.

"Now, Mr. Oglesburg, you need to take this pill three times a day with food," said Nurse Reynolds. Alfred nodded dismissively, his eyes still following the departing Denise. "And I'm going to personally make sure that you take them." She paused to set the pillbox down on his bedside table. "What's this?" she said, picking up the arrow still resting on his pillow. "Oh, Alfred, that's not another magic trick, is it?"

Alfred lunged across the room and snatched it from her. He didn't know what it was, of course, but he instinctively didn't want the nurse taking anything that was in his room. Spying the note attached to the tip, he quickly read it, scarcely believing his luck. His heart hammered with excitement, and he fought to contain a shout. There was hope still.

He hid the arrow behind his back. "It's just a wand," he lied. "Another wand I'm working on, one that can produce messages from the tip like you see. Dr. White lets me keep wands. You know he does."

"I know he lets you keep the one," said Nurse Reynolds. "But after this evening's outburst, I doubt he'd even want you to keep that one. I'll have to ask him about this. He likes to have his patients working on projects, but I should be sure." She finished dispensing the pills into a weekly pill case and offered it to Alfred. "Now come take this medicine."

Alfred didn't move.

"Did you hear me, Mr. Oglesburg? I said come take this medicine."

"No," said Alfred quietly. "No, I don't think I'll be taking any more medicine, Nurse Reynolds. You've held me here far too long under the spell of your potions. I will be bidding you farewell."

"Now, Mr. Oglesburg, don't be silly," said the nurse. "You don't want me to have to call the orderlies in here again to hold you down, do you? I'd prefer to do this the easy way."

"You cannot frighten me with your beastly servants," said Alfred. "My allies have arrived, and their power is great."

"Fine, Alfred, have it your way," said Nurse Reynolds. Marching past Alfred, she poked her head into the corridor. "You two, come here," she said, but she hesitated before coming back into the room. "Hey," she said pointing. "Hey, what's that down there at the end of the hall? That light?"

"Some people call it comeuppance," said Alfred with a smile.

"A wha—?" started Nurse Reynolds, but she never got a chance to finish.

With a crack and a scream, a fusillade of multi-colored bolts came hurtling down the hallway, knocking Nurse Reynolds and the orderlies to the floor. Smoke swept through the corridor as the Roman candles cannonaded the trio of Eisen Gardens' employees with bright fireballs.

Alfred watched with unbridled elation from the doorway of his room. "Huzzah!" he exclaimed, laughing more joyfully than he had in years. Then he burst into the hallway, wand at the ready. "Eat Druid fire!" he yelled, springing away.

The escape was on, and he knew he should join up with his grandson right away, but his feet were carrying him back towards Dr. White's office. He let them lead him. He had some unfinished business with the good doctor, and with Fred and his allies keeping the orderlies off his back, there was time to take care of it before he left this foul place for good.

11

ESCAPE FROM EISEN GARDENS

"Doggone it, where's he going?" Stan asked, dropping a used Roman candle and lighting a new one. "He knows he's not supposed to escape from *us*, right?"

"Maybe he didn't see the note," said Fred. "I'll go get him." He snatched up the magician's cape and the multiplying balls. "Stan, you and Jimmy circle around. We'll meet in the middle. Keep shooting off those fireworks. The more smoke, the better."

"Hey, Fred, take this," Jimmy said before Fred took off. His neighbor reached into his gym bag and tossed Fred something shiny. Fred caught it and stared. He was looking at the trademark T-visor of the best bounty hunter in the galaxy.

"Sweet Mandalorian helmet, Jimmy!" he said.

"It'll keep the smoke out of your eyes and protect you against the light of the fireworks," said Jimmy.

Fred was barely listening he was so amazed by the helmet. It was so cool he didn't need any convincing to wear it. He slid it on and gave Jimmy a thumbs up. Jimmy reached back into his bag and pulled out a Darth Vader helmet, which he handed to Stan. Stan grinned hugely and put it on immediately. Jimmy then slipped off his headband and elf ears and pulled on a replica of Cyclops's visor. "Let's rock this joint," he said, turning the plastic dial on the right side of his visor to full power.

Fred sprinted down the hallway, his hobbit cloak flowing behind him. He leapt over the first two orderlies they had taken out, who were still lying face down on the ground. As Fred sprinted past, he heard the men shout and rise to follow him.

He timed the drop perfectly. The smoke was still swirling thickly in the hallway, so the orderlies never saw the balls Fred had sprinkled along the ground behind him. More balls immediately sprung from those and pretty soon the entire hallway was littered with slippery, bouncing obstacles. Fred might as well have turned the whole hallway into a swamp. The orderlies reached out for Fred, but their hands grasped nothing but air. They gave a startled shout as they lost their balance on the balls and a collective groan as they crashed flat on their backs. Fred left them squirming in pain on the ground. He smiled inside his Mandalorian helmet and kept running, wishing the visor had the capability to block out the pale and bony backside of his grandfather, which was showing through the gap in the old man's robes.

His grandfather turned a corner, but before Fred could reach the intersection, several orderlies emerged from another patient's room and came running towards him. He had no choice but to turn completely around and head back towards Jimmy and Stan.

When they saw Fred being pursued by more orderlies, Stan and Jimmy prepared another round of cover fire. They lit the fuses and loosed another salvo of Roman candles down the hallway. Fred knew they were doing their best to aim above his head, but with the helmet on, he was protected anyway. He could see where the men behind him could not, and he stepped on the bodies of the fallen order-lies to avoid the balls still littering the hallway. The order-lies daring enough to run blindly ahead either took a Roman candle to the gut, slipped on the balls, or tripped on their fallen coworkers.

"We're going to have to go another way," Fred said breathlessly when he finally made it back to his friends.

"It just couldn't be that easy, could it?" said Stan. "Here, Jimmy, keep holding this." Stan handed him his Roman candle, "I'm going to set up for our retreat. We fire and run okay," he said as he tied the trick rope at knee level across the hallway.

"Set phasers to 'kick-a-little-tail,'" Jimmy yelled, firing another round of Roman candles down the hallway. Soon the corridor began to look like a vibrant nebula—smoky and electric with light. The orderlies were too afraid to approach with the tiny bolts of fire flashing all around them, and a few of them even escaped back down the stair-well. Within a few seconds, however, the last of the boys' initial salvo had exploded, and the fallen orderlies started to peek down the hall. Slowly, they started to rise.

"Crap, here they come," said Jimmy.

"Run!" Stan yelled, and the boys took off down another corridor.

The fastest orderlies tripped over the rope Stan had strung across the hallway and fell sprawling on the ground. Unable to see anything ahead of them through the smoke, the next wave of orderlies tripped over their comrades. The men on the ground struck out at each other in confusion, thinking they had caught the invaders.

The boys turned and raced down a larger corridor. Jimmy unhooked his bow as he ran. Some of the patients had been awakened by the commotion, and they had to dodge around those who were already starting to wander aimlessly through the halls. *The more the better*, Fred thought. It will only give the orderlies more to deal with.

He turned another corner in time to catch a glimpse of his grandfather crossing down an intersecting hallway. Though he couldn't see the orderlies hot on his grandfather's tail, Fred could hear them yelling after him and clopping fast in pursuit. "If they catch him, we're toast," he said.

"I've got something for them," Jimmy said, hauling something out of his bag.

Jimmy had attached a cherry bomb to the tip of one of his NERF arrows with duct tape. Even Fred thought it looked way too dangerous, but before he could say anything, Jimmy had lit it.

"Of course, the floor hasn't been properly waxed," Jimmy said. "It's a good thing I wore my track suit pants." Gritting his teeth, he dropped into a controlled slide, shooting across the floor in a blur. Just before he crashed into the wall, Jimmy fired the cherry bomb-tipped arrow into the oncoming orderlies.

His aim had been true again, and his timing perfect: The firework exploded directly in the orderlies' faces, momentarily blinding them. The men smacked into each other, and Fred heard a loud knock as their skulls collided. Their bodies went limp, and they collapsed on the floor. Within seconds, patients were swarming over them like a pack of zombies.

"'Deadeye' strikes again," Jimmy said, regaining his

feet. He pulled out an arrow lined with some nasty looking firecrackers. "You two go on ahead," he said. "I'll throw a few of these orc dorks off your trail and then meet up with you when it's time to haul out of here."

"Wait, how will you find us?" Stan asked, but Fred didn't need to wait for Jimmy's answer. After seeing the archer in action, he knew the elf would be there when they needed him most. He pushed Stan down the corridor after Alfred.

Fred shouted after his grandfather again, but the old man didn't respond. Instead, Alfred turned down yet another hallway, moving fast.

"It may be too late to ask this, but what if your grandpa is actually as nutty as squirrel turds?" Stan asked.

"He's not nuts," said Fred. He's just...complicated, like any good wizard. It's not like Gandalf ever explained everything he did."

"Yeah, I'm not sure running down a madhouse hallway half-naked is the same," said Stan. He stopped suddenly and pointed down the hall. "Oh, crap, here comes shoeless Joe and his braindead buddy."

Stan was right. The two guards he and Fred had tricked out of their shoes were still wandering the halls. Out of sheer dumb luck, the two men had managed to block Fred's path to his grandfather. Fred and Stan didn't have time to find another route—*this place is like the trickiest Halo map ever*, Fred thought—so he started scheming to get past the groundskeepers. He and Stan couldn't just run past them. Even at their fastest and with the gardeners slowed by their slippery socks they might not make it clear.

"I've got an idea," said Stan, holding up the trick mirrors. "Follow me." As they streaked down the hallway, they came up on a giant laundry chute. Stan stopped a few feet past it. "Hey guys!" Stan shouted around the corner. "Let's go this way."

The guards came sprinting down the corridor after them. Before they'd turned the corner, Stan flung open the door to the laundry chute. He hurriedly placed one of the mirrors inside, sticking it securely to the back wall. Then he grabbed Fred and slid to his right, hiding just behind the corner of the wall and out of the direct line of sight of the oncoming orcs. He propped the other mirror against this wall to reflect their images onto the mirror in the chute. Then he started waving his arms to make it seem as if he was trying to use the laundry chute to escape.

"There they are!" shouted one of the men.

The two of them hurried awkwardly down the hallway, slipping on slick parts of the floor. The guard who arrived first leaned into the chute, discovering too late that the boy apparently hanging there was just a reflection. He struggled to catch himself, but couldn't get a grip on the floor in his socks. His partner, who was just a step behind him, attempted to slow down as he approached the chute, but he slipped on the floor and crashed into the other guard. Their momentum carried them straight down the laundry chute. It took a long while for their cries to stop echoing up the vent.

Stan ran over to the chute to shut the hatch and shouted down it: "Why don't you take your shoes off and relax!" Turning to Fred he added: "These guys are dumber than dinosaurs."

A sudden uproar down the hall cut his boasting short. Stan moved to grab the mirrors, but Fred told him to leave them—there wasn't time. They took off down the hall towards the noise.

When they rounded the corner, several things

happened at once. Dr. White burst from his office, a thin scowl on his long face that made him look like one of the Easter Island heads, and Alfred wriggled through a mass of orderlies and escaped patients. Dr. White was looking the other way, but he whirled around in time to see Alfred rushing towards him. Alfred swung his wand wildly at Dr. White's head, but the doctor managed to raise his cane in time to deflect the blow.

"En garde!" Alfred yelled as he thrust his wand toward Dr. White's belly.

Dr. White parried quite smoothly for a man with only one good knee, clicking his heels together as he stepped back into a practiced fencing stance. "I'm very displeased, Alfred," he snarled, twirling his cane expertly.

"You did not think you could keep me here long, did you?" said Alfred. "I'm Alfred the Grand! No hold, however impregnable, can keep me forever!"

He performed another clumsy thrust with his wand. Dr. White once again easily deflected the attempt. "Don't congratulate yourself too soon," the doctor replied as a team of nurses came streaming into the hall, carrying some nasty-looking needles. The nurses were coming right for Fred and Stan, who took off down the hall toward Alfred. The hall was filling up with people—orderlies, nurses, and patients—and Fred really couldn't imagine how they'd ever get out now. His heart was pounding, and he felt foolish for trying to mount the escape in the first place.

When he saw Jimmy approaching fast down the other side of the hall, a firework-lined arrow notched on his bow, Fred knew his neighbor was their only hope.

"Fire, Jimmy. Fire!" he yelled, and the archer did just that, instantly launching a fiery arrow down the hall. The blazing foam shaft flew past Alfred and the doctor, knocking them apart, and then sailed over Fred's head. It went crackling and popping through the midst of the nurses trailing him, who threw themselves to the ground in fright. They dropped their syringes to cover their heads. The deafening sound and flashes of light seemed to disorient everyone in the hall, and Dr. White floundered for a moment, blinking his eyes to try to clear them.

Jimmy ran past them all and went sliding on the ground, scooping up several of the dropped syringes. Popping up to his feet again, he dropped one syringe down the center of a foam arrow until the needle emerged through the tip. He notched the arrow to his blue NERF bow and fired. Before Dr. White knew what was happening, the needle was stuck deep in his thigh.

"Good heavens," he said, his voice quavering as he slumped to the ground.

Fred crashed into his grandfather and wrapped him in a huge hug, which Alfred the Grand returned enthusiastically. Fred hadn't realized how much he had missed his grandfather, and he fought back tears at the sight of him. He knew he couldn't get emotional now—they still had a swarm of guards to deal with. Letting go of his grandfather, he turned around and quickly took in the situation. Things didn't look good—the hall was completely full of the enemy now. Some of them were busy with escaped patients, but there were still too many orderlies for them to take in a straight fight, and Jimmy would not be able to hold them off with the threat of his arrows forever.

To Fred's surprise, Alfred took charge. "Everyone get close to me now!" he shouted, and Jimmy and Stan crouched close to the two Oglesburgs in the center of the hallway.

Dipping into Jimmy's bag, Alfred lit several smoke

bombs and dropped them down. Fred didn't realize that his grandfather had grabbed the cape until he saw it in his hands. As thick billows of white smoke filled the corridor, Alfred swirled the cape around the group. The black fabric looked just like a giant bat-wing cutting through the fog, swallowing the four of them up in the dark folds.

The orderlies charged ahead uncertainly, trying in vain to waft the smoke away with their hands. Several orderlies cried out that they had caught the intruders, but when the smoke finally cleared, there was nothing left of Fred and his friends but a large black cape, crumpled on the floor next to the unconscious form of Dr. White.

12

A WIZARD OF THE HIGHEST ORDER

Fred, Stan, Jimmy and Grandpa Oglesburg dodged through the trees just south of Eisen Gardens, moving fast in the last of the fading light. The woods behind them were clear, but that didn't stop Fred from punching his own personal hyperdrive trying to get as far from Eisen Gardens as he could.

After several minutes of hard running, when everyone but Jimmy was sucking dragon eggs, they stopped at the bottom of a hill and huddled together beneath the cover of some large exposed tree roots. When he glanced back and saw that none of the orderlies had managed to stay on their trail, he decided they could all catch their breath for a minute. To breathe easier, Fred pulled off his helmet and handed it back to Jimmy. Stan did the same, and Jimmy quickly stored them back in his satchel.

"That was expertly performed, boys," said Alfred, putting his hand on Fred's shoulder as he stretched his back.

"Totally wizard," Jimmy agreed.

"That is correct!" said Alfred. "I am a total wizard,

which is to say I am a wizard totally—there's not a part of me that is not wizard, and the wizard I am does not lack any kind of magic. Alfred the Grand at your service." He bowed deeply while the boys tried figure out whether what Alfred had just said made any sense whatsoever.

"Is your family British?" Stan asked breathlessly, inquiring about Alfred's accent.

"Not exactly," said Fred.

"Pray thee, what perilous quest do you boys endure that you require the services of a wizard of my esteem?" said Alfred.

"We are in possession of a powerful ring," Fred said, pausing to gulp in some hair. "One that must be taken to Mordor, California and thrown into the fires of Mount Doom."

Alfred beamed and twirled. "Ah, a journey of most barful strife!" he exclaimed, lifting Fred off the ground as he twirled again.

"Did he just say Bofur?" Stan asked. "Because if he's trying to say you're Bifur and I'm ole big-boned Bombur, that's not the best way to say thank you."

"I see our plight is truly dire," continued Alfred excitedly. "Our path will be hazardous and fraught with unseen dangers at every turn. But in the quest, a bit of true magic." Alfred arched his neck and looked up at the sky, taking in a deep breath, his smile widening. "Ah, I have long pondered just such a venture. I should have known to trust in you, Fred. You have never failed me, and I will not fail you now. I will help you bear your burden, as you carry the very symbol of the Dark Lord's power over men."

Alfred stood up on a nearby tree-stump and held his wand high in the air. He waved it about and then flicked it firmly, pointing it at the heart of the dark forest. The wand-tip sparked and sputtered, but it did not break into flame. Its tiny light struggled like a dying firefly before finally fading entirely.

Alfred's smile darkened too, and Fred shuffled his feet. He had made some pretty bold claims about how good Alfred was at magic, and now he was worried that Jimmy and Stan would think they had just risked their lives to rescue a magician who couldn't even perform a simple spell.

Alfred hit his wand with the butt of his hand a couple more times, muttering under his breath. Then he brought it up with another flourish and pointed it once more at the darkness. This time a small flame flickered at the end of the wand. After an anxious second where it looked like it might die out again, the flame brightened to a full glow. Fred was relieved and disgusted at once because in the small sphere of light the boys could very clearly see the bare buttocks of Alfred the Grand poking out from the gap in his medical robes.

"Uggh," groaned Fred. "How can something so bony and wrinkled still be so bright?"

"He makes Skeletor look like he's got a spray-tan," said Stan. "We need to get him some shorts, a onesie, a raccoon coat, anything."

"I have something he might use," Jimmy said, reaching into his gym bag and pulling out some wizard's robes.

Stan pretended to be annoyed. "Well, why didn't you list that among our assets in the first place?" he said.

Fred laughed in amazement. Jimmy seemed to have everything and then some in that duffel bag of his.

"Why don't you just pull some jet-packs out of there while you're at it?" said Stan. "I've been done with this running."

"I wish," said Jimmy. "Stupid federal regulations."

"Boy, if I had a nickel," Stan said, snapping his fingers.

"I'm almost afraid to ask, but what else do you have in there, Jim?" said Fred.

Jimmy smiled. "Everything an elf lord needs and more," he said, giving Fred a little wink. "I bought that warlock robe for my dad a few years ago...but, uh, he never got around to using it." There was a touch of sadness in the older boy's voice that he tried to erase with a big smile. "Anyway, I thought it might come in handy on our trip. Looks like I was right."

As happy as he was, Fred felt a little sorry for Jimmy and wanted to cheer the archer up. "I'm starting to think that bringing you along might have been the best choice I've made in a long time," he said. "I can't believe some of those shots you made back there. Do you still have some of those needles?" he asked.

"I've got three left, but I'll save them for when we really need them," Jimmy said, wrapping the syringes in a makeshift case of duct tape and placing them in a safe spot in his bag where they would not be broken. "Those servants of Mordor better beware the aim of 'Deadeye' Dingleman."

"Yeah, you said it," said Fred, laughing with excitement, the joy of the successful escape finally hitting him. "Part of me still can't believe we did it. But with Alfred with us now, we can't be stopped. By the way, Jim, this is my grandpa. I don't think you've officially met."

"Yes," said Alfred the Grand as he slipped on his wizard robes, "you're quite right. Introductions are long overdue. Who are these loyal companions, Fred, who have so valiantly rescued me from the vile clutches of the evil Dr. White and his minions of the dark tower?"

"This is Jimmy Dingleman," said Fred, but Jimmy shot

him a hurt face and mouthed "Deadeye." Fred sighed. "Known by his order of elven archers as 'Deadeye,'" he added. "And this is my best friend, Stan. You will not find a hobbit of stouter heart in all of Hampshire Glen subdivision."

Alfred shook their hands in turn. "If you have earned Fred's trust, then you have earned mine," he declared. "I consider it an honor to join this fellowship. May Merlin's luck be with us on this journey."

"Riiiight," said Fred, "but just in case Merlin is busy, we should keep away from the roads and stick to the woods. The Black Riders will spot us on the highways, and now the White Wizard and his minions will be hot on our heels, too," he said.

"A fine plan," added Alfred. "I don't know about you boys, but the spirit of the chase is still upon me. I haven't felt this energized since that *Golden Girls* marathon last month. I suggest we keep moving."

Fred, Stan, and Jimmy nodded that they were ready to go as well. After quickly collecting their things, the four of them stole away into the forest, running as fast as they could in the dark. They had planned to make it all the way to Mordor that night, but after only an hour they had all grown sore and cranky with fatigue.

"Fred, can we stop running like we stole something?" Stan said, dropping to one knee.

"But we did steal something," said Fred. "Two things actually." Saying it aloud only made him anxious to put as much distance between them and Eisen Gardens as they could. But Stan was nearly doubled over, and Fred had to admit that even his own legs were aching. Alfred was probably hurting in every bone and joint. "Maybe you're right," he said. "Maybe we should get some sleep, so we can get a full day's travel tomorrow."

"Yes, yes," said Alfred, wincing as he grabbed his knees, "that sounds like a wise plan. I could use a rest. It feels like someone's replaced my knees with a bag of rusty sporks and my muscles with tapioca pudding."

"I agree with Mr. 'The Grand,'" said Stan. "Fred, I'm down to one bar, man."

"Okay," said Fred. "We'll stop the first good place we find. But we can't stop here. C'mon team, just a little longer."

Luckily for Fred, because Stan was complaining now every step he took, they spotted a good campsite within a few minutes. Fred led his friends to a low ridge of granite rock. It was a short, easy hike up the ridge, and Fred was even more grateful when they reached the top. The site wasn't perfect—it was a little too exposed—but it would do for the night.

The four of them camped there in the open on a bed of moss. They decided to go without a fire. The night air was crisp, but not cold, and there was little wind. The sleeping bags would be plenty warm. As long as a Wompa didn't stroll by, they'd be fine.

Because he didn't want to have to squeeze into a tauntaun sleeping bag with someone else, Fred suggested they rotate on sentry duty.

Jimmy agreed to take the first shift, but the archer was so tired that he fell asleep within minutes, forgetting to wake someone else up to take over. None of the group seemed to mind this, however, especially Alfred the Grand. He slept more peacefully than he had in months, finding the chittering of insects to be much more relaxing than Mr.

Arbogast's snoring. He and his younger comrades slept soundly, each of them dreaming of wild adventures.

If they had known what challenges lay before them, perhaps they would not have slept so soundly or so late into the following morning.

13
PARENTAL PROBLEMS

Fred's mother, Lucy, was up even later than usual. She was trying to finish a final draft of her latest book, send an overdue story to her editor at the newspaper, and grade a stack of papers for the English class she taught on the weekends. In short, she was overwhelmed and exhausted. She couldn't remember the last time she'd gotten a full night's rest, and she'd be lucky if she got any sleep at all tonight. The growing stack of bills on the other end of the table was a sharp reminder that she had no choice but to trudge on.

Calling her little workspace a "table," was actually rather generous. Her makeshift office was really just a small extension of the kitchen countertop held up by a wonky kickstand. There was an old sponge tucked beneath the leg to prevent it from wobbling every time she typed. In order to face the window, she was forced to sit right next to the sink, which always seemed to be full and foul no matter how many times she did the dishes. As much as she reviled the constant stench, facing the dismal interior of the trailer was even worse. It was important for her to see the trees and the creek that watered them. It was important to her to have sunlight fall across her desk as she worked—though these days she was having an increasingly hard time remembering why that was.

There was no sunlight piercing the windows now—night had fallen long ago. So only the harsh flicker of the fluorescent bulbs above and the occasional burst of fireflies in the distance provided any light. When her eyes couldn't take looking at the computer screen any longer, Lucy yawned and stretched and tried to rub the ache out of her eyes. Somehow, that only blurred the computer screen even more. She blinked her eyes fiercely to clear them and then brought her fingers back up to the keys.

When the phone rang the first time, she ignored it. She didn't have time to talk to anybody right now, and if it wasn't a creditor, it was most likely a telemarketer, anyway. When the phone rang the second time, she snatched it up, expecting to have to bark at some poor sap for harassing her, but the caller never gave her a chance to speak.

"Mrs. Oglesburg? Are you there? It's terribly urgent," the caller said in a rush. She didn't have to be Sherlock Holmes to realize something was wrong. The caller sounded frazzled and groggy at the same time.

"Yes, this is Lucy," she said. "What is it?"

"Goodness, I'm glad I've caught you. This is Dr. White, director of Eisen Gardens Medical Facility. I apologize profusely for the hour."

"Don't apologize for the hour, Dr. White, apologize for the call," she said.

"Yes, of course, that is what I meant," stammered Dr. White. "I tried to get a hold of your husband, of course, but...well, I'm sorry to have to relay to you some unfortunate news, Mrs. Oglesburg. Alfred has...left us."

Lucy's breath left her and her eyes really started watering. All her annoyance disappeared in a surge of grief. Alfred had always been a comfort and a joy in her life, especially since her own parents had passed several years ago. He had accepted her fully, and she regretted, now more than ever, that she had not done more to convince Solomon to keep Alfred out of that horrid place.

"When did it happen?" she managed to say, her voice trembling.

"He escaped just moments ago, actually," said Dr. White.

"What?" said Lucy. "Did you just say 'escaped'?"

"Yes, ma'am," said Dr. White. "He's run away."

"Then why didn't you say that to begin with!" Lucy shouted. "You said he left us as if he had died!"

"I'm terribly sorry, ma'am," said Dr. White. "We're all a bit rattled here. It was something of an ordeal."

"An ordeal?" said Lucy. "What happened?"

"Well, it appears he had some help," said Dr. White.

"You mean there was a geriatric jailbreak?" said Lucy, now wondering if she had fallen asleep on her desk and was experiencing a nightmare.

"Uh, not quite, Mrs. Oglesburg—"

"Owen," said Lucy firmly.

"Excuse me?" said the doctor.

"My name is Owen," said Lucy. "Solomon and I are divorced. You were saying?"

"I see," said Dr. White. "Then perhaps I should wait until I can get a hold of Solomon...."

"Let me know how that goes," said Lucy.

"Pardon," said Dr. White.

"That could be the longest wait of your life, doctor,"

said Lucy. "Tell me what happened, and I'll make sure Solomon hears."

"Very well," said Dr. White. "I suppose I should add that our...burglars, so to speak, had some sort of...explosive."

"Explosive!" Lucy exclaimed, now sure she was dreaming.

"Yes, ma'am," said Dr. White. "Well, an explosive of sorts. At the very least they were some pretty powerful fireworks."

"Dr. White, I'm really hoping this is not a joke."

"No, Ms. Owen, I assure you I'm being absolutely serious."

"Who were these people?" asked Lucy. "What could they want with Alfred?"

"They were three young men," said Dr. White. "In fact, two of them were very young—perhaps just boys," he added quietly. "But they proved very resourceful."

"How could a couple kids d—" Lucy stopped herself, realization buzzing in her brain. "Oh, no. Fred!" she whispered.

"Beg pardon?" Dr. White asked.

"N-Nothing," she stammered. "Thank you, Dr. White, for the call. I've got to go." She hung up the phone and quickly dialed Solomon. It went straight to voicemail three times before she finally got a dial tone. He answered on the fifth call.

"What took so long?" said Lucy.

"Hello to you, too," said Solomon. "I answered as soon as I could. My phone died while I was on a call to Singapore, and I just got back home to charge it."

Lucy heard Joanne stir in the background. "That better be somebody dead," Joanne muttered tiredly before Solomon could muffle the receiver.

"Sorry," he said to Lucy.

"It doesn't matter," she said. "Something's up with Fred, and we need to figure out what to do."

"What happened? Is he alright?"

"I think so," she said, "but the folks at Eisen Gardens are a bit shaken up though."

"What do you mean?" Solomon asked. "Eisen Gardens? Did you say we needed to talk about Fred or Dad?"

"What's that waste of space done now?" Joanne shouted in the background before Lucy could explain. Solomon sighed heavily.

"Hold on," he said. She heard him open a door to move to another room.

"It's about Fred *and* Alfred, actually," said Lucy. "Dr. White just called me and said that three boys just broke Alfred out of Eisen Gardens. Considering they blasted the place up with fireworks, I'm guessing Fred was behind this little heist."

"What?" asked Solomon. "You've got to be kidding?"

"No, Solomon. Dr. White called me five minutes ago."

"Good grief," said Solomon. "What a mess. I do not need this right now."

"Nobody needs this right now, Solomon. But we've got to take care of it."

"Why would they do this?" asked Solomon. "It's completely crazy."

"I don't know," said Lucy. "Did anything happen at the party? Did Fred bring up Joanne at all?"

"No, why?" asked Solomon.

"I talked to Fred about your engagement, and he wasn't too excited about it," said Lucy.

"Jesus, Lucy," said Solomon. "What did you say to him?"

Lucy's anger spiked. "Exactly what *you* asked me to say," she said, "so don't act like it's somehow my fault."

"Okay, okay," said Solomon. "Don't get testy."

Lucy bit her tongue so she wouldn't throw the phone across the room.

"Either way it shouldn't have been enough to provoke *this*," said Solomon. "He and Joanne get along fine as far as I know."

"That's because you don't know," Lucy snapped. "They get along like fire and gunpowder."

"That's a bit dramatic, don't you think?" said Solomon.

"All fireworks considered, maybe not," said Lucy. "Did Fred say anything else at the party at all? Did anything else happen?"

"We got into a little bit," said Solomon. "Nothing unusual. I grounded him, which didn't work, of course. He completely ignored me. Carlita told me he was going to stay at Stan's tonight."

"You didn't call Stan's mom to make sure?" asked Lucy.

"I didn't think anything of it at the time," said Solomon.

"Great, now I'm going to have to deal with that, too." Calling Stan's mother, Renee, to explain what had happened was quite possibly the scariest part of the whole situation. Plus, it was yet another thing to do. Lucy was starting to feel like the wonky kickstand trying to hold up a table with too much crap on it.

"Better you than me," said Solomon. "That woman would put the gator in litigator if she ever decided to become a lawyer. I've thought about using her in some negotiations."

"I better have some answers then," said Lucy. "So, let's think. Why would they do this all of a sudden? What's their goal? I know Fred's upset with what's going on at school, but why go after Alfred?"

"Maybe that was the point of the whole thing—just to get Dad," said Solomon. "Either way, Dad will bring them back."

"I doubt it, Sol," said Lucy. "At least not right away. He clearly went along with the escape. And it's like we keep trying to tell you, that place is not fun. I expect he's excited to be out of there."

"Hey, it's supposed to be the best care money—and it's a lot of money—can buy," whined Solomon.

It took some restraint, but Lucy left this alone. She'd fought Solomon on this topic too many times, and this wasn't the time to debate what was best for Alfred. "I think the best thing we can do is figure out where they might be going," she said. "That way we can meet them there and get everyone home safely."

"Clearly, I've got no clue," said Solomon. "I can't keep up with Fred. To me it seems like he always has his head in some new fantasy every week."

Lucy barely heard him she was so deep in thought, but when the word "fantasy" finally registered a second later, she jumped out of her chair. "Oh my god, that's it," she said.

"What?" said Solomon. "What did I say?"

"Fantasy," said Lucy. "I think I know what he's trying to do. The ring, Solomon! Check for the ring!"

"The engagement ring? Why?"

Just check!" said Lucy.

She could hear Solomon scrambling around in his office. A filing cabinet slammed open, and he grunted as he reached into its depths.

"The box is here," he said.

"Check inside," said Lucy.

Solomon cursed. "It's gone," he said.

"That's what I was afraid of," said Lucy. She heard another loud slam on the other end of the phone. "What was that?" she asked, worried Solomon was tearing apart his office in anger.

"Daggone it," said Solomon. "I think Joanne was listening in. JO!" he shouted after her. "Jo, don't go!" He grunted again in rage.

"She just left?" said Lucy.

"If by left you mean stormed off, then yes, she left," said Solomon.

"Yikes," said Lucy. "That's not going to be fun." *Like trying to lasso a swarm of hornets with a wet noodle,* she thought. About the only thing she could imagine being any worse was having to tell Stan's mom that her boy had run off.

"No, it will not," said Solomon. "But it will be better if I've got the ring back by then. So, tell me where they're headed and let's go get them."

"Geeze, Sol," said Lucy, "Fred has read every Tolkien book ten times and watched the movies ten times more than that, and you can't think what he might be up to?"

"Okay, so he's trying to act out the books," Solomon said. "If you know, just tell me. I don't have time for a pop quiz."

"I don't *know* for sure," said Lucy. "That's my best guess at this point. Maybe he thinks that he can destroy the ring and...and things will get better."

"Destroy the ring!" said Solomon. "That's a forty-thou-sand-dollar ring!"

Lucy nearly choked on her own spit. "Solomon, that's

obscene," she said. "That's more expensive than most people's cars!"

"Which is why I didn't shell out for the premium insurance policy. We need to get that ring back, or I could be in real trouble."

"I hope you feel the same way about our son," said Lucy angrily.

"C'mon, Lucy," said Solomon. "That's a given."

Lucy wasn't so sure she believed him.

"So where will we find him?" Solomon asked.

"I'm still trying to figure that out," said Lucy.

"Well, you would know before I would," said Solomon. "You know the stories better than I do. As far as I know we don't have any *mounts* in Bithbon? Do you think he'd just try to throw it away in a creek or park fountain or something?"

"Maybe, but I don't think he'd have gone after Alfred if that was all he planned to do," said Lucy. "He could be going anywhere. We have to call the police, right?"

"I'll call," Solomon said. "But don't expect miracles right away. I know their procedure. Until they know it's a definite missing persons scenario, they'll just send out an immediate notice to all nearby officers and search the area where he was last seen."

"Okay, but these are Bithbon's finest we're talking about," said Lucy. "We can't just leave this up to the pastry patrol."

"They're not Seal Team 6, Lucy, but it shouldn't take special ops to get a couple boys back. With Dad there, everybody should be fine."

"I don't know, Solomon," said Lucy. "I can't just sit here. We need to do something."

"Let's stay calm, Lucy. Think of it as a camping trip. I

know you hate the boy scouts, so think of this as a way for Fred to get the outdoor experience without having to deal with them."

"I think you're underestimating the dangers they could face out there, Sol."

"We'll have them home safe soon, Lucy. Let me hop off so I can call the police and try to get Joanne calmed down."

"Okay," said Lucy. "I need to call Stan's mom, too. But we should talk right after that to coordinate."

"Sounds good," said Solomon, his voice trailing off. "But I've had a few missed calls since we've been talking, so give me some extra time to touch base with everyone."

Lucy sighed. She had seen this show before. Solomon was arming his excuses already. "This isn't a soccer tournament, Solomon. It's our kid's life. You can't blow this off."

"Let's not overreact," said Solomon. "He'll be alright, Lucy. I'll talk to you soon." He hung up before she could say anything more. Lucy cursed him under her breath and tried to call him back, but he didn't answer. After a few more tries, she gave it up. She knew he wouldn't pick up, and she had to admit that at this point she was probably just subconsciously delaying having to call Stan's mom.

She took a deep breath and then dialed Renee, her heart beating faster with every ring of the phone.

When the receiver clicked over, Lucy wasn't sure if she had connected with Stan's mother or a Balrog giving birth. The only sounds coming through the phone were exaggerated groans and bellows of pain. "What's wrong with you?" Renee finally managed to say. "Do you know what time it is? I need my sleep."

Lucy was sympathetic to Dr. White all of a sudden. "I'm really sorry to wake you, Renee," she said. "I wouldn't be calling this late unless it was an absolute emergency."

"It's about to be an emergency if you don't tell me why you're calling me."

"It's about Stan and Fred," Lucy said quickly. "We think they've run away."

"Huh uh," said Renee. "My son doesn't run away from me, okay. He's got more sense than that. Maybe your boy, but not my son."

Lucy had been prepared for upset, angry even, but she hadn't anticipated denial. She wasn't sure what to say next. "Well, I can't really say I know for sure, Renee, but I got a call from the place where Fred's grandfather stays, and the doctor there said that it was a *couple* boys who came by to bust Alfred out."

"No ma'am, I know you did not just say 'bust.' Because that would mean your boy has got my son breaking the law."

"They're not in trouble or anything," Lucy said quickly, "so don't worry about that. Everyone just wants to bring the boys back safely. We've called the police, and they—"

"You did what!"

Lucy had to grab the table to keep from falling out of her seat. "We just, um, made sure the police knew to look out for them," she muttered once she had gathered herself.

"Are you out of your white mind?" said Renee. "They'll put your kid in a blanket and mine in handcuffs, if they don't shoot him on sight first. So, you call them back and tell them we found them, and they can go back to doing whatever they're doing."

Lucy was stammering now. "I'm sorry," she said. "I should have called you first. I'm just so scared for them, Renee. And I can tell you are, too. And don't get me wrong, I've got my issues with the police, but I just want to do everything I can."

"Look, I've seen it, okay," said Renee. "So don't tell me."

"Okay," said Lucy, unsure what to say next.

"You want to do everything you can, then here's what's going to happen," said Renee. "Since your boy got my Stan into this mess, you're going to come pick me up right now, and we're going to find them before the cops use whatever toy he's carrying as an excuse to take a shot at him."

"Uh...okay," muttered Lucy, who hadn't figured on having Renee along for the ride. "I guess I'll be by in a little bit."

"You better make it real little," Renee said before hanging up.

Lucy stared incredulously at the phone. Part of her wished she'd given Solomon some of what Renee had given her. As much as it pained her to say it, she was glad at least someone else was as panicked as she was about the whole thing. That didn't mean that she was looking forward to the next few hours in the car with Renee, though. Quite the opposite in fact.

With a sigh, she shut her computer. Her work would have to wait. She hurriedly poured some cold coffee into a dirty Thermos, snatched up her keys, and rushed out the door into the quiet pre-dawn dark.

Joanne slithered out of bed and crept silently down the hallway on her tiptoes. The moisturizing cream she had slathered over her face before going to bed gave her a ghostly look, but she had other reasons for wanting Solomon not to see her. She crouched, hair standing on end, listening at the keyhole as Solomon spoke with his ex-wife on the phone.

It made her skin crawl every time Solomon had to speak with that hippie hack, so she was already angry. But when she heard that Fred had stolen the ring destined for her finger, Joanne's anger surged to new extremes. The tips of her hair felt like they were on fire, and the veins in her neck throbbed like ticking time-bombs. She ripped the curlers from her hair and stomped her feet on the thick rug.

She did not find her voice until she had lurched back through the hallway and down the stairs. "That monstrous brat!" she spat, no longer caring if Solomon heard her or not. "I'll wring his little neck myself. That's my diamond!"

Wearing nothing but her airy pajamas, Joanne flung open the front door of the house and dashed across the lawn. She jerked open the door to her Mercedes and flopped inside. She fired the ignition and went peeling out of the driveway, leaving black tire-treads on the pavement.

For a long while she drove aimlessly, infuriated beyond measure. She reached down to take her medication, hoping it would calm her. The bottle was empty, so she threw it against the windshield in rage and punched the accelerator. She drove full out until her car got so low on gas it started to sputter, at which point she jerked it into the woods in a fit of blind rage. Losing all control of the car on the grass, she collided with a large tree and knocked her head hard on the steering wheel.

When she came to, her vision was blurry and her head was burning so badly her teeth steamed. She heard sirens approaching in the dark and tumbled out of the car, afraid they *would keep her from her ring. Her mind was spinning now as fast as her vision, and it was empty of all thoughts but one: the ring.*

HER ring! How had it ended up in such a dark and dingy place as this horrid forest? It should be glittering in the bright lights of the mall for all to see and desire. When she thought of Fred soiling her ring with his grubby little paws—or, even worse, losing it in some mud puddle—it nearly made her head explode.

She'd do anything to get it back, anything—even hike through the stupid, nasty woods.

14

THE DIFFICULT ROAD

Fred was the first to wake the next morning. Something caused a big tree branch to fall in the woods, which sent him springing up out of his tauntaun sleeping bag like a turkey timer.

"It's okay, Jimmy, I'm awake," he said groggily. "Everything's ofine. Fokay, I mean. I've got the watch."

When he finally got his senses about him and saw that Jimmy was sound asleep and no one else was looking out, he cursed and jumped to his feet. He checked the area around them nervously as he prodded everyone else awake. The sun was already shining high in a cloudless sky, so he guessed it must have been near midday.

"Jimmy, what happened?" he asked the archer once the older boy had popped his blowzy head out of the makeshift lean-to of his track jacket. "You were supposed to get me up for sentry duty after an hour and a half."

Jimmy rubbed both eyes with his palms and yawned hugely. "Sorry, I must have been more tired than I thought," he said. "I'll have to increase my training regimen. Once I

get my 'Basic Training' obstacle course set up in the backyard, I'll be ready."

"An obstacle course sounds pretty cool, but it doesn't
help us now," said Fred. "There are dark and dangerous foes
pursuing us, Jimmy, and terrible beasts lurking in the
woods that can kill us in a heartbeat. We've got to be more
careful," he urged.

"You're right, Fred," said Jimmy. He stood up and placed
his fist over his heart. "On Galadriel's golden hair, I swear I
will not fail my office again."

"Your bow has served this fellowship well, 'Deadeye,'
do not mistake me," replied Fred. "I fear only for the safety
of the ring and the success of this quest."

"You are surely true of heart, Fred," said Jimmy. "My
bow is yours until that ring drowns in the molten rivers of
Mount Doom."

Visible tears welled in the eyes of Alfred the Grand.

"What's wrong, Alfred—got gunk?" asked Stan, who
was cleaning bits of matter from his own eyes.

"No, my dear boy," said Alfred. "It is enough to make a
wizard weep to see such unflinching loyalty, such stead-
fastness of purpose, such daring courage. I had not realized
how despairing I had grown in the holds of the White
Wizard's tower. To be among this band of intrepid questors
fills with me new hope."

"Well, then I suppose we should just hope the Empire
doesn't strike back anytime soon," Stan quipped tiredly.

Fred rolled his eyes. "It's okay, Grandpa," he said,
patting Alfred on the shoulder. "You're out of there now.
And if we destroy this ring, we can get my dad back, too.
The Dark Lord has spread his reach into distant lands and
even has servants in the Oglesburg household! They have
poisoned my father against us."

"What is this you say?" asked Alfred. "Have worm-tongues corrupted my son with their malevolent mendacities?"

"Sadly, it is so," said Fred.

"Then we should proceed with much haste," said Alfred the Grand as he picked up a knotty, fallen tree branch and tested it against the ground. "This will do nicely," he said.

"I agree," said Stan, collapsing back onto the sleeping bag. "Much haste, much haste—but not before breakfast." He lazily reached into his bag to grab a few of the cookies the widow Thompson had given them. "I can't remember ever being this excited to eat breakfast," he said with a smile, lifting a cookie to his mouth. "At least not since I invented fluffins."

"Puffins?" Alfred asked.

"FLUFFins," said Stan. "They're chocolate muffins with marshmallow fluff spread all over them."

"Wow, put in a course heading for Diabeetus Prime and proceed at warp nine," said Jimmy.

Fred laughed and elbowed Jimmy. "I used to drown my cocoa pebbles in chocolate milk and marshmallows, but Stan just had to one up me," he said.

"Like you complained the first time I handed you a fluf-fin," said Stan.

"No, because those are actually pretty good," said Fred. "But I also had to eat all your horrible creations, too. What with the Pop-tart-cream Sandwiches and French Toblarone sticks and a dozen others, it was like Brunchenstein for the whole summer until you got it right."

"But fluffins are sooo right," said Stan. "Although these chocolate chip cookies are giving them a run for their money, that's for sure. Maybe if I could find some way to combine the two?" Stan tilted his head in thought. Fred sighed as Jimmy chuckled.

"I'll admit, it's nice to eat something with a little flavor," said Alfred, biting into a cookie. "The White Wizard feeds his prisoners only the foulest gruel. Most of it appears to have been recently regurgitated by a bridge troll. But these—oh, these are truly magical morsels."

"We'll have to introduce you to the person who baked them, then," said Fred, winking at Stan. If the cookies were cheering Alfred up, meeting the delightful Dr. Thompson would really cure his blues.

"I would be honored to thank the person who has given me my first true *taste* of freedom," said Alfred.

"And with a witch and a wizard in the same building, Fred is that much closer to his dream of going to magic school," interjected Stan.

"Just eat your breakfast," Fred said.

Stan held out his hands in mock surrender. "No torture curse necessary," he said, swallowing the rest of his cookie in one big bite. Fred had to smile in spite of himself.

After finishing their breakfast, the four of them packed up their bags and ventured deeper into the woods, still heading southwards. The brisk hike soon drove the stiffness from Fred's legs and cleared his head. He was feeling strong and invigorated, and he was looking forward to a long day's travel.

Stan, however, made sure to let everyone know that he wasn't happy about all this physical activity.

"How close is Mordor?" he whined. "We have to be there by now, right?"

"Stan, we're just getting started," said Fred. "So, spare us the whineathon. What kind of a quest would it be if we finished it in a day? That's not a quest. That's a picnic."

"Did you say picnic?" Stan asked, rubbing his stomach. "I could go for a picnic. Fried chicken legs, mashed potatoes, strawberry jam, macaroni-and-cheese. Hey, Fred, gimme one of those sandwiches, would you?"

"No way, we just had breakfast," said Fred. "We can't eat all our food again."

"Why not?" said Stan. "That's what you're supposed to do with food—eat it."

"Because the more we stop for supplies, the more likely we get caught," said Fred. "We have to go as long as possible with what we have. I'm hungry, too, so let's just stop talking about food and concentrate on something else."

"I guess I didn't realize this was going to be like working the night shift in the spice mines of Kessel," said Stan.

"Really?" said Fred. "You're going to compare this beautiful day to a mythical death mine?"

Stan blubbered a bit. "Well, those clouds are just taunting me, looking like marshmallows and all." Fred just rolled his eyes again.

"Keep heart, good Stan," Alfred piped in. "They will hold feasts to honor us once we complete our quest. The tables will spill over with fine puddings, fruited scones and smoked meats. They will toast us as returning heroes."

"I'd settle for a large pepperoni at Chuckee Cheese," said Stan. "One of those pizzas just oozing with mozzarella like you only see on *Teenage Mutant Ninja Turtles*."

"Stan!" Fred shouted.

"I know, I know," Stan said. "I'll shut up. Just don't make me wait too long for lunch."

Fred shook his head and led them on. They climbed over steep rises of rock and scrambled down slopes covered in oaks and ponderosa pines. Colorful wildflowers lined the hills, and Fred ran his fingers over them as he walked, enjoying the warmth of the sun on his face. He couldn't remember the last time he had gone on a hike this long or explored any place this beautiful. It made him realize that Alfred was right—being out here on the quest made him feel truly free for the first time in a long while. He savored every sight and smell.

"Man, it's as hot as an Xbox after a Halo sesh out here," Stan complained, souring Fred's good mood. "How I miss my Xbox. Remind me again why we couldn't just play the video game?"

Fred silenced him with a look. The day was barely half over, and he'd already heard enough complaining from Stan. Stan never wanted to go outside, and that drove Fred crazy. Stan would sleep in the tree house, sure, but that was more out of laziness than a love of the outdoors. Fred always had to work overtime to get Stan to come with him as he explored the local creeks or abandoned barns. Stan hated to be compared to the Borg from Star Trek, so Fred used that move a lot, but it never worked for long, though. After a few hours, Stan would always go right back to the room he called "the bridge," which was full of all his technological gizmos. There were so many old electronic gadgets and crumpled pop cans littered across the room that Fred practically needed to open up a recycling plant just to clear a place to sit down.

Fred sighed. It wasn't going to be easy, but he was glad Stan had come along. Fred knew that if he couldn't convince his best friend that everything was in peril, he didn't stand a chance at convincing anyone else. Plus, he'd never be able to destroy the ring without the help of his best friend. Fred knew that Stan was strong in ways even his best friend didn't even realize. He couldn't think of anyone he'd rather have at his side while he carried the ring.

Thinking about the ring suddenly made him aware that the skin beneath his tunic had already been rubbed raw by the diamond. The flesh was extremely tender and pulsed with a warm pain. He ran his fingers gingerly over the scrapes, trying to hide his discomfort from his companions.

"What's wrong?" said Stan.

Fred dropped his hands to his sides. "Oh, nothing," he covered. "Just a little nipple chafe, that's all."

"Really?" said Stan. "I'm actually getting a little of that, too." Stan grimaced as he shifted his cloak. "I was feeling like a sissy because it's not like Strider would ever complain of nipple chafe."

"No, next to the black blades of Morgul, nipple chafe doesn't sound quite so manly," said Fred, and he and Stan shared a laugh.

His ploy had worked this time, but Fred knew he would have to be careful in the future to hide how painful it was to bear the ring. The closer they got to Mordor, the harder it would be to distract his friends with jokes. And he didn't want anyone trying to tell him to turn back.

In an effort to push the pain from his mind, he took a deep breath of cool air and watched the maple leaves sway in the breeze. He let his worries go and romped up and down the hills. He searched for animal tracks and picked up interesting pebbles and singled out trees good for climbing. Alfred pointed out the different bird songs, and even Stan got excited when they spotted a hawk (although Fred thought Stan might have been pointing it out because he was worried it would swoop down and pluck off his nose).

After spending most of the next hour trooping through

a wide valley, they crested a long, sloping rise. When they got to the top, Fred stopped dead in his tracks. Three dark smokestacks jutted above the tree line ahead, puffing out black crud into the soft blue sky. "Ho, fellowship," he said, pointing to the towers. "The Dark Lord knows of our plot! The fires of Mordor burn hot!"

Jimmy spat. "They forge dark steel and war machines for their orc armies," he said.

"Perhaps those fires have a more insidious purpose yet," added Alfred.

Stan huffed. "They're more likely forging dark chocolate than dark steel," he said.

Fred ignored him. "We must be wary," he said, his eyes locked on the smoking towers. "The Dark Lord's power is growing, and we cannot overestimate its reach."

"We should stay close to the tree line, then," said Stan.

For a moment Fred thought Stan was finally start to get into the whole quest thing. Then he realized Stan was just trying to get them to stay in the shade.

"Smart idea, Stan!" said Jimmy.

"Yeah, smart," added Fred, giving Stan another look. But Fred didn't call Stan out. It was actually a good idea. Staying close to the trees gave them cover if they needed to make a quick escape.

Fortunately, they did not encounter any of the Dark Lord's minions for the rest of the morning. Clinging to the tree line did pose them some other, unexpected troubles, though. Alfred, who never seemed to be able to keep his eyes on the path in front of him, started to have a particularly tough time getting around the many brambles and bushes in his way.

"At the risk of sounding ungrateful, I must say this

raiment is most cumbrous," he said, fumbling as he tried to gather the billowing robes.

Stan looked confused. "Did he just say the robes smell like cucumbers?" he asked.

Jimmy laughed. "No, just that they're awkward," he said. "Sorry, Alfred. You can switch back into your hospital gown, if you'd like."

"NO!" Fred and Stan said in unison.

"If he puts that back on you might as well shine a searchlight up into the sky," added Stan.

"Kind of like a *butt* signal," said Fred, but nobody laughed. "You know, bat signal...butt signal." Still silence.

"Wow, terrible," said Stan.

Jimmy chuckled a little. "I liked it," he said.

"Alfred's butt or the joke?" said Stan.

"Definitely the joke," said Jimmy. "I would do well never to see such a horrifying sight again. I could have gazed directly into the maw of the Watcher in the Water and not been so afraid."

"We'll have to tell Peter Jackson about the Browneye in the Bony Butt for the next movie then," said Stan.

Fred laughed along with the rest of them, and then called for a vote in which the boys decided unanimously to make Alfred keep wearing the billowing fabric despite his complaints. So, they kept moving, and poor Alfred did his best to avoid the snares and snags of the woods. Alas, they were simply too many. The first time his wizard's robes got completely tangled in the thorns of a bush, the group struggled dramatically to free him, imagining that a Barrow-wight was attempting to capture him. They shouted wildly, kicking at the Barrow-wight with their shoes as they pulled Alfred from the clutches of the evil tree-demon. Once they finally freed him, they sprinted away from the bush and didn't slow until they were far away from the plant.

They did the same thing the second, and third, time Alfred got caught by the bushes, but eventually even Fred grew tired of this game. The fourth time Alfred's robes got snagged they all slumped their shoulders and quietly shuffled over to help him.

"It shouldn't take a wizard to tailor a more travel-friendly robe," Alfred complained, tugging and twisting. "The sartorial sciences are surely in a sad state."

"Well, unless Jimmy has a sewing machine in his bag, you'll just have to be more careful," said Stan.

Fred laughed, but couldn't help but look at Jimmy questioningly.

"No, I don't have a sewing machine!" said the archer.

"Then let's just get him clear," said Fred, pulling on a branch.

"No, just pull the branch this way, I'll go this way," said Alfred. "No, you go *this* way. Here I'll just do it." Alfred crouched and mule-kicked himself awkwardly out of the bushes only to sprawl on the ground, his robes flying up over his face.

"Oi!" Jimmy and Stan exclaimed as they averted their eyes from Alfred.

"I think I'm sick of the multiplying balls trick," Stan quipped, gagging into the brambles.

"Sorry," Jimmy apologized, "but the wizard robe didn't come with any underwear."

"That's okay," said Fred, helping up his grandfather with one hand as he covered his eyes with the other. "We'll just make sure we stay on the trails from now on. Until we spot any danger, I think we're safe to do that."

"I say that's a fine idea," added Alfred as he brushed the leaves from his robe.

"C'mon, let's keep moving," said Fred.

A few hours and several miles later, they stopped for lunch. They ate on the edge of the woods, sitting on large rocks and fallen logs. Fred had learned his lesson and suggested that they only eat half of a sandwich apiece. Stan argued fiercely for more but was overruled by a three to one vote. In protest, Stan finished his half of the bologna sandwich in two bites and sat staring hungrily at the rest of the group as they continued to eat.

"You gomma eap da resp ofmat?" Stan asked Jimmy.

"Yeah," Jimmy answered. "I was just moving the sandwich away from my face so that I could finish my first bite."

"Oh, mkay. Jusp asping."

They let their food settle for a few minutes before setting off again. Within minutes, Stan was clutching at his side and breathing heavily. Eventually he stopped altogether.

"What is it?" said Fred.

"Uh, Houston, we have a problem," said Stan. "I've got a proton torpedo in firing bay one that isn't going to wait for the command," he said.

Fred and Jimmy laughed.

"Seriously, what do I do?" Stan asked. "No one ever goes to the bathroom in fantasy books."

"You know, he's right," said Fred. "They go on these epic quests covering thousands of miles, and not once do they stop to drop a deuce."

"I'd be too scared to do any kind of business in Lothlorien, but I don't see why you couldn't pop a squat and do your stuff down a mine of Moria," said Jimmy. "Can you hold it until we get to Dwarrowdelf?" he asked Stan.

"Is he serious?" Stan asked Fred. "I'm about to squeeze out a baby sea-serpent here, and he's telling jokes. Don't you have a toilet in that gym bag or something?"

"No, but lucky for you, I did remember to bring some toilet paper," said Jimmy, tossing Stan a roll. "But we need to conserve that, too!" he yelled after Stan, who began shuffling like a duck into the trees.

"I guess we should hope for some ghost poos then," Stan called over his shoulder.

"What did he say?" asked Alfred, his eyes nervously searching the trees around them. "Do specters haunt this eerie bosk?"

"No, no," said Fred, laughing. "He's just talking about poos that don't leave much...uh...of a trace."

"Very well," said Alfred. "Spare me the scatological specifics. I think I've got the gist of it."

After a few minutes, Stan came skipping out of the woods, a big smile on his face.

"What?" asked Fred.

"Nothing," replied Stan, "I just hope a baby dragon doesn't come by and fall in love."

"You were thinking about that the whole time, weren't you?" asked Fred.

"Pretty much," said Stan. He tossed Jimmy the roll of toilet paper and cleaned his hands in a small stream, and the four of them started up again.

For the rest of the day they hiked without incident, taking only a few brief breaks. When the sun began to slip behind a haze of clouds to the west, they began searching for a campsite. Darkness crept across the land quicker than he had thought it would, which made Fred nervous they wouldn't be able to find a safe place to sleep before night fell. He took a gamble and turned them slightly off course in the hopes that the low hills to the west would lead to better cover. After cresting a rise, he finally spotted a series of small cave openings in the side of one of the larger bluffs a short distance to the west. They hurried towards it and made it to the mouth of the largest cave just as the last of the daylight blinked out beyond the western hills.

Huddling together beneath the cover of the rocky arch, they ate their small supper and prepared their camp for the night. They had gotten lucky again with the weather—it was going to be warm enough outside that they could sleep comfortably without a fire as long as they were shielded from the wind. Fred and his small company laid out their sleeping bags and settled in.

Even though he was exhausted from the day's hike, Fred decided to take the first shift on sentry duty this time. Not only did he want to make sure they got the whole sentry switch concept right this time, but also a lot of heavy thoughts were keeping him awake. He knew that by now his parents would have figured out that he'd run away and would be worried about him. This made him feel more than a little guilty. He didn't want them to be afraid for him. But their divorce had really upset him and now his father was planning on getting remarried, and they didn't really seem to care how he felt at all. So maybe it would be good for them to worry about him for a little while. At least he was giving his dad some time to realize how awful Joanne was, because if he ever married her there was no coming back— not for him or for their family. Fred shivered a little, not because it was chilly, but because thinking about Joanne made him sick to his stomach.

Thinking about her also made him grab the ring anxiously, as if just the thought of her could steal it back from him. He grew short of breath and pulled the diamond out from under his tunic to make sure it was still there. Relieved to find it safe, Fred let out a sigh. He held the diamond up to the moonlight, peering curiously at the stone. It was certainly very clear and shiny, but he didn't really see what all the fuss was about. It didn't *do* anything, like, say, shoot lasers or show the future; it just sat there. He'd much rather have a skateboard with little jet-engines or a new basketball hoop for the driveway instead. A water bazooka would be nice, too, or better yet, a flamethrower. Or, once he thought about it a little more, a pet Komodo Dragon would be really cool. He suddenly realized he could buy all those things and more with the ring. He smiled with mischievous delight as he imagined himself riding a Komodo dragon through the school, carrying a bazooka in one hand and a flamethrower in the other, taking out mutants and cyborg zombie dinosaurs by the thousands.

Then he realized what was happening to him and dropped the ring in horror. With every sparkle and glimmer, the ring was changing him—making him lust for power and things he didn't need. Closing his fist around the ring, he pushed everything out of his mind. He'd have to be more vigilant—the ring knew he was trying to destroy it and would do everything it could to stop him. He took one last look and then tucked it back inside his shirt.

He sat at the cave opening looking up at the stars, which he was just noticing were brighter than any diamond. And there were so many of them! He couldn't help but dream up new and strange beings that lived in those distant galaxies. He wondered if somewhere in all the wide universe there was another boy, just like him, who was on a similar quest to save his family, who was maybe even looking out at the stars and wondering just like he was. Then he thought that maybe he didn't have to look so far to find someone like himself. He knew there were boys on his own world who were suffering worse than he was, and it made him ashamed that he had ever felt sorry for himself. He was lucky. He had a lot more things than most people, and he was sure some of them would think he was crazy or spoiled or stupid for trying to throw away something worth as much as the ring. But that didn't mean it wasn't the right thing to do. And he was also lucky because he had the chance that many other boys did not have: he could fix things. It would take all his strength to survive this quest, but at least he had a quest to go on. At least he had a chance, however slim. He smiled again when he thought about what it would be like to have his parents back together, and then he stopped thinking completely and just enjoyed the beauty of the starry sky.

It was just about time for him to wake Stan for the next shift when he heard the gruff breathing of the approaching bear.

15

BUGS AND BICHONS

Stan's mom lived in a duplex less than a mile from Lucy's trailer. Lucy had actually toured the complex before she'd opted to buy the trailer, so she knew the neighborhood fairly well and had little trouble finding Renee's place. Because there was an old car on cinder blocks filling up the driveway, Lucy parked on the curb next to some broken pieces of furniture and an old television set.

Considering how agitated Renee had been on the phone, Lucy was surprised Stan's mom wasn't waiting by the curb. Lucy thought about honking, but decided against it. From here on out, Lucy planned to avoid doing anything that might irritate Renee—including, but not limited to, issuing loud noises. She was hoping to keep things as amiable as they could be between her and Stan's mom so that she could focus all her attention on finding Fred and Stan. *Better to knock on the door,* she thought, as she killed the engine and started across the lawn.

"Don't stomp on my grass, now," said Renee, who had suddenly appeared in the doorway. Lucy froze in her tracks, feeling as if she'd just stepped on Grandma's glasses or dropped the wedding cake. She dared to look down, and what she saw turned her embarrassment into irritation. She wasn't exactly ruining the rosebushes. She was standing on a pebbly, uncut tuft of sparse grass, next to a faded ceramic fawn and a crumpled Sugar Shark soda can.

Lucy made a show of slowly back-stepping to the car as if she were treading across a priceless painting or a pane of glass. She dropped back inside the car and watched Renee wend her way around the cluttered driveway. Lucy's eyes snapped back to the house when a big man filled the space Renee had vacated in the doorway. "Where you going?" he shouted through the screen.

"You don't need to be stalking me," said Renee. "I'll be back." The man shook his head and then punched the screen door with his palm before disappearing back into the house.

"You stop for a sundae or something?" said Renee as she climbed into the passenger side.

Lucy rolled her eyes. "I know sometimes the rust can look like racing stripes, but don't be deceived, this isn't actually a stock car."

"You ain't never lied," said Renee as she looked around the inside of the car. "But I guess it's going to have to do. Let's get on, then."

"Aye aye, captain," said Lucy. Renee shot her a look that could boil a Boeing, so Lucy quickly added: "I thought we might try Gabden Park first. I've taken the boys there on picnics a couple times, and they always want to stay for hours and hours."

"See, that's what I've been trying to tell you," said Renee. "Boys can't quit, and they don't know a single thing about what's good for them. You can't let them get away with it, because once you do, they'll think they can get away with everything, and they can't."

"I said I take the boys to the park, Renee, not to the casino. Wholesome fun."

"Wholesome?" said Rene, her face twisting with disgust. "That is just more than a notion to y'all isn't it. Don't want to discipline your kids and never think for a minute that if I don't put the fear of God in my boy now someone is going to put a bullet in him later just because he mouthed off. Let me tell you something—the rules are meant for us, okay."

Lucy took another deep breath. "I'm not trying to tell you how to raise your son, Renee," she said. "I would never dream of it. I'm just trying to let you know that I never encouraged them to do something like this. I know how dangerous it is, and I'm worried sick for *both* of them."

"You know how dangerous it is?" said Renee. "Really? Because I don't think you do. My own nephew got thrown in cuffs when he was twelve years old while his mom was pumping gas because he *looked* like a guy who robbed a place down the street. Child had just gotten out of flute practice. Still had cartoon stickers on the case. They cut his lip putting him down on the sidewalk. So don't tell me you're worried because you don't know worry." Renee's voice broke a little at the end, and she was near tears.

Lucy turned her gaze back to the road and kept it there. Renee was right, and Lucy wasn't even going to defend her concern for Fred, as mighty as it was at this moment, if it meant challenging Stan's mom on this point. She conceded as much as she could with her silence and drove on.

They sat in that uncomfortable quiet until Renee asked, "So how far away is this park, anyway?"

"Just a few minutes."

Renee nodded and kept looking out the window.

When they arrived at the park, Lucy pulled into one end of the horseshoe-shaped parking lot and slowly cruised the entire arc of blacktop. Her eyes scanned the tennis and basketball courts, the picnic tables, the playground, and the soccer fields. There was no sign of Fred and Stan. In fact, there was no sign of anyone. The entire park was quiet.

Lucy pushed the despair and frustration out of her heart by holding out hope that the boys were playing somewhere along the hiking trail. She pulled up to the trail entrance and threw the car into park.

"Where you going?" said Renee when Lucy started to climb out of the car.

"We came here to look around for the boys, didn't we?" said Lucy.

"Yeah, but I didn't sign up to go tramping through the weeds in this heat."

"Then stay in the car, Renee," Lucy said as she took off towards the trail. She was actually hoping Renee would stay put, but a few seconds later she heard the car door slam behind her.

"Hold up!" Renee shouted. Lucy stopped at the trail entrance and waited as Renee slowly crossed the field. She dodged every puddle and patch of mud along the way. "Stay close now," Renee said when she finally caught up. "I don't want to end up on the news myself."

"Gangsters aren't dumping bodies here," said Lucy. "It's a family place. Toddlers and dogs."

Renee was too busy struggling to keep her shoes clean to respond. Lucy took advantage of the unexpected silence to scan the area around the trail, but there was no sign of the boys. Absolutely nothing to indicate they'd ever come through the park. Because she was focusing her attention on the ground, Lucy walked right into a large dragonfly hovering over the trail. The bug buzzed directly in her face, and she brushed it aside in surprise. Unfortunately, she knocked it straight into Renee.

Renee screeched so loudly that Lucy had to cover her ears. Stan's mom then started tugging on Lucy's shirt and hopping maniacally, trying to keep Lucy between herself and the bug. The dragonfly must have been amused because it circled them for a few frantic seconds before zooming back into the reeds. Renee didn't let go of Lucy right away. She peeked around Lucy's shoulder, nervously searching for the bug.

"You alr—" Lucy started, but a freshly startled Renee silenced her with a scream.

"What's wrong with you!" said Renee when she'd caught her breath. "You trying to scare me to death."

"Sorry," said Lucy, gingerly peeling Renee's fingers from her shirt. "Just letting you know our little attacker has fled the scene."

"That's funny to you?" said Renee. "Because that didn't look like a toddler or a dog to me."

Lucy smiled in spite of herself. "Well, it was about as big as a Bichon."

"Shoot, that thing looked like it ate a bulldog for breakfast," said Renee. "Girl, I don't know how y'all do this? My hair is already starting to curl and the sun ain't even up."

"I love the heat," said Lucy. "And the quiet. It's usually quiet, you know." Lucy raised her eyebrows at Renee.

"That's because most people got the good sense not to mess with the monsters that live here. I feel like if I take a deep breath, I'm going to swallow something. Or something is going to swallow me."

"Well, we don't have to turn you into Jane Goodall to

find the boys," said Lucy. "Just keep looking and listening. You never know, you might enjoy—"

Lucy had barely gotten the words out of her mouth when she heard chattering voices ahead. Renee had heard it, too. The two women hurried up the trail. Lucy had a vision of the boys standing over a heap of plastic toys at the trail's edge, smiling as if nothing in the world were amiss.

When they rounded the corner, her vision blew away in the wind. Three grown men in suits were huddled on one side of the path looking at a large map and surveying the breadth of the park beyond. As she got closer, Lucy recognized one of the men as John Bonneville, one of Solomon's work associates and Fred's teacher's husband. He was hard to mistake: John Bonneville was a large man whose neck poured over the starched white collar of his powder blue dress shirt like a mound of dough rising over the rim of a pie pan. Even though he had plenty of money to burn, his hair-piece was awful, and Lucy had to constantly remind herself not to stare at it.

After the last heated parent-teacher conference she'd had with his wife, she doubted he'd have anything nice to say to her, but Renee was shouting at the men before she could stop her.

"Excuse me!" said Renee. "Excuse me, but have y'all seen some boys anywhere around here?"

Startled, the men quickly folded the map and tucked it away behind them. One of the men Lucy didn't know said, "Sorry, what was that?" as he stepped in front of the man who was holding the map.

John Bonneville recognized Lucy before Renee could ask again. "Lucy? Is that you?" he said.

"Yeah, it's me, John," she said.

"Where's Solomon?" he asked.

The question rankled Lucy, but she expected nothing less from John Bonneville. "You would probably know before I would," she said. "I don't hold his leash anymore. I've been trying to get him to come help look for our son to no avail. Fred and Renee's son, Stan, are missing right now."

"You don't say?" John said. There was no concern in his voice at all, only the unmistakable hint of perverse satisfaction. "Well, I can't say I'm surprised. I know Lydia has been trying to tell you that your boy has some serious discipline problems, you know. And if you let them get away with small things, eventually something like this is bound to happen."

Lucy looked over at Renee, who she expected to find gloating uncontrollably over the fact that someone was agreeing with her. But Renee was doing quite the opposite, glowering deeply at the businessman.

John Bonneville, of course, completely ignored her. "Just like in business, sometimes it takes a strong hand when dealing with kids," he added.

"Well, if you haven't seen them, you haven't seen them," said Lucy, moving away. She'd already spent more time than she'd ever wanted to spend in John Bonneville's presence. She couldn't resist throwing a barb over her shoulder. "But if you find time between destroying precious wetlands and plotting to ruin our community, please keep an eye out."

"You never know, this might actually be a positive experience in the long run," responded John Bonneville, stopping her in her tracks. "Of course, we don't want the boy to come to any harm, but sometimes it's good for them to learn lessons the hard way. It makes a more...lasting impression."

Lucy could feel Renee's anger coiling like a snake beside her, but she got her response off first. "And how many children have you raised, Mr. Bonneville?" she said.

John Bonneville stammered a little, his moustache twitching. "Well, Lydia and I have not yet been blessed with a child of our own, but we continue to pray. Something I suggest you do, because I would hate to see your child continue on this path. You've got to instill a healthy fear in a child, or else they'll never learn discipline. That's how my parents raised me, and I think I turned out pretty good." He raised the tips of his moustache with a smile and shook the heavy gold watch on his wrist.

"That sounds like a wonderful way to screw up a child, and I hope it works out for you," said Lucy. "But I actually like my son. Heck, I'd even say that I love him. So, for now, I'm going to try spare him the torture."

"It seems to be working quite well, Mrs. Oglesburg," said John Bonneville. "Oh, but I guess I forgot that you go by your maiden name now. What is it again? Oven?"

This time Renee beat Lucy to the punch. "I know you would not talk to an angel that way!" she said. "Are you really trying to beat up on a woman looking to protect her son? What's wrong with you? You better take your stooges and that squirrel on your head and shove off, because I know the way you fumbled with that map you're not supposed to be here."

"Nonsense!" said John Bonneville, smiling awkwardly. "We're just enjoying a pleasant walk before work."

"Yeah, and that thing on your head don't bury nuts for the winter," said Renee.

John's smile broke, and he looked back anxiously at his friends. "Well, we can't be lingering too long," he said. "Some of us have *real* jobs, after all."

"When a white man's stealing, it's for real alright," Renee said.

She was ready to continue the fight, but Lucy gently held her back.

"It's okay," Lucy said. "Just let them go." They watched the men retreat back across the long ditch to the service road that passed behind the park.

Renee was still irate. "They've gotten too comfortable!" she said to Lucy.

"I'll make sure to let Solomon know we ran into you," John Bonneville shouted from his truck, still trying to get in the final word.

"You're a real gentleman," said Lucy, but John whipped around the massive vehicle as if he hadn't heard her. Lucy finally turned away from John Bonneville and his cronies and continued along the path, circling back towards her car.

"Wait—that's it?" said Renee, hustling to catch up with her. "You're just going to let that chubby muppet talk stuff and get away?"

"I gave it back plenty," said Lucy. "And I'm not going to waste any more time on him while Fred is missing."

"Well, the boys aren't here!" said Renee. "You said this is where we'd find them!"

"That's enough!" snapped Lucy, turning on her heel. "I'm not taking any more of this crap from you. In case you haven't noticed I'm on your side. I may even be the only person on your side, and if you think there is any limit to the love I have for my son, you're wrong. I'm not going to stop until I find those boys. So, stop harping on me and start working with me because I'm through with this."

For the first time since Lucy had met her, Renee was at a loss for words. She had taken a step back in shock. Lucy had no idea what was coming next, and she readied herself for another fight.

To Lucy's complete surprise, Renee smiled. "Finally!" she said. "I was wondering when you were going to show up. That's what you should have said to your man the first time, so he'd be out here slugging through the mud."

Lucy shot her a look.

"I'm just saying," said Renee, putting her hands up in the air.

Lucy shook her head and then turned and led them back towards the car.

"So, where are we going now?" asked Renee, hurrying to keep up.

"To Eisen Gardens and then the ends of the earth," Lucy said as she climbed back into the car and fired it up.

"Well then, I'm going to need something to eat," said Renee.

Lucy took a deep breath and threw the car into drive.

A few miles north of the cave in which Fred and his friends lay sleeping, a figure was scrambling feverishly through the thick heath and buckthorn bushes. Its clothes had been shredded by thorns and brambles, and its skin was coated in dirt and grime. Hair that had once been blonde was now blackened and uncombed—curlers dangling like ornaments on a Christmas tree that had been attacked by kamikaze raccoons.

The creature's name was Joanne, but if anyone would have asked she would not have given this or any other. She was beyond all that now—consumed entirely by the diamond ring that had been stolen from her.

The ring must be hers! It must, at all costs, be hers. She knew this because it called to her, and somehow, she knew how to follow it, how to find it. She had experienced this mysterious pull once before. A few years ago, she had forced a group of "frenemies" to visit one of her favorite outlet malls even though they had wanted to go get mani-pedis. After a long fight, which she had won (as she always did), they had gone to the mall. And, lo and behold, she had found her favorite Gucci handbag that day. I mean, it went with absolutely everything. She had fought a ferocious tug-of-war with her best frenemy over that bag, and to this day she always wore it when she shopped with her, just to rub it in. The strange force had not failed her then, so she knew that it would lead her again to what she desired most.

Razor-sharp nettles stung her constantly, but she barely felt them. It was not the sharp pricks of thorns that tortured her but rather the voices of all the gossiping girls she had ever met. They cackled out mean jokes at her just as they had done when she was the new girl arriving at yet another private school. She shouted back at them, and the forest animals ran from this strange, screaming beast.

16

BOY AND BEAR

Fred was on his feet in a flash. He stood frozen at the mouth of the cave, terrified beyond measure. It wasn't until the bear roared again that he found wits enough to move. Somehow, those same wits didn't run away from him like a spice smuggler evading a star destroyer. He barely managed not to scream and bolt. Fred had never heard a bear growl before, but he instinctively knew the second growl was no boast or warning. It was the moan of a tired, irritated, unreasonable beast. He'd heard Joanne make that sound a million times, and a heatstorm of hate usually followed it. And she was just a mallrat with a martini hangover, not a Warg as big as a Waffle House.

Worried that like the Tyrannosaurus Rex the Warg's vision was based on movement, Fred back-stepped as slowly as he could into the cave. Reaching his friends, he prodded them all at once with his hands and feet. Stan and Jimmy's eyes widened in surprise when Fred tapped them awake, but they sat up without a sound. Alfred, however, was not so quiet. He cursed when he sat up, and Fred had to slap his hands over his grandfather's mouth to shut him up.

"What in the name of Guinevere's underbritches is going on?" Alfred asked in a hushed voice once Fred had taken his hand away.

"A vicious Warg approaches the cave entrance!" Fred whispered just as the bear came lumbering up the hillside into the clearing.

Jimmy instantly notched an arrow to his NERF bow and pulled the string back.

"Don't waste your arrows, 'Deadeye,'" said Fred. "Not even the strongest elven steel fired from a bow crafted from the most ancient mallorn tree can pierce this beast's hide. He has been sent by the White Wizard and is protected by his magic."

"He is forcing us deeper into the mountain," added Alfred, "and we have no choice but to go, though I fear the path. Grab your bags boys and get behind me!" he shouted.

Fred's bag was still at the edge of the cave entrance, but he knew he couldn't leave it behind. Food was too precious to them now. He raced as fast as he could back to the mouth of the cave and slid on the smooth rock floor right up to the bag. As he rose back to his feet, the bear suddenly shambled to the top of the rise and stood, teeth-bared, looking in at them. Fred froze again in terror, staring in amazement at the hairy hulk.

"Run, Fred!" his grandfather shouted at him. "This is a most powerful foe, stronger than any of you."

Fred tried to move his feet and failed. Alfred yelled again, and Fred managed to take a small step backwards. His foot connected with a rock, and he fell just as a huge paw swung right for his face. It missed him by mere inches.

Fred rolled to his feet and ran as fast as he could. The Warg growled as it slipped on some rocks, and Fred took advantage of the beast's misstep to catch up with Jimmy and Stan. He followed his friends deeper into the cave, which was getting darker and darker. Soon, he could barely make out the bright yellow of Jimmy's bow. Fred started to worry that Alfred had fallen too far behind because he could no longer hear his grandfather's footfalls over the grunts and snorts of the charging bear. Since there was nothing he could do to help, anyway, Fred put his head down and tried to run faster.

Jimmy and Stan stopped suddenly. Fred had no time to slow himself down and crashed hard into their backs. They pushed back hard against him, waving their arms frantically to keep their balance. "Why are you stopping?" he asked breathlessly. "Mordor's hound-dog is right on top of us!"

"There's no more light!" said Jimmy. "Not even my magical elven eyes can pierce this Eru-forsaken darkness."

Jimmy was right. Fred looked past him into utter blackness.

The bear's next growl was so loud and close it made all of them jump at once. They wheeled around in fright, searching for the beast. A moment later, Alfred the Grand's wand broke the total gloom of the cave. It sputtered and flared up as Alfred slid in front of them protectively. Fred had to shield his eyes from the wand light. Squinting in pain, all Fred could really make out of the bear was its size. The beast filled the entire cave like a hairy boulder. There was no room to sneak past it—even if they had the courage to try. They'd have to face the bear or risk venturing deeper into the cave. Luckily, the light seemed to have stunned the bear for a second, too. It shook its head and rubbed its massive paws over its eyes. Then it reared up on its back legs and let loose another growl that shook the rock walls of the cave. The fur of the beast seemed like it was on fire where the light from Alfred's wand hit it, and the shadow on the wall behind the bear looked like giant black wings. When it roared again, rows upon rows of teeth gleamed wickedly in its massive maw.

"You will go no further, foul beast!" Alfred the Grand shouted at the bear, raising his walking stick high into the air. "You shall not..." For a moment everything in the cave was still, and then Alfred brought the stick crashing to the ground. "PaAAAAAAH!" He shouted in agony. Somehow, he had managed to miss the cave floor completely and had instead smashed the stick down right onto his big toe. He hopped backwards on one leg, clutching the injured foot in his hands. He stepped on a rock and lost his balance completely, colliding with the boys and sending them all sprawling.

The darkness at the back of the cave had been hiding a sharp drop, and the four of them went somersaulting down the rocky slope away from the bear, their legs and arms flying up, scattering rocks and dust. As he rolled, Fred caught glimpses of his friends falling alongside him into the blackness. He wondered if they would ever stop falling, or if the drop went on forever. He was worried either way. If they fell into an underground lake, they could drown. If the floor suddenly gave out and dropped them down onto some sharp crystals or rocks, they would be crushed to death. Soon the pain of the rocky cave floor became too much to bear and his mind shut down. It took all of his strength just to keep sight of his companions.

They were all tumbling together, and then, in an instant, Alfred was gone.

17
SPELUNKER? I BARELY KNOW HER...

The boys continued to fall for what seemed like an eternity. The hard cave floor scratched and bruised Fred's arms and legs with every roll. Finally, just when he thought he couldn't take it any longer, the slope leveled and dumped them onto a dusty cavern floor. They skidded to a halt, lying together in a heap, dust swirling up around them.

They spent a few moments coughing and trying to catch their breath. Fred's already injured shoulder ached from the fall, but he tried not to clutch at it in pain. He rolled some soreness out when no one was looking. "Is anybody hurt?" he asked, his tongue still heavy with dust.

"Everything *but* my pride, I think," Stan replied, reaching a hand to his back. "No, no, that hurts too. It just had to be a bear, didn't it? I've seen too many crappy camping movies for it to be anything like a playful koala bear with hugs and hamburgers for all of us."

"We lost Alfred," Jimmy said gravely. "I saw him fall down another passageway."

"I know," said Fred, a bubble of emotion rising into his

own throat. He was truly scared that he would never see his grandfather again. He was even more terrified that it was his fault. "I saw it, too," he managed to say. "How are you, Jimmy?" he asked.

"Bow and bollocks and everything in between," Jimmy replied. He reached over to examine his satchel. "Everything in the bag seems to be okay, too. I managed to slide most of the way."

"Isn't that nice," Stan said as he dug a large pebble out of the skin of his leg. "We must have gone on different rides because I managed to bounce on jagged spikes most of the way."

"At least you didn't bust a lip," said Fred. "I don't know how we'd ever make it if you couldn't tell us how you felt every second."

"You asked," said Stan.

Fred slowly stood up and gave his sore muscles a good stretch as he searched the shadows around them. "Well, at least the Warg had enough sense not to follow us. This place makes Angband look like Aruba. C'mon. Let's see if we can't find my grandpa and get out of this place."

"One second," said Jimmy. He reached into his gym bag and pulled out a firework and lit it.

"A sparkler, Jimmy?" Stan asked, unimpressed.

"It's not mine," said Jimmy defensively. "It must have gotten tossed in with the rest of Alfred's fireworks. Besides we need something that stays lit for a while, nothing flashy." Jimmy handed the tiny torch to Fred and lit another one. They slowly let their lights pass across the small room.

"There!" yelled Stan, pointing to an opening.

Stan's eyes hadn't failed them—it was clearly a passageway. But there was no way anyone would say it looked particularly inviting. Darkness seeped out of it as if from a scab that hadn't healed. Fred looked desperately for another route out, but there was nothing. He reluctantly led them down the path, lighting a new sparkler whenever one would burn out. The route grew so narrow in places that they had to hold their breath just to squeeze through.

"Nothing like an endless 'chokey' to make you want to give up fluffins," Stan said after the boys had to push each other through a particularly tight spot.

"You tell but a fraction of the tale," said Jimmy. "Even the most frightening elvish bedtime stories fail to describe the horrors of this dank place. And I couldn't sleep for a week the first time I heard the tale of Rotgrin the Goblin Witch, bane of the cliff-pine elves."

"Let me guess," said Stan. "Her smile could enslave a dragon and slay an elf in his tracks."

Jimmy went wan. "And I wouldn't dare tell you what her cackle may do to a misbehaving elf or a sarcastic hobbit."

Stan looked unafraid. "Have you met my mom?" he asked. "Because I think I've got a pretty good idea."

Jimmy shivered. "Rotgrin's tongue is made of rust and razorwire," he said.

"She must be beating the boys away," said Stan.

"She and her Mudborn Brigade build their foul warrens out of wurm scales and dragon dung deep in the hearts of mountains like this," said Jimmy.

"Well, then, I can see why she's so hostile," said Stan. "Poop huts are always tough to move on the market. Even the eco-friendly stylings can't make up for the lack of curb appeal and, you know, basic hygiene."

Stan was making fun, but Jimmy's story had Fred spooked. He started stepping a little more cautiously around every dark corner and checking the shadows for the glow of goblin eyes and the glint of hooked goblin blades. Getting skewered on a goblin blade was not how he hoped this whole adventure would end, but that possibility was growing more and more likely the longer they lurked in these nasty caves. All things considered, Fred had to agree with Jimmy and the elves. Being stuck underground was making him realize just how much he truly loved the open air.

"We're running out of sparklers," Jimmy said when Fred reached back to grab a replacement.

"That's something I never thought I'd be sad to hear," said Stan.

Fred was really desperate to find an escape route now. He didn't want to be stuck without any light this deep in the lair of the goblin witch. He stretched his sparkler as far out in front of him as he could and peered intently into the shadows. It may have been his imagination, or the after-glow of a passing sparkler, but he finally thought he'd spotted something. "There!" he said, charging down the rocky corridor towards the faint band of light at its end.

"Careful!" yelled Jimmy. "That's all we've got!" The light in the cave hall died as the last of the sparklers burned out with a pathetic little sizzle.

Fred slowed to a crawl. Feeling blinded, he tried to activate his other senses like Daredevil to help guide his friends to safety. To his surprise, it actually started to work. He could feel the rock's bitter chill on his skin more intensely, and he could hear even the most distant drip and whistle echo through the cave passageways. If the noises hadn't been so terrifying, his plan might have worked. When some bigger rocks shifted, a low rumble reverberated through the caves. Fred stopped in his tracks and held his breath.

"What was that?" said Stan, all sarcasm gone.

"The Mudborn Brigade," said Jimmy. "They beat their war drums with hobbit bones and seek to wake the slumbering dragons at the bottom of the cave with their grotesque elf-hair harps. Let us hope that they have not captured Alfred and that we do not cross paths with one of their hunting parties."

Stan grabbed Fred's arm and then bolted past him down the corridor. Fred had to rush to keep up. Twice he thought the dagger-like tongue of Rotgrin the Goblin Witch was snapping at his legs, but when he reached to fight her off, he realized he had simply run into a sharp rock.

The cave wended on and on. Just when Fred was starting to think that they were utterly lost and would never see light again, the boys spilled suddenly into a high-arching cavern. Escaping the narrow walls of the passageway felt like removing a lead vest. Fred lifted his chin to the cavern ceiling and took in a deep breath.

There was just the smallest amount of light in the cavern and Fred used it to take a good look around. He couldn't believe how much there was to see. He'd always imagined caves as just a bunch of rock, but this room was full of weird growths and shapes. Crystals hung like icicles from the ceiling and rose like spikes from the floor. Little black streams flowed over and through the rocks. To his dismay, the one thing Fred couldn't see was a way out. He huddled next to Stan and Jimmy in the center of the cavern and pondered what to do next.

"Do you think we could climb the walls and reach one of those cracks in the ceiling?" Stan asked.

"Maybe with Jimmy's aerial bridge," said Fred. "We're hobbits, not Spiderman."

"Fine," retorted Stan. "No more helpful ideas from me. You got us into this mess. You get us out of it."

Fred didn't get a chance to defend himself because Jimmy suddenly bolted away. "Something's shining over there," he said as he ran. "Look!"

Fred followed him towards a faint shimmer at the far corner of the cavern. He dared to hope it might be something that could help them get out, or find his grandfather. They were surprised to find a large chest with its top slung open. Spilling out of the chest were swords and daggers, coats of chainmail, helmets and countless other weapons of war.

"Whoa, is this what I think it is?" Jimmy asked.

"Holy Sword of Omens, I think we just found treasure," said Fred, smiling broadly.

"So, are we still hobbits, or are we pirates now?" Stan asked.

"We're still hobbits, Stan," said Fred. "This is troll treasure, or maybe the goblins stole it from the elves." Fred pulled one of the daggers from its sheath and slashed through the air. "I think we're looking at authentic elven weaponry here."

"Yeah, right—let me see that," Stan said as he dug into the chest and pulled out a short sword. It rang a clear note as he unsheathed it and shone a silvery blue in the slivers of moonlight. "Whoa. Most triumphant," he said.

Fred was spellbound, too. He dove into the chest, rummaging for anything of value. He was so absorbed in his search that Jimmy had to tap him twice to get his attention. "Listen," Jimmy whispered, once Fred had finally turned around. Jimmy held his ear to one corner of the cavern.

Fred listened in the same direction. A few seconds later, he heard voices echoing softly down the passage. They were in a distant chamber, but they were getting closer. "It's a trap!" he exclaimed. "Hide!"

The boys scrambled around a large, waxy growth and ducked behind it. Fred's eyes were locked on the treasure chest. He was expecting a goblin war party to drop down on top of it in full ambush mode. Instead, two figures lumbered into the cavern from a hidden door, carrying another chest. One of them was enormous—his thick arms covered in brands and tattoos. The other man was much shorter than the first, and his bent nose was studded with metal.

"You know how I know this is legit?" said the larger man. "It's heavier than your mama."

The other man snarled and snorted, his long thin nose twisting in irritation. "Las mujeres de verdad tienen curvas, acho," he said. "And you think I'd waste my time casing that joint if it wasn't a big payday? They been watching all the ice, man. This is the only stuff worth anything you can get."

"Because it's already been stolen once," said the bigger man.

"Ain't that the truth," said his friend.

"But you can't just go to the pawn shop for golden sippy cups," said the hulk. "And brothers ain't exactly walking the streets with *Braveheart* swords."

"No sense selling to them small-time fools, anyway," said the smaller man. "You got to have serious cash for this. They stop being stolen when they become 'antiquities.' And I got a guy who deals with them old time money types all the time."

"How do you know no one's going to come poking around here?" asked the big man.

"Because they do tours through caves across the

border," said the smaller man. "And people like doing what they're told and going where they're supposed to go."

"You act like no one ever crossed a border."

"Don't even start with the Mexican jokes," said the smaller man. "My dad is from Colorado and my mama is Puerto Rican, and if you say one more word about her I ain't showing you the way out."

Fred pulled his friends down behind the rock as the two men continued to bicker.

"Why are we hiding?" said Stan. "They just said there's a way out. Let's pretend we got lost and never heard a thing."

"That's quite a gamble," said Jimmy. "They'd have good reason to not want us to reveal where they've hidden their loot."

"Jimmy's right," said Fred. "Too risky. Plus, we haven't found Alfred yet. No, we've got to trick them into the sunlight. Trolls turn to stone in the sunlight."

"That's our plan?" Stan asked in disbelief. "Besides the fact that it's still the middle of the night, those guys looked pretty tan. Maybe our think-tank should reconsider?"

"Of course their hides are dark, they're trolls!" Fred exclaimed quietly. "Their skin is as tough as oliphant hide. And I am not a think-tank."

"Blast it, Fred, they're not trolls," said Stan. "The small guy said he's Puerto Rican."

"Well, if they're not trolls," Fred said, "then they must be the biggest goblins anyone has ever seen. He's probably one of Rotgrin's goblin chieftans. Goblins and Olog-hai working together," he said, rubbing his chin, "things are worse than I thought."

"It'll be a whole lot worse if those guys hear you calling them something racist like a troll or a goblin," said Stan.

"Shhh," Jimmy hushed them, glancing worriedly towards the two men.

"Did they hear us?" Fred asked, peering cautiously over the hide himself.

"Doesn't look like it," someone answered him.

"That's goo—" started Fred before it registered in his brain that the voice that had answered him was five levels deeper than Stan and Jimmy's voices combined. Two enormous paws as heavy as a suit of armor came to rest on Fred's shoulders. He turned his head and slowly let his eyes drift up. And up. And up. The troll was even bigger than the thief with branded arms. Sitting atop the skyscraper of bulk was a huge, moony face with a bright orange beard. It was curved in a big, broke-tooth smile.

Fred didn't even bother trying to make a break for it. They were captured.

18

BATTLE IN THE CAVERNS

"Y'all might want to come look at this," said the colossal carrot-haired man as he picked the boys up by their clothes and dragged them out from behind their hiding place. "These little punks been listening to everything y'all been saying."

The shorter man dropped the spear he was polishing and immediately came to get a look at the boys. "What? Where did they come from?" he asked.

"I just found them there," said the ginger giant, pushing Fred forward as he did.

"Now, I know what you're thinking," Fred started, "but contrary to popular belief, hobbit meat really isn't all that tender and juicy. In fact, it's quite gristly and rotten. I mean, I've never had it, of course, but I've heard."

"And elf meat won't fill you up," Jimmy added. "You'll just be hungry thirty minutes later."

The small thief's eyebrows rose. "What, is there a madhouse around here or something?"

Fred had the good sense not to answer that question.

"There must be," said the small goblin, "because

Halloween ain't for six months. Larry, help Dwayne tie them up, while I figure out what to do with them."

The two huge men grabbed some rope from near the chests and bound the boys' hands while the little goblin paced around the cavern.

"What we gonna do, Ricky?" Larry asked.

"You say they heard everything?" Ricky asked.

"And then some," answered Dwayne.

"Then we can't let them go," said Ricky. "They'll just go telling the cops where to find the merchandise, and we can't risk moving it right now."

"So, what you reckon we do?" Dwayne asked.

"We'll just tie them up and leave them," said Ricky, his voice cold. "Nobody with any sense is going to come looking down here."

Fred looked at Stan, but his friend was staring at the cavern floor. The rotten feeling in Fred's stomach crept into his toes and hair and even the hair on his toes. For all he knew, his grandfather might already be dead, and he and his best friend could be joining him soon. It was hard to find anything positive about the situation, but Fred was glad, at least, that the goblins hadn't seen the ring. *We would be dead already if they had any suspicion,* he thought. And he took small solace in the fact that the goblins hadn't considered that somebody without any sense might come to rescue them. They'd been given just the slightest chance, and Fred knew he had to take advantage of it.

Fred's mind ran through all the things they had that might help them. The trolls had taken Jimmy's bow and gym bag, but Fred still had the knife he'd found in the treasure chest, and he thought Stan might still have the short sword tucked away in his cloak somewhere. If the goblins didn't

search them, they might be able to work together to escape.
Jimmy's bag was lying in plain sight, and they didn't seem
too worried about what might be inside it. Apparently, after
dealing with dwarves and dragons the goblins didn't think
the boys were that dangerous. Fred hoped that he and his
friends could use that to their advantage too. If they could get
back to Jimmy's bag, they might be able to pull off an escape.

"C'mon, let's get moving," Ricky said to his henchmen.
"Grab some more rope, Larry." The three men prodded the
boys forward down a shadowy tunnel. "We've got to take
them deep enough to make sure no one will hear their
screams," Ricky said, and this time a smile turned up his
long, hooked nose.

The thieves marched the boys forward into the bowels
of the mountain. The ropes were biting into Fred's wrist,
and one of the trolls kept prodding him sharply in the back.
He was getting more and more frightened every second. If
they ever managed the miraculous and broke free, they'd
have a hard time finding their way out. Fred worked his
arms, trying to loosen the rope, but it was hopeless. He'd
never be able to reach the dagger on his own. He looked
over his shoulder at Stan, trying to get his attention, but
Stan was looking dejectedly at his feet.

Stan didn't even look up when they entered another
domed cavern filled with crystals. Cursing silently, Fred
searched desperately for anything that might help them.

"Let's just leave them here," said Ricky. "It's deep
enough."

"I'd expect nothing less from a goblin!" Fred yelled at
him, merely trying to stall until he could think of something better.

"What did you call me?" Ricky asked him. "I wouldn't

be calling people names if I was dressed like I just got off the short bus."

"Your greed couldn't even fit on the short bus," Fred said.

"What?" said Dwayne.

"He's as treacherous a goblin as the White Wizard of Orthanc ever dug up from the muck!" Fred yelled. "You all should know we've bested your master, and we'll best you, too."

"How they know about The Lion?" asked Larry. "I thought you said no one knew who he was?"

"Shut it, man!" yelled Ricky. "They don't know a thing. They're just crazy."

"Something ain't right with these kids, bro," said Larry. "Too many skittles done messed with their brains. Let's get rid of them and get out of here."

"Fine, I'm just gonna teach Mr. Hero here a lesson before we go," Ricky said with a wicked sneer. He shot a hand out and tugged Fred forward by his shirt. Fred fought against him, and as they jostled about the ring fell out from under Fred's tunic. Fred gasped and struggled harder against the thief's grip, but he could not break loose.

"What the—" said the goblin, grabbing at the ring. "Man, this kid has forty bands of ice around his neck."

The two trolls whistled.

"I guess you weren't a total waste," said the goblin, inspecting the ring. "Good cut, nice clarity..."

Fred pulled away again, trying to break Ricky's grasp, but he couldn't get free. The thief was wiry but extremely strong—there was no way Fred was going to be able to overpower the goblin. Unless Fred suddenly learned to turn into the Hulk or unleash the power of Grayskull his quest was over.

Ricky laughed maniacally as if he knew the despair blooming in Fred's heart. The thief reached for the ring again. "Thanks for the bling, kid," he said, his hand wrapping around the ring. Fred closed his eyes to keep himself from crying.

"Unhand that hobbit you frothy, fat-kidneyed flap-dragon!" A voice boomed from the back of the cavern, the echoes rebounding forcefully off the rock walls. Fred's eyes shot open and the thief leapt back in fright. *Grandpa! You're alright!* Fred yelled silently. *And you're just in time to get us out of this mess!* A surge of hope and energy filled him, but he stayed quiet, letting the goblin fear the worst.

"What the heck was that?" Ricky exclaimed as he and his two trolls searched the dark cavern.

As if in response, the crystals on the cavern walls suddenly started to glow brightly, filling the area with a mystical light. Once the whole cavern was flickering, the shadow of a hooded figure appeared at the top of a nearby promontory. Fred knew it was just his grandfather using some of his old magic tricks, but the goblins had no idea that it wasn't a great and powerful wizard. He hoped it would be enough to scare them away.

"This is the type of crazy stuff that goes down when you hang in caves," said Larry.

"Shut up, Larry," spat Ricky, who didn't seem scared at all. "Who is this, one of your friends?" he asked Fred, grabbing the front of his tunic again.

"You have angered a wizard of unspeakable power," said Fred, trying to sound confident. "Your wicked goblin ways will not go unpunished."

Ricky guffawed. "Folks is crazy as hell in the suburbs," he said. "Alright come down from there, kid, and you won't get hurt," he yelled.

"Do not mistake me for some two-bit tregetour!" Alfred bellowed as he sent several small explosions popping off throughout the cavern. When the smoke cleared, they saw that Alfred had somehow moved from one rock outcropping to the next, and he was now holding his staff and wand in hand.

"What?" Dwayne asked, scratching his head.

Alfred lowered his wand and sighed. "Tregetour," he said again.

Dwayne and Larry shook their heads in confusion.

"Fine," Alfred said through gritted teeth. "Do not take me for some conjurer of childish tricks!" he shouted again, but this did not have the frightening effect he had clearly been hoping for. Unfortunately, the dramatic moment had passed.

"Well, what you waiting for?" Ricky said to Dwayne and Larry. "You're the muscle. Go get him."

"You go get him," said Larry, his huge legs shaking a little.

"It's just an old man—dude can't even walk without a cane," said Ricky. "You telling me you couldn't take down old man Withers by yourself?"

Dwayne and Larry started creeping cautiously towards Alfred.

"Halt!" Alfred commanded, and the two big men jumped back in fright. "Your conduct, sirs, is most unmanly. It is clear that you are servants of the Dark Lord. He has corrupted you and consumed you with his spells of greed. You have pillaged and now you plan to murder to keep your pockets full. Well, no more shall you flout the honor of the just. No more, I say! Your goblin tribe should fear my wrath, for I am Alfred the Grand and foe to your kind."

"Your conduct, sirs, is most unmanly," Ricky mocked him in a high-pitched voice. "Just come quietly, you old fart," he said. "If you was gonna do something, you'd have done it already."

Alfred's confident façade broke just a little. "I was merely deciding what spell would befit such dankish, dog-hearted dewberries," he said quickly. "I could transmogrify you into bats or into gobs of snot. Or I could invoke an army of cave-dwelling beasts to attack you, or freeze you in ice or burn you with the flames of...of..." Alfred stammered, searching for the word.

"Anor!" Fred shouted.

"Yes, I could burn you to cinders with the flames of Anal," said Alfred.

Stan winced. "Not that I don't think that might actually be possible after a few uranium-grade wings from Buffalo Explosion, but if we get out of this, you really should get him a hearing aid," he said.

Fred was glad Stan had snapped out of his funk. It was going to take a team effort to get them all of there. He didn't get the chance to say that to him, though. The light Alfred had been burning in the cave crystals suddenly blinked out all at once. The three thieves stopped completely, afraid to climb the wet slope in darkness. Fred strained his own eyes trying to find Alfred in the dark. He was just starting to make out shapes in the shadows when two columns of blue fire flared with a crackle and a hiss on either side of Alfred. Fred had to cover his eyes. The two large thieves turned their backs, but Ricky pushed them forward up the slope. Standing his ground, Alfred brandished his wand at the approaching thieves and muttered a spell in a strange language. He flicked his wand as he finished his spell, and the thieves ducked again.

Fred was still tied up at the bottom of the slope, but even he flinched. Once he heard Ricky laughing, he knew it was safe to open his eyes...and that they were screwed again. Alfred had cast his "spell," but there was no fire, or ice, or anything dangerous at all shooting from his grandfather's wand. Instead, Alfred's wand had produced a small bouquet of flowers. Alfred was smacking his wand with his other hand the way someone hits a fuzzy television set, trying to fix the problem with brute force, but nothing seemed to be working.

"He must be trying to kills us with allergies," Ricky mocked him. "Or are there bumblebees in there? You see, Larry, he's just a crazy old man with some crappy magic tricks. Now let's grab him and get this over with."

If this gave Larry and Dwayne any extra confidence, it didn't show. They inched ever so slowly towards Alfred, kicking away loose rocks as they climbed.

Alfred kept smacking his malfunctioning wand against his knee. He finally got the flowers to disappear and then squared himself to the oncoming thieves. He chanted his strange spell again and flicked his wand at the approaching thieves. Again, no fire or ice sprayed from the wand. *Maybe the core crystal needs replaced,* thought Fred, because all that Alfred had cast were some globs of a foul-smelling liquid. At least the putrid liquid had landed on the two gargantuan men. They struggled for a second, pulling at their clothes as if they had been burned with some sort of acid. Once they realized the liquid wasn't burning them, Larry and Dwayne started sniffing at their shirts.

"Smells like gas," Dwayne said.

"Balderdash!" said Alfred. "That's liquid milked from a dragon's fire-gland." He started fussing with his error-prone wand again.

"I'm sure all the kiddies believe that one," said Larry in a clear attempt to raise his own confidence.

"Yeah, maybe if the dragon is named Exxon, and if by fire-gland you mean an oil pump," Dwayne joked feebly, and his heavily muscled body shook with laughter.

"It's called a derrick," Jimmy corrected him.

"Your name is Derrick," Dwayne fired back, redness coming to the small patch of pale skin not covered by his orange beard and mess of long hair.

"Squidward has made better comebacks than that," Fred spat.

"I'll come *back* down there if you don't shut up," yelled Dwayne.

"Good, then you can tell us what it's like to be a giant ginger Gorg," said Fred. Dwayne's mitt-sized hand flew to his rope of red hair. Fred didn't care how mad the man was as long as it bought Alfred some time. Unfortunately, the aging magician was their only hope of escape, and there was no telling how long it would take him to get the spell right that would take care of the goblins.

Dwayne took a step back down the slope. "You're a giant pain in the—" he started.

"Dwayne!" Ricky cut him off. "Man, just get the old man. The toddlers ain't going anywhere."

The orange troll looked threateningly at Fred for a second more and then started back up the slope towards Alfred, who was still striking his wand. The thieves were almost within arm's length of the magician when a sharp blow knocked loose the flint Alfred had hidden in the trick wand. The metal went tumbling down the rocky rise, showering the dark cave with fiery sparks as it fell. One of the sparks caught Larry where Alfred's "dragon saliva" had soaked him, and the man's sleeve quickly burst into flame.

The thief thrashed about frantically, causing the fire to spread wherever the gas had landed. He lost his balance and crashed into Dwayne, whose shirt caught fire in turn. The both of them started to flail about crazily, which only caused the fire to spread over them more quickly. Rather than stop, drop and roll, they ran figure eights throughout the cavern, screaming so loudly that they could not hear Ricky tell them to jump into one of the larger underground pools.

Fred used the distraction to shuffle over to Stan. "Grab the dagger in my front pocket!" he yelled.

"There's got to be a better way to say that," said Stan, cringing. His hands still tied, he fumbled with Fred's cloak, but got the dagger free. He held the knife while Fred sliced his ropes on its edge. The rope frayed and then fell away. His hands now free, Fred grabbed the dagger back from Stan. He cut away Stan's bindings and then did the same for Jimmy.

The boys were now ready to make a run for it, but Alfred was still taunting the thieves from the ledge. He was bowing deeply and blowing kisses as if to a roaring ovation.

"No time for a curtain call, Grandpa!" Fred shouted. "C'mon!"

Alfred blew one last kiss and then bounded nimbly down the slope on his wiry legs. The four of them took off together back through the tunnels.

"There has to be an exit back where we were," Fred yelled as they ran, "because those goblins were lugging that treasure in from somewhere." Fred tried hard to remember the turns they had taken as he led them back through the underground paths. The channel twisted and turned so many times, Fred was sure there was no way they'd ever make it back, but he kept running. The fire would not hold the goblins for long.

Somehow, they made it back to the cavern where the goblins had initially captured them. Alfred and the boys bent over and put their hands on their knees, chests heaving. A howl of rage from somewhere in the channels behind them cut their break short. Scooping up their gear on the run, Alfred and the boys took off again down the dark tunnel.

19
WHITEWATER

As winded as he was, Fred pushed Stan and Alfred forward at a faster pace. "We've got to hurry!" he yelled. "Goblins are stupid, but very fast, especially when they've just been scorched by dragon fire."

"Alex Lassiter is the fastest kid in the sixth grade, maybe his mom is a goblin," Stan joked breathlessly as he adjusted his gear.

"You should ask him if we ever escape," said Fred as he led the group down the tunnel.

After a hundred yards, the passage veered sharply to the right. They bunched together like an accordion at the turn and then sprung into a long straightaway. A thin crease of light at the end of the tunnel guided them the rest of the way, and soon they burst from the darkness of the cave into the immense brightness of an oak forest. Pain stabbed Fred behind both his eyes. It felt like he had watched the entire extended Tolkien trilogy in the theater and then stepped out onto the surface of the sun. He rubbed his eyes, trying to massage the pain away and clear his vision. But when he heard angry goblin grunts echoing down the tunnel, he knew he didn't have any time to let his eyes adjust. He forced his eyes open and scanned the forest.

"Where do we go?" Stan asked, gasping for breath.

Fred was just going to pick a direction and run, but then he thought he heard something besides troll taunts. He cupped his ear, listening intently. "I hear water running!" he said. There must be a river close by. C'mon!" He bolted through the trees, everyone else close behind.

The thieves tumbled out of the cave a few seconds later. Larry and Dwayne clutched at their hurting eyes. Smoke was rising from their backs as if they were a pair of smoke-stacks on an old riverboat. The two larger men looked like they could barely stand, but Ricky was hardly breathing at all. His small, dark eyes scanned the forest before him.

"There!" he said, pointing straight at Fred, who felt his heart crash like Humpty Dumpty down his ribcage. "They're making for the river." The three thieves took off after the boys, trailing smoke behind them like trick airplanes.

Fred ran as hard as he could for the riverbank. But the closer he got, the more he began to realize how wide the river actually was. He'd been hoping to swim to the other side, leaving the giant trolls dog-paddling like Andre the Giant through eel-infested waters, but now he knew that plan was useless. He was completely out of ideas and actually looked skywards hoping to see a flight of giant eagles diving down to rescue them. But the skies were as empty as Fred's brain.

But just when he'd lost all hope, Jimmy cried out: "Hey, over there!" He was pointing downriver. "Follow me."

Fred was happy to do just that, even if Jimmy's path took them down a riverbank lined with slick stones. He focused hard on keeping his balance, looking up only to check on Alfred, who was, surprisingly, moving along just fine in his hospital sandals. Jimmy was practically prancing ahead of them, his feet barely touching the stones. Wherever he was leading them, he was determined to get there fast.

Hearing voices ahead, Fred peered around Jimmy. He finally saw what Jimmy's elven eyes must have seen from afar. A group of people in helmets and life-preservers were chatting on the riverbank, a set of rafts floating in the water beside them. Fred was expecting Jimmy to stop and ask them for help, but instead Jimmy dashed right past them and jumped into one of the rafts.

"Get in!" Jimmy yelled, and Fred had no time to second guess him.

He, Alfred, and Stan went flying past the bewildered raft party, who were too stunned to move. The three of them jumped into the yellow vessel and Jimmy pushed away from the riverbank and started oaring furiously. The raft guide, who had been grabbing more life-preservers from a shed, saw what they were doing and came running down the bank, shouting after them to stop.

"Sorry, River Folk," Fred yelled to the rafters, "but the needs of the fellowship are great. Delay the goblin horde if you value your clear rivers and green banks."

"What?" screamed the raft guide, as he waded a few feet into the water. "Get back here! It's dangerous!" He stopped when the boys showed no signs of turning around, putting his hands on the top of his head in exasperation and defeat. The thieves were just coming upon the rafters, and Fred shouted at the guide to look out. The guide turned around in time to see the thieves, two of them still steaming, jump into the other raft. The guide yelled even louder at them, lurching towards the raft.

Fred was hoping the man would be able to stop the thieves, but he wasn't holding out much hope. Sure enough, just as the guide reached for the raft, Dwayne heaved one of the extra paddles at him. The guide had to duck to avoid it and slipped on a wet rock, falling onto his rump. Waist-deep in the water, the guide looked dumbfounded as he watched the two rafts float downriver.

In the boys' raft, Jimmy had taken charge, moving to the back of the vessel so that he could steer. "Fred, you and Stan get on the left side," he ordered. "Alfred, you paddle on the right, and I'll steer. Try to paddle together, guys—we'll go faster."

Fred was so glad Jimmy had some idea what he was doing, he didn't think twice about following his neighbor's orders. Stan and Alfred did the same. They were so scared they had the raft moving at a fast clip within seconds. Fred had seen the size of Larry's arms, and Dwayne's were even bigger, so he knew the thieves would be fast rowers.

Jimmy took a look back and confirmed this fear. "They're gaining on us fast," he said.

"No crap," Stan said. "That ginger giant alone weighs as much as an Olympic rowing team. Great idea, Jimmy," he said, but everyone was too busy rowing to argue with him.

Getting into the rafts had bought them some time, but the goblins would catch up to them fast if they didn't push it as hard as they could. The river began turning south, bending like a dog's leg, and the thieves moved inexorably closer. Fred doubted they had much more than a minute before the goblins would overtake them. It felt like their raft was moving as slowly as a Sandcrawler in a pod-race. His arms were already growing tired and heavy. He risked a glance over his shoulder and was horrified to see that the goblins were only twenty yards behind them now.

As they rounded the dog-leg, Fred turned his gaze back forward. If he thought he had been afraid of the goblins, it was nothing compared to how scared he was when he saw what lay ahead. A hundred feet before them, the river, which had been as smooth as a giant pane of green glass, broke into raging tempests of water. The river frothed and churned, spraying high where it crashed against foreboding rocks. Stan immediately started back-paddling.

"What are you doing?" Jimmy shouted. "We've got to get into those rapids. They're our only chance to lose them."

"I'll take my chances with the goblins," Stan said. "That sign said this is a Class 6 rapid, and I'm guessing the skull-and-crossbones aren't telling us we should keep our eyes open for some pretty flowers as we cruise down the river."

"Do not despair, young Stan," Jimmy yelled over the roar of the rapids, which were growing very close, despite Stan's back paddling. "No goblin can match my skill in the rapids. I swear that I will see us safely to the other side."

"Jimmy, if this is a *GUTS* thing, I'm going to kill you!" Stan shouted angrily as the prow of the raft dipped into the first white-cap. "You know we don't have a womp rat's chance in Hoth of making it out of this alive," he said to Fred.

"Never tell me the odds," Jimmy said determinedly.

Stan rolled his eyes, but Jimmy seemed not to notice. "Fred and Stan, when I say left, you paddle hard," the older boy ordered, yelling over the thunderous rapids. "Alfred, when I say right, you paddle with me."

Fred turned his attention to the river and saw Stan do the same a moment later, though his friend was still grimacing in anger. Jimmy took another look over his shoulder and saw the thieves follow them into the rapids. "Come join the party, boys," he said with a smile. "It's sure to be a smashing good time."

Time seemed to slow as the raft sat perched on the cusp of the next huge rapid, and then, when they started surfing down the wave, everything suddenly rushed forward. The rampaging river caught them up in its flow and did not let go. The bright yellow craft heaved as spouts of water crashed into it, nearly throwing Fred overboard. He fell into the belly of the raft, groping wildly for a grip on the slippery sides, trying not to choke on the water thrashing overboard. He regained his balance in time to see a large boulder jutting from the swirling water directly ahead of them.

"Jimmy, what do we do?" he hollered.

"Left side paddle!" Jimmy yelled, and Fred and Stan responded by oaring as fast as they could.

Jimmy jammed his paddle into the water, using it as a rudder, and the raft banked slowly to the right. Based on his neighbor's grunts, Fred could tell Jimmy was putting all his weight behind it, but the water was pulling them the other way with enormous force. The paddle shook in Jimmy's hands. "Left, left!" he shouted.

Fred and Stan gave as much effort as they could muster —their paddles turning like the pistons on an old iron train. Alfred slid across the raft and helped them paddle. Jimmy pulled even harder on his oar, but the current was so strong it didn't seem to matter. The stone loomed ever closer. They were starting to bank, but not fast enough. *We're going to crash,* Fred thought. But at the last second, they caught a current and their direction changed just enough to get them past the rock. They didn't have much room to spare, though. Fred's paddle scraped against the side of the stone as they rushed by it. He was near enough to touch the boulder, and he pushed against it with his hands trying to give them more space. The raft brushed the rock but did not hit directly, and in the blink of an eye they were past it.

Jimmy had been holding his breath and exhaled sharply. "Good job, guys. That was our first big test," he said. *"Around the first buoy,"* he said in a whisper Fred barely heard.

Fred had been hoping that the rock would stop the thieves, but a quick look back showed him that Ricky and his troll companions had managed to skirt past the boulder, too.

He could only keep his eyes from the river for a second, though, because the rapids were growing more intense. The boys had dropped into a canyon, and the tall cliffs of layered rock rose up on both sides and closed them in. The narrowing of the river seemed to speed everything up even more. They were being buffeted on either side by whitecaps, and it required all their effort just to keep from tipping over.

"Right side, right side!" Jimmy shouted to Alfred. Fred looked to the right and saw that the path was full of jagged-looking rocks and fallen trees spiked with broken branches, and the current was forcing them directly into it. They needed to swerve to the left, and fast. Alfred responded quickly, paddling as hard as his skinny limbs could manage. Stan and Fred jumped across the raft to help him paddle. Again, at the last second, Jimmy managed to steer them clear of this second hazard.

Unfortunately for the boys, he had accidentally led them straight into a far more dangerous situation. They had veered right into a hole, one of the deadliest perils of whitewater rafting—a fact Fred was learning the hard way.

The small maelstrom was caused by huge undercut rocks, which could pin the boys if the swirling water sucked them under.

Fred was getting dizzy as the twisting rapids spun them in place. No matter how hard they paddled, they couldn't break free from its grip. Escape seemed impossible. Even Jimmy was unable to hide his fear. Fred knew if they didn't break free soon, they'd grow too exhausted to stay afloat and would drown. They had already almost used every last bit of their energy just trying to prevent the current from sucking them under. Stan was working so hard he didn't even have enough spare energy to yell at Jimmy.

To make matters worse, the thieves were headed straight for them at full speed. The larger men had taken the turn away from the fallen trees at a sharper angle and were hurtling towards the hole at a much higher speed. Apparently realizing they were moving too fast to dock with the boy's raft, they tried to back-paddle. But the current was far too strong, and they rammed straight into the boys' stalled raft.

The impact shook Fred's bones and knocked both rafts free from the grip of the hole. The yellow watercrafts both dropped back into the rushing rapids. The boy's raft was spinning, but Jimmy had everyone paddling instantly, trying to straighten out and gain some distance from the thieves. The three thieves took a little longer to recover from the crash, but they were almost within arm's length and keeping pace now with the boys. Dwayne was trying to grab hold of the boys' raft, but he couldn't get a grip on the slick vessel. He was trying to get solid footing to leap into the boys' raft, but before he could try, a large wave pushed them apart again.

"We need a plan!" said Fred. If one of the trolls managed to jump into their raft, they were done for.

Jimmy scanned the river ahead and gritted his teeth. This gave Fred little comfort. "Right side!" he ordered. "Take us all the way across to the left side of the river, Alfred."

Alfred responded once again by paddling hard, brushing his wet hair back from his eyes.

"Get ready to paddle hard, left side, it's going to be a sharp turn," warned Jimmy. "On my mark," he said.

Alfred took them skimming across the water away from the thieves, who turned clumsily in the strong rapids to continue chasing them. Fred gripped his paddle tightly, waiting anxiously for Jimmy's order. *We're gaining too much speed*, he thought. If they weren't careful, they'd run up against the canyon wall and splatter against the limestone. He wanted to scream a warning to Jimmy, but the river was roaring like a tornado now. The rocks were nothing but a blur, and the canyon wall seemed to be coming at him impossibly fast

"Engage!" Jimmy shouted at the last second, and Fred started paddling furiously. The raft slowly turned sideways but continued drifting left towards the canyon wall. Fred thought they had turned too late, and he braced himself for impact.

But the crash never came. The raft whipped around at the last second, and they passed between the large boulder and the canyon wall completely sideways. There was no room to spare. The front of the raft scraped the boulder, and Jimmy's bow knocked loose pebbles from the cliff-face behind them. Fred couldn't believe it. For a second, he just marveled at what they were doing, and then the current shot them out of the turn at breakneck speed.

"Right side, right side," Jimmy shouted and Alfred paddled until the front of the raft was facing forward again.

Fred thought he heard Jimmy say, "Around buoy two," but he couldn't be sure with the water rushing around him as loudly as it was. He looked back and saw the goblins' raft smack into the canyon wall and then crash into the boulder. He cheered, thinking the chase was finally over. But somehow the thieves managed to stay on board the raft. They were up and paddling quickly. Fred slumped in his seat. They had just pulled off one of the most amazing maneuvers imaginable in a raft, and if that didn't help them escape, he doubted anything could.

"They made it," he told Jimmy. "Not cleanly, but they made it."

"Stay ready," Jimmy replied. "I've still got a few more tricks up my sleeve."

"I believe that's my line," Alfred piped in tiredly.

Everyone managed a feeble laugh even though the rapids were intensifying again. The water was splashing so high, Fred could barely see anything at all, so it was no surprise that they all missed the small rock. Jimmy called out a warning at the last second, but it was too late. The rock struck them a glancing blow and spun them completely around. They fought to right themselves, but the slip-up had allowed the thieves to catch up.

By the time they had the raft moving in the right direction again, the thieves had pulled up beside the boys. The thieves rammed them from the side, and two stray Velcro straps locked the rafts together. Ricky shouted nasty words, and Larry balanced himself for a leap into the boy's raft. Alfred swung his paddle wildly at Larry, trying to keep him away. Stan and Fred moved to help him, sliding to the other side of the raft and pushing against the thieves' ship with their paddles, but no matter what they tried, they couldn't break free.

A loud roaring sound caused everyone to look downriver. Things were only going from bad to worse. Logs and large rocks closed off both sides of the river, and the only safe path through the obstacles was just a narrow opening between two imposing boulders. It was difficult for Fred to tell with the water gurgling about, but he was pretty sure that there was only enough space for one raft to pass safely through the rocks. The gap was two meters wide at most, and maybe not even that (Fred didn't really get the metric system—he was mostly working off the little video of green blips that rebel leaders showed in *A New Hope*). He imagined it would be difficult enough to guide a raft that *wasn't* being attacked by goblins and trolls through the gap. And he was sure that if the boats stayed stuck together, they'd both crash.

As if all the obstacles weren't perilous enough, the rapids had turned into a series of small waterfalls. The boys went down a couple of rib-rattling drops that tossed them about like nameless ensigns on the bridge of a Federation starship. Fred felt as if he'd been thrown into a blender, yet somehow the goblins were still stuck to them. He hadn't used Velcro since the second grade, but now he was thinking he should get some for the window in the treehouse that never stayed shut because the stuff really worked.

But treehouse improvements aside, the situation was getting dire, and time was running out. The rocks were only a short distance ahead, and Fred had no idea what to do. He looked back to Jimmy, hoping he had a plan. Suddenly, the older boy stood up in the raft. His eyes were bright with what Fred hoped was a brilliant stratagem.

"Stan," Jimmy shouted, "the short sword! Throw it to me."

Stan grabbed the sword from beneath his cloak and flung it to Jimmy, who caught it and unsheathed it with a single smooth twirl. "What are you gonna do?" Stan yelled, but to everyone's horror and amazement Jimmy had already jumped out of the raft.

At this point, Fred's brain took a moment to catch up, because Jimmy hadn't leapt into the thieves' raft, he had jumped off the other side, straight into the rapids. At least that is where he should have landed. Jimmy should have disappeared beneath the white-caps, but instead he was running on top of them, right alongside the craft!

Fred was sure his mind was playing tricks on him. Surely, the thrill of the chase was causing him to halluci-nate. Or maybe they had already crashed, and he was delirious with head trauma. He closed his eyes and shook his head. When he opened them, Jimmy was still sprinting beside them. *He's running on flipping water*! thought Fred. Elves were light enough to run on top of snow, sure, but water was a different story.

To make sure he wasn't going crazy, Fred leaned over the side of the raft for a better look. It turned out Jimmy wasn't running on water. He was actually running on top of a long, flat rock that only stuck out a few inches above the surface of the river. It wasn't a miracle, but it was still really cool—the rock was only a couple inches wide and looked extremely slick. Surprising Fred again, just before Jimmy reached the end of the rock, he leapt again. This time he soared completely over Fred's head, twirling the sword as he flew.

"Cowabunga!" Jimmy's shout rang out as he glided through the air. He seemed to hang forever, and then he dropped like a stone, burying the sword in the side of the thieves' raft. There was a loud popping sound as air blew out from the gash in the yellow fabric. The eruption flung Jimmy all the way back across the boy's raft. Fred and Stan had to reach up and grab him before he toppled over the opposite side.

Losing air fast, the thieves' raft was now spinning out of control. With an unexpectedly high-pitched scream, the thieves crashed into the tangle of fallen tree-trunks and rocks. Fred wanted to shout for joy, but he and his friends were still heading for the rocks at breakneck speed. He whipped his head around, thinking he still might be able to steer them through the boulders, but there was no time— the rocks were only a few yards away. He shut his eyes tightly and waited for the end.

But instead of the agonizing pain of pulverizing every bone in his body, he felt only a rush of air as they slipped through the narrow gap between the boulders.

"Yeehaw!" he heard Jimmy scream and opened his eyes. Fred couldn't believe what he saw. The rapids had ceased, and the river was carrying them along smoothly again. A small wave dumped them into completely calm water.

We made it! Fred thought. They had survived a Class 6 rapid and escaped from the goblins!

Fred let loose another weak shout of triumph and gave Stan a limp high-five. He could tell by the force of the hand-pound that his friend had also spent every last ounce of his energy. A good thing, since Stan was probably not happy at all about what had just happened. Fred would avoid a fight with him for a little while at least.

Alfred had fallen back against the side of the raft, tired but beaming. Together, the three of them all looked down at Jimmy, who was still lying on the bottom of the raft, clutching the sword close.

"And 'Whitewater' goes to 'Deadeye' Dingleman—he's got six hundred points and stays in the lead," Jimmy said, smiling. And then he collapsed in exhaustion.

Joanne hated having to leave the caverns. They were so dark, so cool. The sunlight burned. She scratched at her skin as if to brush away a swarm of insects. This nasty place was so different from the cool, sterile white of the tanning beds, and she wanted to retreat back into the darkness. But the ring had come this way, so she must follow it.

Lurching through the bushes, she traced the ring to the river, where she stopped. She knew the ring had crossed the river, but there was no catamaran moored anywhere close. How did they expect her to cross? She wheeled about in confusion. The last thing she wanted to do was swim in the cold, murky water. That's why people bought yachts, for Ayn's sake!

She screamed, totally enraged. It was the same scream she had been using her entire life. A long time ago she had learned that it was a surefire way to get whatever she wanted from her father. And she had perfected the tantrum over the years. What had once gotten her a doll or an easy-bake oven could now easily get her a Mercedes sedan or a set of pearls.

She had always wanted these things, though she had never really known why. Most girls usually shopped to spend time with their mothers or their friends, but she had never had either. Still, the impulse to buy something nice was always there waiting for her in the morning. In fact, shopping was her only real pastime, and her life had always seemed empty without expensive things. Frighteningly empty. And she would fill that emptiness any way she could. The scream had worked well so far—there was only one thing she hadn't gotten. Realizing that her childish screams weren't working this time, the howl she made turned even uglier.

The voices in her head had come back. They attacked her with mocking riddles: "Why did the little rich girl cross the river? Because no sailor would give her a ride!"

She pulled at the few curlers still stuck in her hair, trying to be rid of them. But the mocking laughter only got worse.

"What a ghastly ensemble!" said the voices, making fun of her tattered clothes. She tore at the rags, trying to rip them from her body.

"Poor thing, I guess she'll have to buy her own diamond," the voices cackled again.

Joanne continued to scream, and then she dove into the water, thrashing furiously.

That ring would be hers. No matter what.

20

REVELATIONS ON THE RIVER

Fred decided not to wake Jimmy right away. The thieves were down for the count, and it had been a crazy night. Fred figured that his friends hadn't slept more than an hour or two before the Warg had attacked, and he hadn't slept a wink. The river was running smoothly and carrying them south, just the direction they needed to be going, so he decided they could all use the rest. Before he nodded off, Fred caught Alfred and Stan fighting to keep their eyelids open, too. He couldn't tell if they fell asleep before he did.

It was well into the afternoon when he finally woke. The sky was still clear. The sun was up. Birds were chirping all along the pine-covered riverbanks. There was a cool breeze blowing. What had been a dark and frightful evening had become a rather pleasant afternoon. Fred checked the sun to make sure they were still flowing south-ward and was glad to find that they were. With any luck they could keep riding the river deep into California, cutting precious time off their journey.

He lifted the bookbags to see how much food they had

left and frowned when he felt how light they were. He didn't need to check inside to know they had almost run out of food.

He didn't get much time to dwell on it. Alfred, Stan, and Jimmy were all up within a few minutes.

"That was a good bit of sport, old chap," Alfred said, patting Jimmy on the shoulder as the archer rose. "Enough to make the heart race."

"That's putting it mildly," Stan said with a yawn.

"I'm with Stan on this one," said Fred. "Jimmy, how on Middle-earth did you know how to handle the rapids?" he asked.

"In preparation for the 'Whitewater' event on *GUTS*, I took rafting lessons," said Jimmy, "although we normally stuck to easier rapids for the class. And we were expressly forbidden to do anything more difficult than a four without an expert guide. I had only heard my instructor talk about the Class 6. The *Devil's Lore*, I think he called it. And it proved to be a ghastly tale for those goblins, didn't it?" Jimmy said with a smile.

Alfred laughed hard. "An excellent new chapter for the *Devil's Lore*," he said between hearty chuckles. "Those waters froth with fury at our escape, but we taunt them with our cries of victory."

"The *Devil's Lore!*" Stan exclaimed. "Are you insane? I couldn't think of a scarier name if I tried. Do me a favor and leave me out of your next rafting trip, alright. You guys can go down *Satan's Entrails* or the *Gorge of Horror,* or whatever you want, all by yourselves."

Fred was confused. "So, wait," he said. "If you had never been down it, how did you know that rock was going to be there when you jumped out of the raft?"

"Oh, my instructor talked about the *Running Rock* all

the time," said Jimmy. "So, I knew exactly where it was going to be."

"The *Running Rock*?" Fred asked again.

"Yeah, that's what they call the flat rock right before the *Widowmaker*," explained Jimmy. "In the olden times Native Americans would jump out of their canoes and run on it. They have another one down my favorite Class 4, but my instructor never let me try it."

"The *Widowmaker*!" Stan exclaimed again. "This just keeps getting better and better. You're suicidal, man. It's official. And what was that bit of theatrics at the end?"

"*Super Smash Brothers*," Jimmy said with a smile.

Of course! Fred thought, chiding himself for not making the connection sooner. He knew he had seen a figure with a bow strapped across his back performing that downward strike with a short sword many times before. Fred always chose to fight as Link when he and Stan played the video game *Super Smash Bros*, and Jimmy had pulled off Link's finishing move to perfection. What was even better, Jimmy had knocked all three of his opponents clear off the map—the best outcome in the game!

"It was a perfectly executed down-sword, Jimmy," said Fred, and Jimmy beamed with pride. "Stan is just mad because I've beaten him with that move a hundred times, even when he's cheap and picks Kirby or Ness."

Stan shot him a look, and Fred decided to back off a little. Apparently, Stan was still not in the mood for jokes.

"Still, it was Stan who found the Master Sword amongst many other weapons in that pile of treasure," said Jimmy. "You chose wisely, Stan." Jimmy offered Stan the sword.

Stan waved it away. "No, you keep it, Jimmy. You obviously know how to use it better than I do."

"You are truly an honorable and generous hobbit,"

Jimmy thanked him, strapping the sword belt over the elastic waistband of his tracksuit.

"Don't mention it," Stan replied.

He wasn't sure why, but Fred was suddenly wondering about the thieves. Even though the goblin and trolls had wanted to do nothing but kill him, Fred was hoping Jimmy's down-sword hadn't actually sent them to a watery grave. "Do you think the goblins drowned?" he asked.

"I hope so," Stan said, "because they were going to do a whole lot worse to us."

"I know, but I still hope they didn't drown," said Fred.

"If they got a hold of one of those long branches, they could have pulled themselves to safety," Jimmy assured him. "Either way, they aren't going to be able to follow us, and that's the most important thing."

This satisfied Fred. As long as they gave the thieves a chance to get out of there alive, he didn't need to spend any more time worrying about them. He needed to focus all his attention on the quest, anyway, because there was always something new with his crew. Captain Picard made it look easy, but Fred was starting to understand why the man had gone so (beautifully) bald so young.

Everyone was starving, so Fred passed around the last of the sandwiches. As he started eating, Fred realized suddenly that in all the commotion he had not thanked Alfred for helping them escape. He also hadn't found out what had happened to his grandpa after they had lost him in the caves. "Grandpa, how did you ever find us in those caverns?" he asked.

Alfred sat up, excitement twinkling in his eyes. "Well, the tale is a thrilling one, if I do say so myself. As you know, I came within inches of the foul beast as he thundered down the dark tunnel. I was close enough to feel the dreadful behemoth blowing its hot breath directly upon my face. The fires were so intense, it was as if I was roasting on the spit. And I could see my very reflection in the gleaming razors of the Warg's innumerable teeth."

"At this rate, we'll be older than he is when he finally gets to the part of the story when he finds us," said Stan.

Alfred ignored him and stood up in the raft to act out the rest of his story. "I raised my staff to challenge the fiend, but even as I did, the beast pounced, shaking the very ground so that my spell miscarried, and I myself was thrown into the utter darkness of the caves. I tumbled head over heel into the depthless abyss, my senses so discombobulated from the battle that I heard not your calls nor anything that would orient me in the cold silence into which I was plummeting. I cannot tell you with what tenacity I clung to my wand and staff, for I knew they would be my sole salvation in those inhospitable climes."

"Come to think of it, I was clutching my staff pretty tightly too," said Stan. Fred and Jimmy laughed, but Alfred was too engrossed in his story to stop.

"When I finally stopped sliding," Alfred continued, "I was so bruised and battered I could barely stand, and I had not the faintest clue what had become of you. I feared the worst, yet steadily did I make my way through those labyrinthine passages. What wonders did mine eyes behold in those rarely trod regions, I have not the eloquence to express, but they were not soothing to my spirit, for still I feared for the safety of my grandson and his indomitable company. What's more, there was a residue of ancient magic all throughout the rocky innards so potent my seeking spells had no effect.

"I was losing hope, and then I heard one of those savages relieving his bladder in an underground pool but a short distance away. In order to ascertain his purpose, I followed him stealthily, but to my dismay, he discovered you before I did. I heard the blackguards' plan and then waited for my chance to free you from their capture. They were leading you back to a part of the cave I had already explored, so I surpassed them in the dark and planned my gambit. I needed to draw those gargantuan villains away from you, so I enticed them towards me with trickery and deception."

Stan rolled his eyes at this part of the tale, but luckily Alfred did not notice. "The rest," he said. "I believe you know."

"Yes, we do," said Fred. "And we would have been lost but for you."

Alfred waved away this expression of gratitude. "Those were caitiffs of a most ignoble sort," he said. "Our cause was just and so we prevailed. Woe to the wicked!" When Alfred raised his arms high in the air he lost his balance, and Jimmy had to grab him to keep him from falling over the side of the raft.

"Take care, Sir Knight," said Jimmy. "These waters can be perilous, even for the wizardly."

By the time Alfred had finished his tale, Stan had eaten his fill and finally seemed to have forgotten to be angry about the dangerous ride down the rapids. He even retold his own favorite part of the rafting trip with enthusiasm, describing their perfect drift-turn with some energetic hand gestures of his own.

"And, Jimmy," Stan continued, "that down sword—whoa, what a move. It would make Link jealous. I've only ever knocked all three opponents off the map with a single move a couple times playing the video game, and you did it in real life! I can't believe you don't have your black belt! That move itself should earn you an honorary one."

Fred was glad Stan was finally enjoying himself now, but he couldn't help noticing Jimmy wince at the mention of his black belt. Jimmy had made sure to keep laughing, but Fred could tell that the last few chuckles were faked. Fred was hoping Stan had noticed this too, but Stan charged ahead. "So why don't you have the black belt, Jimmy?" he asked.

Jimmy studied the floor of the raft, fiddling with his new sword. "I can't do the break," he said, his voice cracking a bit. "They'll give you all the other belts if you can do the form and answer the vocabulary, but not the black. Once you're past a certain age, I mean. At least that's what they've told me. I haven't seen anyone else have to do it. But I just can't do the break. I've tried five times. It's just impossible for me."

"Why is it so difficult?" Stan asked again before Fred could change the subject.

"It's a multiple board break," said Jimmy. "Well, bricks, actually. You've got to break a brick with your Admiral Ackbar (Jimmy once again called his left fist the Calamari rebel leader), turn and break one with your Salamandastron (Jimmy had named his right fist after the legendary badger's keep), break one with a flying front kick, then two at the same time with both feet. But it's the last break that is the most difficult. You've got to break a hanging brick with a wheel-kick." Jimmy's head dropped even deeper. "As much as I try, I just can't get that break. But maybe that's what they want. They might not want me embarrassing their school."

"I think if they saw the moves you just pulled, they'd be

embarrassed not to have you," said Fred. "Right, guys?" he asked Stan and Alfred.

"Totally," said Stan.

"Indubitably," said Alfred.

"You'll get it, Jimmy," said Fred. "Just keep trying."

"I don't know," Jimmy replied. "I'm tired of not breaking and watching all the eight-year-olds get their belts. I don't think I want to go through that again."

"Well, next time you try, we'll be there," Fred assured him. "And no matter what, we should go get pizza afterwards to celebrate."

Jimmy nodded and offered a weak smile. Because it was obvious Jimmy was growing uncomfortable with the attention, Fred let the matter drop. He quietly finished his sandwich and then kept his eyes on the riverbanks for any signs of trouble.

Midday quickly lengthened into early afternoon, and luckily the weather remained sunny and fair. The raft ride was quiet and serene, and Alfred and the boys enjoyed spotting deer grazing along the riverbanks and hawks soaring in their wide loops high in the sky.

Although they were glad to be off their feet after a day and night of hiking and running, Fred could tell that everyone was starting to feel a bit claustrophobic in the raft —including him. Only a few comics had not been totally ruined by the rapids, and soon even he grew tired of rereading those. So, they played every game they could think of to pass the time. Stan made war-paint faces out of his sun screen, and they sped through rounds of "twenty questions," "paper-rock-scissors," and "I spy." They invented new travel games and played those too. But the river ride was long, and eventually Alfred and Jimmy dozed off again out of boredom.

At several points the raft got slightly bogged down in massive algal blooms where dead salmon floated in a thick green film, their bulging eyes staring blindly at the sky. Fred had to carefully steer them clear of the nasty water. He tried not to look at the floating bodies and puckered mouths of the dead salmon. They just reminded him of the goldfish Alex Lassiter had cruelly stomped. But as the foul smell lingered, it was hard to think of anything else.

Annoyed that he was having to do all the navigating, Fred suddenly noticed how hot it had grown in the raft and how thick the stench was floating in from across the cattle pastures. His skin was uncomfortably sweaty and itchy, and small clouds of gnats were clustering overhead, stinging his eyes and clogging his mouth. The bugs seemed to be targeting him specifically, and soon he couldn't fight his irritation any longer.

"Hey, man," he said to Stan. "Why did it take you so long to help me go after the goblins?"

Stan laughed. "Because if there's one thing I've learned from my mom it's that you don't mess with people who can hurt you, and that counts double for her."

"But what about the Firebirds?" said Fred. "You went after them."

"They're sixth graders not six foot six," said Stan. "I'm sorry I don't have a death wish."

"That's not what I mean," said Fred. "I was just trying to get your attention to come up with a plan."

"Next time some murderous maniacs threaten to kill you, here's the plan—shut up and do what they say."

Fred shook his head and clenched his jaw. "I'm tired of doing what other people say," he said. "What *mean* people say."

"That's life, man," said Stan. "Nothing's fair."

"No," said Fred. "No way. That's not the hero's way. That's what they want us to think. That's how they win. We're too exhausted or hopeless to fight back. That's why we're doing this, to show mean and stupid people that we're not just going to give in and do what they say anymore. That we're willing to go the distance."

"Who are we talking about?" said Stan. "Joanne? She's not going to learn anything—she's just going to be the same beeya she always was and make your life even more miserable if you manage to lose her ring."

"Maybe," said Fred. "And maybe after all this my dad sees her for what she is. And it's not just Joanne, it's people like Alfred's doctor and Mrs. Bonneville."

"They're all bloody mad," Alfred interjected, surprising them both. "And I know a cell in Eisen Gardens that just came available." He smiled mischievously.

Stan laughed, but Fred was still boiling. "The thing I want to know is why? Because I really don't get it. Why are they so Mordor-bent on turning us into a cruel army when everything inside of me wants to help when other people hurt. How can we see the Dark Lord's plan and they can't? What spell has he cast upon them?"

"The most insidious kind," said Jimmy, looking up from a comic. He leaned forward in the raft and beckoned them to come closer so that he could speak with his voice just above a whisper. Fred grabbed Stan and Alfred and leaned in to hear him. "The Dark Lord knows it is far easier to win the battle in the mind," Jimmy tapped his noggin with the tip of the Master Sword, "than on the battlefield. So, he has cast a spell that makes his subjects think they are working for their own glory, when they are really working for his. All the while, he grows stronger by sapping their lifeforce. And once this spell has infected his subjects' minds, they can't even imagine being free and will work only to enslave others in the Dark Lord's army. But we must not give the Dark Lord what he wants and make enemies of those he has enthralled. Instead, we must free them. For there is still good in them, and they could be good again, if we could just show them another way."

The raft was quiet for a moment as everyone pondered Jimmy's words.

"Well, he's either a genius or a Jedi," Stan said finally. "Who knew?"

Everyone laughed. "Thanks...I guess?" said Jimmy.

"Stan is right," said Fred, pouncing on the opportunity to boost Jimmy's confidence. "We are lucky to have such a wise elvish scholar in our company."

Jimmy shrugged. "Ah, my parents are the smart ones. I just read a lot. My library card looks like a cave troll tried to eat it."

"You may not have the credentials, but what you say is illuminating, 'Deadeye,'" said Alfred. "In fact, I was just saying the same thing to Dr. White."

Fred and Stan whipped their heads around and lifted their eyebrows at Alfred.

"What?" said Alfred. "Well, mayhap not verbatim, but the sentiment was the same."

Fred rolled his eyes. Alfred was smarter than he looked, sure, but Stan was right—Jimmy sounded like a genius.

"Your elvish is certainly too advanced for me, master archer," said Fred. "But I think that what you are trying to say that most people are more like...Darth Vader than the Emperor?"

Jimmy chuckled. "That's one way to put it, Fred," he said. "But, yeah, like Anakin they've been deceived. They've been manipulated. They've been broken and tamed and forced to serve an evil empire. But it's not their fault. And we shouldn't give up on them."

"What can we do to show them?" asked Fred. "To bring them back...to the good side?"

Jimmy put his hand on Fred's shoulder. "Exactly what we're doing, my dear hobbit. We must travel to the Dark Lord's den to show him and all his unwitting subjects that people matter more than things. That it is better to create friendships than possess a cruel power over others. That adventure is the jewel of life. Such is the glory and honor of our quest."

Jimmy's thought was so beautiful it made Fred smile. Jimmy is so smart, he thought, and Stan was right—who would have known? Jimmy worked at a grocery store, and he spent most of his free time plotting to enact his revenge on kids from an old game show. But Jimmy had been saving his deepest thoughts for himself. Fred knew he had underestimated 'Deadeye' Dingleman for the last time. He was happier than ever that he had decided to bring Jimmy along.

Stan shook his head. "How is someone so smart stacking sauces at the supermarket?" he blurted.

"Stan!" Fred said.

"It's okay, Fred," said Jimmy. "I get what he's trying to say. And I don't know, really. I guess I get to meet lots of people when I'm on register, and when I'm monitoring the store, I get to read most of the day. Plus, the comic book store didn't have any openings."

"Bummer," said Stan. "Bet you could teach at the Jedi Academy, or you know, a more boring college."

"Ah, I don't know," said Jimmy. "Both of my parents are archaeology professors, which is not as cool as it sounds. They don't have a single whip between them. And when I was growing up, they were always so concerned with finding new artifacts and publishing books, that they didn't really have time for too much else. When they weren't away on expeditions, they were in terrible moods about something or another. Funding mostly. It just turned me off of the whole business. I'd rather study and think on my own, in peace and quiet. I'm not interested in any glory or anything, just understanding."

Fred was starting to feel really sorry for Jimmy. Come to think of it, he had never seen Jimmy's parents more than a handful of times in all the years that they had been neighbors. He had never known how sad their being gone all the time had made Jimmy. It made Fred even more afraid that if he didn't get his parents back together now, he'd end up mopping up messes in aisle nine. And as much as he was impressed by Jimmy's smarts, he definitely didn't want to end up with pictures of kids from an old game show on his parent's garage wall when he was his neighbor's age.

Still, all that *GUTS* nonsense aside, Jimmy wasn't off his rocker any more than Alfred was. Like the old magician, Jimmy was just sad. Fred resolved to cheer him up. "You have counseled us very wisely, 'Deadeye,'" he said, "and helped us to better understand our enemy. Is it true, then, that the elves keep scrolls of ancient texts, and that they are the protectors of magical lore?"

"Oh, yes," Jimmy answered. "There are many that are written in runes and tongues not often spoken among men and some that can only be read by candlelight. And though the lieutenants of the Dark Lord cannot comprehend them, they seek to destroy the message in those tomes because they are as afraid of what they contain as we are terrified of what lies at the center of the Dark Lord's heart."

"What else do they say?" Fred asked.

"Those scrolls prophecy a time when the Dark Lord will no longer hold dominion," said Jimmy. "But they also warn that there are many who will want him to reign forever, for he heaps riches upon them and makes them like kings. But I have joined your quest because I believe that if you throw away the ring, we fulfill the prophecy of those ancient manuscripts. Only the bravest and wisest among us will be strong enough to cast away what so many prize. That is what the Dark Lord and his minions fear most. That is why your quest must succeed."

"No wonder we have been pursued so relentlessly," Fred said gravely. "The Dark Lord's reach is everywhere. Those thieves were clearly his servants, but he has many more spies, and they are cleverly disguised. We must be cautious. Your wise words will not go unheeded, 'Deadeye.'"

"I don't know about all that," said Stan. "But I'd much rather have you for a teacher than Mrs. Bonneville."

Jimmy rubbed his chin thoughtfully. "Well, I learned from the best," he said. "Apart from all the philosophers I've read, no one can introduce an event like the mesmerizing Mo Quirk."

Fred laughed. It hadn't taken long for Jimmy to get back to normal.

"Quirk? Isn't that the dude from Star Trek?" Stan asked. "With the big ears?"

"If you were any other hobbit, I'd have your hide for mistaking my sweet Moira for a Ferenghi," Jimmy told them. "That's Quark, not Quirk."

"Not this again," said Stan. "My bad, okay."

"Who is this Moira you speak of?" Alfred asked.

"A woman so beautiful she makes your Guinevere look like Gothmog the deformed orc," said Jimmy.

Alfred huffed angrily. "You speak of the fair queen of

Camelot, brash archer. Mind your tongue. I will be forced to defend her honor if you question her unrivalled muliebrity again."

"Wait, did you just call her a mule?" asked Stan. "Is that a good thing?"

Alfred threw his hands up in exasperation.

"I meant no offense and do not wish to anger a wizard of your skill," said Jimmy. "I intended only to praise my damsel's great beauty."

"As all chivalrous knights do," Alfred said, his anger gone. "Both our ladies are worthy. To their fortune," he said, raising an invisible cup as if to toast. Unfortunately, this only reminded everyone of how thirsty and hungry they had become.

"Do we have any more Capri suns in there?" Stan asked Fred.

"No, we're out of everything," Fred said despondently, reaching into his mostly empty bag. "I think there is only one cookie left."

"What in the heck are we going to do for dinner?" Stan asked.

"I think you're more worried about going hungry than you were about taking on the goblins," said Fred.

Stan offered fake laugh. "But seriously," he said, "what are we going to do?"

"I say we follow the river for as long as we can," suggested Fred. "It's moving us a lot faster than if we were hiking, that's for sure. Let's just hope we find something along the way. We'd be in the same boat if we were moving on foot. Well..." Fred paused, realizing how silly that sounded, "...you know what I mean. We'll have just as good a chance of spotting food from the river, so there's no sense in getting our legs tired or slowing down."

"That doesn't give me much hope," Stan whined.

"I'm sure something will turn up," Fred assured him.

However, for the rest of the afternoon, nothing did turn up. The sun began to drop, and they still hadn't seen any opportunity for dinner. To make matters worse, the river had carried them into a large, flush forest, making it difficult for Fred to see anything through the tangle of the trees. Because they had not spotted any signs of civilization all day, Fred was really starting to feel like they had traveled to a strange and distant land. As much as he was excited by this, he was equally scared. He was the leader of this expedition, and if they went hungry or came to danger, it was his fault.

On the flipside, it gave him an odd sort of comfort to be going through such hardship. Being "molly coddled," as Alfred would put it, would do him no good. A proper quest was full of dangers and terror, and if his own journey was too easy, it wouldn't work, Fred was sure of that. If putting up with a pinched stomach, Stan's griping, and a chest chafed raw by a giant diamond meant he'd get years of happiness with his family, he would endure all of it gladly.

Well, maybe not gladly. But he'd do it. Realizing he truly meant this gave him a much-needed boost of energy. He kept imagining leading his parents back to their house, arm in arm, triumphant, from the Dark Lord's den.

Within the hour, the last of the sunlight had faded into the trees lining the western bank, and the river had become just a shining ribbon of moonlight draped across the shadowy hills. Forced to give up his daydream up for the moment, Fred was growing desperate now. The darker it grew, the harder it would become to safely steer their vessel, let alone find food.

"Do you think it's safe to stay on the river?" Alfred asked, voicing the concern they were all feeling.

"Not for too long," Fred answered. "Without the sun, there's no way to know if we're still going south."

"What about the Northstar?" Jimmy asked.

"I thought about that," said Fred," but I don't know which one it is."

"Isn't it the brightest one in the sky?" Jimmy asked again.

They all rocked their heads back and looked for it.

"Is it that one?" Stan pointed.

"I don't think so, that's where the sun just set," said Fred.

"That has to be it," Jimmy said, pointing to what was clearly the largest, brightest star, a shining orb positioned in the sky behind them. "So long as we keep that to our backs, we should be fine," stated Jimmy.

"Slow down there, Capitano," said Stan. "I may not look like Leonardo DiCaprio, but I'm smart enough to be worried about rocks in the dark."

"That's a good point," Fred agreed. "I can see pretty well in the dark. I'll look out for rocks."

"Why don't you use this to help you see, my boy," said Alfred, handing Fred his wand.

The tip was already glowing, so Fred just pointed it towards the water right in front of them. "That'll really help, thanks, Grandpa," said Fred. "You guys keep checking the horizon for food."

"A float-thru would be nice," Stan suggested. "That way we wouldn't even have to get out of the raft. I'd order a double cheeseburger and a milkshake. Chocolate. No, vanilla. No..." his smile grew, "...cookies-n-cream."

Fred cut Stan off. "Just keep looking for lights," he said

tersely. He wasn't about to listen to Stan talk about food for hours. His own stomach was growling and twisting fiercely.

Another hour passed and still they hadn't seen any sign of a town. Not even the slightest hint of civilization. Fred didn't dare hope for the white cliffs of Minas Tirith, but the gates of Bree would be a welcome sight. They had been riding the river all day, and Fred was sure they were now deep inside California, getting closer to Mordor every second. He knew things were only going to get worse the longer they traveled into that dark country, but he was hoping they could get one last hearty meal before taking on the enemy, at least. Even if a bacon cheeseburger was out of the picture, he would happily settle for a couple of cheese sticks and some peanut butter crackers. He would need all the strength he could get if he was going to see this quest to the end.

"Guys, we're starting to veer east," Jimmy warned suddenly. "It's just slight right now—we're still mostly moving south—but if the river continues to turn, we need to get off the raft."

"Yoda's moldy undershorts!" Fred cursed. He'd been hoping to ride the river just a little longer. He didn't think any of them had the strength to hike very far on an empty stomach.

Night's dark curtain fell swiftly. Soon the raft was swallowed up in total blackness. Only by the light of the stars and the faint glow of Alfred's wand could the boys see enough to keep from running up the riverbank. As the hours drew on, Fred began to worry that they'd have to go all night without food. His eyes were starting to hurt from straining to see in the dark, and he had to fight to keep them open now. He was about to collapse from exhaustion when Stan suddenly stood up in the boat, peering intently at one point along the coast.

"What is it?" asked Fred. "What do you see?"

"Lights, I think!" Stan said. Fred looked in the same direction, but he couldn't see anything. After a moment, Stan exclaimed again, "Those are definitely lights! Lots of them. Look!"

Fred saw them now. He could make out the faintest glimmer of lights among the shadowy branches of the towering trees. As the raft drifted closer, he could see the lights were huge and multicolored, blinking and spinning festively.

"It's a carnival!" Stan shouted. "That means funnel cakes and cotton candy, cherry slushes and root beer floats. The power of prayer really does work!"

"It is perfect," Fred agreed. "We'll definitely blend in more at a carnival."

"So, what are we waiting for?" Stan said, smiling hugely.

Fred looked at Alfred and Jimmy, who both nodded their approval.

"Alright, take us in, Jimmy," he said.

21

A MOTHER'S LOVE

Sherriff Elmer Marshal was a man who enjoyed lively conversation. His job often put him in serious, even dangerous, situations, but he saw this as no reason at all to be impolite. In fact, during his long career in law enforcement he had seen it proven time and again that bad manners were the first stepping stone down a bad path. Setting a good example might not ever be enough to prevent kids from going down it, but it sure was worth a try in his mind.

His motives weren't entirely pure, however. Long days sitting behind a desk could be incredibly dull, and Wynnie, his newest deputy, wasn't much of a conversationalist. When she wasn't doing push-ups and crunches at her desk, she was reading biographies of Jackie Chan or Bruce Lee, practicing punches and kicks from a seated position. A few times he had caught her trying to move desks and filing cabinets with nothing but her mind. When she was concentrating that hard, to ask her a question was to risk getting a pair of scissors flung his way. According to Wynnie, dodging projectiles was the best way to keep him on his toes. He wasn't sure about that, but it did help him keep a clean office. The less there was to throw, the safer he felt.

At that very moment, Wynnie was trying to twist her fingers into a special death grip she had been attempting to perfect for a week, so Elmer let all hope of a conversation go and 'turned his attention back to work. As he flipped through his growing case-file, he lingered on the most recent addition: three boys missing and presumed to have crossed state lines. The fact that one of the boy's fathers was in prison made him nervous, but he chided himself for making that assumption. Other than the dimpled chin, he shared no qualities with his own father. He had been happy to see, at first, that the other boy's father was a well-respected lawyer, but he had been unable to reach Solomon Oglesburg at work all afternoon—not even to leave a message.

He decided to dial once more before calling it a day. He'd been on duty going on 36 hours, after all, working overtime trying to evacuate civilians from the path of a wildfire and bring some big-time thieves to justice, and he really needed to grab some shuteye. The phone rang several times, and then several more. He was just about to hang up when Solomon's administrative assistant finally answered.

"Hello," she said in obvious irritation.

Surprised at the harshness of her tone and by the fact that someone had actually answered, Elmer stammered, "Uhm, fine...I mean, hello...how fine are you this afternoon? Er...How fine is your afternoon this time?"

After a moment of silence, she sighed deeply. "What do you need?" she said.

"Apologies—I'm not normally so tongue-tied," he said,

"I must just be happy to be talking with someone." Another uncomfortable silence. "Anyway, I was hoping to speak with Solomon Oglesburg. My name is Sheriff Marshal, and I run things down here in Chadarras County. I have some information concerning his missing son."

"You expect me to believe that one?" said the secretary. "What—are you calling from the Wild West? I mean, which one are you—a sheriff or a marshal? You should really have that figured out before you call. It at least makes you sound more believable. I don't even want to guess what sink hair news site you work for."

"Well, actually—" Sheriff Marshal tried to correct her, but she talked over him.

"Mr. Oglesburg is a busy man, and pretending to know something about his son to get a quote for your clickbait bologna boat is just awful!"

Sheriff Marshal rushed to explain, but she had already hung up the phone. He stared at his own phone for a second, half-expecting to find that it had just grown teeth. Then he hung it up and tried to call Solomon Oglesburg's office again, but the assistant did not answer. Knowing that Solomon was at the office at least, he flipped through the report again, searching for an alternate number. He finally found one hastily scrawled in chicken scratch on one of the last pages. It had the name Lucy Oglesburg and the letter *m* next to it, which he assumed stood for *mother*.

Wondering if his inept deputies could have hidden her number any better, he dialed her, kicking his boots up on his desk as the phone rang. He reclined deeply in his chair and took a big sip from his coffee mug.

"Hello? Hello?" Lucy answered before the first ring had ended, startling him again.

In order to respond, Sheriff Marshal had to swallow his steaming hot coffee much too fast, burning the back of his tongue in the process. "Miff Oggeburr," he said, wiping some liquid from his chin, "you cobb me opp guarr."

"I caught you?" she asked, clearly annoyed. "You called me."

Sherriff Marshal shifted in his seat and dabbed his tongue with a napkin. "Yes, but I've been trying to get a hold of your husband all day and haven't been able to," he said once the pain had subsided a bit. "I was just surprised you picked up."

"My *ex*-husband gets very busy at work," she said. "What is this about Mr...?"

"My apologies, Miss," said Sheriff Marshal. "My name is Elmer Marshal, and I'm the sheriff down here in Chadarras County. I think I have some news about your son."

"Chadarras!" Lucy exclaimed. "But that's so far. I've still been looking in Oregon. Are the boys okay? Do you have them?"

"Now, as far as we know, they're alright," said the sheriff, even though that wasn't exactly the whole truth. Lucy already seemed worked up, and he didn't want to startle her. "Our office got a call this morning from a raft guide who called to report a theft. He said that some strangely dressed boys stole one of their rafts and took it downriver. I cross-checked that information with reports made in Oregon and Northern California over the last few days, and the computer pulled up a missing persons claim made by your husband."

"So, you don't have them?" Lucy asked, hushing someone else on the other side of the phone.

"No, ma'am," said the sheriff. "But—"

"But the rapids must be dangerous?" Lucy interjected. "How can you be sure they're alright?"

"It can be a tough ride, ma'am," said the sheriff, "There are some pretty good-sized rapids down the river, but we have reason to believe the boys made it down alright."

"What do you mean?" Lucy asked.

"Well, the tour guide said that a couple men stole a second raft and followed the boys down the river," said Elmer. "Anyway, we only found the remains of one of the rafts."

"The remains!" Lucy exclaimed.

Sheriff Marshal slapped his forehead. "Yes, ma'am, but don't be alarmed," he said, trying to recover. "Like I said, there's no sign that the boys have been harmed in any way. The tour guide said the men were dressed in black, and at the site we found a black shirt, sized triple extra-large, snagged on a tree branch. Unless one of your boys is big enough to box a buffalo, it's more likely the men's raft crashed, and the boys made it through the *Widowmaker* just fine."

"The *Widowmaker!*" Lucy exclaimed, and Elmer Marshal cursed himself beneath his breath again for letting the name slip. *Get it together you tired old fool!* Because he thought it would take a little longer to calm Lucy down after telling her about the *Widowmaker*, he signaled to Wynnie to put on another pot of coffee as he picked his boots off the top of the table. Wynnie apparently misunderstood this gesture, because she rolled her head around in imitation of someone drunk and then continued pumping out reps on her thighmaster as she flipped through a book of advanced Aikido postures.

Sheriff Marshal didn't get a chance to ask her again because Lucy and whoever she was with were both yelling incoherently in his ear now. At least he had not accidentally told her that the men chasing her son were criminals potentially working for the biggest crime boss in the West and that a huge manhunt was now underway to find them. That would have really set her off.

"The *Widowmaker's* bark is worse than its bite," Elmer finally managed to get in. "And we've got thirty officers combing the riverbanks. With any luck we'll have your boy and his friends by nightfall."

"I've heard that before," said Lucy.

"Not from me you haven't," said Elmer. "Trust me. They are as good as found."

Suddenly another woman was screeching at him through the phone. "And to make sure they're still good when you find them, we're coming there."

He heard a little scuffle for the phone and then Lucy had the phone again: "That was Stan's mother, sheriff. Sorry."

"Quite alright, ma'am," said the sheriff. "I can imagine she's mighty worried. I know she didn't mean nothing by it."

"Oh, she meant every word, sheriff," said Lucy. "And I mean it when I say we'll get there as fast as we can." With that Lucy hung up on him.

"Dagjummit!" he hollered. "I never been hung up on so much in my umpteen years. Wynnie, I want a report from the field now! Find out if those Combe County knuckle-heads have found those thieves or those kids. If they haven't, tell them they durn well better."

He stomped over to the table and snatched up the empty coffee pot. Shaking his head and muttering under his breath, he reached for the coffee beans to make another cup. As he did a pencil sharpener struck him directly in the back of the head.

"Too slow, boss," said Wynnie. "Way too slow."

As Sheriff Marshal rubbed the fresh knot swelling on the back of his head, he wondered just how much had been sent to test him. Then he turned and smiled at Wynnie before putting on another pot of coffee.

22

A FESTIVAL OF LIGHTS

Jimmy slowed the raft and steered it towards the river's edge. Just before they reached the bank, Fred and Stan jumped out and helped ease the craft onto the sandbar.

"We should carry the raft inland a bit and hide it," said Fred once everyone had climbed onto land. "We don't want trolls or goblins or anyone else tracking us."

"That's a good idea," agreed Jimmy. "Now that we're out of the water, the raft is basically just a giant yellow homing beacon."

"Why don't we just push it down the river?" said Stan.

"That's not a bad idea either," said Jimmy.

"What if we have to make another run for it?" asked Fred. "I know the river isn't going exactly the way we need to go, but I'd rather have a plan B than not."

"Excellent point," said Alfred. "Preparation is the marrow of action!"

"Rrrright," said Stan. "Whatever that means. So, I guess Jimmy won't be popping a sword sized hole in the raft to make it easier to carry, either."

"Probably not," said Fred. "I'm guessing that would make it tough to ride again."

"Well, then let's haul," said Stan, grabbing hold of one side of the raft. Together, the four of them hoisted the craft over their heads and marched into the woods towards the carnival lights. A few hundred yards into the woods, Fred found a dense clump of bushes, and everyone else agreed that this would be the best place to hide the raft. They placed it in the middle of the shrubs, taking care to lift some fallen leaves and branches over the top of it to complete the camouflage. Even Fred had trouble finding it when he stepped back to examine their work. Someone would have to be searching very closely to spot it.

"That looks good," he said, dusting off his hands. "Let's get to that carnival before it closes for the night."

But Stan was already scooting off through the woods towards the noises of the festival. "Popcorn and candy apples, ice cream cones and flavored ice!" he shouted. "I can taste the pretzels and hot dogs and nachos already."

"Easy there, Augustus Gloop," Fred shouted after him. "Or you're going to lead us into a giant chocolate tube of orc torture."

Everyone stopped and looked side-eyed at Fred.

"Yeah, that didn't sound quite so weird in my head," he said. "Sorry."

"It's alright, my boy, we're all tired and hungry," said Alfred. "Even the most stalwart of knights cannot fight hunger forever."

Grandpa, you couldn't be more right, thought Fred, whose stomach was rumbling out loud. He hoped the carnival had something to eat besides bologna sandwiches and choco-late chip cookies. He had been surprised to learn that the two snacks didn't actually go together very well, and, as hungry as he was, the thought of eating bologna again made him want to hurl. Swallowing deeply, he reminded himself to stay sharp. There were going to be a lot of people at the carnival, and even though the fellowship would blend in better amongst the carnival-goers than anywhere else, there was still a risk that they would be recognized. As soon as Stan caught a whiff of a freshly baked pizza or slow-roasting hotdog he was likely to throw caution to the wind and give them all away.

They moved quickly through the woods, happy to stretch their legs after spending the entire day sitting down in the raft. After a few minutes of brisk hiking, the trees began to thin before them, and they strolled onto a wide field of grass. The little glade was completely filled with brightly colored tents and sparkling carnival rides.

"Try not to draw too much attention to yourselves," Fred warned. "Don't forget that there are enemy spies everywhere."

No one seemed to be paying him any attention. They were all awestruck by the sight of the carnival. Fred looked up as they passed beneath the flashy entrance sign, which read:

THE KASSIRBANN BROTHERS, ART AND JULIAN

TRAVELLING CARNIVAL AND CIRCUS

The fair grounds were bristling with people, but Fred was happy to find that no one was even looking twice at them. As far as he could tell, they were the only ones in costume, but to people who had just seen one of the circus performances, he imagined that the four of them would not have seemed that out of place. The ticket takers even let them pass through without asking them to pay.

At the front of the carnival there were all kinds of brightly lit game booths. Of course, Stan could not have cared less about the games; he had his nose stuck out like a cartoon hound dog, sniffing feverishly for a food hut. He was practically lurching and drooling as if he had been zombified by all the hearty smells. A little girl who was carrying a globe of cotton candy in one hand made the mistake of walking too closely to Stan, and Fred had to hold him back so he didn't snap at it.

"We're going to get food in two minutes," said Fred, "so try not to bite anyone's fingers off before then."

"I'm not making any promises," said Stan.

Hearing the loud thunk of an arrow caused Fred to look around anxiously. He relaxed once he realized it was just a sharp-shooter booth and not Uruk archers launching black arrows at them from the trees. Two young kids had just fired rubber-tipped arrows from a wooden bow and both had missed the targets completely.

"Well, that's just bad form," said Jimmy, craning his neck to get a better look. "Their stance is too wide, their nock too high, and their release is clumsy as all get out."

"Yeah, well we're not running a bow-hunting clinic," said Stan.

Jimmy nodded, but his eyes lingered on the targets as the fellowship slowly drifted past them.

"Not now, Jimmy," added Fred. "There's no time."

"I was only looking," said Jimmy, hurrying to catch up.

Still on the hunt for food, they continued strolling through the fairgrounds. They passed a Ferris wheel and then an octopus-themed carousel, which Fred warned everyone to stay away from. Water or not, he wasn't going to be caught unawares around a giant monster with flailing tentacles.

Finally spotting a large snack hut nestled between the two rides, Stan sprinted towards it. Fred whispered another warning to him and then hurried to catch up.

Stan was already ordering by the time Fred, Jimmy and Alfred got there.

"I'll have a large popcorn, two, no, three corndogs, nachos with double cheese and extra jalapeños, and a full pepperoni pizza," Stan said to the squat middle-aged man behind the counter. "You guys want anything?" he asked the rest of the group.

The man grunted and put on a show of going to great lengths as he started to prepare all of Stan's order. He moved sluggishly from counter to counter and pretended like the cheese ladle was as heavy as a cave troll club.

"That'll be fifty dollars," the carnival employee said with a huff, once he had placed all of the food items on the counter.

"No problem," Stan said looking back at the rest of the group. "Anybody have any money?"

Fred winced—he hadn't thought about money at all. He was so worried about being caught that he had forgotten that they would need to find some way to pay for the food. He shook his head. Alfred did the same.

"Jimmy?" Stan pleaded.

"Sorry," Jimmy replied. "What little money I did bring was torn to tatters in my pocket when we went down the river." He held out a few green rags that looked more like troll bogies than dollar bills.

The employee was getting angry. His big, pink cheeks were growing redder by the second. "What are you guys, some kind of fellowship of the inane?" he said. "Did you think that you could pay with marbles or trade some mana for all this food? Or maybe you thought I could just ask the ship's computer to make it all in the replicator, and voila! Free nachos with jalapeños and Klingon meat sauce for everyone. Or maybe Mr. Wizard back there could 'Not the corndogs you're looking for' me?" Alfred huffed, but the employee wasn't finished. "Well, unfortunately, here in the real world, you have to pay with money!"

"Sorry," Stan said. "But you looked so much like a bridge-troll, we thought we would get it for free so long as we answered your three questions."

This really set the guy off. "Bridge troll, huh?" he said. "Three questions? Okay, why not? Here's the first one, and it's for you, Buzz Lightyear." He stuck his finger in Stan's chest. "Why do they call them nachos?"

"Because they're not yos!" Stan said as he snatched the nachos off the counter.

The employee came sprinting out from behind the snack hut. Fred cursed Stan's hot temper as he and the rest of his group took off. They had to dodge in and out of carnival goers as they evaded the snack hut worker, and Fred was worried the extra attention could do them in. That was assuming the snack hut guy didn't catch them first. They were all exhausted and hungry, so even though the carnival worker was husky, he was gaining on them. He was an arm's length away when an older couple passed in front of him, blocking him off. He crashed into them, and the three of them went sprawling.

Fred took advantage of this collision and pulled Stan, Jimmy and Alfred down a small alley between two carnival rides. He turned left as soon as they passed the rides, hoping this would throw the snack hut worker off their trail for good. He pulled everyone to a stop and peered cautiously around the corner. A second later, the snack hut worker stumbled into the mouth of the alley, but after looking in all directions, he threw up his arms and started back towards his hut.

Fred waited a second to make sure the coast was clear before he turned around to tell everyone they were safe. Before he could get the words out of his mouth, he found himself staring at the largest creature he had ever seen. Its deafening trumpet shook the very ground, and Fred slipped on some mud trying to scamper away. The huge animal ramped back on its hind legs, letting out another roar as its trainer struggled to calm it. For a second, Fred thought the beast was going to crush him with its hooves, but his friends pulled him to safety at the last second.

"Oliphaunts!" Fred exclaimed. "The Southrons are here! Keep running," he yelled as he scrambled to his feet and darted around the elephant pen.

Fred ran until he could barely hear the oliphaunt's trumpet, and then he took cover behind a small clump of trailers. He and his friends lay on their bellies in the shadows, gulping in air as quietly as possible. They watched for the snack hut employee and the Southrons, ready to take off again at the sight of either one.

After a few minutes, when it was clear they had not been followed, they cautiously stood up to step out of concealment. When two pairs of boots came marching right up to the trailer they were hiding beneath, they ducked back into the shadows. The owner of one pair of boots knocked loudly against the trailer door, and the boys hardly dared to breathe.

Fred eventually gathered enough courage to take a quick look. Banging on the trailer door was a short man, whose jet-black hair was slicked back into a ponytail. The man was wearing funny pants that ballooned out at the thigh and a long overcoat that looked like a sparrow's tail. "Stupid drunk magician!" he yelled at the door no one had come to answer.

"What are we going to do?" asked the other man. "The performance is supposed to start in ten minutes."

"How long can Dmitri stall with the lions?" the man in the long overcoat asked.

"Only a few minutes longer," the other man replied. "Jorge is getting agitated."

"I can't afford to refund the money from the tickets," the man in the coat said. "I'll have to think of something."

"Perhaps I might be of service," said Alfred, stepping out of the shadows and bowing deeply.

Fred had to do a double take because he simply couldn't believe Alfred would do something so reckless. Then he cursed silently and crouched deeper in the shadows of the trailer. As much as he wanted to keep Alfred quiet, he couldn't risk getting the rest of them caught. All he could do was bite his tongue and wait.

"Who in blazes are you?" the man in the coat asked, putting on his top hat.

"Al—" he began, and this time Fred had no choice but to intervene. He jumped up from the shadows and elbowed Alfred in the ribs before the old fart could give them all away. At this point, though, Fred was just hoping the man in the top hat was in too much trouble himself to bother turning them in.

"Al...low me to introduce the greatest wizard since Merlin himself!" said Fred. That was as far as he had thought ahead, so he made some dramatic hand motions to give him some extra time to think. He dove into his memory banks, mentally scrolling through everything he had seen or read for a good wizard's name. Gandalf, Belgarath, and Allanon were the first wizard names that came to mind. *Bah!* he thought. Everyone knew the first one. And the second two just didn't fit—they were much too serious and scary. "Schmendrick!" Fred exclaimed at last, hoping once again that the ring master and his assistant had not read or seen *The Last Unicorn*.

"Schmendrick?" the ring master said questioningly.

"Schmendrick?" Alfred whispered to Fred.

"I saw it in a movie," Fred whispered back. "Just play along."

"Schmendrick the Magnificent at your service, sir," Alfred bowed deeply and conjured a pigeon in a flash of smoke. The bird went sailing over the head of the ring master, dropping a big glop of white poop onto the shoulder of his coat.

"Aack!" the ring master exclaimed, brushing the waste off his shoulder with his top hat.

"My apologies, good sir," said Alfred.

"How is it that you happen to be here tonight?" the other carnival employee asked.

"Call it providence," said Alfred. "Regardless, I don't believe you have any time to be concerned. You are in need of a magician, and a magician I happen to be."

"He's right," the ring master said with a sigh. "You go on in ten minutes. I'll tell Julian about this later. I'm Art Kassirbann." He extended his hand.

"A pleasure to make your acquaintance," Alfred said as he shook Art's hand. Fred elbowed him in the ribs again. "Yes, of course there is still the matter of payment left to discuss," wheezed Alfred. "As much as the true magician lives solely for his art, I am afraid the stomach does beg for more."

"Yes, of course," Art said, thinking quickly. "I'll give you ten percent of the ticket sales."

"My assistants and I ask only that you replenish our food stores," countered Alfred. "Like you, we are a travelling band and have come to find that the road can leave even the hardiest of travelers hungry from time to time."

"Assistants?" said the ringmaster. When Jimmy and Stan stepped out of the shadows next, he raised his eyebrows. "I see," said Art. "Well, if you can keep the audience from revolting, I'd be glad to give you as much food as you can carry. Ten minutes, Schmendrick."

A lion roared nearby, and Art tore across the carnival grounds without another word.

"So much for not drawing attention to ourselves," said Fred, giving his grandfather a look. "But it just might work. It's kind of like hiding in plain sight."

"Kids always say that they're going to run away and join the circus, right?" said Stan. "No one would think we'd be stupid enough to actually do it."

"My thoughts precisely," said Alfred.

Fred rolled his eyes.

"Alright, Alfred," Stan said seriously. "We need a plan. And I think we can all agree to leave the pooping pigeon trick out."

"Geez, you really must be hungry to be going along with this," said Fred.

"Stop wasting time," said Stan. "By my clock, we've got nine minutes to come up with a magic show that is going to please a whole circus tent full of people."

"Well, technically all we have to do is prevent them from uprising," Fred corrected him.

Stan pointed at Alfred and raised his eyebrows.

"Right," said Fred, "we've got some work to do. Any ideas?"

"Boys, boys," said Alfred. "Fear not. I am a peerless prestidigitator!"

"You're a rest-stop janitor?" Stan asked him. "I guess that will help us clean up after the lions, but I don't see how it will help us with a magic show."

"I am a lord of legerdemain," Alfred continued, ignoring Stan, "an icon of illusion, an expert of escapology."

"Well, at least I know how to introduce you," Fred said. "But you haven't performed in years, Grandpa. You're more an expert of early-bird specials than you are of escaping."

Alfred guffawed. "My wand may not get as much use as it once did, I'll admit, but I assure you my performance still rivals that of any younger magician," he said.

"Alright, alright," Stan interjected. "All we need are a few opening tricks, just little things like card tricks and stuff like that."

"Consider it done," said Alfred.

"Then we need one pretty sweet trick and one grand finale," Stan said, biting his thumb in thought.

"What about a catch-an-arrow trick?" Jimmy suggested.

"What do you mean?" said Fred.

"You know how some magicians catch bullets with their teeth?" Jimmy said. "Well, I can shoot an arrow at Alfred, and he can catch it!"

"Sure, and after that miracle, I'll marry Beyonce," said Stan. "Thanks for nothing, Jimmy."

"It'll work, Stan," said Alfred. "Although we cannot afford to waste our archer's fabled arrows."

"The game booth!" said Jimmy.

"Jimmy, c'mon, we don't have ti—" started Fred.

"But those nub-ears were using a common bow!" said Jimmy. "Exactly what we need."

"Then run swiftly, 'Deadeye,' and grab that bow and make sure to grab three arrows," Alfred said. "Fred, perhaps you should accompany him."

"Don't you think I should be here to help pl—" Fred started.

"We got this, Fred, go help Jimmy," said Stan. "All you need to do is say how dangerous and great the tricks are when we get on stage."

"I don't know," said Fred.

"Just go," said Stan. "Let me be your Lando, man."

Stan made a good point. Sometimes you just had to let a scoundrel do his thing. "Alright, let's go, Jim," said Fred. "They're right. No one should go off alone this close to Mordor, not even an elf."

"Go, my boy, go," said Alfred. "Time is running short. With any luck we'll have the final illusion decided by the time you return."

Fred was still anxious about leaving Stan and Alfred to plan the magic show without him, but Alfred was right, time was running out. Arguing about it would only make sure they went hungry tonight. He and Jimmy sprinted back through the fair-grounds towards the archery booth, the lights of the carnival rides drifting by them in a blur. Avoiding the snack hut on purpose, they skidded to a halt in front of the archery booth. The little crowd standing nearby stopped to look at them.

"Brothers, I am an archer from a distant forest," Jimmy said to the game attendants, two pimply-faced teenage boys. "I come to you in a moment of great need. I must borrow one of your bows and three of your arrows."

"It costs five bucks to play, dude," one of the boys said sleepily.

"We do not have the time to play your games!" Jimmy exclaimed. "We need the bow and arrows now!"

"Just what you see on the wall, man," said the other attendant. His eyelids were drooping halfway down over his eyes like a Hutt who had just gorged himself on a bowl full of Nala tree frogs.

Jimmy wasn't getting through to the workers, and he was getting frustrated. "They must be elves from a different wood and do not speak my tongue," he said to Fred.

"We want the bow and three of your arrows, not any of your silly kid's prizes," Fred said, trying to help. "And we're running out of time."

"You mean you'd rather have some crummy bow-and-arrow set than one of these prizes?" the first boy asked, waving his hand in front of all the stuffed animals behind him.

"Yes, please, I cannot stress how important it is that I get this bow," said Jimmy. The crowd around the booth was growing, making Fred a little uneasy.

"Whatever, man," said one attendant, who didn't seem to like the extra attention either. "But to get the bow you've got to hit all five targets."

Fred could tell the boy felt this was a sure bet. Judging by all the giant teddy bears left no one had hit more than three targets all day. And there wasn't a single scuffmark on the smallest target. Fred wondered if anyone had ever hit it.

"Five bucks," said the attendant, extending his hand.

"I do not have conventional money," said Jimmy. "I offer my own bow as collateral."

"Geez, man!" the other attendant exclaimed, "You don't even have money!"

"This bow is priceless," said Jimmy. "It has seen more battles than you have seen years, young elfling."

A little boy, who had been standing nearby, looked at Jimmy's bow and said, "Cool!" Seeing this, the two attendants stepped back and had a secret conversation. At least they thought they were whispering quietly enough not to be heard. Fred could hear everything they were saying.

"How do the whackos always find us?" said one attendant.

"I don't know, man, but let's just let him play," said the other. "If he loses, I bet we get twenty bucks out of that little kid's dad trying to win this idiot's plastic bow."

"Yeah, alright. We've always got the backup set if we lose."

They turned back to Fred and Jimmy. "Okay man, knock yourself out," said the droopy-eyed attendant, handing Jimmy the wooden bow and five arrows.

Jimmy slipped four arrows into his quiver and notched the fifth. He took aim at the largest target, which was only about the size of a soccer ball and fired. Before the arrow hit the metal, he had another arrow flying through the air. A few seconds later a cheer arose from the crowd behind him. He had hit every target, including the last one, which was a little smaller than an apple, within the blink of an eye.

The little boy in the crowd said, "Cool!" again, and the two booth attendants looked at each other in astonishment.

Jimmy flipped open the top of his plastic *Millennium Falcon* watch to check the time. "We've got two minutes," he said to Fred.

They grabbed both the plastic bow and the wooden one Jimmy had just used to win the game and made sure to collect three of the wooden arrows. As they rushed back to the main tent, Fred bit off the protective rubber stoppers on the arrows, exposing the thin metal tips beneath. The barbs were razor sharp. Fred really hoped his grandfather knew what he was doing.

They made it back to the meeting spot within seconds, but Alfred and Stan were nowhere to be seen. Fred looked around frantically. Jimmy checked his watch again. "No time," he said.

Just then, the ring master's assistant called out to them from a short distance away. Fred and Jimmy rushed after him, slipping inside the main tent. Following the man, they hurried along the side of the tent, past the crowd, which was frighteningly large. Fred swallowed hard and kept his eyes down. The assistant led him backstage where he found his best friend and grandfather waiting just behind the curtain.

"Did you succeed, Deadeye?" Alfred asked.

"Do Galadriel's blonde locks make the very sun jealous?" Jimmy answered.

"I—" Alfred stammered. "Yes?" he ventured an answer.

Jimmy held up the arrows with a big smile on his face.

"Great, just give me one," Alfred said as he grabbed an arrow and made it disappear into his wizard's robes so quick Fred and Stan rubbed their eyes to make sure they were working properly. "The first arrow you'll fire is just to show the crowd that they are real," Alfred explained and Jimmy nodded. "With the second arrow you're going to graze my right shoulder."

Stan and Fred both opened their mouths to protest, but before they could say anything, the timer on Jimmy's *Falcon* watch beeped. With a screech of pulleys, the curtains swept wide, and the stage lights fell on them with blinding intensity.

23
MAGIC TIME

Fred's legs were wooden and his palms wet. His stomach was clenched and aching. Stage fright gripped his entire body. He tried and couldn't move. *At least I don't have to take on a Hungarian Horntail or anything*, he thought, trying to calm his nerves. But once he saw how many people had filed into the tent, he quickly reconsidered. Compared to speaking in front of a crowd, a dragon didn't seem all that frightening.

It took everything he had, but he finally got his legs to work and stepped out into the spotlight. The glare from the lights was so bright he had to shield his eyes with this palm. By the time his vision adjusted, he was wishing he was blind. There were even more people than he had thought. The whole thing made speaking in front of the class seem as easy as taking on a team of Jawas in a game of basketball. When he realized that the crowd had stopped applauding and was now waiting for him to begin, he got really scared. Stan and Jimmy looked even more nervous, but Alfred was standing very calmly at the front of the stage with his head bowed and his hands held together.

Fred's mind had suddenly gone blank. He had no clue what to say, and he grew more nervous with each second of silence. He could hear every groan and murmur in the crowd. The pressure was too much! He was about to run off stage when Alfred slowly turned his head to look at him. His grandfather looked like he might say something, but he just winked and smiled.

Fred couldn't help but smile back. The man had confidence; nobody could deny that. And if his grandfather could do it, there was no reason Fred couldn't manage either. They were of the same blood, after all. He swallowed hard and pulled the microphone from the stand.

"Ladies and gentleman, boys and girls," he said. "The usual magician will not be performing tonight." He paused while a gasp went through the crowd. "Instead, the Kassir-bann Brothers are proud to bring you a sorcerer of the highest order. Many years ago, he was banned from performing his magic because the act you are about to see tonight was considered too dangerous."

He wasn't being totally honest with his grandfather's story, but he needed to make him sound expert and mysterious. If he told them that Alfred had been twiddling his thumbs in an old folks' home after accidentally shooting a firework through his neighbors' window, they'd probably all head straight for the doors.

"As a result," Fred continued, "he performs very rarely, emerging from his secret keep only on special occasions. Occasions like tonight! Ladies and gentleman, I give you Schmendrick the Magnificent!"

As the audience applauded, Fred stood back and crossed his fingers. If Alfred botched the initial set of parlor tricks, the jig was up and they'd go hungry tonight. He hadn't been there to hear the rest of the plan, so Fred had no idea what Alfred was going to do. But now that he thought about it, he couldn't remember the last time he'd seen his grandfather perform a trick correctly. *If there was ever a good time to start, it's now,* he thought.

After the claps had ceased, Alfred slowly raised his head and removed his hood. Then he flashed his hands and a deck of cards fanned out in a wide arc through the air. For a moment, all the cards were suspended in air, and Fred didn't see how anything could keep them from flying into the crowd. But Alfred caught them all in his other hand. Fred was amazed, but the crowd responded with nothing more than some spotted claps.

A second later, Alfred tossed the cards back to his other hand, fanning them through the air in the same way. Once again, he caught them all. Alfred was really gaining confidence, maybe too much confidence. He was starting to showboat. Fred wanted desperately to whisper a warning to his grandfather to stay focused, but he couldn't disrupt the show. He could only watch and hope.

Smiling from ear to ear, Alfred caught the cards and went to fling the deck back into his other hand again. The trick started out well—the cards floated through the air—but something went wrong as they hit Alfred's left hand. He fumbled the cards badly, spraying the entire deck into the audience. *Oh no!* Fred screamed silently.

Everyone in the circus tent laughed, and Fred flinched at the sound. He could already feel the pull of one of those giant cartoon hooks on his neck. They hadn't even made it through the first trick, and Alfred had already blown it. Alfred looked at his empty hands, mimicked the card toss, and then scratched his head as if trying to figure out what went wrong. The crowd laughed harder. A pretty woman in the front row had caught a single card, and Alfred pointed to her. "Miss, could you stand up and show the audience what card you have?" He asked her.

She stood up and held the Queen of Hearts high above her head, turning around so that everyone in the audience could see.

"Thank you, Miss," said Alfred. "I, uh, must confess that I don't really have a trick. I just noticed you in the front row and wanted to get a better look at you. I must say that dress is very becoming."

The crowd rolled with laughter, and several men whistled and jeered. The woman blushed and sat back down. *Good cover, Grandpa,* Fred thought. *A little creepy, but that just might buy us some more time.*

"If you would just write your phone number down on the card, I'll have my assistants come pick it up at the end of the show," Alfred said, smiling. The crowd laughed again. The woman pulled out a stick of red lipstick and played along with the joke, writing her phone number on the back of the card.

At a signal from Alfred, Stan went backstage and then rolled out a cart, which he placed just beside the magician. A black shroud was draped over the cart, and jiggling on top of it were several large water balloons. Alfred picked up three of the water balloons and began to juggle them. He tossed them slowly at first, but soon he was launching them higher and faster into the air. Eventually he had all five water balloons soaring. The crowd, and Fred, watched in stunned silence. The balloons were flying so high Fred thought that they would surely burst as they struck Alfred's hands. But the magician continued to catch them and fling them back into the air. Alfred started to sway back and forth on the stage as he struggled to keep the water balloons from falling. The crowd gasped nervously.

Alfred seemed to have found his balance and rhythm. He turned and smiled at the crowd as he launched one of the balloons almost to the top of the tent. That's when his foot slipped on the front edge of the stage. He toppled backwards, losing control of all the balloons. They splattered all across the first few rows of the crowd, soaking everyone, including the woman in the dress.

Fred was prepared for the audience to rush the stage in anger, but the audience wasn't angry at all. Quite the opposite. They were roaring with amusement.

"You're stealing the show, my dear," Alfred said to the woman in the soaked dress, whose cheeks turned an even deeper shade of red. The crowd was already in tears, but now they were collapsing in the aisles with laughter.

"I don't know what's wrong with me tonight," said Alfred. "I appear to have caught a bad case of the butterfingers. Oh well, the show must go on," Alfred said as he whipped away the shroud to reveal a bunch of large, shiny knives.

Several people in the first few rows got up out of their seats and retreated to the back of the circus tent, while those safe in the back continued to chuckle. The woman in the dress clearly didn't want to stand up. She grabbed at her friends' arms, trying to hold them back as they broke for the back of the tent. Unfortunately, this only brought more attention to her, since she was now the only person left in the front row.

"Be still my heart, she's got faith in me," Alfred said to another round of laughter. "Which is more than I can say for you cowards." He pointed to the people clustering in the aisles at the top of the bleachers.

Alfred picked up the knives and started juggling. The audience whooped and laughed. Fred couldn't be sure if

Alfred had intended all the slip ups or if his grandfather was just great at turning mistakes into jokes, but either way it seemed to be working.

Alfred juggled the knives up higher into the air for a few moments, and the audience gave a shout every time he caught one. As Alfred juggled, Stan went backstage again and rolled a wooden target, placing it about ten yards behind Alfred. Without looking, Alfred hurled the first knife at the target before Stan had even let go. Stan's eyes opened wide when the knife landed squarely in the center of red and white circles. Alfred's arm jerked again and the second blade hit mere inches from the first. He spun around as he released the last knife. It struck directly between the other two knives.

The crowd went silent in amazement—the knife had struck a playing card that had not been there a second ago! Even Fred was stunned as he watched Alfred walk over to the board and remove the card. Fred glanced back at the woman in the front row. *It couldn't be her card*, he thought.

"If you would please stand up and show the audience your card once more, Miss," Alfred commanded the woman.

She followed his directions and stood up, waving the card so that the entire audience could see. Surprisingly, it was still the Queen of Hearts, and some grumblings of uncertainty rippled through the audience. Fred figured that they, too, had thought that Alfred had somehow nailed her card with the knife. Now they were all wondering, Fred included, if Alfred had really messed up the trick.

"Oh...you didn't think this was her card did you?" Alfred asked them, holding up the card he had hit with the knife. "Now that would have been amazing," he guffawed. "But clearly the real trick was getting her to stand up again."

The tent actually shook from the sound of laughter.

"Schmendrick the Magnificent, everybody!" Fred remembered to say at the last moment.

He had to wait a long time for the applause to die down. When the audience had finally grown quiet again, Fred introduced the next trick. "And now, Schmendrick will perform a feat so dangerous that it has claimed the lives of a dozen lesser magicians. That's right folks, he is going to catch an arrow with his bare hands!" The audience gasped. "'Deadeye,' if you would please show our audience how very real and how very sharp the arrows are?"

Jimmy stepped to the front of the stage and held up the two arrows before the audience. He tapped his finger against the tips of the arrowheads, and then scraped them both against the wooden stage, pulling up pale shavings to show how sharp they were. Then Jimmy notched an arrow, pulled back the string of the bow and fired it straight into the center of target, which was still sitting at the back of the stage. When the crowd saw how easily the arrow drove through the wood they tittered again.

Giving the audience time to quiet down, Alfred strolled slowly to the far end of the stage. Jimmy took position at the opposite end. When Alfred nodded, Jimmy notched the second arrow and pulled back the string. Fred's pulse spiked—there was no room for error here. He wished they had had time to practice this or that Alfred had explained the trick because one minor misstep could spell death. Fred thought he saw Jimmy's hands shake for the first time.

Just before the archer was about to shoot, Alfred shouted, "Wait!"

Jimmy released the tension on the bowstring immediately and took a deep breath. For a moment Fred thought that his grandfather had lost his nerve and no longer wanted to do the trick. Apparently so did the audience, because they started muttering again.

Alfred raised his hands and addressed the crowd. "Wait, archer, wait—I'd hate to have you pierce this," he said and held up a card for the audience to see. It was the Queen of Hearts! "It is not every night that I get the phone number of a beautiful young woman who is being such a good sport," said Alfred. On the back of the card the magician was holding up were numbers written in red lipstick. The woman in the dress held up her hands and shook her head in befuddlement.

Alfred placed the card on the cart and then returned to the end of the stage. "You may proceed, 'Deadeye,'" he said.

Jimmy once again pulled the string back. He took a moment to steady his aim and then fired. The arrow shot across the stage with a thwip and a whoosh. Fred was standing a little to the left of Jimmy, so he saw the arrow go flying within a few inches of Alfred's shoulder and sail safely past him, disappearing into the shadows backstage.

Alfred missed! Fred thought at first. But when he looked at his grandfather, he saw that Alfred was clutching an arrow in his left hand. Fred rubbed his eyes, thinking he was seeing things. How had Alfred done it? Jimmy's arrow missed him completely; there's no way he could have caught it. Then it hit him like a wompa's paw. The arrow Alfred took from Jimmy before the show! He must have pulled it from his sleeve just as the other arrow passed him, and to the audience it must have looked like he caught it.

The people in the bleachers were standing and cheering. Fred couldn't believe it. They were just one grand finale away from completing an entire magic show!

"What a catch!" Fred bellowed over the applause. "And now, Schmendrick the Magnificent will perform one final illusion. A display of sorcery so astounding it will change your world."

Stan rolled his eyes at this. Fred just shrugged his shoulders.

Alfred pulled his wand forth from within his wizard's robes. He brandished it as he addressed the audience. "I am the last of an order of druids who have long kept many ancient secrets," he said in a bellowing voice. "Today you will be privy to one of our most guarded rituals. The 'Fire-Conjuring!'"

Now Fred was really worried. The last time Alfred had tried to produce fire the closest he had come was a sunflower. Fred was hoping that when Alfred screwed up the trick this time, he would just make a joke out of giving the bouquet to the woman in the dress. He held his breath as Alfred flicked his wand.

A small fireball instantly shot from Alfred's wand and hovered in the air before him. Alfred moved his wand in a circle and the fireball started to turn.

The audience oohed and aahed when Alfred made the single fireball split and then split again. He kept them turning in a circle for a moment, and then he sent all four fireballs soaring into the crowd. The audience ducked as the flames passed close overhead. They screamed again when Alfred beckoned the fireballs back to the front of the stage. There the flames came together into one larger fireball, which flared for an instant and then disappeared back into the tip of Alfred's wand. After a moment of stunned silence, the crowd applauded raucously.

"Child's play!" Alfred bellowed. "Now shield your eyes from the great flame of Endor!"

"It's Anor, for Bilbo's sake," Fred said under his breath. "Get it right for once, Grandpa."

Muttering an incantation in some bizarre and poetic language, Alfred swung his wand like the conductor of an orchestra. He said the final rhyming word with a shout and pointed his wand at the stage. Just like in the cave, nothing happened. Fred screamed silently. They had almost made it! All Alfred had to do was get this trick right, and he'd blown it. Now they'd be thrown back into the woods without a bite to eat.

"I'm sorry folks, but it appears the spell is a bit more ancient that I thought," said Alfred, and the crowd laughed. Alfred started striking his wand again, trying to get it to work. He swung the wand too forcefully and fumbled it in his hands. He mishandled it, and it fell to the ground with a clatter. The wand rolled behind him, and he whirled around groping for it. He bent over to grab it, putting his butt squarely before the audience. As he did, he accidentally let slip a rumbling toot. It sounded something like a startled Fell Beast trying to play the tuba, and a large flame erupted just behind his backside, nearly lighting his robes on fire. Alfred jumped up sharply and then slowly turned to face the crowd, which was laughing harder than ever. He pretended to be embarrassed as he said, "Well, I guess that incantation was actually quite simple—only one syllable, in fact."

The audience rose again and cheered even louder than before. Alone at the front of the stage, Alfred smiled and bowed deeply.

After a moment, Fred realized that he was laughing, too, and clapping, and Stan had to remind him to say his line.

"Schmendrick the Magnificent!" Fred said, gesturing with his arm. And then the curtains dropped.

24
A FEAST AND A FRIEND

The first thing Fred did when they were safely hidden from the audience was give Alfred a huge hug. Stan and Jimmy wrapped him up too. Fred even heard Stan promise Alfred a piece of his pizza. Stan made sure to add that it would be the smallest piece, but still, when Stan was this hungry, that was saying something.

"You were great, Grandpa, really great," Fred told him. Alfred the Grand just winked at him. "How did you do—?" Fred started to ask.

Alfred wagged his finger and clicked his tongue. "Now, what kind of wizard would I be if I revealed my secrets?" he asked with a smile. "Besides, those were all just parlor tricks. I couldn't risk showing them real magic. They'd know who we were in an instant if I did."

Fred beamed at him.

Art Kassirbann, and another man who looked so similar that Fred figured he had to be Art's brother and co-owner of the travelling carnival, Julian Kassirbann, came running up to them smiling broadly and clapping.

"Excellent, excellent!" they chorused.

"That was wonderful!" said Julian. "We've never seen a show like it! And we've been in the entertainment business for as long as you can imagine."

"What do we have to do to get you stay on permanently?" Art asked Alfred.

Fred's mouth fell open. He couldn't believe the two ringmasters were offering his grandfather a permanent job! Just a couple of days ago Alfred was locked up in a dark wizard's keep, and now he was being offered a chance to do magic again. Fred was absolutely elated for him.

"Well, now, that is an interesting proposition," said Alfred. "And I'll need some time to think it over." He looked down at Fred. "But you must know that I have a previous engagement that I cannot break. Once I have fulfilled that obligation, I would very much like to speak with you on the matter."

Fred was surprised to hear his grandfather turn down such an amazing and unexpected offer. Alfred had always loved performing magic more than anything. It warmed Fred's heart that Alfred had chosen to finish the quest.

"Of course, Schmendrick, of course," said Julian Kassir-bann, handing Alfred a small business card. "A magician of your caliber is most certainly in high demand. Please do call us soon. We think you'd make a fine addition to our family."

The two brothers still hadn't mentioned food, so Stan coughed to get Alfred to remind them.

"Yes, we will talk soon enough," said Alfred. "But, in the meantime, I believe we were promised a meal...."

"Absolutely—anything you want," said Art. "Mr. Burtman will take care of everything you need."

Art waved to the assistant who had been following him around all night. Mr. Burtman quickly scurried over from the far end of the tent, where he had been helping the next act—several short-statured performers—prepare for the stage. The figures were small enough Fred almost mistook them for children at first. Then he took a closer look. Not children—dwarves! Dressed in matching costumes, they were limbering up for their performance. A nearby promotional sign told Fred they were the "Fantastic Flipping Lees," a family of acrobats. *Just like the Graysons! How cool,* Fred thought.

A younger member of the troupe suddenly burst into the tent, struggling to get her costume all the way on. A man with "Papa Lee" written on his shoulders immediately started yelling at her to hustle. The girl couldn't have been that much older than Fred, and although she was a little shorter, Fred had to admit she looked much, much stronger. Fred stared at her bulging shoulder muscles and unconsciously grabbed his own scrawny arms. The dwarf girl looked so sturdy, Fred was surprised to hear her choking back tears as her father scolded her. Her corded shoulders slumped, and her eyes tracked the floor.

Thankfully, Art called out to "Papa Lee" after a moment, breaking up their spat. "Time to go on," said the ringmaster.

The older dwarf shoved his daughter to the back of the line. Then, taking the lead, he led the troupe of acrobats onstage. Fred offered the still sobbing girl a comforting smile as she passed, but the young circus performer did not look at him.

After the acrobats had gone onstage, Fred turned back to his friends. While he had been watching the spat between father and daughter, his friends had made their way across the tent and were already following Mr. Burtman out through a slit in the back. Because he was famished and didn't want to miss any part of dinner, Fred hurried to catch up with them.

Stan was already listing food items directly into Mr. Burtman's ear. The assistant scribbled as fast as he could as they walked to a picnic table behind the circus tent near the trailers. Alfred and the boys collapsed on the bench, and within minutes they were feasting on as much carnival food as they had ever imagined.

"It makes a Redwall Abbey feast seem like cafeteria leftovers," said Stan with an almost maniacal smile as he piled food high on his "plate," which was actually an entire pizza box. He scooped over pretzels and popcorn, cheeseburgers and chocolate cake.

There weren't any treacles or scones, but Fred had to agree with Stan. This feast was better than any they had ever cooked at Redwall. He shoveled pizza into his mouth while Stan dipped his corndogs in nacho cheese, eating them two at a time. The pizza was great, but Fred thought that the freshly baked blueberry pies were the best food the fair had to offer, and he helped himself to several pieces.

"Now that's more like it," said Stan, finally pushing himself away from the table after devouring as much as his stomach could comfortably hold and then some.

"A feast fit for an elf queen," said Jimmy.

"And Stan will still be hungry in an hour," said Fred.

"But thanks to Alfred, that's no problem at all—I can have as much as I want," Stan said, still chewing a mouthful of pepperoni pizza.

"And more importantly, Art promised to give us food for the road," said Fred.

"Very true," said Stan, "which is why *Alfred the Grand,*" he whispered the name, "is my favorite magician in the whole world. I just wish I had brought a larger bookbag.

Hey, Jimmy, you think I could rent out some of your gym bag?" he asked, slurping the last few drops of his extra-large soda.

"I think there's a spot open by my dirty socks," Jimmy offered sarcastically.

Stan shrugged. "That's fine, three-day old pizza tastes a little bit like socks, anyway."

"That does bring up a good point," said Fred, standing up to go find a restroom. "We should definitely pick food that isn't going to spoil after five minutes."

Walking away, he heard Stan ask Jimmy if nacho cheese would stay fresh for a while and laughed to himself.

Fred found the portable restrooms just beyond the last of the trailers. As he was opening the door to one of the port-o-lets, he heard a shouting match start up nearby. He flinched at a loud crash, and then his curiosity got the better of him, and he turned to check it out. Interestingly, the racket was coming from the magician's trailer where they had hidden earlier that night. He crept quietly around the outside of the small aluminum box until he found a low window. Standing on a cinderblock, he peeked over the ledge. Inside, a tall, dirty-looking man paced around the small trailer, yelling at a boy who looked to be about a year or two older than Fred.

"I ask you to do one thing—one thing!" yelled the magician, holding up a finger. "And you can't even do that. And because you didn't wake me up, I don't have a job anymore. I hope you're happy."

"I didn't make it back because I was out working like you told me to," said the boy. "Look at all the loot I got." In the boy's hands were several wallets and a couple watches, which he offered to the magician. "One guy caught me picking his watch, and I had to run and hide. I'm sorry I didn't make it back in time to get you."

"Good-for-nothing little leech," the magician said, grabbing the stolen items from the boy. "I should have never promised my sister that I'd take care of you. What do I get for my trouble? You get *me* fired."

"You were the one passed out drunk!" The boy yelled.

The man slapped the boy hard across the cheek. Fred was amazed that the boy did not scream or whimper. Instead, he stared back coldly—saying nothing even when his cheek started to blush a deep red.

"Don't give me any lip, boy!" the magician spat in his face. "And if you think two watches and a couple wallets are going to be enough to cover my lost wages, you're wrong. I'll barely have enough to eat, let alone feed you, too. But maybe it will do you some good to go hungry."

Looking around the house, Fred noticed that a majority of the trailer floor was covered in crumpled beer cans. This made him doubt that the magician was that worried about food.

"We need ten times this," the magician continued. "If you're not that good of a pick-pocket by now, then there's no sense in keeping you around."

"I'm getting better, but if I push it, I'll get caught," the boy pleaded.

"I don't want to hear excuses," the magician said as he cracked another beer open and sucked down the fountain of foam that came spewing from the mouth.

"That could go on for hours," said a scratchy voice behind Fred.

Startled, Fred toppled back clumsily off the cinderblock. It was a short fall, but he landed flat on his back, and his cloak flew up over his face. He brushed it back clumsily, struggling to get a look at who had startled him. When he finally got himself clear, he was surprised to hear laughter. He looked up to see the dwarf girl rocking back on a barrel and holding her sides.

"Nice dismount," she said between chuckles.

"Nice unitard," retorted Fred, who was more than a little embarrassed.

"Touché," said the girl, snapping the straps on her uniform. "I'm sorry for scaring you, but I was just trying to save you some trouble. Those two fight every night—tonight's nothing special."

"Not quite," said Fred. "You might not have heard, but Art fired the magician tonight."

"Really?" asked the girl. "Well, it's about time he got rid of Ivan. Hopefully Art lets Miroslav stay, though."

"And I didn't mean to eavesdrop," said Fred. "I just heard some shouting."

"It's okay, I won't tell," the girl said with a wink. "You can practically hear them from across the carnival grounds, anyway."

"And we didn't mean to get Ivan fired," said Fred. "We just needed some food and performing the magic show seemed like the only way to get it."

"Are you kidding?" said the girl. "Don't apologize. I hate Ivan. I'm glad Art fired him. He treats Miroslav even worse than my dad treats me. He even makes him steal when he doesn't want to."

"That's terrible," said Fred.

The girl laughed.

"Why are you laughing?" asked Fred.

"Because that's what we call him: Ivan the Terrible. Of course, he calls himself Ivan the Incredible. But the only thing incredible about him is how stupid he is."

It was Fred's turn to laugh. He was starting to like the dwarf girl, who reminded him a lot of Stan in a weird way. "What's your name?" Fred asked her.

"I'm Gemma," said the girl. "Gemma Lee."

"I'm Fred."

"Nice to meet you, Fred," Gemma extended her hand. Fred took it and tried in vain to match the strength of her fierce grip. Shaking out his hand so she couldn't see, he sat down on a barrel beside her.

"So, you work for the circus?" Fred asked. "That must be really cool. Don't all kids dream about that?"

"You would think so, but it's not," Gemma said. "You never stay in one place for longer than a couple weeks, and you do the same thing every night. Not to mention you train for the same routine day in and day out—on top of doing schoolwork. I'm sick of it. I never wanted to be in the circus, anyway."

"What do you want to do?" Fred asked.

Gemma looked like she was about to say something and then stopped. "It's stupid," she said.

"I bet it's not," Fred told him. "Heck, I wish I knew what I wanted to do. If you do know, I'm jealous, no matter what. I like to do so many things I don't think I'll ever figure it out."

"My dad doesn't seem to think it's great. *The Lee's have been a circus family for generations*," Gemma said, imitating her dad's voice. "*Why would you ever want to be a guitarist in a rock band, girl? We're the 'Flipping Lees,' not the 'Picking Lees.'* " Fred chuckled. "But, to tell you the truth, Fred, I'm an ax-woman at heart, and all I've ever wanted to do is play in a rock and roll band."

"I don't think that sounds crazy at all," said Fred. In fact, he would have been surprised if Gemma had wanted to be anything other than an *ax*-woman. "I think if that's what you love to do, you should give it a shot."

"Oh yeah, well how many women do you see playing lead guitar for a major band?" Gemma asked him.

"A few, I think," said Fred.

"Okay, how many little people do you see playing guitar for a major band?" she asked again.

Fred scratched his head. "Uh, well..."

"Exactly," said Gemma. "It's better than it used to be for little people—not all of us are carnival attractions, you know—but some doors are still closed. And that doesn't even take into account the whole biracial thing," the dwarf girl added.

Fred wanted to ask her if by biracial Gemma meant she had both Harfoot and Stoor ancestry, but after Stan had responded poorly to that line of questioning, he thought better of it. He didn't really care what line of dwarves Gemma was descended from, anyway. Fred simply wanted to help her out. "So why can't you be the first?" he said.

"I guess so," said Gemma. "But if I'm stuck in the circus, I'll never get the opportunity. I mean, maybe if we ever travelled to southern California, I could at least have a chance at being discovered by somebody. But, of course, we never do. They've got big arenas there, so they don't need our crummy travelling circus."

Fred was starting to think maybe meeting Gemma wasn't pure coincidence. Although he doubted that there would be someone good-hearted enough to make Gemma's music dreams come true in that smoky orc den, it seemed like they both wanted to go the same place. Fred thought that they could help each other. But he didn't want to speak too soon; he needed to make sure Gemma really wanted to go before letting her know about the ring. There was always the risk that Gemma would think they were lunatics and turn them in as soon as she heard him talking about a great quest. They had come so far, now was not the time to blow the whole quest by acting rashly.

"You could always try one of those reality music shows," Fred suggested, even though he personally thought this was a fate worse than Mordor's dirtiest dungeons.

"Let's get serious, Fred," said Gemma. "I'm not *that* desperate," she smiled. "Besides, I like to think I actually have some real talent."

Fred laughed again. Gemma was really funny, and though he had only known her a short while, he knew the dwarf would be great for the fellowship. *I mean, she's a dwarf who calls herself an "ax-woman," how could I not let her join us?* He decided to trust his instincts.

"As luck would have it, my friends and I are travelling to southern California," Fred said. "We are on a great quest to destroy a powerful ring. If you are brave enough to join us, we would greatly desire your help."

"No way," Gemma said. "You're kidding, right?"

"I'm gravely serious," he said. "We journey to dark and dangerous lands on a quest of the utmost importance. But we must go to southern California to destroy the one ring and break the Dark Lord's enchantments which threaten this great land."

"Hey, if you're going to so-Cal, I'm in," Gemma said excitedly. "I've been waiting for this chance for a long time. I don't think I can stand another minute in this place."

"You're sure?" asked Fred. "This is no small undertaking. We have faced great perils and will face greater still."

"Am I sure?" Gemma asked incredulously. "Does a bear poop in the tent?"

Fred cocked his head to the side. "Umm..."

"Sorry, circus humor," said Gemma. "Of course, I'm sure! I don't like leaving the rest of my family, but there's no other way."

"So, we have your ax, then?" asked Fred.

"Yeah, man, you have my ax," Gemma said, jumping off the barrel and playing a killer riff on her air guitar.

"Great!" exclaimed Fred. "We're glad to have you."

"When do we leave?" asked Gemma.

"We'll camp here tonight and leave first thing in the morning. If I were you, I'd pack as much food as you can carry and go hide in the trees south of the grounds. That way you don't get caught. We'll pick you up at dawn and continue moving south."

"That's a good plan," agreed Gemma, "because if my dad catches me, that could be the end of it for all of us."

"Exactly," said Fred seriously. "Which is why it is really important that you don't tell anybody that you're leaving. I'm taking a big risk telling you about this, but I think we could really use your help. Don't make me regret it. Not a word to anyone, got it?"

Gemma laid her hand on the air guitar. "On my ax, I swear it."

"And we will hold you to your oath as we hold ourselves. You are bound now to the fellowship." Forgetting how strong Gemma's handshake was, Fred stuck out his hand and Gemma grabbed it and shook. Fred instantly regretted it. Gemma's hand was as tough as old leather, and for such a small person her grip was like iron. Her training on the ropes and guitar had certainly hardened her. *She'll be good to have in a fight,* Fred thought. The dwarf would probably have Alex Lassiter crying for his mommy if she ever got her hands on the Firebird's neck.

"I will go straight away to tell the rest of my party that

one of the great Lords of Moria will be joining us on our quest," said Fred, nearly tripping over himself as he started back to camp. "I'm sure they will look forward to meeting you in the morning."

"Are you sure they'll be okay with a..." Gemma started.

"A dwarf?" said Fred. "Well, I should tell you that we have an elf in our company," he said. "And just as I expect him to treat a dwarf with respect, I would ask that you do the same."

Gemma looked confused. "Uh, I meant a girl," she said, shouting now because Fred was still moving away quickly. "And, you know, dwarf isn't really the preferred...," she said, but Fred was already too far away to catch the rest.

Fred found himself alone again in a strange part of the circus grounds. Ivan and Miroslav were still fighting in the trailer, and although Fred was still curious about the poor boy, he had already been caught eavesdropping once and didn't want it to happen again. He still had to use the bathroom, too, so he crept around Ivan the Incredible's trailer as quietly as possible.

Before he had made his way to the other side of the small clearing, the door to the trailer flopped open with a loud crash, and Miroslav burst from the house at a dead sprint. To avoid being seen, Fred dove back behind the trailer. Lying on his stomach, he watched Miroslav stagger across the courtyard and throw himself into the grass. The magician's nephew buried his face in his arms and sobbed uncontrollably. For a moment, Fred wondered if he should go console the older boy, but he decided against it. He hadn't forgotten how many nights he'd spent crying into his pillow since his parents split, and he knew how angry it would have made him to have a stranger see him like that.

No, it's better to leave him alone for now, Fred thought. He crept back into the shadows and tiptoed his way around the opposite side of the trailer. Surely, he would find another set of restrooms if he kept moving. Only when he could not hear Miroslav's weeping did Fred relax and stroll more freely through the carnival grounds.

When he finally made it back to the picnic table, Fred found his friends lying about like a family of Brandybucks who had eaten one too many honey-scones for "second supper." Alfred was slumped over the table, snoring loudly into his arms. Jimmy had slid back into his chair, his head fallen back and his mouth open. Stan was on the ground, lying on his back with his hands on his stomach.

"What happened to you?" Fred asked.

"I think it was the chocolate-covered banana that did it," Stan groaned, not even lifting his head from the ground to answer.

"Of course, you'd blame the one fruit they tricked you into eating by covering it with chocolate," said Fred.

"I had a cherry-flavored shaved ice, and you don't see me blaming that, do you?" said Stan, rubbing his hands over his sore stomach.

"If that had any real fruit in it, that would make a good argument," Fred laughed. "If you can, roll yourself over here and listen up."

With great effort Stan picked himself off the ground and ambled over to the table. "This better be important," he said. "I'm very busy digesting at the moment."

"It is, Sarlacc Stan," Fred replied. "Our fellowship is about to grow in number."

"Hey, I'm full, not pregnant," said Stan.

"You could have fooled me, but that's not what I mean," Fred continued. "I have just met a dwarf of great strength and character. Upon hearing the nature of our quest, this courageous dwarf has offered to lend a fearsome ax and join us on our quest."

"Most excellent news," opined Alfred the Grand. "If recent history is any indication of what travails yet await us on our voyage, we could use a sturdy dwarf and his redoubtable ax."

"Thanks, Grandpa," said Fred. "But it's, uh, *her* ax, technically."

Stan belched loudly in surprise.

"Good question, but I'm going to come back to you," said Fred. "Jimmy?" he asked pleadingly.

"Well, I can't say I'm thrilled to have a stubby-legged cave-dweller slowing us down," said Jimmy. "Dwarves are notoriously ill-tempered in the open air, you know."

"A dwarf *girl?*" Stan added before Fred could tell Jimmy not to worry. "I mean, are we trying to be the dorkiest group ever? Why don't we just ask the one-legged ballerina or the bearded lady to come along while we're at it? Or does she have a beard, too? Don't answer that. I don't want to know. I do want to know just exactly what kind of operation we're running here."

"I get it," said Fred. "We've got a great thing going here that we don't want to mess up. I don't know what you've heard, but, personally, I've been hearing Dream Team comparisons. But I think you're going to like Gemma. She's really cool and really funny, and, let's not forget, she is a flipping dwarf. Literally. She flips in the circus for a living and could grind any one of us into dust with her bare hands, so I dread to think what she can do with her ax."

"I don't know, man," said Stan. "Seems like an Arwen slash Tauriel gimmick to me."

"Things are bad for her here, Stan," said Fred. "She needs to get to Mordor, California as badly as we all do."

"Too right, Fred," said Alfred. "All people and all races are threatened by the Dark Lord, and each should play a part in our noble attempt to destroy the ring. I welcome this noble dwarf to our fold."

Jimmy raised his fist to his heart. "So long as she does not slow us too much and keeps her roguish tongue in check, I do not oppose her joining our fellowship," said Jimmy. "If it is the will of the ring-bearer, let it be so."

"And as you ask of her," said Fred, "be kind to her ways, though she prefers the darkness of caves and the ringing of steel upon to steel to the glow of the sun and the whistling of the wind through golden leaves."

Jimmy took a step back in surprise. "You speak with an eloquence beyond your years, Fred," he said. "There is more to the burden of the ring than meets the eye. If this dwarf can help us see it destroyed, then I welcome her." He bowed deeply.

"And you, Stan?" Fred asked. "Whose counsel I value above all others, do you agree?"

Stan shrugged. "Looks like I don't really have a choice, but I guess she can't be a bigger geek than any one of us."

"Then it's settled," Fred said with a smile. "She'll be waiting for us south of the circus grounds at dawn. We'll leave early so that no one sees which way we're travelling. Pack up the food you want before you go to bed. And don't overpack, Stan. It'll just make you hungrier if you're carrying fifty pounds on your back."

"Yes, your supreme high commandership," replied Stan, offering a fake bow. "Is there anything else you'd like me to do before you retire?"

Fred smiled. "Wipe the mustard stains and that goofy grin off your face."

"As you wish, your eminencyness," Stan said with a flourish of his outstretched hand.

Fred packed his bookbag full of potato chips and popcorn, thinking they would keep fresh for a longer time on the trail than anything else Mr. Burtman had brought. Then he threw his tauntaun sleeping bag on the grass and lay down to go to sleep.

"What are you doing, ya hobo?" Stan asked him, who was still busy packing food into his own bookbag. "Art came by while you were making new friends and offered to let us sleep in one of the extra tents."

"Thanks for letting me know," said Fred, struggling back to his feet.

"Well, it's not like we can get a word in when you're around," said Stan.

"I'm just happy we don't have to sleep out in the open," said Fred, trying to avoid getting into it with Stan. He was too tired for another fight. "Show me to the tent because I'm beat."

Alfred led the way through the trailers to a smallish tent, which stood just behind the larger one covering the stage. Inside, Art Kassirbann was telling several workers where to spread out some cots. The employee from the snack hut who had been chasing them earlier was helping set up their beds. Stan grinned mischievously. "It looks like we didn't need to answer your riddles after all," he said.

The worker unfolded the cot with such anger he nearly broke the hinges. "Looks like you've been eating all the circus animals' kibbles."

"Your mom is a circus animal," said Stan.

The man threw the cot to the ground and started towards Stan, rage boiling in his eyes.

"Oswald!" Art yelled. "What do you think you're doing?

Get those cots ready on the double. These are our honored guests. You don't want to have to clean up the elephant stall again, do you?"

"No, Mr. Kassirbann," the man said meekly, backing away from a grinning Stan.

"Good, because if our guests aren't completely satisfied with their night's rest, I'll hold you personally accountable," Art declared.

"Yes, Mr. Kassirbann," said Oswald, keeping his eyes down and continuing to prepare the sleeping quarters for Fred and his friends.

Art turned and addressed Alfred. "Schmendrick, Julian and I desperately want to retain your services," he said. "That magic show was truly magnificent! Whatever we can do to keep you here, just let us know."

"You and your brother have been most kind, Mr. Kassirbann," Alfred replied. "As I said before, I have a previous responsibility which I must honor." Hope visibly faded from Art's face. "But if luck would have it, this engagement will not keep me long. I am hoping that within the week, we can begin contract negotiations."

"That's great news, Schmendrick," Art said. "Great news, indeed. Will you be joining us for breakfast?"

"Unfortunately, I must decline. Our affairs are most pressing, and it would be better if we were on our way before first light."

"Very well," said Art. "I will wish you safe travels then. And don't forget to call. We want you back as soon as possible."

Art followed Mr. Burtman and the other carnival workers out of the tent. The snack-hut employee gave Stan a leer as he exited. Stan patted his belly and stuck out his tongue.

"You know, Stan, we've got enough enemies already without you making new ones all the time," said Fred.

"Well, you're so busy making new friends, I'm just trying to keep up," Stan said as he slipped into his sleeping bag. "Besides, that guy's an idiot. He's nothing to worry about."

"I sure hope not, because I doubt we'll be getting any party invitations from him anytime soon," Jimmy added.

"No big loss there," Stan said, rolling onto his side. "You guys should be thanking me for improving the class of your friends. None of you are exactly Orlando Bloom, ya know."

Fred looked at Alfred and Jimmy, who just shook their heads. Too exhausted for a fight himself, he decided to let the matter drop. It had been another crazy day. Add in a full stomach and you had one tired boy. He slipped into his sleeping bag, hoping a good night's sleep would improve Stan's mood.

As Fred slowly drifted off to sleep, he wondered what they might face tomorrow. He hoped Gemma could escape without her father noticing and that Stan and Jimmy would be able to get along with the dwarf girl. Most importantly, he hoped that another day's hiking would bring him that much closer to Mordor and the end of his quest.

His hand went to the ring, and he nervously worked it between his fingers. For a few peaceful minutes he imagined how happy he would be once he was rid of it, and then he drifted off to sleep.

25
SEEDS OF DISCORD

The following morning Fred was shaken awake from a wonderful dream. He and his parents had been enjoying a picnic. His father had been reading a book out loud while Fred acted out every scene. Fred had played a brave knight facing his mother, who had played both the dragon and the damsel. After she had drawn out a noisy, painful death as the dragon, she had flipped her hair and thanked Fred in a silly voice for saving her "beautiful damsel life." Laughing, Fred had taken his mother's hand and led her to safety on the picnic blanket, where she had kissed his father on the cheek. Fred's father had just started to read the next story when Alfred had woken him up.

"Fred, my boy, it's time to pack up," Alfred said with a smile. "You'll waste the day away, my darling dewdropper."

"Thanks, Grandpa," said Fred, trying to hide how sad he was to lose the dream. He looked around the tent and saw that Stan and Jimmy were already busy packing up.

"Art told me I could keep one of these sleeping bags, so it looks like we won't have to keep switching," said Alfred.

Fred was glad to hear that. His tauntaun sleeping bag wasn't exactly a bed at the Ritz, but it sure beat sleeping on the ground. He didn't know if Gemma had a sleeping bag, and if they only had three to split between five people, that meant that they'd have to share or someone not on sentry duty would be sleeping on the bare earth without covers. Having a fourth bag meant they'd have extra room to carry food as well. "That'll be a big help," said Fred.

"And I'll gladly carry a few extra pounds if it means waking up without aches all over my poor old body," said Alfred.

"Not to mention it gives us plenty of extra space for grits and gravy," Stan said, yawning.

"Glad to see your mind is in the right place this morning," said Fred.

Stan grinned tiredly. "Always," he said.

Fred rolled up his sleeping bag and slung it over his back along with his book bag. Stan did the same, and Alfred agreed to carry Jimmy's sleeping bag, because Jimmy was carrying his bow, quiver, short sword and gym bag already.

They left the tent and crept through the silent circus grounds, taking care to make as little noise as possible. There was a chill in the air, and the flags at the tops of the tents fluttered lightly in the morning breeze. Fog lifted up through the spokes of the Ferris wheel, and several ponies snorted and stamped in their pen.

Fred's eyes lingered on Ivan's trailer as they passed it, and he couldn't help but wonder about Miroslav. The boy was another poignant reminder for Fred that he shouldn't take things for granted. No matter how bad life might seem, it was important to remember that there was always somebody else who had it worse than he did.

The fog swallowed up the trailer as they continued

walking. Fred led the fellowship past the last of the carnival rides and then stepped across a strip of dewy grass into the forest. He searched the trees intently as they walked, searching for Gemma.

"Where's your wonder-dwarf, Freddy?" Stan asked after a few tense minutes of fruitless searching.

"She'll be here, I promise," said Fred.

"No doubt this treacherous furface sold us out," Jimmy whispered, reaching for his bow.

This time Fred didn't get a chance to respond. A sudden gust of wind parted the fog, and in a small clearing ahead a hand was waving to them.

"See, I told—" Fred started, and then the fog retreated some more and a second figure appeared beside Gemma. Fred's words caught in his throat. Jimmy had an arrow notched on his bow in an instant. Stan turned halfway around and prepared to bolt. Fred grabbed Stan's arm to hold him and told Jimmy to hold his fire, although he had to admit he was just as anxious. Fred squinted, but the distance was too great and the fog too thick to make out the second figure. Gemma was running towards them, the neck of her "ax" poking out over one shoulder and bobbing a little as she moved. She was waving her hands.

"Gemma, I told you not to say *anything*!" Fred said.

"I know, Fred, and I'm sorry," Gemma said. Even though Fred believed her, he was still angry. "But you heard Ivan," continued Gemma. "You know I couldn't let Miroslav stay there."

Fred looked up again, and now that the other boy was closer, he recognized Miroslav.

"Fred?" Jimmy asked, training his sights on Miroslav.

"It's okay, he's a friend, too," said Fred.

Jimmy didn't lower his bow right away and Miroslav

kept his hands raised in surrender. "I thought you said they would be fine with this?" he said to Gemma. "Maybe I should just go back."

"No," Fred blurted. "Don't go. Jimmy, 'Deadeye,' please, save your arrows for foes. I assure you this is a friend to the fellowship."

"Looks like now you've got too many friends for your own good, Fred," said Stan through his teeth.

"I didn't mean to cause any trouble," said Miroslav. "Gemma just said that you all were taking...well, I mean that you all were running away. And I..." his voice quivered, "...I can't go back there. Not now."

Fred looked at Stan. He saw the anger on his friend's face melt into pity. He could tell Stan was feeling the same things he was—as much as they might not like having a stranger join them, they couldn't turn Miroslav away. Fred knew that as soon as he told Stan about Ivan, Stan would be won over completely, but that would have to wait until he got a free moment with him. Stan nodded in response to the question Fred didn't even have to ask, and Fred looked back across his shoulder to see what Jimmy and Alfred thought as well. Alfred nodded too, which wasn't surprising. As much as Alfred had wanted to get out of Eisen Gardens, Fred knew he could sympathize with Miroslav, who was as much a prisoner of the evil magician as Alfred had been of Dr. White. Jimmy seemed more hesitant. His brow was furrowed deeply as he looked over Gemma and Miroslav, but eventually he nodded as well.

"It's okay," said Fred, "you're both welcome to come with us."

Miroslav and Gemma smiled at each other. "Thanks, Fred," Gemma said.

"And you can thank Stan, Jimmy and Alfred as well," Fred introduced them in turn.

Gemma and Miroslav shook hands with each of them. "I'm Gemma Lee, and this is Miroslav Borowski," said Gemma, who seemed happier than ever. After having an arrow pointed at him, Miroslav still seemed a little nervous.

"It seems that at every new turn along this journey, I am more impressed," said Alfred. "Here the fellowship finds two new courageous companions ready to risk everything to aid the ringbearer on his quest. I see the forge-fires of your ancestors' burn bright in your eyes," he said to Gemma, "and you have legs made for long journeys," he said to the lanky Miroslav. "We are honored to have you among us."

"Uhh...thanks," said Gemma, confused. "I guess I forgot that I told Fred my mom's side of the family used to do metal work. People say I look like them all the time."

"A compliment sure," Alfred smiled again.

"I'd love to stay for the rest of the tea-party," Stan interrupted. "But I'd like to get a little farther away from the circus before everyone starts waking up."

"Good idea," seconded Fred. "Let's get moving."

The newly formed group quickly disappeared into the swirling mists and thick leaves of the forest, finding it difficult to see at first. Thankfully, the rising sun soon started to provide more light. As the heat of the day melted the fog away, Gemma and the boys were able to pick up their pace. With Fred in the lead, they hastened south.

Despite the growing warmth, there wasn't much conversation, and Miroslav was especially quiet. Fred could feel the group getting tenser the longer they went without speaking, and this worried him. If they were to defeat their many foes and make it successfully to Mordor, there could be no doubt or division among the fellowship—they would have to trust each other completely. He just needed to get them talking. After a little conversation, they'd soon realize they were all as thick as thieves. In the end, he figured Jimmy was the easiest mark.

"Hey, Jimmy, we know you call your fists 'Admiral Ackbar' and 'Salamandastron' but what do you call your kicks?" he asked.

"I call this one 'Ragnarok,'" Jimmy said, throwing a sidekick with his left leg. "And this one," Jimmy threw a right legged wheel-kick, "I call 'Betty Sue.'"

Everyone laughed at the name, even Miroslav. "Betty Sue" didn't sound intimidating at all.

"That's a terrible name, Jimmy," said Stan. "Couldn't you come up with anything better?"

Jimmy smiled. "Of course. But you are obviously not familiar with the Ninjutsu art of deception."

Jimmy thought he was being very clever, but Fred wasn't buying it.

"'Betty Sue' is actually my deadliest weapon," Jimmy went on. "But if I called a kick from this leg 'Thunderbolt,' 'Shaq-Fu' or 'Yukon Cornelius,' I'd give away how powerful it is. Always make your opponent think you are weakest where you are strongest, grasshopper."

"That way you can blast their hairy Bumble hides right back to the North Pole, right Jimmy," Stan said to even greater laughter.

"You laugh now, but wait until you see what 'Betty Sue' can do," Jimmy said, wagging his finger at them.

"If Ragnarok can make a Firebird drop a plopper in his pants, Betty Sue might bring about the zombie apocalypse or blow up the Death Star," said Stan to another round of laughter.

"Well, we've got enough trouble with trolls and orcs, so let's not add zombies to the mix," said Fred.

"Yes, sir," said Jimmy. "I'll only use Betty Sue as a last resort. Certainly not before the final event."

"Speaking of," said Fred, "Gemma, have you ever heard of Nickelodeon *GUTS*?" He was hoping Gemma and Jimmy could find something to bring them together.

"Yeah, but I never liked it that much," Gemma said bluntly.

Jimmy turned white as a ghost. Fred winced—his plan had backfired. Hard.

"I always thought *Legends of the Hidden Temple* was a thousand times better," continued Gemma. "That one actually required a bit of intelligence to win," she added with a condescending laugh.

"A simple hammer-jockey like you *would* prefer the shadowy confines of a temple," Jimmy said. "But *GUTS* is a true test of wits and physical endurance. Your temple games were more like glorified stunts, and they paled in comparison to the Olympian events on *GUTS.*"

"Tough words there, Spock, especially for someone who I doubt would have even made it to the temple games," said Gemma.

Jimmy's hand shot to his plastic elf ears. Fred could tell his neighbor wanted to say something, but he was too angry to form words. His mouth just hung open and his head shook in rage.

Gemma took advantage of this and continued to slam the elf's favorite show. "No, you'd never have seen the inside of the temple because first you would have had to answer some trivia questions to conquer the steps of knowledge—a tough task for somebody whose brains have been rattled by too many bungee jumps. *Legends of the*

Hidden Temple was for smart kids, you know, aspiring archaeologists like *Dr.* Indiana Jones. *GUTS* was for dumb jocks and *Double Dare* rejects, everyone knows that."

Jimmy's jaw clenched. "You better watch what you say about *GUTS*, shortstack, or I'll beat you with 'Betty Sue' until your barracudas turn blue," he said, stretching his hamstrings.

"I'd like to see you try, you big clumsy baby giraffe," Gemma fired back.

"At least my show wasn't hosted by a bunch of rocks," said Jimmy.

"You know you've got a point. A scruffy, middle-aged goofball is *way* cooler than a bloodthirsty rock-god."

"O'malley!" Jimmy yelled, so angry now all he could do was shout the *GUTS* commentator's name.

"Olmec!" Gemma shouted back the name of her favorite show's host.

"O'Malley!"

"Olmec!"

"Hey!" Fred shouted, stepping between them. "Enough. They were both good shows, so there's no reason to get into a fight over it." Unfortunately, this didn't seem to make either one of them any happier. *Fantastic*, Fred thought. The rumor was true: elves and dwarves naturally hated each other. He had hoped that because Gemma and Jimmy were closer in age, they'd have an easier time getting along, but this feud must have gone back to before the Years of the Trees. Stirring old animosities back up was exactly what Fred had been hoping to avoid. He had wanted Jimmy and Gemma to become better friends, not find new reasons to dislike each other! Now he had to think of some way to get them back on friendly terms.

Fred turned around at the bottom of a small rise and

raised both his hands. "You guys need to let this go. Those shows aren't even on television any more for Pete's sake," he said.

"*The Adventures of Pete and Pete?*" said Jimmy. "That show was okay, I guess, but it wasn't even a game show."

Fred didn't know what he was talking about. Stan was confused, too.

"Yeah, just so-so," Gemma followed. "Nothing like *SNICK*."

Fred wasn't sure what had happened, but he had stumbled across something Gemma and Jimmy both agreed on, and he wasn't going to miss this opportunity. "What's *SNICK*?" he asked quickly, hoping the conversation would take off in a new direction.

"It means Saturday-night Nick," said Jimmy. "And it was really good. But...I'd say the second set of programs was the best."

"Definitely," said Gemma. "*Ren and Stimpy* and *Are You Afraid of the Dark* were always my two favorite shows on *SNICK*."

"Same here," Jimmy said, smiling broadly.

Fred breathed a little sigh of relief. It looked like Jimmy and Gemma might be friends after all. But Miroslav still hadn't said much, and he was the most unpredictable one of them all. Fred needed to get him chatting, too. "Miroslav, what was your favorite show growing up?" he asked.

"Uhh, I don't really know," whispered Miroslav. "All those ones you guys are talking about were good, I guess."

"C'mon, there must have been a couple you really liked?" Stan asked again.

"I just can't think of any others right now," said Miroslav.

"Well, what about video games, what's your favorite one of those?" Fred tried again.

"I don't know, okay!" said Miroslav, his voice rising. "I never had a television or Nintendo or anything, alright!"

Fred felt like he'd been punched in the stomach. Stan looked horrified.

"Sorry, man," said Stan and Fred at the same time.

"Whoa, that sucks, bro," Jimmy added.

"If it makes you feel any better, I didn't have a Tinbendo growing up either," said Alfred, but his attempt to cheer Miroslav up didn't work. All the fun had been sucked out of their conversation, and the six of them began marching in silence again.

Fred had only seen a little bit of Miroslav's life, but none of it seemed very happy. Fred knew he had been lucky to grow up with everything he wanted, and he also knew that a lot of kids like him didn't realize how fortunate they were to have toys and video games. Miroslav had given him yet another reason to destroy the ring: reminding other kids that there were boys and girls out there who got nothing from their parents but slaps in the face. There was so much pain in the world. Fred couldn't understand why no one else was truly trying to stop it. *How powerful a spell had been lain upon them*, he thought. He just hoped he could keep his little fellowship together long enough to break that spell. That part of the quest was proving much more difficult than he would have thought.

The group continued to march in awkward silence until Stan spotted the largest turtle that any of them had ever seen as they were crossing a small creek. At first, they thought the turtle was just a small log, it was so large. The huge reptile was sunning itself on a shelf of rock, its green, leathery eyelids closed tightly in slumber.

"Morla's moldy marbles—look at the size of that thing," Stan said. "Keep your eyes open for a canister of green ectoplasm," he joked. "We might be able to coat an arrow with it or something."

Everyone but Alfred and Miroslav laughed at this joke. Fred realized with another pang of sorrow that Miroslav had probably never seen *Teenage Mutant Ninja Turtles* either.

"Speaking of turtles, who was your favorite?" Jimmy asked the group.

"My favorite ninja turtle?" Fred asked.

"Yeah," said Jimmy. "It's something I ask a lot of people. Rank the *Teenage Mutant Ninja Turtles* in order."

"Hmm...that's tough," said Fred.

"No, it isn't," Stan countered. "Raphael was the best, Michelangelo was second. Donatello was a close third, and Leonardo was the worst."

"You see, I like Donatello best, Raphael second, Leonardo third and Michelangelo last," said Jimmy.

"No way, Raph is the best for sure" Stan said. "And Leonardo was such a pain. He's like Cyclops man, just a boring goodie-goodie who's always bossing people around."

"Hey, I like Cyclops," Jimmy said, clearly hurt.

"No offense, man, but I can name ten X-men that are cooler than Cyclops," said Stan. "I mean, Jubilee is almost as cool as Cyclops."

"I could make a strong argument against that, but we still haven't heard Fred's answer to the turtle question," said Jimmy.

"You go first, Gemma, I'm still thinking," said Fred. Now that he knew Jimmy was going to ask everybody, he was going to wait. He wanted to make sure no one slipped up and accidentally asked Miroslav. If they did, Fred could always butt in with his choices, saving Miroslav any more embarrassment.

"I liked Michelangelo best," Gemma said quickly. "Then Donatello, Leonardo and Raphael last."

"Interesting," said Jimmy. "Alfred?" he asked.

"Sorry, my boy, but I believe that was past my time," answered Alfred. "But if you were to ask me my favorite Knights of the Round Table or perhaps how I would rank my favorite Danny Kaye movies—"

"Err, maybe later," Stan said, interrupting him. "Fred, what's taking so long?"

"I think I've got it," said Fred, knowing he couldn't delay any longer. "Michelangelo is first," he started, and Stan gave him a look of surprise. "Leonardo is second, Raphael is third and Donatello fourth."

"Hey, we both have Mikey at number one," Gemma said and gave Fred her a high five.

"Big deal," Stan burst. Then he added, "I mean, it's just a stupid game, it doesn't mean anything."

"Actually," Jimmy explained, "I ask that question because it's a great way to get a psychological profile. The way you answer tells me a lot about how you see yourself, because each ninja turtle has such a distinct personality type. Leonardo is the responsible leader, Donatello is the inventive engineer, Raphael is the brooding, passionate one, and Michelangelo is the happy jokester."

"Cool story, *Jeopardy*-teen," Stan said sarcastically. "Somehow I doubt that they teach the crackpot ninja turtle method at medical school."

Jimmy laughed. "I didn't say it was something all psychologists do," he said. "It's just something fun I like to do to learn more about people."

"Fine then, *Dr.* 'Deadeye', of the famous ACME college of cartoon medicine, please give us your thoughts on our favorite *Ninja Turtles*," said Stan.

"Well, you picked Raphael first and Leonardo last," Jimmy pointed out. "My personal experience with you notwithstanding, I'd say you have a problem with authority, and can be hot-headed at times."

Fred whistled. "I'll be a Balrog's uncle!" he said. "Jimmy, you got it spot on."

"Yeah, Dr. Phil would be jealous," Stan muttered.

Jimmy smiled. "Of my silky elven hair or my innovative methods," he said.

"Ha ha," Stan said. "I thought you picked Michelangelo last, so what's with the jokes?"

"I did, I did," said Jimmy. "I'm normally more like Donatello, tinkering in my workshop, or like Raphael, bent on my *GUTS* revenge. But I can still joke every once in a while. After all, I needed to be able to say something funny to Moira during my victory interview."

"Plus, there's not a lot of money in the revenge business," said Fred.

"Too true," said Jimmy.

"Yeah, well, you made up the game, so it's not surprising you'd look good with your choices," Stan said.

"Gemma, I'm interested as to why you picked Donatello second?" asked Jimmy, ignoring Stan.

Fred was happy to see the elf trying to get along with Gemma.

"I like electronics a lot," Gemma answered, grabbing the neck of her guitar and rotating it around. "This is my ESP AX-401FM. I'm talking pure electric mayhem in midnight black with obsidian tuner pegs."

Fred gawked. Gemma wasn't kidding—the ax was

massive and boasted four jagged spikes. Like any normal
guitar it had strings, but unlike most guitars, which were
smooth, Gemma's ax had long, crooked barbs. Fred had no
doubt that it could cleave an orc skull with a single blow.
He was glad Gemma was not an enemy. It was a good thing
the ax was cleverly disguised as a guitar, too, for the enemy
would probably be eager to get their hands on such a
formidable weapon.

The instrument of rock and war gave Fred a few ideas.
He had been asking his parents for a flame-thrower for
years, but of course they'd always said no. He'd never
thought about disguising the weapon as something else,
though. If he could get the flame-thrower made to look like
a vacuum cleaner, he just might get away with it.

"Now, you can just plug this in to any old amp and get a
pretty intense sound," continued Gemma. "But that's like
ordering a pizza and settling for just the crust."

She paused while Fred and Jimmy laughed. Fred
thought for sure Stan would laugh at a pizza joke, but Stan
kept staring at the ground with tight lips.

"So, I started thinking about all the delicious toppings I
could put on this *ax*tra-large, Rock City-style pizza,"
Gemma went on, "because I wanted to play heavy metal
the way the god of thunder intended it to be played."

Fred and Jimmy laughed even harder. Fred thought this
was the most obvious thing Gemma had said. Of course, a
dwarf would play *heavy metal*. After centuries of
hammering away in caves they weren't going to be cutting
smooth jazz records or covering show-tunes.

"So," Gemma said, "the first thing I did was buy a Kerry
King model Marshall amp, and I know what you're thinking, and the answer is yes—they do go up to eleven. I can
rock out so loud with that amp that if you listen, your

grandkids will be born with their hands covering their ears." She paused for more laughter. "But that's just the beginning. There are literally dozens of things to make your sound even more thunderous. You add a Korg Kaos Pad, a Klon Centaur Overdrive, a Boss Compressor, and a Digitech Whammy Pedal and you could start a mosh-pit in a school for the deaf or a riot in an old-folks' home."

Fred shared a private smile with Alfred. Alfred winked back.

"But getting all that technology to translate into pure metal can be tricky," said Gemma. "Thankfully, like Donnie, I like a technical challenge."

"That's awesome," Jimmy said. "And I can also see now why you picked Michelangelo first. You're not so bad, you know that, for a...well, you know."

Gemma laughed at him. *"Little People, Big Sound*—that would be the name of my reality T.V. show," she joked. "That is, of course, if I ever got repeatedly hit over the head with a tack-hammer enough times to make me stupid enough to be on one."

"More like *Little People, Big Mouth*," Stan said under his breath.

Fred hoped he was the only one close enough to hear him because they didn't need another argument.

"What?" Gemma asked.

"Uhh, I just asked if we were still going south," Stan covered quickly.

Fred frowned at his best friend and then checked the position of the sun. They were still heading in the right direction, but this was little comfort in light of Stan's comment. After Stan's remark everyone's attention was redirected to staying on course, letting their conversation fizzle.

Eventually, the woods thinned and the terrain leveled. For a majority of the early afternoon, they covered mostly open grassland. Low hills and long valleys stretched out as far as the eye could see. They crossed a few crumbling country roads but made sure to avoid passing cars. There was one tense moment when they came to a large barbed-wire fence, and Fred was reminded of a none-too-pleasant instance during which Alfred's wardrobe had malfunctioned. Luckily, with the added help of Miroslav and Gemma, they were able to hoist Alfred over the fence without a repeat show.

With the food from the carnival, at least the meals were a lot better, even if their mouths were too full to say much. Fred was torn between keeping Stan happy or warning him to ration his food. He decided to keep quiet and let Stan eat his fill for another day. Stan was upset about the new companions already, and Fred thought Stan would absolutely hate it if he gave him orders around people they hardly knew.

As they finished dinner and prepared to camp for the night, Fred tried to make his way over to his best friend. He hadn't yet had a chance to tell Stan why Miroslav had to come along, and he wanted to do so before they went to bed. The boys had made camp in a small clump of trees nestled between two small hills, and Stan was laying out his sleeping bag between the large roots of a tree a short distance away from the rest of the group. Fred took a seat on one of the roots.

"Hey," he said.

"Just get to it, Fred," said Stan.

"Alright," he said, "I know things are getting a little crowded around here."

"You noticed?" Stan gibed.

"Look, Miroslav's mom died, and the drunk magician is the only family he's got. The jerk is making him steal from people at the carnival. I heard them fighting when I met Gemma."

"What are we going to do, round up every kid who's had it rough?" said Stan. "I feel bad for the guy, but why are we doing this? Is it about stopping Joanne and your dad from getting married or rescuing everyone who's down on their luck? It's your deal, so it's up to you, but I think you better figure it out quick."

"It's not my *deal*, it's our quest—all of us," said Fred. "Truly our most important goal is to destroy the grip of the ring on my father's mind and—"

Stan interrupted him. "Why don't you cut the hobbit-speak when it's just us okay. I'm getting sick of the goodie-two-shoe leader act, too. I mean, what happened to you? Just a few days ago we were leading a rebellion, just the two of us fighting against the machine, and now Leonardo is your second favorite *Teenage Mutant Ninja Turtle*! You sold out man."

"Yeah, well a few minutes ago you thought that whole thing was bogus, and now you're using my choices against me," Fred retorted. "Who's the sellout, now?"

Stan played as if he was checking his watch. "Let's see, it's a quarter to bogus, so...still you."

Fred looked off into the trees. He had been trying to make sure Stan was cool with everything, but now Fred was getting angry. It felt like he was always had to babysit his best friend. They were on an epic journey and unexpected things were bound to happen along the way. Stan agreed to come along, so he should be ready, and even *excited*, to deal with the changes as they came. Fred didn't have the time or the energy to put up with his attitude. He had more important things he should be focusing on. "This isn't even about Miroslav, is it?" he said. "You're just upset because it's not just me and you."

"Don't flatter yourself," said Stan. "I'm upset because I'm realizing how stupid this whole thing is. All this talk of throwing away something expensive so people see what truly matters in life. I mean they go after *treasure* in *The Hobbit*, or did you forget about that?"

"But it was never about the gold," said Fred. "It was always about the adventure. About finding a home, a family."

"Well, they didn't have a mom or a creepy principal ready to kill them as soon as they made it back again, did they?" said Stan. "If I'm even lucky enough to make it back alive that is! So stupid!"

"The only thing stupid here is your attitude," Fred replied.

Stan kicked his sleeping bag. "My attitude?" he spat. "I'm the only one around here who isn't completely bonkers. We've got a glorified bagboy, a delusional Nelwin, a total weirdo, and a magician so old his wand is made of dinosaur bone."

Fred wanted to say that he thought a velociraptor talon or tyrannosaur tooth wand was probably the coolest thing he'd ever heard of, but Stan didn't give him the chance.

"I should have never let you guilt me into coming along," Stan said. "I should be at school, making sure I don't fall behind and get placed on custodial track so I'm just like old greasy Filch cleaning up poltergeist poo for my entire life."

Fred was taken aback. "What?" he said. "School? You're saying you'd rather be taking boring job quizzes than doing this? You're either mental or you're ornamental, Stan."

Stan threw up his hands. "That's what you don't get! For some of us it's better to be ornamental! Some of us don't have our own personal Gringotts for a father. It's better for us to just blend in to the background and not give people a reason to.... Look, it's just different for me, okay? I can't afford to just take off whenever I want to and tick off the principal every week."

"What are you talking about—afford?" asked Fred. "We can't *afford* to lie down while they try to turn us into minions of the Dark Lord. Have you forgotten why we're here?"

"No, I know exactly why we're here. We're here because you're a spoiled rich kid with spoiled rich kid problems. I didn't see you starting a revolution after Mrs. Bonneville made us play slavery chutes and ladders, or whatever that stupid game was. No, you just got all hot and bothered when it finally inconvenienced you."

This hurt Fred more than anything, probably because he was worried that there was a shred of truth to it. "No, you're here because I'm the only friend you've got!" he yelled. "I'm the only one who'll put up with all your crap!"

"Look, if you want to play mind-doctor, too, do it on someone else okay," Stan yelled back. "I'm fed up with your games." Stan started stomping away into the trees. Before he made it too far, he turned around, grabbed a tub of popcorn, and then stomped off again.

"Where the heck are you going?" Fred yelled after him.

"I'm going home," Stan yelled over his shoulder, "and I'm going to grab every stray shoe I see along the way on the off-chance that it's a portkey. If that doesn't work, then I'm hitching a ride on the first bus I come across, magical or no. The sooner I get back, the better. I think you and your new gang will get along just fine without me. Send me a postcard from Mordor or from the madhouse, whichever one you get to first."

Fred's anger reached a fever pitch. "Fine," he said. "Some loyal friend you are. Happy trails."

Stan was already out of earshot. Fred stood up from the root and started to walk back to his own sleeping bag, but he only managed a few steps before he stopped. He cursed under his breath. As much as he was frustrated with Stan, he knew he couldn't just let his friend go away on his own. It was too dangerous out there to be alone. Plus, Fred knew that leaving things as they were would gnaw at him and make him anxious and uneasy the whole rest of the trip. For Stan's benefit and for his own, he decided to catch up to him and apologize. He sighed and turned around again, jogging in the direction Stan had taken, shouting after his friend.

But darkness had crept through the woods, and with only slivers of moonlight to guide him, Fred had to grope blindly as he moved among the trees. With every second, Stan's trail became harder to follow. Bumping into branches and thorns only irritated him more. *What I wouldn't give for a pair of night-vision goggles,* he thought. If he had a pair of military grade Knight Owl Assault Series goggles with infrared stealth technology, not only would he have found Stan by now, but he probably could have spotted every orc sentry posted from here to Mordor's doorstep. Talk about the kind of gift that kept on giving, too —once they'd made it back home, he could use night vision goggles every time he and Stan made their late-night smuggling runs on the *Windlord*. An Imperial blockade would be easy to slip past with that kind of technology. Really, he couldn't see how he had gone without them this long. There was simply no other option, he decided finally; he had to have them no matter what the cost.

As he stumbled through the shadowy grove, he was so distracted by his plans to use the goggles, and by the constant pain coursing through his chest where the rough edges of the ring had scratched the skin raw, that he didn't bother to look behind him. Not even when he thought he heard twigs snapping.

26

LIKE WILDFIRE

S till unable to find Stan in the dark, Fred was starting to worry. He'd had to leave the cover of the trees to continue his search, which would completely expose him to the enemy. Plus, the farther he traveled, the harder it was going to be to safely find his way back to camp.

He shouted out for Stan again, but there was no answer. The only thing Fred could hear was the eerie blowing of the wind, which he was starting to realize was strangely warm, and getting hotter. Dark clouds were sweeping in fast over the plains, covering the little valley in scary shadows. When Fred crested the top of the hill, he looked out into total blackness.

"Stan!" he yelled into the valley. "It's too dark to be running around in the borderlands of Mordor, ya meathead!" He looked desperately in all directions, but there was no sign of his friend. It was so dark, he could barely make out the shape of the next hill. *Finding anything smaller than an oliphaunt or an AT-AT at this time of night is impossible*, he thought. He was about to turn around and head back to the camp when suddenly the top rim of the hills flared in a bright orange line. The sun had just set, but to the east an orange glow appeared along a stretch of the horizon, and Fred could now see the hills and vales around him as clearly as if he *were* wearing a pair of night vision goggles.

Chill bumps rose on the skin of his arms and neck. "What black magic is this?" he said. And then, when the fiery glow on the horizon began to swell and advance with a terrible fury, he yelled out for his friend as loudly as he could. "Stan! Fire!" he screamed.

But he worried that it was too late already. The Battle of Sudden Flames had already begun. The blaze was jumping on the hill now, spreading from one edge of the plains to the other. Dry grasses crackled as they burned, and smoke billowed up into the night sky. Terror washed over Fred, as hot as the winds that blew the wildfire in all directions. He took a step back, covering his eyes from the light of the blaze. Things had just gone from bad to worse, and he had no clue what he should do. He wanted to find Stan and make sure he was safe, but he needed to warn everyone back at camp, too. If he didn't let them know about the danger, that fire could reach Jimmy, Gemma, Miroslav and Alfred in minutes.

Hope fading, he cried out for Stan one more time. Again, no response. He cursed and reluctantly turned back towards camp.

Fred crashed into something solid and toppled to the ground. Terrified that he'd stumbled into an enemy ambush, he rolled to his feet quickly and prepared to bolt. But it wasn't goblins or orcs blocking his path; it was a familiar face he'd run into. "Miroslav, you scared me half to death," he said. "What are you doing out here? Did Jimmy send you to come get me?"

"No," Miroslav answered quietly, looking down. The sound of Miroslav's voice and the tension in his fists worried Fred. The magician's nephew looked haunted and afraid. There was a circle of puffy redness beneath his eyes as if he had been weeping.

"Well, then we need to warn them!" said Fred. "The Dark Lord has started a great fire to stop us. We need to get out of here now!"

Mirsolav grabbed Fred's arm. "Give me the ring," he said quietly.

"What?" Fred said, shaking Mirsolav's hand off. "What are you talking about?"

"Just give me the ring, okay," said Miroslav.

Fred wrenched his arm free and backed away slowly from the larger boy. "No. You know I can't do that. I have to destroy it to save my family. To save everyone."

"You want to just throw it away, but do you know what it's worth?" Miroslav's voice broke. "What it would mean to someone like me? You say you're doing this to save your family. Well, I don't see how throwing away something worth so much could help them. I've never had a family. I have to make it on my own. I've always had to. And that ring is more valuable to me than to you. You can just tell them you threw it away—they'll never know the difference. You'll get what you want, and Ivan will finally be happy when I bring him the ring. We could eat for a year with the money we could get for it."

The story broke Fred's heart, and he wanted to do everything he could to help Miroslav, but he knew he couldn't give in. To give away the ring wouldn't do him or Miroslav any good. Everything would just stay the same. As he looked for a way around the older boy, he noticed how tall Miroslav was for the first time. Miroslav was at least a half a foot taller than Fred, and although he was wiry, his arms were taut with lean muscle. *If this turns into a wrestling match, I'm screwed,* Fred realized. He was going to have to try talking Miroslav down, but he didn't have much time!

A great gust of wind blew from the west and whipped the fire across the plains. It felt like a Furnace Dragon was breathing directly against Fred's cheek, and he started to sweat. *Someone just cast the mother of all Flame Waves,* he thought, gaining a new hatred for red magic. "I know Ivan makes you steal, Miroslav, and I'm sorry about your family," he said. The heat was so stifling, Fred could barely get the words out. "But this isn't the right way to fix things. Don't you see that this is exactly why the ring has to be destroyed? We need to show people like Ivan that life is about people, about love, about family and friends. Not about expensive things. We need to show him that money isn't the answer to all of his problems, or else he'll just keep treating you the way he's always treated you. Even worse, men just like him will keep beating on boys like you long after you and I have grown up. I know you're not the same as Ivan. I know you don't really want to steal from people."

"Just shut up okay," Miroslav interjected. "You don't know anything about me. You're a nice kid, and I don't want to have to hurt you, so just give me the ring, alright." He reached out and grabbed Fred's arm again, and this time Fred couldn't wrench free.

"You're cool, too, Miroslav!" Fred was now yelling over the crackling sounds of the encroaching wildfire. "And you don't deserve what's happened to you. But taking the ring won't solve your problems. It will only make you feel worse. You get addicted to gold and jewels like anything else. Once you have some you only want more, but you can never have enough. If you come with us, we'll figure something else out. We'll find you new parents. There are lots of good people looking for a son like you."

Miroslav shook his head violently. "No, Ivan would find me! Just give me the ring!" he said as he lunged at Fred with his other hand.

Fred dove away in desperation. The ground rose up to meet him quickly, sending jolts of pain up through his elbows and into his shoulders and neck. He tried to roll away and stand up, but Miroslav grabbed hold of Fred's cloak and held on fast. The two boys grappled, and their momentum caused them to totter off the side of the slope. They started to roll and bump and slide down the hill. They tumbled one over the other, gaining speed as they continued to wrestle for control of the ring. Knowing he could not overpower the older boy, Fred reached out a desperate hand, hoping to catch anything to stop his slide. His hand flailed, snagging nothing but air.

And then he caught something—the branches of a small bush, maybe. Fred clenched his fist hard, holding on to the plant with everything he had. It felt like his arm was going to explode, but he didn't let go. He kicked out furiously.

One of his kicks hit Miroslav on the forehead. The older boy lost his grip on Fred's cloak and fell down into the ditch. Some of the pain left Fred's arm, and he was able to pull himself a little higher up the slope. But he wasn't safe yet. The fire suddenly coiled itself and rose like a snake into the sky. It began spinning and bending like a twister, turning directly towards him. "Dark forces of Morgul!" he exclaimed. "It's a fire whirl."

The winds from the cyclone of fire blew the flames

wildly about, and the raging inferno swept in fast and circled Miroslav, who inhaled a large breath of hot smoke and collapsed on one knee. Fred frantically climbed away from the flames, but they only came at him faster. There didn't seem to be any way Miroslav could escape the fire, and Fred thought he was a goner, too. *So much for being a hero,* he thought. *I'm just Smaug bait, now.*

Then suddenly the fire seemed to pause, as if it really were some huge dragon deciding which way to turn next. Fred was momentarily safe at the top of the hill. Realizing this could change at any second with the fire whirl so close, Fred's first thought was to run back to camp and help his friends escape. But when he looked again at the coughing Miroslav, he knew he couldn't leave him there trapped by the flames. The ring of fire was slowly tightening around the magician's nephew, and soon he'd be roasted alive.

Fred drew in a deep breath, wrapped his cloak tightly around his body and ran down the hill—straight towards the tunnel of heat. When he reached the edge of the fire, he took a big leap and sailed over the flames. Coughing uncontrollably now, Miroslav was on his hands and knees, unable to rise to his feet. Fred came up underneath him and threw the older boy's arm over his shoulder and wrapped his cloak around them both as best he could. *Let's hope the whole blanket shield from the fire gag works as well in real life as it does in the movies,* he thought. Then he began the slow haul back up the hill using the cloak to protect them from the flames. Fred was completely exhausted by the time they reached the top of the hill. With one final agonizing push of his legs, he threw himself and Miroslav over the ring of fire and rolled in a heap on the grass. The vice grip the flames had clamped on his lungs lifted slightly, and the grass felt as cool as ice-water. A few small embers clung to Fred's cloak, and he beat them against the ground until they died.

Then the brief respite was over, and the heat was hammering him worse than ever. Looking across the plains, Fred expected to find a clear path back to camp. But the fire whirl had wheeled about and another wall of flame had reared up before them, larger than the one they had just escaped. There was no way out now—the fire whirl was swelling larger and whipping about like a power cable suddenly cut loose. Water began to well in Fred's eyes, and smoke clouded his vision. He grunted as he picked up Miroslav again and started to run, but his lungs, wracked by the heat and smoke, gave out immediately. He fell to one knee, losing his grip on Miroslav. Fred tried to get Miroslav off the ground again and keep moving, but it took every ounce of his strength just to breathe. He only managed to crawl a few feet before he fell again, this time flat on his face. Black spots appeared in the corner of his vision, and his face felt as if it had been battered by an Inferno Titan's flaming morning star. Exhausted and helpless, he lay down, waiting for the end—for the dragon jaws to close one final time.

Just before Fred lost consciousness, he felt a sharp tug under his arm and heard someone yelling at him to get up. His eyes were still too blurry to see who it was, and the roar of the fire was too loud to make out the voice, but with the help of the stranger Fred managed to coax himself up with his last remaining strength. Using his free arm, he yanked Miroslav to his feet and started moving as fast as he could, letting the faint, mysterious voice guide him. Each supporting the other, the three of them moved slowly across the field. Fred could see nothing but a bleary gate of fire barring them in, but whoever had rescued him seemed to know where he was going, so Fred followed him.

It wasn't a Flame Wave. It was a Worldfire. And Fred was convinced the quest was going to end in failure. He knew the fire whirl was seeking him out, and that he'd never escape it. But he kept running. And just when he thought he was going to burn up altogether or pass out from fatigue, the flaming twister sped away in a different direction and coolness swept over him. He kept running as far as he could stay on his feet, and then he fell over, letting Miroslav slide off his arm.

"Are you alright?" the person who led them from the fire asked him, and now that the roaring flames had retreated, he could tell that it was Stan who had saved them.

Fred tried to respond but only managed to cough. "Yeah, I'm alright," he said after a while, once his throat had calmed. "Thanks to you."

"What in Rivendell are you guys doing a fire dance for?" Stan asked, but Fred was too tired to respond.

Miroslav was hunched over and coughing up black blood, but he was alive and breathing at least. He turned to look at Fred. There was a tired peace behind his eyes. He looked like someone freed. "You both saved my life," he said, once he caught his breath. "I'm sorry, Fred, I don't know what came over me."

"It's okay," said Fred. "It's not your fault."

Miroslav coughed again. "Yes, it is. You're right, about Ivan, about everything. I don't ever want to be like him, and I almost just.... You're braver than anyone I've ever met."

Fred was going to tell him that this wasn't true, that Miroslav was braver than he would ever be, but he heard shouting coming from somewhere in the distance. Stan immediately ran to the top of the hill to see what it was.

"It's Alfred, Gemma and Jimmy!" he shouted down to Fred and then called out to the other members of the fellowship, hailing them with a waving arm. "They look like they're running from something, but I don't see the wildfire blowing over that way."

"You've got to go," said Miroslav, standing up shakily. "I'm not proud of it, but I told Ivan you had the ring. He probably followed me in case I couldn't bring it back. I can guarantee that's what they're running from. I can stall him, but you guys have to get out of here."

"No way," said Fred. "You're too weak. We're not leaving you. You're coming with us."

Miroslav put his arm on Fred's shoulder. "Thanks, Fred," he said. "I'd like nothing more than to go with you, to be a part of what you're trying to do, but I have to stay. No one else will be able to stop Ivan, and I won't let him get the ring. You get that rock to where you're going, and then *Throw. It. Away.*"

Stan had run back down the hill and was helping Fred up. "He's right, Fred. We've got to get out of here."

Fred exchanged one last look with Miroslav. "Good luck," he said. "You stay away from the fire. We'll come back for you once this is finished."

Miroslav smiled tiredly and then went limping away. Fred watched him go for a moment, and then Stan helped him back up to the top of the hill, where Alfred, Jimmy and Gemma were just arriving.

Jimmy got there first, chest heaving. "Some drunk Russian and that guy Stan ticked off at the carnival just attacked us," he said, wiping ash from his face. "If Gemma hadn't beaten them away with her ax, they would have had us for sure."

"It was Ivan," Gemma said.

"I know," said Fred. "Miroslav told him about the ring, but he's going to stall them now."

"I'm really sorry, Fred," said Gemma. "I almost ruined your whole plan. I shouldn't have told Miroslav."

Fred was preparing to console her, but Stan spoke first. "Do not say such things, Master...er Mistress Dwarf," he said. "It was in the spirit of our journey to accept one as troubled as Miroslav into our fellowship. You hoped as did we all that he might find comfort among us. You did what your noble heart demanded of you, and for that you deserve praise."

Fred was utterly stunned. Despite the fire fight he had just been through, hearing his best friend speak those words filled him with energy and excitement. He was proud and thankful to have such a good-hearted friend. A small part of him felt like the quest had just begun.

"If any man, wizard, elf or dwarf ever said hobbits were not poetic in speech, he was surely proven wrong just now," Alfred said teary-eyed.

Fred wasn't sure if it was the heat, ash stinging his eyes, Stan's comment, or Alfred's naked emotion, but tears were forming in his own eyes, too. He looked down at his feet so that his companions would not see. "You do not lie, Alfred," he said, hoping speaking would help him choke down his own emotions. "But let us not waste Miroslav's sacrifice." He finally took his arm off Stan's shoulder and tested his weight on his own feet. His legs were aching and more than a little wobbly, but they held. "We should put some distance between us and Ivan."

"Smartly said," Gemma added. "Though my ax has

felled them, it will not keep them down for too much longer. Here, take these." She handed Stan and Fred their book-bags. "We didn't have time to grab all the sleeping bags, but we made sure to grab as much food as we could."

"You're going to make me hug you if you keep that up," Stan said with a smile.

"Then I probably shouldn't tell you that she knocked out that snack hut employee with one blow from her ax," Jimmy added.

"Well, if you weren't my favorite dwarf, you sure are now," Stan said as he and Gemma exchanged a high-five.

Watching Stan and Gemma smile at each other, Fred felt as if the entire ordeal with the fire had almost been worth it. Then he felt a stabbing pain in his lungs and shook some more soot from his hair. *Almost*, he thought.

"Alright, we need to get around this fire," he said. He pointed to the sky, where planes and helicopters were skimming by, dumping water over the rolling conflagration. "The Dark Lord has sent his Fell Beasts to drop boiling pitch on this fire to keep us from getting to Mordor. We must hurry before it bars our path completely."

"It looks like the wind is blowing the fire east," said Jimmy. "I think if we keep going south we'll be alright. There's enough light we should be able to see fine."

"Sounds good—let's go," said Fred and then the five of them set off on a jog. Every hundred yards or so Fred would glance over his shoulder for signs of Ivan, but he did not expect to see him. All he could see was the dark silhouette of the hills and the ever-growing crown of fire above it, but he knew Miroslav would do as he had promised and would hold off Ivan, or misdirect him. From the start Fred had known that Miroslav was really a very kind boy who had simply gotten unlucky with his uncle. After seeing what the magician's nephew was really like, he regretted that the boy could not accompany them, because Miroslav needed this quest as much as any of them did. Fred was glad, at least, that he had the chance to talk with Miroslav, and he hoped that he had given him some hope and comfort.

The fire brought down a large tree behind them, and the sound of the limbs crashing reminded Fred that he needed to pay attention. Not only could they not risk stopping while Ivan was still so close behind them, but the fire could still shift direction at any moment. Fred wanted to distance himself from both threats. Ignoring the weariness in his legs, he quickened his pace, and his companions followed suit.

Because the still-billowing smoke had blotted out the stars, they had no way to be sure they were still travelling south, but Fred had an unexplainable feeling that they were still on the right path to Mordor. The light from the wildfire guided them for a few hours, and then dawn broke colorful and quiet, catching the boys still loping across the plains.

"Fred, we've got to stop," said Stan. "Alfred is getting tired. So am I, if you're keeping score. I feel like I literally just ran the Kessel Run. 12 parsecs, my butt."

"You're right," Fred answered. "I just wanted to make sure we put enough space between us and Ivan in case Miroslav couldn't stall them for long. But I think we've lost them. Not even Wolverine could track anything through that fire. Let's find a place and camp. We'll each take a one-hour watch while the others sleep and then we'll move out again. We'll camp early tonight and catch up on our rest then." After pausing for a moment, he added, "Unless, of course, someone else has an idea?" His spat with Stan had made Fred realize he had been giving orders, much like Cyclops or Leonardo, and, considering what happened after their last conversation, he wanted to make sure he gave everyone a say.

"I'd say that sounds like a smashing good idea," Alfred said, putting his hands on his knees to gather his breath.

"Gemma, Jimmy?" Fred asked.

"I follow the Ringbearer without prejudice or reservation," Jimmy answered. "You know that."

"Yeah, sure, same here," Gemma agreed. "Whatever you think is best."

"Let's find a place to nap then," Stan said. "I'm beat."

"Yeah," said Fred, which was all he could manage to say, as he was suddenly overwhelmed with emotion. Never in his wildest dreams had he ever expected to have such loyal friends. It made him feel very lucky and very safe. Over the course of the past few days, he had discovered that questing was a much more difficult business than he had ever imagined, and he knew that he would have never been able to make it this far on his own. It was quite possible that he had the most amazing and courageous friends on Earth, Middle-earth, Third Earth, or any other Earth, but at that particular moment he found himself unable to tell them how much he valued them.

I will honor them better by seeing this quest to the end, he thought, and then he led them on into the smoky light of the morning.

She had not eaten for days, but the thought of slipping into a size zero wedding dress filled her with a feeling far more wonderful than food. For a moment she felt something near happiness— and then she remembered that her engagement ring was in the grubby paws of that child. And that made her angrier than she'd ever been (and she'd once kicked a valet in the shins for not spraying air freshener in her car after he'd been in it!).

The trail of the ring had eluded her for a while, for how long exactly she could not calculate. Day and night had begun to blend together, for the only light she saw was that of her diamond ring. She had picked up the trail leading from the west bank of the river, but some strange sense had warned her to stick to the shadows. Soon she'd found out why.

As she had approached a glade, she'd come upon several dumpy men in horrendously ugly uniforms. The fabric, if it could even be called that, was a horrid shade of mustard. It was as if they were trying their hardest to look like human Twinkies! Based on their ghastly attire alone, they were enemies, and she had decided to avoid them at all costs. It had not been difficult to imagine how painful a torture session with them would be. They would dress her in the same hideous clothing and put her in a white washed room with iron furniture. No curtains, no throw pillows, just harsh fluorescent lights. Oh, the insanity! She could imagine only a few worse fates than this, so she had skulked around the men, using the cover of the trees to stay hidden.

They had failed to capture her this time, but they were surely hunting her ring, too, probably because they thought that the ring would give them better fashion sense. She feared that, like the "hungry tigers" that had always used her to better their own reputations, these enemy guards would only keep coming after her. In fact, there were probably hungry tigers hot on her trail out here, too. They'd just love to get their paws on her ring! That would make them the new "it-girl" in a hot second.

But she'd dealt with hungry tigers before, and she wasn't going to let them take what was hers this time either. She hadn't shared a single thing with anybody her entire life, and she certainly wasn't going to start now. Not when she was so close to having it all! Not when she was so close to proving to everyone once and for all that she was the prettiest, most popular girl in the whole world!

27
GIRLTALK

"Where did you say this place was again?" Renee asked.

"Chadarras," said Lucy.

"And how far did you say we have to go?" said Renee.

Lucy shot her a look.

"Don't take that tone with me," said Renee. "You heard the police say they're out hunting for my boy."

"I don't know if *hunting* is the right word," said Lucy.

"Oh, you don't think so?" said Renee.

Lucy was not eager to start that conversation up again. "Sorry," she said, "it's just that, as a writer, I try to be very precise with my language."

"My language is about to get *real* precise then," said Renee, arching her eyebrows.

Lucy shook her head and sighed. "I honestly don't know how far it is, Renee. Check the map." She popped the glovebox.

"What's this?" said Renee, pulling out reams of crumpled paper.

"A modern cartographical artifact," said Lucy.

"Say that again?" said Renee.

"A map," said Lucy.

"Do they know it doesn't have to be as big as the real thing?" said Renee, whose face suddenly disappeared behind the huge folds of paper.

"What does it say?" asked Lucy.

"It's a piece of paper, so it doesn't say anything," said Renee. "But a smartphone will tell you just how to get there and where the nearest Starbucks is, too."

"You know what I mean," said Lucy.

"You're the one who likes her language precise now," said Renee.

Lucy sighed. "Touché," she said. "So how far does the map indicate we have to travel before we reach Chadarras?"

"I don't know," said Renee. "The only thing I can find on this thing is the cheese puff someone left the last time they bothered with it. You don't have a phone we can use?"

"Do you?" said Lucy.

"Shoot, they don't even give you a discount on them for signing a contract anymore," said Renee. "So, I said forget it, I'm on the phone all day at the office anyway."

"Well, this is what I have," said Lucy, passing her embarrassingly cheap phone over.

Renee looked at the phone with mock curiosity. "Uh, unless you're trying to reach 1999 this ain't going to help," she said, pulling out the antenna on the phone and shaking it.

"You asked," said Lucy, snatching for her phone.

Renee pulled away. "If you don't mind, though, I'd like to check in with my little girl real quick."

Lucy lifted her glasses and rubbed the rim of her nose to

mask the irritation on her face. "Sure, Renee, go right ahead," she managed to squeeze out.

"Alright, thanks." Renee flipped open Lucy's phone and dialed. "Hey, Marie," Renee said after a moment. "Could I talk to Amber real quick?" Lucy tried her hardest to be polite and not eavesdrop, but in the small car the gesture was useless.

"No, we haven't found him yet, but we're getting close," said Renee after a pause. "Thanks again for letting Amber stay with y'all." There was another pause. "Hey, baby girl!" Renee exclaimed when her daughter got to the phone. "What are you and Maddie doing?" Lucy couldn't make out the daughter's garbled response. "That's good—I know they've got that big T.V. over there," said Renee. "Are there any little black girls in *Frozen?*" Another brief pause. "Then why are you guys fighting over who gets to be Elsa? Sounds to me like the other one is better, anyway. Elsa just took off and abandoned everybody like that brat Simba." Lucy could hear little Amber's voice rise in protest. "Alright then, just take turns—I don't want you giving Miss Marie any grief, you hear. I'll be back soon with your brother. Okay, love you, baby girl."

Renee collapsed the phone and made a show of slowly pushing the antenna back down. "Anything else I got to do to shut this thing down? Turn a crank or something?"

"That's fine," said Lucy. "Unless you need to call... anyone else?"

Renee looked at her. "You mean that knucklehead eating up everything in my house? He doesn't need to be in my business." She handed Lucy the phone back.

"He won't be worried?" asked Lucy.

"How should I know?" said Renee. "But it ain't my problem."

"Okay," said Lucy, surreptitiously checking to see if Solomon had called before she put the phone back in her pocket.

"He hadn't called yet has he?" asked Renee.

"Uh...no," said Lucy.

"That's the gift of goodbye, girl," said Renee. "He's not your problem either."

"That's an interesting way of putting it," said Lucy.

"That's real talk," said Renee. "And if I'd have married your man, I would have been since retired."

"It doesn't quite work that way," said Lucy.

"Yes, it does," said Renee. "If you could get out of your own way."

Lucy huffed.

"What do you want to do?" said Renee. "Just tell me that, because I know it's not drive around in this p.o.s. cleaning up his messes."

Lucy wanted to say: "Kick you out of the car at the next stop and carry on with my life," but she stopped herself.

"First, I'm not doing anything for anybody," said Lucy. "I'm looking for my son the same as you."

"Okay, so what do you want to do after that?" asked Renee.

"I just want to write," said Lucy. "And to make it on my own steam."

"You were right the first time," said Renee. "The rest is you trying to prove something."

"And maybe it's something worth proving," said Lucy.

Renee laughed. "Hey, it's your little red wagon, girl. You can push it or pull it."

Lucy rolled her eyes.

"I can't even imagine you ever getting married," said Renee, still laughing.

Lucy's eyes narrowed. "What's that supposed to mean?" she said.

"It means you're a brass-knuckle bi—"

A car swerved into her lane, and Lucy laid on the horn. "Orchole!" she said.

"See what I mean," said Renee.

"You ever hear that one about throwing stones in glass houses?" said Lucy.

"You better have good aim?" said Renee.

"Something like that," said Lucy.

"Orchole?" said Renee, laughing. "I've never heard that one before."

"I think my dad used to say it."

"Was he funny?" said Renee.

"He could be," said Lucy.

"Good story," said Renee. "I thought you were a writer."

"Well, it's not a good story."

"That's okay," said Renee. "I'm used to those."

Lucy took a deep breath. "Fred reminds me a lot of my father, actually. Dreamer gene, I guess you could say. Which terrifies me, because my dad couldn't keep a job. I mean he worked constantly, but he just never cared about anything except the 'unique and elusive triumph of invention.'" She did her best imitation of her dad's voice.

"That's better," said Renee.

"I'm glad you approve," said Lucy. "I guess I didn't understand what my dad was up against until I was older. The thing is, people don't want miracles. Not really. They'd rather not be bothered with the truly new or the radically improved. It takes too much effort and attention to change one's ways. So, they told him no again and again, and every time it broke him a little more. And every time he drank a little more. And my mother knew just how to dig into his wounds."

"The best ones always do," said Renee.

Lucy sighed and nodded. "My mother had training, too. She came from a ragged line of defeated aristocrats clinging to the scraps of a dignity they never earned."

Renee's eyebrows lifted. "Wow. It's like that? Now we're getting to the good stuff."

Lucy shrugged. "So, she left my dad for a man with no dreams and lots of money."

Renee's face twisted in thought. "You're Belle," she said after a second.

"What?" Lucy said.

"Oh, don't act like you don't know," said Renee. "I've got an eight-year-old girl, so I've seen all the princess movies a hundred times. You're a smart little brunette whose dad was a poor, crazy inventor," said Renee laughing. "You're Belle."

Lucy waved her away, but Renee just shook her head and kept laughing. "Well, now I know why you won't just take your man's money and do you," she said.

"Why's that?" said Lucy.

"Look," said Renee. "You loved your daddy because you're just like him, and you think your mom killed him because she wanted money. But she was just scared. And you can't change what happened between them no matter what you do."

Lucy shifted in her seat and looked out her window, away from Renee. She had a rotten feeling that Renee actually made a good point, but she wasn't ready to admit it yet. There was still the same anger, the same bitterness eating at the edges of her memories like acid. She thought it was strange how fully it became a part of you. How it propelled you in hidden ways.

"And what would you change?" she asked Renee to shift the focus away from her. "If you could?"

"I'd listen to my mom," said Renee. "She was a doctor like her parents, and she always told me to get my papers. You see Black women run the house. We've always worked. And if you want to have any peace whatsoever you need your degrees."

"So, you didn't go to school?" asked Lucy.

"Oh, no, I went to the best schools in D.C.," said Renee, "and then Stan's dad came along promising paradise, and I thought I could step out for a little while, live another life, but you can't. You can't take it off. You can't get out of it. And I know that now."

"You could go back—finish your degree," said Lucy.

"Not with two kids and no money, I can't," said Renee.

"Your parents can't help," asked Lucy.

"They passed," said Renee. "Whatever money they gave me, the government has now, thanks to Stan's dad."

"Sorry," said Lucy. After a moment of uncomfortable silence, she asked: "So is Stan a family name?"

"No, honey," said Renee. "It's just the whitest name I could think of. I see kids come into the clinic named Kannabus and Maryjuwanna, and I just can't. Set a kid back from day one. My son doesn't need any help getting behind. That boy is stuck on stupid."

"He seems like a good kid," said Lucy.

Renee huffed. "Just whistlin' in a t-shirt."

"I'm sorry," said Lucy.

"Me too," said Renee.

"No, I mean I don't know what that means."

"At Stan's old school they had a concert with those

recorders," said Renee, "and the teacher told them they had to bring two things to the concert: a button up white shirt and their recorders. What do you think my Stan managed to bring?"

"Neither," said Lucy.

"Exactly," said Renee. "But, God love her, the teacher told Stan to get up there, anyway. So, there he was, front and center on stage in his ratty t-shirt just trying to whistle along while everyone else played an instrument. My ex-husband shows up twenty minutes late and asks me what he's doing, and all I could say is: 'Whistlin' in a t-shirt.'"

Lucy couldn't help but laugh at the image. Renee laughed with her for a moment, but then she closed her eyes and shook her head, her lips trembling slightly. She turned away and covered her mouth with her hand. Lucy could see her jaw working to fight back tears.

"Fred doesn't have many friends, you know?" Lucy said to break the silence.

Renee took a moment to wipe her eyes before she responded. "Yeah, neither does Stan, I guess."

"You think that, um, your hungry friend is good for Stan?"

"I don't even think he's good for me," said Renee.

"So why are you with him?" asked Lucy.

"Because he's a Leo, and I've always been attracted to fire signs."

Lucy laughed at first, but when Renee didn't say anything else, she realized Renee had been serious. "Wait, that's it?" she said. "He just has to be born in the right month?"

Renee laughed. "I knew you wouldn't like that." She sighed. "No, I guess it's more than that."

"He makes good money?" asked Lucy.

"Lord no," said Renee. "They never do. Except for Stan's dad, every man I've ever known has been mad at money. No, that's not it. I'm 39, girl, and I feel 93. I married a white man because I thought it was a safe bet, and he got tossed in jail. I'm just trying to hold on to the closest thing to romance I can find at this point because I'm not sure what comes next. You know what I mean?"

Lucy was suddenly ashamed she'd been so harsh with Renee. Renee had her wounds, too, and they were deep. "Yes," she said. "I know exactly what you mean. That's why I write. Even when it feels so often like no one is listening."

"I ain't mad at you, girl," said Renee. "Whatever revs your engines."

"What?" said Lucy, a chuckle slipping out. "No, no, that's not what I—" She chuckled again. Then the tension broke and she was laughing full out, unable to finish her sentence.

"What's so funny?" said Renee.

"It's just that," Lucy was still laughing and only managed to squeak out a few words at a time, "men never really know...as much about engines... as they think they do."

"You ain't never lied," said Renee, and then she was laughing full on herself.

They were still wiping tears from their faces when they saw a sign for the Chadarras County Sheriff's Office.

"There it is," said Lucy.

"Rev those engines then, girl," said Renee.

Laughing uncontrollably now, Lucy accelerated towards the exit.

28
A BATTLE WITH DINOSAURS
(WELL, SORT OF...)

Gemma woke Fred for the final hour of sentry duty just before midday. Fred had offered to take the first shift, but after what happened the night before, they all agreed that he should get to sleep right away. He had been secretly thankful for the break and had fallen asleep within seconds.

Waking now, he felt as if he hadn't slept at all. His muscles ached, and his stomach felt like a ball of rubber bands that had been bounced around a spiked room for hours. Shelob's venom, or something just as caustic, was burning his throat, too. He swallowed hard, hoping he'd feel better in a few minutes.

As Fred unzipped the sleeping bag, Stan rolled over and tooted out some noxious tummy bubbles.

Fred pinched his nose. "I thought...they smelled bad... on the outside," he said.

Gemma laughed weakly and then sighed. She didn't look excited at all to share a sleeping bag with Stan.

"Thanks for waking me," said Fred, rubbing his eyes sleepily. "Did you see anything?"

Gemma shook her head. "You can see the smoke still on the horizon, but it's moving away from us."

"Good," said Fred. "Well, I'm up—you can get back to sleep. We'll move out in an hour, so sleep fast."

But Gemma didn't respond. She had already collapsed on the sleeping bag, trying to slide as much of the tauntaun cover over her while still keeping as far away as she could from Stan's backside.

Smiling and yawning, Fred left his sleeping companions and started walking around their camp in large circles. He wasn't just making sure the perimeter was safe—keeping his legs moving was also the only thing keeping him awake.

After circling the camp several times, he relaxed, for nothing seemed amiss. Miroslav must have managed to stall Ivan and the snack hut worker long enough to throw them off their trail. Fred didn't think he had to worry about Ivan, but still, he couldn't shake the feeling that someone—or something—was following them. He tried to put the thought out of his mind as he sat down near his companions for the remainder of his watch, but his eyes kept drifting to the north as if he expected an attack to come from that direction. No attack came, however, and when the sun had reached its peak in the sky, he slowly woke his companions.

"Instantly refreshed," Alfred said, rising shakily from the ground and lifting his arms in a stretch. "But don't push us too hard today, Fred-O, my old bones feel like bashed bottles and my muscles ache like minced mutton."

"Don't worry, Grandpa," Fred replied. "We'll take it easy today and camp early. So long as nobody attacks us, that is," he added.

"And the way things have been going, I wouldn't make any promises," Stan added.

Worried that Stan made a good point, Fred packed up his things quickly. He and his friends left the small cluster of trees to start hiking across the grassland once again. The rolling hills stretched out before them in all directions, wildflowers and patches of trees dotting the landscape every few miles. Birds of all types and colors rose and swirled in the light blue of the sky. Because they were climbing a lot, Fred kept the pace slow, hoping this would help them save energy.

They crested the rise of a larger hill, and Fred paused. That nagging feeling that they were being followed was back even stronger than before, and the hill was tall enough to give him a good view of everything around them. He took a long look in every direction. Again, to his consternation, he found nothing. Everything was clear—open and blue as far as the eye could see. He told himself he was just being paranoid, but still, something inside him wasn't quite convinced.

Just as he started to turn, a flash of white in the corner of his eye stopped him. He looked in its direction, but it had disappeared as quickly as it had come. Ultimately, Fred guessed that it had probably just been a small animal of some kind—a bird or maybe a rabbit.

Everyone else had almost made it all the way down the other side of the hill, and Fred had to hurry to catch up with them. He started to follow them through the meadow, but then he stopped again. "Hey guys, hold up a second," he said.

"What's up?" Stan asked. "Bowel break?"

"No," said Fred. "It's just that I suddenly looked behind us and something is there. It's probably nothing, but I want to make sure no one is following us."

He fully expected Stan to make fun of him for being

skittish, but after everything that had happened so far on their quest nobody was going to take any chances. They followed him without protest as he dropped down on all fours and did a soldier crawl back up to the top of the hill. Like outlaws planning an ambush in an old Western movie they poked their heads up just over the ridge.

"I saw it just over there," Fred pointed. "Like I said, it was probably just an animal or a leaf or something, but for a while now I've had this feeling that someone, or something, is following us."

"I think it's best that we take every precaution," Alfred whispered to Fred. "Our quest is too important not to, and the dark lands grows nearer by the minute."

They watched in silence for several minutes, their eyes carefully searching the plains, but nothing appeared. Strangely, the more they searched, the more Fred hoped that they'd find something. The longer they went without spotting anything the sillier he felt for getting spooked. They could afford no delay (their food was already running low), and if there was nothing following them, he'd feel really stupid for making them stop. He shifted nervously and scanned the area again. He'd been wearing the ring for a long time now, and he didn't want his friends to start to believe that it was making him loopy. They couldn't expect him to lead them safely to Mordor if he was losing it.

"Sorry guys, it must have been nothing," he said, standing up, but Stan pulled him back down and cursed in surprise.

"Great big dragon balls, I see it," Stan said. He pointed just a little to the west of where Fred had first seen that flash of white. Sure enough, about a mile or so away, a crazy-looking figure in tattered shreds of clothing was crawling on its hands and knees, sniffing the ground as it went along. Fred had been momentarily relieved to find that he wasn't imagining things, but now that he saw what was following them, he was even more terrified than before.

"What the heck is it?" Gemma asked.

"Is that who I think it is?" Stan whispered to him.

"I don't think so," Fred said. "At least it's not her anymore. What was once Joanne is now the mother of all bridezillas, and I don't think she's happy with the place settings or the cake."

"Who is it?" Gemma asked again, more insistently this time.

"It's the woman, or it *was* the woman who this ring was meant for," Fred answered. "Her name is Joanne, and she's been casting a spell over my dad so that she can marry him and throw me out on the street. She's the one who helped the White Wizard imprison Alfred."

He paused while Gemma and Jimmy cursed Joanne.

"But her greed has consumed her and transformed her so that now her outside mirrors her inner ugliness," said Alfred.

"Yes," said Fred. "I used to hate her, but now that I have seen what the ring has done to her, I feel nothing but pity."

"What I don't understand is how your wannabe evil step-mother has been following us?" Jimmy asked. "We've gone through caves and across rapids, over the hills and through the woods. We even stopped at a grandmother's house for Eru's sake."

"The ring calls to her," Fred answered. "All of her desire has been focused upon this one object, and it has taken away her sanity. She won't stop until she gets it back or it's destroyed."

"Should we try to capture her?" Stan asked. "Lure her in

with a Louis Vuitton handbag or something and then pounce on her or, you know, have Jimmy shoot her with one of his arrows?"

"I'm not getting my arrows anywhere near that thing," said Jimmy.

"And I don't know about you, but I left all my Louis Vuitton stuff at home," said Gemma sarcastically. "I've got nothing but Prada, and I doubt that will be enough."

"You know what I mean," said Stan. "If we leave her alone, she could sneak up on us at night and snuff us out, or worse, dress us up for her crazy fake wedding."

The boys stuck their tongues out at the thought.

"I don't think we should try to catch her," said Fred. "She's off her rocker, and I don't know how we'd keep a hold of her. She could probably lead us straight to Mount Doom, but if we had her with us, she could still turn on us at any moment. I think we should avoid her." Fred turned to look at the land to the south. "Let's stay hidden in the valley between these two hills for a while. It looks like the ridge turns south after a while, anyway. So, it won't be too much of a detour. So long as she doesn't actually see us, I think we'll be okay. After that, give me your best ideas about how we could throw her off our trail."

"If she managed to follow us down the river, I'm not sure if anything will get her off our backs," said Jimmy.

"Still, we've got to try," said Fred. "I'd love for my dad to see her all crazy like this, but we've got to worry about getting the ring to Mount Doom first."

They all took one last look at the pitiful, tatterdemalion figure of Joanne, and then they slid down the hill on their backsides. Once they reached the bottom of the slope, they adjusted their packs and started moving along the gully. Fred set a slightly faster pace than before, wanting to get as far away from Joanne as possible. After a few minutes, they rounded the bend in the gulch and started jogging south once again. Fred kept looking back, worried each time that he would see Joanne on the horizon chasing them. But he never caught sight of her again. Soon the ridges on each side of them flattened and they strode out onto a wide, flat plain of higher grass. Anxious that they were suddenly very easy to spot, Fred started to move even faster, hoping to find cover quickly.

Before he could find any sort of cover, they came to a large, barbed-wire fence. Fred hesitated. He didn't know if they should cross the fence or attempt to go around. He looked in both directions, but the fence stretched as far as he could see. He stamped his feet nervously. They didn't have any time to waste. Joanne could crest a rise at any moment and spot them, and then they'd be in serious trouble.

"We need to go across," he said, planting his foot on one of the wires.

"No way," Stan said. "Not with those things running around in there."

"What are you talking about?" Fred asked.

"Look over there," Stan said, "by that tree."

"What, the ostriches?" Fred asked, spying the tall, flightless birds.

"Yeah, the *ostriches*," Stan said again. "It's too dangerous to cross with those terrors running around."

"They're just birds, Stan," Fred said laughing. "They're not exactly Ancalagon the Black. They don't even fly. Do you run into the other room every time Sesame Street comes on the screen?"

"Just birds!" Stan exclaimed. "You act like you've never seen *Jurassic Park*. Those things are practically velociraptors. You wouldn't want to cross an alligator farm or a shark tank, would you? Well, it's the same thing!"

"Look, we can't stay here," said Fred, "and the fence is too long to go around. We either go through the ostrich farm or we go have a little convo with Joanne."

"Fine," Stan relented, "but we stay as far away from those beady-eyed deathbirds as possible."

Fred couldn't help but laugh. Compared to what they'd already faced on this journey, some giant feather dusters seemed like no trouble at all.

"I'm not kidding now, Fred," said Stan. "As far away as possible."

"Don't worry, we'll just say hi to Elmo and be on our way," Fred joked. Jimmy and Gemma laughed with him. Stan shook his head angrily.

Fred went over the fence first, placing his hands carefully around the barbs, launching himself from the ground with a powerful leap and landing with a thud on the other side. Stan came over next, and then Jimmy and Gemma helped Alfred up while Fred and Stan helped ease him down on the other side. Once they were all over, Fred checked behind them one more time for signs of Joanne. It was clear for now, but that could change at any moment. They would have to move quickly if they wanted to make it to the other end of the farm without being spotted.

They started running across the pasture keeping their heads low so they wouldn't be seen. The first few ostriches they saw were standing around a large tree, which had the name 'Bulong Farm' and the words 'Keep Out' scratched into it in a scary jagged script. Fred stayed as far away as he could from them without bringing them too close to the barn. Fred had been focusing so much on the first group of birds, he accidentally drifted nearer to a second group of ostriches he hadn't noticed. Stan spotted them first and bumped into Fred as he turned away in fear.

"Mind watching where you're going?" said Fred.

"Yes, I do," Stan replied in a whisper. "And I'd like to mind it farther away from those dinosaurs."

Most of the ostriches didn't seem to notice them and continued chewing on whatever tasty bit of grass they had found. This didn't stop Stan from keeping his eyes trained on the birds the entire time as if he expected them to attack. The rest of the fellowship was more entertained by Stan, and they continued to poke fun at him.

They were almost all the way across the farm when Fred said to Stan, "You see, I told you, they're just giant pigeons, nothing to be scared —"

He stopped mid-sentence. There were two large ostriches standing only a few feet away, and they were staring straight at them. Fred had never actually looked into the eyes of an ostrich. As he did for the first time, he saw that they looked nothing like a pigeon or any other bird he'd seen around Bithbon. The ostrich's eyes were just as beady and black, but where a pigeon's eyes were wide open and dumb-looking, the ostriches' eyes saw right through you. And the way the huge birds peered downwards around their large beaks made them look completely unhinged and seriously angry.

Fred hardly dared to breathe, and he realized with a start that the farm had grown eerily silent. "Umm, maybe Stan has a good point," he said, backing away slowly. "I don't think this is a petting zoo."

"Yeah, and I don't hear anyone singing the ABCs," Gemma agreed.

"Why don't half of us go around this way and half the

other way," said Fred. "That might confuse them enough that they'll leave us alone."

"Does anyone know if ostriches eat meat?" Gemma asked nervously as she began to shuffle.

"I don't know, but I'm not waiting around to find out," said Stan.

Jimmy and Gemma started moving slowly around the left side of the ostriches, while Fred, Stan and Alfred sidled around the birds on the right, keeping their eyes trained on the large birds the entire time.

They were looking at the ostriches and nothing else, so when they'd made their way around the birds, the two groups bumped into each other. Stan let out a frightened gasp as they did. This noise startled the ostriches. Both of the birds made a terrible cawing noise and puffed up their feathers, which only frightened Stan even more. He gasped again, and the birds finally charged. Screaming, Gemma and the boys went dashing in five separate directions away from the birds. Fred had to run as fast as he could to avoid being stomped by the ostriches' large clawed toes.

The five members of Fred's party sprinted across the farmland, the ostriches driving them towards the south end of the large pen. Dashing through a small garden, Stan plucked a carrot loose from its stalk and lobbed it back at the ostriches. Unfortunately, just as Stan himself had done many times before, the birds ignored the vegetable and kept chasing the boys from their territory.

Fred finally spotted the south border of the fence a hundred yards away and yelled out some encouragement to his friends, who were breathing too hard to reply. One of the ostriches had singled out Stan and was nipping its beak at his heels, causing him to leap into the air every few seconds like a cartoon character. The other ostrich was chasing Gemma, who was pumping her shorter legs extra hard to keep up with the rest of them.

Although he was growing tired and short of breath, Fred tried to think of the best way to get them all over the fence before the ostriches caught them. He knew that although Jimmy had the most to carry, the elf was still the fastest. His neighbor could have quickly run past them all, but he was hanging back in case one of them should fall behind.

"Jimmy, run ahead and jump the fence first so that you can help the rest of us over," Fred hollered, and Jimmy shot ahead. "Stan and Gemma, we'll get you over next," he yelled again. Stan was concentrating too hard on avoiding the snapping beak of the ostrich on his tail to say anything, so Fred had to just hope that they would all be on the same page. "Run out a little ways and then come towards me," he shouted.

They were now only fifty yards away from the fence. Fred hoped they had enough space for his plan to work.

Stan and Gemma must have heard his order, because both of them peeled away from Fred and Alfred.

"Hang back, Grandpa, I'm going ahead," Fred said, and he used the last of his energy to sprint ahead.

Jimmy had already jumped the fence and was cheering the rest of them on. Fred raced forward but did not follow Jimmy over the barrier. Instead, he stopped a few feet in front of the fence, dropping down on all fours and bracing his back. Stan and Gemma both seemed to catch on to his plan and came sprinting directly towards him. Gemma arrived just before Stan and put her left foot down on Fred's back. Clutching her guitar and pack to her chest, she pushed off hard and went flying over the fence, rolling expertly as she landed. Stan's foot met Fred's back a second later, and he leapt, too, sailing clear of the barbs and into Jimmy's hands. Jimmy helped break his fall, and both boys went tumbling.

Fred had first been looking for a way to get his friends safely over the fence and had not considered that his plan left two fully grown ostriches running straight for him. He only had a moment to regret this, however, for the ostriches had not been far behind Stan and Gemma. They were both charging fast.

Ducking his head and curling into a ball, Fred waited for impact. The ostriches cried out sharply, and then Fred heard a heavy collision. Strangely, he felt no pain. He opened his eyes to find that while trying to avoid the fence, the ostriches had slipped on the grass and crashed into each other, missing him completely. Stunned by his unbelievable luck, he stared down at the ostriches lying next to him. They were shaking their Martian-like heads groggily and pedaling their long legs slowly in the air.

Fred knew he should get away from them, but he was frozen in place. Then Alfred was picking him off the ground and helping him to the fence. With the help of their friends, the two of them were both up and over the barrier before the ostriches could get back on their feet.

Finally safe, the boys lay piled in a heap on the other side of the fence panting heavily.

"Big Bird he says...like feeding the ducks at the park he says," Stan muttered between deep breaths.

"Sorry," Fred apologized, "I did not think that the Fell Beasts had taken such shapes."

"Yeah, well, now you know," said Stan. "If Jimmy hadn't caught me, I'd be flat as a Stancake by now."

Jimmy laughed. "That doesn't sound that tasty," he said.

"They're actually delicious," Stan said with a smile. "Better than fluffins even. Seriously, though, I barely made it over—but, Gemma, you cleared that fence by a couple feet."

"Nobody tosses a dwarf," said Gemma. "But that's just because little people got hops, too."

Everyone gave a tired laugh. "That's for sure," said Stan. "And apparently so do elves. Jimmy, I don't know how you leaped over that fence without help."

"I've been training for 'Over the Top' for some time now," Jimmy said. "And I needed to keep my lead going into the last event. I'm not just looking to win. I want the perfect score."

Fred laughed again. He couldn't believe it. While the rest of them were running for their lives, Jimmy was still pretending to be on an episode of *GUTS*.

"Sure thing, Jimmy, whatever you say," Stan said, sucking in another gust of air. "I'm just glad we're safe from those beaked terrors."

"As I was saying before," Alfred added, "we never can be too cautious. It will do us no good to underestimate the enemy."

"I say we just avoid ostriches altogether from here on out," said Stan.

"I agree," Gemma laughed. "Or any other friend of the dinosaurs."

The ostriches had finally gotten all the way up and looked funny wobbling away, still dizzy from their collision. Gemma laughed even harder at the sight of them, and her cheer seemed to ripple through the rest of the group. Fred was amazed at how simply laughing made him feel so much better. He almost forgot that they had just been running from the terrifying birds.

"Alright, let's get a move on," he said after they had all wiped away their tears.

As soon as he turned around, however, his smile disappeared. A giant wall of gnarled trees rose before him: an impenetrable tangle of vines and shadows that seemed to go on forever. Behind him, he heard his friends grow silent as they, too, caught sight of the forest. Fred felt a chilling breeze knife in from the woods to cut at his skin. The bright spring afternoon seemed a distant memory as he peered into the black center of the forest.

"Let me guess," Stan said. "There's no chance of us going around the 'fire swamp' is there?"

Wishing there were some other route, Fred slowly shook his head no.

"I didn't think so," Stan sighed. "Next to spiders and centaurs and giant rats, we'd probably love to run into an ostrich in there."

"You might be right," said Fred. "But if we want to make it to Mordor before we run out of food, we have to go through."

"Then lead the way," Jimmy said.

Fred thought even the elf sounded a little scared, which did little to boost his own confidence. Other than Ents, elves knew forests better than anyone, but it seemed as if even Jimmy had never seen a wood this foreboding.

Fred took a moment to muster up his own courage. He pulled his cloak over his shoulders and tightened the straps on his book bag. "Alright, everybody stays close," he said, and then he pushed aside some brambles and stepped into the trees.

29
COWBOY CARPOOL

The Chadarras County Sheriff's Office was tucked away behind a boarded-up Burger King on a dusty back road. It was nothing but a small, brown building marked only by a faded sign. Lucy missed it initially and had to spin the car around in the road, bouncing Renee a little bit in the passenger seat.

"You trying to hit every pothole or something?" asked Renee.

"Yeah, why?" Lucy deadpanned.

"Cause I think you missed one," said Renee.

"Nobody's perfect," said Lucy, pulling the car into the visitor's spot.

"You know how I know there isn't another Black person around for miles?" said Renee.

"How?" said Lucy.

"Because the Burger King went out of business," she said. "Y'all are afraid of flavor."

"I'm a vegetarian," said Lucy as she led them up the stairs.

"Of course you are," said Renee.

Because no one was in the lobby to greet them, they marched down the hall and pushed open the door marked "S-eriff's Office."

Before Lucy could introduce herself to the man sitting across the room at his desk, she was tackled. The collision knocked the breath out of her, and she felt the cold hard tile digging into her bones as someone wrangled her arms behind her.

"I got 'em, sir, don't worry," said a large woman as she placed a meaty knee squarely between Lucy's shoulders, sending jolts of pain up her spine. "We must be getting close if they're sending assassins after us."

"Lord have mercy, they're brutalizing white women now," said Renee, dropping to the floor and putting her own hands behind her head.

Lucy, who was pinned to the ground facedown, couldn't speak. She struggled to keep her eyeballs from popping out of her skull.

"Would you get off her, Wyn?" said the sheriff, covering the receiver of the phone. "How many times do I have to tell you, ain't no daggone assassins coming after us."

"That's the thing about assassins, sir, you never see them coming," said Wynnie, grabbing her handcuffs.

"Put those away right this minute and let the poor woman up," said the sheriff, "before we get sued."

"Oh, you're getting sued," said Renee.

"See?" said the sheriff. "It's another six months behind that desk if you don't!"

Wynnie groaned and then reluctantly rolled off of Lucy. Renee helped Lucy up. Lucy dusted herself off, shooting lasers from her burning eyes at deputy Wynnie. Surprisingly, the sheriff stayed on his phone call.

"Can you believe the manner of him?" said Renee. "Like we ain't even here."

Before Lucy could bark her displeasure at him, a voice blared across the line. The sheriff had to hold the phone a foot from his ear while a shouting voice pierced the air. Lucy assumed the sheriff was getting chewed out by his boss, and, based on how she had been treated so far, she figured he probably deserved it. An audible thud ended the phone call. The sheriff studied the phone for a moment as if he had never seen one before, and then he laid it softly on the table.

"You ready to talk about this lunatic yet?" said Renee. "Or do you need to make another call?"

Wynnie took a threatening step towards her. "You better center yourself," said Renee, pointing at the deputy. "Crazier than 40 going north," she said to Lucy. "And he's probably no better," she pointed at the sheriff. "I don't even know why we're here."

"I offer my sincerest apologies," he said, finally standing up. "As you probably know, we're swamped. What with the fire, and we're working on a very important case right now. We just haven't slept, so we're both just a little on edge. If you have something to report, Wynnie will be gl—"

Lucy finally got her breath back and cut him off. "I'm Lucy Owen—we spoke on the phone earlier," she said, stretching her neck. "Renee and I are here looking for our sons."

The sheriff banged his knee against an open drawer in surprise as he hurried to round his desk to greet them. He smiled forcibly through the pain of his bruised knee and offered his hand, stammering nervously. "We meet at long last," he said. "A great pleasure this is, well, not that your sons are missing, I mean, certainly that doesn't give me pleasure. What I mean is, you give me pleasure, err pleasure me to meet...." He took a deep breath. "It's a pleasure to meet you both," he said as he shook their hands. "Please sit," he pointed to the two seats in front of his desk. "Can I offer you some coffee? Wynnie puts as much energy into making our brew as she does protecting the office from assassins."

Neither Lucy nor Renee returned the sheriff's smile. "I'd test the pot for drugs, then," said Renee, throwing Wynnie a venomous look. "And if you said you all had a fire, I know who I'd peg as the number one suspect." The deputy narrowed her eyes right back but didn't say anything.

"Oh, no, we didn't have a fire here," said the sheriff. "You haven't heard about the wildfire?"

"From who?" said Renee. "Mr. Fox?"

The sheriff looked confused.

"We've been in the car the entire time," said Lucy.

"Oh, I see," said the sheriff. "Well, another wildfire has been spreading like...well, wildfire all over the state, and we've been working nonstop trying to contain it. I'm surprised you didn't see anything from the road."

"We didn't know," said Lucy, suddenly fearful. "H-have you found anything about the boys?"

"Well, quite a bit, if I do say so myself," said the sheriff. "I don't normally like to toot my own horn, so to speak, but I think we've done a bang-up job...so to speak." He coughed and pushed papers across his desk nervously. "Well, for example, we're positive the men who were chasing your son are some thieves that we've been looking for...and we're positive it was their raft that we found."

"Those both sound like negatives to me," said Renee.

"You best watch your tone, there, Missy," said Wynnie.

"I'm sure you'd love to beat a little on me with that

baton, huh?" said Renee. "C'mon sister, let's get this place shut down for good."

"Hold up now," said the sheriff quickly. "No need for that. You'll be happy to hear that we're following some leads right now. Yeah, we've got some real promising leads."

"Like what?" probed Lucy.

"Well, I'm not really at liberty to say at the moment," said the sheriff.

"Sheriff, I'm not in the mood for making threats," said Lucy. "I'm tired and scared for my son. Now with this wildfire..." she trailed off. "But, if I were you, I would not underestimate a mother's love for her child. My ex-husband is a really, really expensive lawyer after all, and I'm already starting to feel some pain in my neck." Lucy grimaced and massaged her neck.

The sheriff shifted uncomfortably in his seat. "We, we're doing everything we can, Mrs. O—" he stammered.

"No, you're not," Lucy cut him off again. "Tell us what you know, so that we can help. There's no sense in wasting us. Nobody knows the boys better than we do. I've come this far, and I'm not stopping now."

The sheriff leaned back in his chair and rubbed his forehead. There were dark circles under his eyes and tension in his brow. "Alright," he said after a moment. "But only on the condition that you do not interfere with my investigation. And everything and anything you figure out you tell me about it, understand?"

"Yes, of course," she replied.

"Okay." The sheriff leaned across his desk. "The big news is we also found a second raft," he said. "But don't worry, this one was perfectly intact. It was also nowhere near the first one. If the boys were in that one, they managed to float quite a ways south on the river—so far, in fact, that they are now well out of my jurisdiction."

"See, I told you," said Renee. "We're just wasting our time here."

"Wait a second now," said the sheriff. "Because this wildfire is cutting across the whole danged state, the commissioner has put me in charge of the surrounding counties as well. What that means is I can have my men all over the state searching for the boys as they look for the thieves and help to deal with the fire."

"Good, let's go to where they found the raft," said Lucy, standing up.

"Hold those horses, now," said the sheriff. "I was just fixing to say that the boys hid the raft, which was a smart move if they're trying to hide from the thieves, but it also made it tough for my officers to find. Now we can't be sure, but we think they got off the river to visit a travelling carnival. Unfortunately, the carnival has already started moving. We're going to intercept it, of course, and investigate. But with all the other kids who probably visited the carnival over the last few days, it's doubtful that anybody would have remembered your boys specifically."

"They were dressed as hobbits, Sheriff Marshal," said Lucy. "I think it's worth it to ask around."

"And we will, I'm just telling you not to get your hopes up," the sheriff added.

"Trust me our hopes couldn't be any lower if your deputy dragged them to the ground," said Renee. Wynnie glared back at her.

"I wish I had better news," said the sheriff. "But the carnival caravans and the fire have eradicated any other trails. If the boys aren't with them, we're back to square one."

Lucy's phone rang suddenly. She was entirely surprised to see Solomon's name scroll across the screen. "It's my ex-husband, sheriff—I should take this. If you can, try to prevent your deputy from attacking me when I return."

"I suggest a leash, or perhaps a treat for good behavior," said Renee.

Wynnie glowered at them both as Lucy stood up from her chair and walked into the hallway, shutting the office door behind her. "Hello," she said into the phone.

"Hey, Lucy, it's Solomon. What's going on? I haven't heard anything in a while."

"I'm not surprised," said Lucy. "Your secretary hasn't been answering the phone for anybody. Not even the cops."

"What?" he exclaimed. "I told her to put anybody through who had information about Fred."

"Can you be sure Leo didn't countermand your orders?" Lucy asked. "Regardless, I would have expected you to have called sooner."

"I tried, I meant to," Solomon stammered. "It's just... with work...I lost track of time. But I can't even begin to tell you how much I've been worrying about Fred."

"I don't think I believe you anymore," said Lucy.

"C'mon, Lucy, of course I'm terrified for him," Solomon continued. "I just don't see what I can do. I feel almost like I'd go sick from worrying if I didn't have work to distract me."

"Yeah, you keep telling yourself that, Solomon," said Lucy.

"You can hate me all you want, but please, tell me if you know anything more about Fred," said Solomon.

Lucy was fuming. "Oh, nothing much—only that he went down the most dangerous rapid in California in order to escape some murderous thieves and then may or may not have been consumed by a raging wildfire!"

"What!" Solomon exclaimed. "Is he alright? Do you know if he's alright?"

"I can't be sure, but I think so," Lucy answered. "Though at this rate, there's no telling how long he'll stay that way. But don't you worry about it, Solomon. I wouldn't want you to suffer just because your son is missing. I'm down here looking for both of us, so you can just go back to your distractions."

"Lucy, I—" he started, but she hung up the phone. She turned it off completely and stormed back into the sheriff's office once again.

Sheriff Marshal was just getting off the phone as well. "There you are," he said. "Good news—Combe County deputies have found the carnival. They've actually been travelling in our direction. I'm going to speak with them now."

"We're coming, too," said Lucy.

"Like heck they will," said Wynnie.

"Be quiet, Wyn," said the sheriff.

"There's no way two civilians get to go out in the field, and I've got to stay here reading documents," the deputy whined.

"Not enough pictures for you," said Renee.

Wynnie grabbed a throwing star and cocked her arm, but the sheriff stepped in front of her. "Enough!" he said. "I've been up four days straight managing ten times the people I should, and I'm at my wit's end with this childish behavior. In my department you earn the right to be out in the field, you understand me?"

Wynnie dropped her head. "Yes, sir," she said quietly.

"I'm moving out, so if you want to come with me, now's

the time," said the sheriff, grabbing his hat from the coatrack.

"So, it's the cowboy or the crazy?" said Renee. "Lucy, let's just look ourselves. We're going to end up missing, too, if we keep messing around like this."

"Ma'am, since I've been in charge of this office we haven't had a single police misconduct claim brought against us," said the sheriff.

"That just means you haven't been caught yet," said Renee. "You can't fool me. I was twelve the first time I saw a cop drag a man to the ground and nearly beat him to death. I stood there crying and throwing my weekly allowance at him trying to get him to stop."

The sheriff stopped before getting into his car. "Ma'am, I can't tell how sorry I am you had to see that. I know you're tired and worried, so I won't feed you any empty lines you've heard a million times before. All I can say is that I, me, Elmer Marshal, the man, not the officer, I've got your back. And I've got your son's back."

Renee shook her head and looked off into the distance.

"I understand if you don't want to come, Renee," said Lucy. "But I'm going with the sheriff. I want to be as close to the search for the boys as I can. If you want to take my car and follow or look elsewhere, you can." Lucy handed Renee the keys and then dropped into the passenger seat.

"Hold up," said Renee. "If you think I'm riding in the back of this thing, you've lost your mind, too."

Lucy sighed and climbed back out of the car. She took her keys back and got into the backseat of the sheriff's cruiser while Renee took the front seat.

"Y'all ready," said the sheriff, "or do you want to run another Chinese fire drill?" He beamed back at Lucy, but when she didn't show even the slightest amusement, he tried Renee, who gave him an even more disgusted look.

"Not okay," said Renee.

His smile disappeared. "Okay, why don't we just get a move on then," he said, throwing the car into first and pulling them out of the parking lot.

30
A DARK WOOD

The forest's gloom deepened, making the trail more difficult to follow the further the boys travelled into the dark heart of the wood. The thick leafy canopy kept out nearly all sunlight, so the woods were cold, dank and dreary. Ferns cast long shadows everywhere, and the mosses on the ground squished with freezing water. Soon Fred's socks were soaked completely through.

The fellowship had formed a line, with Fred in the lead and Jimmy pulling up the rear. They stepped carefully on the sodden black leaf-litter, constantly pushing aside overgrown shrubs and vines from their path. The brief cheerfulness they had felt after escaping the ostriches seemed to be draining from the group with every passing minute.

"I don't think I could imagine a more depressing place," Stan said after stepping into a deep puddle. He tried to shake the slop from his shoe but it stuck. "This mud stinks worse than Nazgul poop, too."

"Well, it's not like I like it either," Fred said defensively. "But what else could we have done?"

"Relax, man—I'm not saying it's your fault," Stan replied. "I'm just saying that I'd rather spend a night in a real tauntaun's belly than camp here. I bet there are Imperial prisons more heartwarming than this place."

Fred and Stan both seemed to realize that Stan had said the word "prisons" at the same time. Stan's eyes dropped, and he started chewing his lip nervously. The mention of the word made Fred choke back his next comment, which, once he had a chance to think it through, was going to be a lot meaner than it really needed to be. *Why am I getting so angry for no reason*? he thought. Fred was beginning to realize that the glum surroundings were to blame. He also knew that the dreary woods would keep turning them against each other unless he did something to stop it.

"You're right," he said to Stan. "This place is worse than the Doldrums, so we need to think of something to cheer us up, or else we'll be stuck here forever."

"Like what?" Jimmy asked.

"I don't know," Fred said. "Anything. But we have to be creative. That's the only way out of the Doldrums. Anybody know any jokes?" he asked.

"I've got a good idea," said Stan. "Why doesn't everyone try to come up with a really bad joke."

"What do you mean?" Gemma asked. "Like a dirty joke?"

"No, no," said Stan. "Just like a dad joke."

"I guess that's a little better," said Gemma, "though my dad hasn't told a single joke his entire life."

"Oh, sorry," said Stan. "Maybe it was a bad idea."

Fred could feel the energy ebbing even more from his friends. "I think it's a great idea," he said. "And it just might keep us away from each other's throats. Although I have a strange feeling Stan is cheating and already has a good 'bad' joke lined up."

"Maybe," Stan said with a grin. "I haven't tried it out yet."

"Well, don't keep us in suspense, man," said Alfred.

"Okay, knock, knock," said Stan.

"Who's there?" said Fred.

"Merry dol! Derry dol!" Stan replied.

Fred sighed. "Merry dol derry dol who?"

"Tom bom, jolly Tom, Tom Bombadilloo," Stan said as he did a little jig.

"Archimedes' beak, that's one bad joke," Alfred said with a chuckle.

"Yeah, pretty terrible," Stan agreed, smiling. "Which is a good thing in this game, remember? Anyone else have one?" he asked.

"Okay, okay, I think I've got one," Gemma said after a few seconds. "What do a ninety-five-year-old Shrek and the garbage masher on the Death Star have in common?"

Fred and Stan both considered themselves serious authorities when it came to *Star Wars* trivia, but even they were perplexed by Gemma's riddle. "I don't know, what?" they all asked together.

"A dianoga," said Gemma. No one laughed. "Get it? A dying oger. A dianoga."

"Yeah, we get it," they said, laughing a little as they shook their heads. "That's pretty bad, too."

"I don't know which one is worse," said Fred.

"Yeah, well, we don't have all the entries now do we, so let's not get ahead of ourselves," said Stan. "Let's hear yours, Fred."

"I'm still thinking," said Fred. "Jimmy, you go."

"Yeah, let's hear yours, Deadeye," said Gemma. "Bet you can't beat a dianoga joke."

"You might be right," said Jimmy, smiling. "I might have too much self-respect to come up with a joke as bad as those."

"Just give it a try," said Stan.

Jimmy shrugged. "Okay, here goes. Why didn't the Backstreet Boy cross the road?"

Stan rolled his entire head and groaned.

"Oh, c'mon," said Jimmy.

"I don't know, why?" Fred asked, although like everybody else he thought he could guess the punch line.

"Because he didn't have any GUTS!" Jimmy said, grabbing his belly.

Stan groaned again and everyone laughed weakly.

"My dad tells that horrible joke every year on Halloween, except with a skeleton," said Fred.

Jimmy shrugged. "Like I said, Michelangelo, I ain't."

"Well, it was still pretty bad, Jim," Fred told him with a laugh. "If that's any comfort."

"It was a better slam than it was a joke," Stan said. "Time's up, Fred. Let's hear it."

"Alright," said Fred. "Knock knock."

"Who's there?" said Stan.

"You know," said Fred.

"You know who," said Stan.

"That's right you filthy mudblood, *Avada Kedavra!*" Fred pointed an invisible wand at Stan, who played like he'd been cursed and fell over into the leaf litter.

"That one is actually kind of good," said Gemma as she and Jimmy pulled Stan to his feet.

"I can't tell if it's so good, it's bad, or if it's so bad, it's good," said Jimmy.

Gemma laughed. "You know what would really get me in the doldrums?" she asked.

"What?" said Jimmy.

"If my beloved J.K. Rowling ever did anything to tarnish the legacy of that series," said Gemma.

Jimmy scoffed. "Don't be ridiculous," he said. "I can *guarantee* that will never happen."

"Yeah," said Gemma. "I don't know what I was thinking."

"It's just the woods," said Jimmy, patting her on the back. "Pay no heed."

Fred was extremely satisfied with himself for having helped Jimmy and Gemma to get along. He was hoping they'd continue chatting, but Stan wasn't finished with the game. He turned to the oldest member of the fellowship.

"Alright, Alfred," he said. "You're the last to go. Give us your joke."

"Let's see here," said Alfred, tapping his finger against his chin. "No, that one's too good. Hmm, and that one's not bad enough. I could do that one, but no, that's for a slightly more advanced crowd. Yes, yes, that's the yeoman's yoke! Here it is, boys. How do Welsh longbowmen eat their cheese?"

Gemma and the boys looked at each other in confusion.

"I feel like I should know this," Jimmy said, adjusting his own bow.

"I don't know, how?" they asked together.

"Caerphilly," said Alfred, grinning from ear to ear.

Gemma and the boys were stunned silent by the horrible pun. Fred was so confused he wasn't even sure that the joke made sense enough to be considered a good 'bad' joke.

"Carefully, Caerphilly," Alfred said the words slowly.

"It's a pun. Caerphilly is a type of Welsh cheese...." He looked away and whistled uncomfortably. To his relief, everyone finally broke into wild laughter, stopping in their tracks to slap their knees.

"Okay, whoa, Alfred wins by a landslide," Stan said between convulsions of laughter. "I don't think that joke was ever funny, even when you first heard it a century ago. Or is that what you guys talk about over at Eisen Gardens when pinochle gets cancelled?"

"I prevailed in the contest, did I not?" Alfred asked, but the boys just kept laughing.

For a moment Fred forgot that they were wandering through a strange and scary forest, and, judging by the laughter, it looked like his friends had, too. *How about that —being creative really is a great way to get out of the Doldrums,* he thought. He spent the next few minutes trying to come up with another joke, but the forest was so overgrown, he had to pay too much attention to where he was going and quickly gave it up. Within minutes the group's laughter had faded again into silence.

The sun was dropping, and the chill of the forest had turned bitter cold. Fred and Stan pulled their cloaks more tightly about them, and Jimmy searched in his bag for the matching jacket to his track-suit pants.

"I guess we should start looking for a place to camp," suggested Fred. "It looks like it's going to be a cold night, so keep your eyes peeled for something that might keep the chill out."

"What about a fire tonight, Fred?" Stan asked.

"I don't know," said Fred. "I want to, but I think it's too risky. I'm not about to put everyone in harm's way again. We can go two of us to a sleeping bag to conserve heat. It'll be snug, but better than going cold."

"Great," said Gemma. "Another night in the methane missile."

"Yeah, what are we going to do when Alfred starts baking stink pies in his Dutch oven," said Stan.

"Hope they're any flavor but chocolate, I suppose," said Fred.

"What the purple pimpernel are you talking about?" exclaimed Alfred. "An oven would be much too heavy to carry, and if I had one, I don't know why you'd think it would be Dutch over any other." He was shaking his head. "Boys today, sometimes I just don't know."

The younger members of the fellowship were all laughing, but Fred was surprised to find that Alfred looked like he was actually really upset. He looked as glum as he had those first few months after Fred's grandmother had passed, and with every passing minute he seemed to be getting sadder and sadder. The dark wood seemed to be affecting him more than anyone else. The old magician slowly fell to the back of the line and even started muttering to himself.

When he dropped behind Jimmy, the archer ran forward to tell Fred. "Something's up with Alfred," he said. "I think you should go talk with him."

"I was worried about that," said Fred. "Okay, you take the lead. Alfred and I will bring up the rear."

Fred hustled back down the trail. Alfred had wandered off the path completely and was now just staring aimlessly up at the sky. Fred had to grab his arm and redirect him back on course. "Grandpa, what's wrong?" he asked.

"Oh, it's nothing, my boy," said Alfred. "Nothing. I just got to thinking about your grandmother is all. She loved her walks in the woods, you know."

Fred didn't know what to say. Tears were welling in

Alfred's eyes, and Fred's own throat clenched in sadness. He had been hoping that all the excitement and adventure would help Alfred find happiness again, but he was beginning to realize that some things were a little harder to get over. He couldn't even begin to understand how much it hurt his grandfather to lose someone he'd been married to for over forty years.

Alfred must have recognized Fred's discomfort because he broke the brief silence. "I know it's the last thing a grandson wants to hear from his grandfather," he said. "But she was...well she meant more to me than anything." Alfred wiped away tears. "I'm sorry for being such a grump on your great adventure."

"You don't have to apologize," said Fred, patting Alfred on the back.

"I just feel so tired all of a sudden," Alfred said, his shoulders slumping. "So tired. I don't know if I can go on. I'm afraid I'll only slow you down."

Fred looked around; he was starting to realize what was going on. H*ow could he have been so stupid?* They weren't in the Fire Swamp or the Doldrums any more. They had wandered into the Swamps of Sadness! If he didn't lift Alfred's spirits right away, he might lose him in a quagmire just like Atreyu lost Artax. "You've got to buck up, Grandpa," said Fred. "I know it seems bad now, but all quests get tough at some point, don't they?"

"I'm not sure, I—" started Alfred.

Fred cut him off. "The way I see it you've got two choices—keep marching on or go home," said Fred. "And the second option just seems kind of boring to me. I mean, you could be back in Eisen Gardens gobbling gruel, remember?"

Alfred issued a light chuckle.

"Besides," said Fred. "We *need* you if we're going to see this thing through. We never would have made it this far without you, and we won't make it to Mount Doom if you quit. You can't stop now."

"I don't know, Fred," said Alfred. "I thought this whole thing might be the best way to honor your grandmother, but I wonder, well I wonder if anyone will even notice. It's just one more thing you know, and then on to the next one. If you knew what I'd been through in that awful place, you might see how blind and stubborn people can be. They're so set in their ways, Freddy. So willing to be dishonest. It just makes me feel so foolish to think we could ever change...anything."

"You can't talk like that, Grandpa," said Fred. "Not now, not after all we've done. We're not doing this for the people who will never change. We're doing this for everybody else, and I think that's more people than we've been led to believe. The Dark Lord wants us to think we have no hope, that he has already turned everyone to the Dark Side, that things are too far gone, that nothing else is possible. But there are good people out there who need our help. We can't let them down. What would Grandma think if we did nothing to help?"

Alfred was silent for a moment, deep in thought, and Fred was worried that he'd lost his grandfather for good. It looked like the quest was going to end right there, but just then the tiniest bird Fred had ever seen shot through the grove, hovering for a moment above a gnarled bough.

"Look, look," said Alfred excitedly, pointing to it.

"What is it, Grandpa?" asked Fred. "Is it a fairy?"

"No, no my boy, but close—it's a Calliope Hummingbird. It's the smallest bird in North America and your grandmother's favorite. She always wanted to see one, and she never did."

The hummingbird seemed to regard them for a moment, then it buzzed away as quickly as it had come, following the trail south out of the forest.

"It's a sign from her, Grandpa," said Fred. "She wants us to keep going. There's so much more to see, so much more to do. She's showing us the way."

Alfred smiled through his tears. "Well, of course she is!" he said finally, some of the glow returning to his face. "Do you think Vera would just stand by while we had all the fun? That's just not her style."

Fred smiled. Alfred was back.

"She's probably just dropping by to tell me I should be looking after you and not the other way around!" added Alfred.

"I think she'd be proud of you for that performance you put on back at the carnival," said Fred.

"Do you really think so?" Alfred asked.

"Definitely," said Fred.

"I think you might be right," said Alfred, smiling. "And she would have loved that bit with the thieves—especially the part with the rapids."

"That's the spirit, Grandpa," said Fred. "And don't forget, my dad still needs us. Somewhere deep inside I know he still loves my mom as much as you love Grandma, and you know more than anything how precious that is. We can't let Joanne and Leo ruin it."

"You truly are a noble squire, Fred, and a brave boy," said Alfred. "You've got the best of your father in you." Alfred clicked his heels together and straightened his back. "You can count on me."

"Good," said Fred. "And we can talk more about this later. Oh, and when you're ready, the boys and I have someone we'd like you to meet."

"You don't say?" said Alfred, his eyes twinkling. Fred gave him a wink.

Alfred stepped back in line, and the group resumed hiking through the woods. Just before sundown they chose their campsite for the night. Several elderly oak trees had grown up together, and their bases had fused into one large semicircle at least three hobbit-lengths high and six across. Part of the trunk had been eaten away or destroyed and now formed a small alcove within the hollow of the trees large enough to fit everyone.

Fred helped Jimmy to lay out the bags while Stan and Gemma set out dinner. As they worked, Jimmy started whistling a song Fred did not recognize. He liked the tune, so he asked Jimmy for the name of the song.

"That's 'Ramble On' by Led Zeppelin, man," Jimmy told him. "I can't believe you haven't heard it. It's a classic, and it's all about *Lord of the Rings*. It goes, 'And in the darkest depths of Mordor, I met a girl so fair, but Gollum and the evil one, crept up and slipped away with herer! Herer! Yeah!'"

"Those are the actual words?" Fred asked excitedly.

"Yeah," Jimmy replied. "Led Zeppelin had all kinds of Tolkien references in their songs. 'Misty Mountain Hop,' 'Over the Hills and Far Away,' 'The Battle for Evermore,' and 'Stairway to Heaven' all allude to the books in some way."

"That's so cool," Fred said. "I've never listened to them. Do you have their music, because I'd really like to hea—" he started, but was interrupted by Stan, who appeared in the opening of the hollow, looking frightened.

"Fred, we've got a problem," he said.

"What, are we already out of corndogs?" Fred asked.

"No," Stan said and stepped aside.

A larger figure filled the face of the hollow. Fred dropped the sleeping bag in total shock.

It was an elf.

31
WHERE THE RUBBER MEETS THE ROAD

Lucy didn't remember falling asleep. But she must have been fairly deep in sleep because it took a rough patch of highway to jostle her awake. She was embarrassed to find drool on her sleeve. To hide it from Renee and Sheriff Marshal, she pretended to be bending over to look for something in her bag.

Her ruse didn't seem to work because the sheriff said, "Well, rise and shine, Frankenstein."

Before she could answer, Renee yawned hugely and stretched her arms. "That's how you talk to a woman?" she said. "You call her a monster as soon as she wakes up? No wonder you're single."

The sheriff's smile disappeared. "Well, that's not, I didn't mean," he stammered. "You both look...fine...real fine...if you don't mind me saying. It's just a funny rhyme. Funny because no one looks their best...not that you don't look your best...it's just that sleeping...well, at least for me, I look a little rough when I wake...but that's just me."

Lucy decided to spare him his slow death. "He's the doctor," she said.

"No, he's the fool that woke me up just to insult me," said Renee.

"No, Frankenstein is the doctor that creates the monster," said Lucy. "The monster is just called the monster—the fiend."

"There you go," said the sheriff. "Not really an insult after all when you think about it." He smiled at Renee.

"Oh, good lord," said Renee. "My psychic warned me, but I didn't believe him," she said. "He said trials are coming, Renee, trials to test you like no other."

Lucy yawned. "Please tell me you don't really waste your money on that nonsense," she said.

Renee whipped around with a disgusted look on her face. "I don't know why I thought you'd say anything different," she said.

"My late wife used to spend all kinds of mon—" started the sheriff, but he changed his course midsentence when he felt Renee's gaze, "—I mean, time talking with one."

"Did she?" said Renee. "That just tells me you weren't listening. Poor woman. And look, I'm not saying there aren't a lot of bad psychics. I went to this one psychic, and she was just awful. My friend loved this lady, so I went to her and I must have looked at her wrong or something because she hated me instantly. She told me I was going to have a heart attack, so I told her she was cross-eyed and never went back."

The sheriff rocked back in his chair in laughter.

"I guess I must have looked in the wrong eye," said Renee, and the sheriff laughed even harder. "But that can happen. She didn't like me for some reason, so she gave me bad readings. What I'm saying is you need to have a connection with somebody. I suppose that's the whole point, really. The guy I have now he prays with me before a reading and calls me out for being too anxious or too eager, and it works, I'm telling you."

"Okay," said Lucy, dismissively.

"There they are," said the sheriff before Renee could respond. He pointed to a bunch of cruiser lights blinking and spinning in the road ahead.

The sheriff pulled off the road and parked his cruiser in front of an elephant carriage, nearly pinning his nose to the window trying to get a better look. Lucy hadn't come along for the petting zoo, so she was out of the car in a flash. Because there was a crowd of deputies around them, she strode straight for the Kassirbann brothers, Renee hot on her tail. Finally realizing that the two women were well ahead of him, Sheriff Marshal rumbled out of the patrol car and hastened after.

Though he was still a few feet behind, he shouted out so that he could be the first to make introductions to the Kassirbann brothers. "Hi there, I'm Sheriff Marshal!" he said, pushing past Lucy and Renee and shaking Art's hand first and then Julian's. "Sorry to disrupt your traveling troupe here. Looks like you guys have a mighty fine carnival. Afternoon, boys," he said to the other officers, who just muttered and sniggered in reply.

"Thank you," Julian responded. "And we're happy to do whatever we can to help. But I hope you understand that we do have scheduled shows, and if we miss them, we don't get paid."

"Of course, of course, we'll get you on your way in no time," said the sheriff. "But we've got some big-time thieves on the loose, and we'd like to catch them as soon as possible."

"Well," said Art, "like I told the deputy, we never saw

the three men you described, so I don't know how much more help we can be."

"But what about the kids?" Lucy asked.

"Pardon?" Art asked, confused.

"The missing boys," Lucy continued, "surely the deputies have asked you if you've seen the missing boys?"

"You got some new detectives, sheriff?" said one of the deputies. The other officers laughed.

"Where are my manners today?" said the sheriff. "Anybody seen them?" He made a show of looking around his feet and checking his pockets. "Pardon me a thousand times. Officers, misters Kassirbann, allow me to introduce Lucy and Renee, the mothers of the two boys missing from Oregon."

"I guess one Deputy Dyke wasn't enough for you?" said another deputy.

"Excuse me?" Lucy and Renee said in unison, but Sheriff Marshal stepped between them and the other officers.

"Go," he said, pointing to their cruisers. They shuffled their feet and one deputy puffed his chest out at Sheriff Marshal. "Boy, you're lucky I don't have the time," said the sheriff. "Get on. Now."

"Jesus, it's a joke," said the deputy, backing away. "Just like your whole department."

Sheriff Marshal just stared back at him with stone cold eyes.

"He don't mean nothing by it," said one of the other officers wrestling him away. "He's just tired."

"Well, I guess that's when it gets real doesn't it," said the sheriff.

"You ain't never lied," added Renee.

Once the other officers had finally pulled away in their cruisers, the sheriff turned back to Lucy, Renee, and the

Kassirbann brothers and said, "I'd love to apologize at length for that inexcusable behavior, but we've got bigger flames to fence, so to speak."

"I'm still a little lost," said Art Kassirbann. "Would someone please explain what's going on?"

Lucy wasn't going to wait for the police any longer. "My son ran away several days ago," she said. "He and his friends came down the river. The criminals the police are looking for were chasing them, but we think the boys got away and came to your carnival."

"I'm really sorry to hear that, ma'am," said Art Kassirbann, "but, like I told the deputies, a lot of people come to the carnival. Heck, even half of our employees are temporary and change from week to week as we move along. We pick up teenagers who need work to run the booths on the weekends. I probably couldn't identify half of them, let alone remember specific patrons. Asking us to remember three people, even three criminals, is like asking a three-legged mule to win the Kentucky Derby."

Sheriff Marshal laughed. "Three-legged mule, Kentucky Derby, I'll have to remember that," he said between fits of giggles. "Well, if that's the best you can—" he started to say, but Lucy cut him off.

"Mr. Kassirbann, I can appreciate how difficult a task this might seem," she said, "but these boys were dressed very strangely. They'd be in cloaks, and they'd have an older man with them. He'd be in his late sixties with long white hair."

Art and Julian shared a look of surprise that Lucy did not miss. "What is it?" she said.

"No, it couldn't be," said Julian, shaking his head. "The boys with Schmendrick looked eager to help him. There's no way they were there against their will."

"Are you saying you recognize that description?" Lucy asked. Sheriff Marshal shifted uncomfortably.

"Our house magician couldn't perform last night, so a magician named Schmendrick and his three young assistants put on one heck of a show," said Art. "They had the crowd rolling."

"An old magician and three strangely dressed assistants, that has to be them!" Lucy said.

"If you say so," said Renee.

"Schmendrick's not the right name, but they could have given fakes. Are they still here?" Lucy asked.

"No, ma'am," said Julian. "Schmendrick, or whatever his name is, said that they had a very urgent appointment elsewhere and that they had to leave first thing in the morning. He's not accused of kidnapping the boys, is he?"

"Uh, no, sir," the sheriff said, now just trying to be part of the conversation. "The elderly gentleman in question would be the one boy's grandfather."

"That's a relief," said Art, "because we really liked the performance."

"I'm glad someone feels relieved," said Renee. "Because it doesn't look like we're any closer to finding my son, and clearly the cops out here don't know fat meat's greasy. No offense," she added, gesturing in the sheriff's direction. The sheriff could only lift his hands, shake his head and mutter.

"Did they tell you where they were going?" said Lucy. "Or did they mention anything else important that you can remember?"

"No, I'm afraid not," Julian answered. "And we've actually had some of our people go missing, too. The main attraction in our family of acrobats and another employee, a guy named Oswald, didn't check in before departure this morning. Gemma Lee, the girl, has run away before, but not for several years now. I didn't think she'd ever do it again after what her father did to her the last time."

"You can be sure she's with my son," Lucy told him.

"Well, we can't know that for sure," interjected Sheriff Marshal. "We don't even know that it was your son Mr. Kassirbann remembers."

"It's them, sheriff," said Lucy.

"I do hope you find them, ma'am," said Julian. "But we've got a long way to travel still to our next show."

"Of course," said Sheriff Marshal. "Sorry to have kept you so long. If you come across those thieves you let my department—my direct department—know." He handed them his card.

Julian took the card and slipped it into his front pocket. "If you find them," he said to Lucy, "tell Schmendrick that we still want him to come back. Good luck."

"Yeah, thanks," said Lucy, but she wasn't really listening. She was already trying to figure Fred's next move. Without realizing it she had already started for the car.

"Looks like the sun's going down," said the sheriff, jogging to catch up. "Y'all want to head back, and I'll get you set up with a bed for the evening?"

Renee turned sharply on her heel. "You still haven't figured it out, have you?" she said. "We don't rest until we've got our boys back. And you should know why by now." She looked over to the group of cops loitering by their cars.

The sheriff followed her gaze and when he turned back, looked desperately at Lucy.

"She's right, sheriff," said Lucy. "You're taking us to that carnival site. And we'll see if we can't pick up their trail from there."

The sheriff looked off into the distance for a moment

and then threw up his hands again. "Okay then," he said. "But we'll be in the car for a little while, so if you need something to eat or drink, now would be the time."

"I'm fine," said Lucy.

"Well, I could do with a cup of coffee," he said as he pulled away from the caravan. "Without my coffee I'm no better than a porcupine without her petticoat."

"What on earth?" said Renee.

"Sorry, I meant I'm no better than a princess without her pricks," said the sheriff. He shook his head. "Wait a second now, I've got it wrong again."

Renee laughed. "What day were you born?" she said.

"First of December," said the sheriff warily.

"Sagittarius," said Renee. "I knew it."

"How's that?"

"Because you're a fire sign," she said.

"And?" he asked.

Renee sighed and shook her head. "And I get along with fire signs," she said.

"How 'bout that," said the sheriff, beaming as he pulled on to the highway.

32
THE PROTECTORS OF
THE WOOD

A tall, slim male elf with fair skin and long blonde hair held back in a tie-dyed bandana was staring back at Fred from the hollow of the tree. Fred looked to Jimmy out of the corner of his eye, hoping his neighbor might recognize his elven kindred, but Jimmy only shrugged, which made Fred more than a little anxious. Sure, they had an elf with them, but they had also trespassed upon sacred lands and brought a dwarf into hallowed wood. If the elf had been angered by this, Fred and his friends were in deep trouble.

The elf must have noticed Fred's nervousness, for he spoke first. "It's alright, little dude," he said, speaking in Common Language, although Fred detected more than a hint of the ancient elven accent on his tongue. "I didn't mean to crash your little hobbit party."

"It's okay," answered Fred, more than a little relieved.

"Shaka, brah," said the elf. "You know when, like, I first saw the camp I thought you guys were, like, totally working for Rychter, because he's been sending spies in here to spook us out from our tree house. But once I heard you singing Zep, man," the elf smiled hugely, "I knew right then and there that there was no way you guys were with that totally bogus buttmuncher." The elf laughed and shook his long hair back over his shoulder.

"You speak the truth," said Fred. "We know not of this Rychter, but it sounds like he is a servant of the Dark Lord."

"Whoa, gnar speech man," said the elf with another laugh.

Fred was delighted by the fact that he must have picked up some of the elvish tongue himself after travelling for so long with Jimmy. He fought to hide how proud he was of himself. Few mortals were smart enough to master elvish.

"And Rychter is, like, totally a servant of the Dark Lord!" the elf continued. "He and his heinous crew of barnwallers have been threatening to crush this forest for months, man. They want to build a bunch of condos or a Wally-Mart or whatever. And we're the only ones keeping him out!"

Fred had finally been convinced that the elf meant to help them, not harm them. Apparently, Jimmy's brethren had also been battling against the forces of Mordor for some time. "Well, those who care for all worthy things in peril, I call my friends and allies," Fred said, extending his hand. The elf looked a bit confused but slapped Fred's hand in greeting. Fred was ecstatic to have made such a legendary comrade. "I'm Fred," he introduced himself, "and this is Jimmy, one of your kindred from the North, it was his song you heard."

"Oh yeah!" exclaimed the elf. "Put her there, man!" He held his hand up high for Jimmy to slap. Jimmy had to jump a little, but he managed to slap the tall elf's hand. "I love that tune, brah," said the elf. "I'm a total Ledhead. I could rip it to 'Stairway' all day."

"Yeah, they're really great," Jimmy said. "I was just

telling Fred about them. He had never heard anything by them."

"Really?" asked the elf. "Say it ain't so, brah."

"Yes, sadly, I have not yet heard the songs of the Lindar," lamented Fred. "Though I dearly wish to do so."

"Hey, don't sweat it, my dude," said the elf, "You're just a little grommet, after all, so you got plenty of time. But def listen to Zep. Rock and roll for the soul, man." The elf extended his thumb and pinky and shook his wrist. "So, who are the rest of your broheims?"

Fred introduced Stan, Alfred, and, lastly, Gemma.

"Pleasure to meet you dudes and dudette," said the elf. "They call me 'Radical Hal,' but 'Hal' will do just fine. That's a killer ax, sis," he said to Gemma, who beamed back happily. "The kind we don't mind around here."

"Thanks," said Gemma.

"It is nice to meet you, too, Hal," said Fred. "Although I wish we could have met during happier times. We are beset by many foes already, and now it appears we must be watchful of this Rychter."

"Is he a most loathsome enemy?" asked Alfred.

"Totally loathsome," said Hal. "He's like one of the most heinous barneys I know, man. We have to keep a constant watch, or he'll chop the whole thing down. We even have to sleep up in the trees!"

"The legendary tree-keep of the elves!" Fred whispered excitedly under his breath to Stan.

"Yeah, well this guy smells more like a Wookiee if you ask me," Stan replied, wafting the air in front of his nose. "He probably can't wait to make us chase a couple angry katarns up a wroshyr tree."

Fred rolled his eyes—this was too deep a reference, even for nerds.

"It's fitting when you think about it," continued Stan. "You've basically dragged me along one large hrrtayyk ceremony as it is."

"Yeah, I keep hoping once you find your rrakktorr you'll stop complaining," said Fred.

"Geek touché to you, sir," said Stan, offering a short bow. "Rrakktorr...? Sounds Klingon, don't you think?"

"Now there's a fight I'd like to see," said Fred. "Worf vs. Chewie."

"Pff, no contest," said Stan. "Chewie's got at least a foot and a half plus a hundred pounds on Worf."

"Um, does the River of Blood mean anything to you, or how about undisputed champion of Klingon's biggest bat'leth tournament?"

"River of Blood—that's the Klingon name for the Devil's Lore if I'm not mistaken," said Stan. Fred playfully punched his shoulder. "Plus, I don't care how many painstiks the guy can take, Chewie would totally house him."

"I disagree," said Fred. "But this will have to wait. We've got an elf ambassador among us in case you didn't notice. And P.S., you don't exactly smell like a mallorn blossom yourself."

Stan sniffed his armpits and looked ready to retort, but Fred had already turned back to Hal, who was carrying on as if he was catching up with old friends. "I mean, don't get me wrong, I dig it here," said Radical Hal, "but I'd be rippin' it up out there in the wild blue if I had my choice. I've got a sick case of the roonies, bros—it's been, like, an eternity since I've felt the waves. But when Ariel says hop to, it's hard to say no. Plus, Lorne would turn me into shark bait if I didn't come along."

"Who's Ariel?" Jimmy asked excitedly.

"She's the crewmaster general of our whole lineup,

man," Hal answered. "She's the one who's had us out here dirt-baggin' it for so long."

"The Lady of the Wood," Jimmy said in a shocked whisper. "Never in my wildest dreams did I think mine eyes would ever behold her."

"Lady of the Wood?" Hal looked confused. "Yeah, I guess she is, more or less. She's always talking about saving the planet and whatever. I've eaten so much organic food it's like a flippin' miracle I haven't turned into a radish myself. Hey, you guys should come meet everybody. We're just getting ready to chow down, and I'm sure we got enough for the whole crew. I can't wait to see the look on Phinney and Miller's faces when they see I found some hobbits. They're gonna totally flip their wickets, man! Hey, you dudes should bring your bags, too, 'cause our campsite is way more chill."

Fred didn't need to ask any of his companions if they wanted to take Hal up on his offer, since it was obvious that everyone was excited to meet more elves. Jimmy was especially eager to go and kept asking Hal about Ariel as they packed up their belongings. Within a few minutes they had all filed in behind Hal, who led them through the forest. Hal's laugh was infectious, and the mood of the company instantly improved. He was as pleasant an elf as they could have met, and the boys spoke over each other trying to ask him questions.

Hal was in the middle of telling them a very funny surfing story when he suddenly grew quiet. The boys stared at him, wondering what was wrong. He slowly raised his arm and pointed across the glade. When Fred saw what the elf was pointing to, he gasped. To the west, a whole swath of the forest had been cleared away. Wood chips littered the ground and ugly tree stumps dotted the landscape.

"Great ghosts of Fern Gully," said Stan.

"They murdered Mirkwood!" said Fred.

"Yeah, and they don't intend to stop there," said Hal. "Rychter won't rest until this whole forest has been chopped to the ground."

"That's terrible!" said Fred. "We've got to stop him."

"Well, that's the goal, bro," said Hal, as he started across the ruined forest.

Fred picked his way carefully through the clearing, not wanting to step on any of the slaughtered trees. Fallen comrades deserved such respect, and he certainly didn't want any angry Ents coming after him for accidentally stomping on their slain cousins. When they finally reentered the trees on the other side of the clearing, Fred took a long look over his shoulder. He wanted to remember this scene, this massacre, this disaster of the Gladden Fields, when he confronted the orcs of Mordor. It would give him strength when he needed it most.

As they continued walking through the trees, Fred felt a transformation come over the forest. The dismal and frigid fern-groves gave way to warmer stands of birch and holly, and the sounds of birdsong replaced the eerie silence. The melancholy that had been gripping the boys slowly began to lift. Soon they could see the fires of the elven camp, and Hal led them into a grove ringed with silver maples, where a bonfire snapped. Around the fire sat three male elves, dressed in the same strange multi-colored tunic as Hal (Fred guessed it was a special magical fabric made from some immortal Lothlorien silkworm), stirring a small cauldron from which drifted a delicious smell. Fred had to forcibly call himself down. Never in his wildest dreams did he think he'd ever be invited into the Fortress of Trees.

"Hey, dudes, look what I found," Hal said to his friends. Fred and company followed him into the firelight.

The elf who had been stirring the stew stood up. He looked surprised and more than a touch nervous. "You were supposed to be keeping an eye out for Rychter's goons, Hal," he said. He looked over Fred and his companions suspiciously, who examined him warily in turn. The elf looked strong and dangerous. His features were sharper and more angular than Hal's, and he carried more weight on his frame than did any of the other elves. The two elves still sitting by the fire, who must have been Miller and Phinney, were laughing at the sight of Hal's new friends. Fred figured that, to the tree-dwellers, his companions must look as strangely dressed as the elves did to him.

"Chillness, Lornestar, chillness," said Hal. "I *was,* like, totally looking out for Rychter, that's how I came across these righteous minnows. But they're cool, brah, and they were just going to camp on their own, so I thought it would be safer for them to join us."

The big elf relaxed a little. "Well, I wouldn't want Rychter's men to find them on their own and think they were with us," he said. "Come on over and sit down, guys." Lorne pointed to some seats by the fire. "Sorry that we're a little jumpy, but there's no telling what that madman will do just so he can chop down this forest."

"We doubt it not," said Fred. "We have fought many servants of the Dark Lord as vile as Rychter on our journey. We are glad to find such brave allies still battling against our great enemy."

"My brave companion speaks the truth," said Jimmy. "Like you, we count ourselves stewards of all things that might grow fair or flower again in the days to come."

The two elves sitting across the fire fell over in a fit of

giggles. "Daggone, they talk almost as crazy as you do, Hal," joked Lorne.

"Lorne, be nice," said a silky sweet voice from behind them. Every one of Fred's companions snapped their heads around. Fred could scarcely believe his eyes. The most radiantly beautiful woman he had ever seen stepped into the firelight. She might as well have stepped out from the pages of a comic. The elf maiden's long, flowing hair glimmered like raven feathers. Set against glowing almond skin, her garnet eyes shone like bright cups of honey in the sunlight. They were shot through with notes of copper and flecks of deep green. She wore a long, airy gown and no jewelry except for a single flower with white petals above her left ear.

"Where's your sense of hospitality?" she said.

Once the initial stun wore off, Jimmy was the first to fall into an awkward bow, kneeling and placing his right fist over his heart. Fred, Stan and Alfred followed suit and knelt before her.

"Good grief," said Gemma, rolling her eyes.

Hal, Lorne and the two other elves chuckled at the boys. The elf queen's laughter was musical. She placed a delicate hand over her mouth to hide it.

"At least someone around here still has some manners," she said to Lorne with a smile. Turning to the boys she said, "And although I am flattered by such a grand display of chivalry, I assure you it is not necessary. It is pleasure enough to have such honorable guests."

"It looks like they're smitten, Ariel," Lorne said, but she silenced him with a look.

"It is we who are honored, Lady," Jimmy said rising from the ground. "And we do not mind such heavy speech, for we are on a great quest to preserve the land."

"Are you now?" Ariel said. "Then we will add courage to your list of virtues."

Jimmy's eyes lit up, and he fought hard to contain a smile.

"But I have not yet learned your names," she said.

Jimmy spoke first: "I am Jameson Fletcher Dingleman of the Northern Wood, and these are my companions and friends," he said. "Fred Oglesburg and Stan Weiss, two doughty hobbits. Alfred the Grand, a wizard of the highest order. And Gemma Lee, a most companionable dwarf...as far as dwarfs go."

Gemma moved to kick Jimmy in the shins, but Fred grabbed her arm and held her back.

Ariel laughed and gave a slight curtsy. Fred was slightly taken aback by the name Jameson—he had never heard Jimmy use his full name. Apparently, the Lady's beauty could make elves and men alike act strangely.

"We're delighted to meet you all," said Ariel. "We've just made a little dinner, so everybody relax and we'll bring it out."

Without hesitation, the boys did as she said. Fred sat down between Stan and Jimmy.

"I told you she was beyond the realm of earthly beauty," Jimmy whispered excitedly. "She makes the tips of my ears tingle with a strange feeling, and I feel almost as if I've been hit with a Petrificus jinx below my beltline."

"Easy, Jimmy," Gemma whispered. "Don't get your arrow in a knot."

Hal and the two other Elves had pulled out a box of cheap wine, and they were pouring large amounts of the liquid into several goblets.

"Is that *miruvor*, the cordial of imladris?" Fred asked excitedly.

Hal threw his friends a cheeky grin. "Of course, my hobbit-brah," he said. "You didn't think we'd drink the cheap stuff did you."

"I would very much like a taste if you can spare it," Fred said.

"Hey, be my guest," Hal said with a chuckle, standing up to fill Fred's glass.

"Hal, don't you dare," Ariel said as she reemerged from the tent with platters of food. Hal immediately halted his pour and downed the wine in one gulp.

"Sorry, dude, Queen's orders," he said.

Fred guessed that the cordial must be too strong, and that although it was invigorating to the larger elves, it would make him sick. No matter—he was more hungry than thirsty, anyway. He was practically drooling by the time Ariel handed each of them a dish with a salad mix and a plate covered in mixed fruit, and he had nearly cleaned both plates by the time Lorne ladled some vegetable stew into a bowl for him. The healthy meal was surprisingly good, but what Fred found even more surprising was that Stan didn't complain at all that Ariel was giving them only salad and fruit for dinner.

"Delicious," Stan said as he licked his plate clean.

"Well, will wonders never cease," Fred said through the corner of his mouth. Stan gave him a sheepish look.

"So, Hal has told us briefly about this evil orc-lord Rychter and how he befouls your fair streams with his metal forge-machines, but he said you would be able to tell the tale better, Ariel?" Jimmy asked the elf queen.

"Well, we certainly don't like what he's trying to do," Ariel replied, "but I try not to call anybody bad names."

"Yes, of course, my lady," said Jimmy. "My sincerest apologies. In every wood they sing of your benevolence."

"Uh...I'm not sure about that," she said with an embarrassed smile. "But I think we should all try to set a good example. And I want to believe that Rychter is not a bad man. I think we have to believe that. It's not the men. It's the system." She paused and looked up. "Do you boys like this place?" she asked.

"Oh, yes," they spoke over one another, trying to please her. "It's wondrously beautiful," they said in unison. You could not have pried the attention of the boys away from Ariel with a free trial for a real lightsaber or with a practice run on a Firebolt.

"Yeah, we think so, too," Ariel continued. "I can hardly bear it to think these ancestral lands might soon be destroyed."

"May we never witness the empty garden of Elrond," said Jimmy.

"Sadly, I don't think we'll get that lucky," said Ariel.

"The plight of your fair race moves me," Stan said, surprising Fred once more.

"Curse the slavish greed that whips these villains to such deeds," Jimmy spat.

Fred certainly felt the same anger as his friends, but he was surprised to find that, unlike his companions, he wasn't sure if he agreed with the elves' plan of action. He understood why the elves had come to the peaceful wooded glade, and he hated those minions of the Dark Lord who had ripped and gutted the land to fill their own coffers. Yet something told him that to defeat the Dark Lord, the elves needed to do something else—something more. His feelings must have been easy to read because Ariel asked him what he was thinking.

"Well, I don't know..." Fred started hesitantly, not wanting to say anything to upset the elves. "Let me first thank you for the food and fellowship. We've been travelling for some time, and hard miles at that, so this kindness means more than you know."

"You're most welcome, honey," responded Ariel, smoothing the hair on the top of his head. Fred blushed and gulped hard. "Go on," she said.

Fred had to recollect his thoughts. "Well, I understand why you love it here—it is much more beautiful than the gray havens from which you have traveled," he said. "And what you do, what you have done, staring the enemy in the face, shows a bravery possessed only by the best of us." Fred paused and watched his hosts closely. "But...I'm not sure it is the best way to defeat the Dark Lord and his horde."

"What else can we possibly do?" said Lorne, frustration in his voice.

"How long until Rychter and his masters bring their wormtongues and order you to move, or worse still, take you away and lock you up?" said Fred softly, keeping a watchful eye on his elvish hosts to make sure he hadn't angered them. "I'm just a humble hobbit, but I can see that the War of Wrath is upon us and that Beleriand may soon sink beneath the sea." He looked ruefully in the direction of the forest already destroyed. "We've lost so much already, and we could lose more still. All the Ents and their tree herds all over the world."

Alfred started sobbing and Ariel came over to comfort him. She sat down on the log beside him and held his hand. "What do you propose we do, Fred?" she asked quietly.

"Scattered, the elves are weakened," said Fred. "But together, you are strong beyond measure. You must resume the Great Journey and reunite with long lost kin, for we need the whole host of Valinor to win this battle. We need you to do everything you can to bring them together. To speak with one voice of many chords, so that all races see what threatens us. And so that they believe we are strong enough to stop it."

For a moment, nobody spoke. Fred figured they must be conversing telepathically because after a few seconds they all started smiling.

"These hobbits are wondrous creatures are they not?" Alfred the Grand said with a smile, patting Ariel's hand.

"Yes, indeed they are," Ariel agreed. "You make some good points, Fred, and... I think you're right."

Fred smiled. The other boys glared at him, their faces green with envy.

"As much as I hate to say goodbye to this specific place, because I have such fond memories of it," she threw a knowing look to Lorne, and the boys' jealousy was quickly redirected, "we can't do this alone. We need to rally the troops," she said, winking at Fred.

"You sure, babe?" Lorne asked.

"Yeah, I'm sure," she said. "People have been watching what we've been doing here, but no one else has come. We have to try something different. Let's just enjoy this one last night here. The stars are out, the birds are singing. In the morning we'll go back to the city, and we'll try to make people listen."

"Sounds good to me," said Lorne.

"You mean we'll be back rippin' the surf tomorrow?" Radical Hal asked.

"Yes, Hal," Ariel answered, "but only after we do everything we possibly can to make a difference. Because if we don't, I think I know one brave hobbit who will come looking for us." She smiled at Fred.

"Yes, ma'am," Hal said, saluting playfully. "From henceforth I will be known as 'Difference-maker' Hal, because making a difference is radical, too."

"More radical than dropping off a chopper into a bomb and hanging eleven into the soup?" said Phinny as Miller mimed surfing a big wave.

"You bet your best board," said Hal. Miller and Phinney threw their empty cups at Hal and everyone laughed.

As the evening wore on, Fred's company and their new friends enjoyed some pleasant conversation and more healthy food as they soaked up the warmth of the fire. Ariel said it was okay if Gemma played some songs on her "ax," and she delighted their hosts by playing tunes they knew by heart. They sang with her long into the night. Having drunk an entire case of "miruvor," they sang as loudly as they could and rocked arm in arm as she picked some cheerful songs. Hal, Miller, and Phinney clapped and cheered after each song, raising their goblets in grand toasts.

"Here's to dwarlfs and hobbitses and widzards and whi —" Hal hiccoughed drunkenly, "—hitches."

"And gryffindydunblydores and yoo—" Phinney burped loudly, "—neecorns."

"And girls with flowers in their hair," Miller finished and they all hooted with laughter and pointed at Ariel who smiled brightly and clapped her hands. Soon, the Elves began to grow drowsy from the miruvor, so Gemma strummed some mournful songs. The Elves' voices grew soft and sweet as they followed along. When she played "Going to California," Miller, Phinney, and Hal wept as they sang and then promptly passed out, snoring where they lay on the ground.

"It's a good thing there's not going to be any rain tonight," Lorne said as he grabbed some blankets and draped them over the sleeping Elves. "You guys are welcome to put your sleeping bags in their tent—they won't need it." Then he grabbed Ariel's hand and led her to the other tent, bidding Fred and his friends goodnight.

Grabbing their bags, the fellowship accepted Lorne's offer and spread out inside the other tent. Even though he knew that the forces of the Dark Lord would not leave the picturesque glade standing for long, Fred was able to enjoy the crisp night air and forest sounds.

Fred was glad that everyone fell asleep within minutes. He had pushed them hard, and they deserved a good rest. If possible, he had come to love them all so much more. They were the very best of friends, and he'd done nothing but drag them into great peril. Fred was suddenly overwhelmed with shame at his selfishness. He realized, too, that this was the last time he wouldn't be worried sick for his friends, for he was leading them into even greater danger. The thought that they might come to harm trying to help him burned worse than any wildfire ever could. He couldn't bear to see his friends suffer on his account any longer, and after dinner with the elves, Fred realized that the forest dwellers needed plenty of help, too. He was starting to think it would be safer if he left his companions to travel the rest of the way with their new friends instead. They'd have a better shot gathering allies if they worked together, especially if he was distracting the forces of Mordor.

It was settled, then. As soon as the elves fell asleep, Fred would set off alone.

33
RYCHTER ATTACKS

Fred slipped out of the tent well before sunrise. He left a little note to his friends explaining why he had to go the rest of the way on his own. He told them it was for their own safety and implored them to help the elves on their journey. He promised he would see them back in Bithbon or by the Waters of Awakening where the first elves were born. Either way, he would see them again.

His heart was heavy as he began his moonlit march through the woods without his friends. It was as if the diamond on the ring was a weight pulling his heart down into his stomach. He wanted to throw it away right then and there—cast it deep into the dark of the woods. But he couldn't. Someone might find it and wield it with evil purpose.

Unfortunately, there were still many hard miles left to go. He marched on into the darkness.

The sun had still not risen when he heard a first terrible woody crunch and the low-pitched groan of massive gears. He ducked behind a tree, searching all around him for the source of the noise, his tired eyes struggling to make sense of the shadowy figures milling all about the forest. A second later, bright lights flooded the area, and a deafening noise rumbled through the forest as many engines revved up at once.

Orcs! They were attacking the elves in the middle of the night. They truly had no honor. Fred had no choice but to race back to camp to warn them. His heart thumping furiously now, he sprinted back the way he had come, his shadow stretching out in front of him. The gnashing machines rumbled behind him, knocking down everything in their paths.

By the time he made it back to the campsite, Lorne and Ariel had already emerged from their tent.

"The orcs are coming now!" Fred yelled, and the elves sprang into action, rousing their companions.

"It's Rychter," Lorne called out, "the maniac is trying to cut down the forest now. We've got to get to the tree house!"

The scream of saw-blades was drawing ever closer. Fifty-foot-tall oaks and hickories were falling like dominoes.

"Fred, you've got to get everyone out of here," Ariel called out over the metallic roar. "It's too dangerous."

Fred agreed. A piece of splintering wood, or a chip of a sawblade could end the quest faster than you could say Lond Daer Enedh. "Orcs!" he cried out into his friend's tent. "Everybody up, we've got to move now!"

Stan, Jimmy, Gemma and Alfred scrambled out of the tent, lugging their bags behind them. Stan shoved on his shoes without tying the laces. After all their hiking, only one tattered shred of hobbit hair was still clinging to the heel. Fred snatched up another bag from the ground and threw a sad wave to Ariel, Lorne and the other three elves, who were still struggling to rise. "Thanks," he said, "and goodbye for now. Fight well."

"Later, dudes," Hal groaned painfully, grabbing his head as he followed Lorne towards the lights. Ariel returned Fred's wave with a sad smile, and then she too hurried to their makeshift tree house.

"We must stay and help the Lady!" cried Jimmy, starting after her.

"This is not our battle," Fred yelled, grabbing his arm. "As much as I hate to leave our elven friends to fight alone, we must think of the quest first."

"You got no chance, Jim," Stan added, "so let's get moving before we get mulched." He winced as another enormous tree came crashing down.

Jimmy looked like he might fight them for a second, but then he gritted his teeth and let his shoulders drop. "I do not like to leave the Lady," he said. "It is like a black orc's arrow has pierced my heart, which I would gladly suffer for her honor. But I know we must go."

Fred put his hand on Jimmy's shoulder. "She'll be alright, 'Deadeye,'" he said. "She has power still that we know not of." Jimmy nodded but was too choked up to say anything. "Let's get a move on, then," Fred added. "Or else those orcs will be having us for elevensies."

The five of them stole through the forest, away from the lights of Rychter's forge-machines, regretfully leaving Ariel and the other elves to fight alone. They ran full out until they could no longer hear the screams of dying trees. After a while, Jimmy fell slightly behind. When Fred glanced back, he thought he saw tears dripping down his neighbor's cheeks, but he couldn't be sure.

Dawn broke within the hour, and they marched on

through the brightening forest. It was nearing noon when the trees finally thinned, and the fellowship left the forest for a dry shrub land. The grass was sparse and brown, and the dirt was cracked and covered in pebbles. Soon the greens of the grasslands and forests were gone completely. In some places the ground was blackened and burnt, where the great fire had just swept across the plains, scorching everything in its path. A dirty, wet heat blanketed everything, and soot drifted through the air, making the boys burst into fits of coughing every few minutes. A thick smog floated just beneath a sky completely grey with clouds—a cement-colored haze that choked Fred's lungs. The sun was nowhere to be found.

Mordor was close.

He reminded everyone to be extra cautious, for they were now nearer to the seat of evil than any force of good had ever been.

As they continued on, the land grew more yellow and cracked. The fires of Mordor had burned the world and built on its ashes giant gray roads that crisscrossed the area like stiches. The metal caravans of the enemy roared by in droves, carrying whatever wicked things the Dark Lord had planned for them.

The company's pace slowed to a crawl. More and more roads appeared, and soon Fred was struggling to pick a route for them that would avoid the sentries of Mordor. Searching for cover, he led them underneath the crumbling columns of an old overpass, which he thought may have once belonged to a hall of kings long since gone. They followed the columns for a short while, the ground rumbling on all sides of them as the fires of Mount Doom burned beneath. As they emerged from under the concrete, a sudden gust of wind swirled the dark mists of the sky and huge spires appeared in the distance.

"Holy Thangorodrim," said Fred, pointing to the horizon. "The black towers of Mordor rise up through the ash and smog of Gorgoroth."

"Wretched hive," Jimmy spat.

Overhead an airplane flew low, roaring loudly as its massive engines flared.

"Take cover," Jimmy said. "The Fell Beast carries its Rider towards the fiery peaks of Mordor. We cannot be seen."

The boys ducked and swirled their capes over themselves, waiting with breath held while the Fell Beast flew overhead. Once the wraith steed had flown away, the boys emerged.

"We will require a bit of magic if we are to get any further into the land of the Dark Lord undetected," said Alfred. "I know a very ancient and complex spell which will mask us from the eyes of the enemy. We will appear like orcs, but only to those who serve the great evil. We will still appear ourselves to friends and allies."

"I cannot ask you to risk it," said Fred. "Your magic could bring the whole host of Mordor upon us."

Fred looked gravely into the distance, to the dark towers of Mordor, sharp as dragon fangs. The orc ambush had disrupted his plans to set out on his own, but he knew he had to do so now. It was just too dangerous. "You have all proven most valiant," he said, "and I could never have made it this far without you. But I'm afraid I must finish this last leg of the journey on my own. One hobbit alone can better travel unseen."

"Is that why you were already dressed this morning?"

Stan said. "Is that why you left this?" He held up the note. "Planning on leaving us behind?"

"That's not how it—" Fred started.

"Well, forget it." Stan cut him off. "If I've come this far, I'm sure as heck going to be there when you get rid of that doggone ring. That's the only way I'll know for sure we can get back to life as usual."

"It is a noble gesture, Fred," added Jimmy. "But you think too little of us. The Dark Lord is powerful, sure, but there are no powers he possesses that we cannot oppose. We will see this to the end. Together."

Fred's lip was quivering. "Gemma?" he asked.

"Hey, I haven't shown you what this ax can do yet," she said with a smile.

"Grandpa?" Fred asked.

"This is just getting interesting, my boy," said his grandfather with a smile. "It'd be a shame to turn back now."

Fred was touched beyond measure by the loyalty and courage of his friends. He had to look away to wipe his tears. He still didn't like putting his friends in danger, but now he knew that with their powers combined, they would succeed.

"Then do your magic quickly, Grandpa," said Fred, "before the whole host of Mordor is upon us."

Alfred raised his wand and once again muttered an incantation in a language that Fred did not understand. As his grandfather spoke, Fred closed his eyes and waited for the magic to change him. A slight breeze washed over him and chill bumps rose on his skin. He figured this was the magic taking effect. When Alfred finished with his spell, Fred opened his eyes. He wasn't sure what he was expecting, but his friends looked just the same. At first, he thought something had gone wrong, then he remembered what Alfred had said—they would be disguised to the enemy, but not to each other. Jimmy and Gemma were looking at their arms in wonderment.

"Who needs an invisibility cloak?" said Gemma. "Not us —that's who."

"Good work, Alfred," said Fred.

"Elementary, my dear boy," said Alfred.

Now that they were invisible, Fred got them moving quicker. It only took them a few more minutes to get to the edge of the city. Climbing over a short concrete wall and dropping onto the sidewalk, Fred quickly took a look around. The streets were swarming with orcs of all shapes and sizes. They were wearing rags stolen from their human victims. Such bizarre clothes made them both horrifying and humorous.

Fred approached the first group of orcs very slowly at first, wanting to make absolutely sure Alfred's spell had worked. Much to his relief, the passing orcs did not attack them or call out the alarm. The sentries threw them a confused look, laughed a little, and then continued on their rounds. Not wanting to draw any more attention to the fellowship, Fred did not risk a look over his shoulder, but proceeded along at the same easy pace.

The enemy territory only got messier the longer the group marched. The orc's wretched den was covered in refuse—the remains of their meals strewn along the sidewalks. There were dark puddles of oil and tar everywhere. Styrofoam cups skittered through the gutters, and food wrappings blew about in the wind. The stench was so foul, Fred drew his cloak across his mouth to block it. "This place smells worse than one of Stan's chilidog farts," he said.

"And that's saying something," agreed Stan.

"Foul orcs," said Alfred, "who defile their own lair and live in filth."

"I will be glad to be rid of this place," Jimmy said as he backed away from several goblins in Spongebob Squarepants tank-tops.

"We have wandered deep into the stronghold of the enemy," Fred said, gripping the ring. "I feel the weight of the ring grow heavier than ever before."

"I hope we find the mountain of fire quickly," said Jimmy.

The words were hardly out of his mouth when all five members of the company froze in their tracks.

"No way, it can't be..." Stan said as he and the others looked upon the strangest and most frightening sight they had ever seen.

Written on the side of a huge brick building, blazing like the single eye of Sauron, were giant neon letters spelling M-O-R-D-O-R.

"The Dark Lord taunts us," Jimmy spat.

"He is over-confident," said Fred. "He did not think we would make it this far. But his arrogance will be his undoing."

"Still, his bastion is formidable," chimed in Alfred. "That outer wall spans many score of acres, and the inner chambers will be brimming with those most loyal to the Dark Lord. And that is an abhorrent lot, I can assure you. This is a most dangerous final leg, friends, for we will be tempted by the Dark Lord's spell at every turn."

"You counsel wisely," said Fred, "but no matter how impregnable his fortress or how impossible the quest, I must see it done. And if my courage fails, I will need my brave companions to pick me up and help me to the edge of Mount Doom."

"We'll be there all the way," Stan said, and the other members of the fellowship nodded as well.

"Then what are we waiting for?" Fred asked. He turned on his heel and marched through the squads of orcs towards the black gates of Mordor.

34
THE WISDOM OF SOLOMON

Solomon Oglesburg felt like a man shot from a cannon. He had started before dawn again and each meeting had rolled into the next without any chance to brake or breathe, and now his assistant was handing him lunch as if passing a baton in a relay because he had yet another meeting to go to.

The meeting was nothing groundbreaking—Leo's company was taking over several corporations in southern California, and Solomon was facilitating the legal aspects of the exchange—but Solomon was suddenly, gravely, aware of how frenetic his life had become, and he was dreading every second of the walk to the conference room.

He was so unsettled, he couldn't even bring himself to snatch a bite of his lunch before he burst into the conference room, where Leo, John Bonneville, and three senior members of the board of trustees for Richmond Industries sat in leather chairs in front of a long, gleaming table. Across from them sat several depressed-looking businessmen.

"Ah, Solomon, finally," Leo said as he leaned back in his

chair and smoothed his sky-blue tie between two huge fingers. His broad chest tested the buttons of his silk shirt, and he sat with his arms resting on his belly. "Please hurry, I'd like to get this over with quickly," he said.

The men on the other side of the table shifted uncomfortably in their seats.

"Of course," Solomon said as he placed his briefcase on the table and popped it open, reaching inside for the documents. "Um, as you all know, we are here to negotiate the matter of a property transfer from the holdings of Goldacker and Silverwell Incorporated, worth sums estimated to exceed fifty million dollars, to the ownership of Richmond Industries. As a matter of record, I will read the properties in question."

Solomon's voice sounded to him like it belonged to someone else as he began reading the list of properties. "Arthur's Alehouse on Astin Avenue. Bed, Bench and Bannister on Bloom Boulevard. Dennie's Dairy on Davies Drive. Mordor Wholesale Clothing and Manufacturing Center in McKellan Mall Commons. Wild World of Waterports on West Woodwar—" he stopped midsentence, too stunned to speak. The name of the second to last store had just registered in his brain. He scanned the page again with his finger, thinking his eyes were playing a trick on him. But there it was in black ink: "Mordor Wholesale Clothing."

"Mordor," he whispered to himself. "Sonuva—" he started. "Where is McKellan Mall Commons? What city?" he shouted at the men sitting across from Leo and John Bonneville.

"Alhambra," one of the men answered. "Just outside of L.A. Why? Is there something else you'd like to steal from us?"

"No, I..." Solomon's head was spinning. His whole world

was in disarray, but he was starting to realize why. He knew where Fred was going, and something deep inside him knew that he would do anything to meet his son there and bring him home. "I'm sorry everyone, but I have to go. My son is missing, and I think I know where to find him."

"Solomon!" Leo shouted, falling forward clumsily in his seat. "What are you doing? There are authorities who can take care of your son. Let's just finish the meeting."

Solomon did not even slow as he continued towards the door.

Leo threw his considerable bulk up out of his seat. "Solomon, if you take one more step you're fired!" he roared.

Solomon called over his shoulder. "I'm going after my son, Leo. You should do the same for your daughter."

Leo fumed, stuttering unintelligibly, his jowls turning red. The great vein that ran down the middle of his bald head started to swell.

"Wait! Mr. Oglesburg," said the oldest of the three members of Goldacker and Silverwell, who had followed him out the door.

"I don't have time!" Solomon said, moving down the hallway. "I'm leaving immediately for Alhambra."

"It looks like you're in need of a job, and I'd like to hire you to represent us," the man offered. "Or rather to represent me," he corrected himself.

"Beside the conflict of interest, I think I'm retiring from corporate law," said Solomon as he pushed the button for the elevator.

"That's why I want to hire you," said the man. "Being on the other end of one of these takeovers has made me lose my taste for it as well. I don't want you to defend me against Leo. I'd like to get my company back from those

vultures in there, so I can do something good with it. Why
don't you borrow the company helicopter," he offered. "I'll
be selling it as soon as I can, so you might as well get some
use out of it. It sounds like you need to get to L.A. in a hurry.
It's parked on the roof. Just tell the pilot you're my new
lawyer. My name is Denton. Theodore Denton."

The elevator arrived and the doors popped open.
Solomon stepped inside, mulling things over. "Thanks,"
Solomon said, pushing the button for the roof. "I can't
make any promises, but I'll owe you one."

"Don't mention it," the man said. "I've got a son, too."

The elevator doors shut, and Solomon went hurtling
upwards to the top of the building. He pulled out his cell-
phone and dialed Lucy's number. His phone beeped. It was
almost out of batteries, and he cursed it. He had been so
bothered the last few days, he had forgotten to charge it.

The phone started ringing as soon as he stepped from
the elevator and ran up the small flight of metal stairs
towards the roof. Lucy didn't answer, so he left a message
explaining exactly where he thought Fred might be and a
guess at how long it would take him to travel there by helicopter. He started to apologize for not traveling south
sooner, but his phone died before he could finish the
message. Cursing the device another time, he shoved it
back into his pocket. He had planned to call the police, too,
but his lifeless battery nixed that idea. Hopefully, Lucy
would turn on her phone and listen to his message. She
could then relay to the police where to look for Fred. Either
way, Solomon would be there in no time thanks to
Theodore.

The helicopter operator was reading a magazine when
Solomon arrived. Solomon introduced himself breathlessly
to the pilot.

"Who?" the pilot asked.

"I'm Theodore's new lawyer. He told me you'd take me to Alhambra."

"New lawyer?" he asked. "I haven't heard anything about it. I'd have to clear it with Goldacker and Silverwell."

"My son is missing, and I think I might finally know where he is! You get this thing in the air or you're out of a job—those are Theodore's words."

"Look, mister, I can't just take off in a helicopter every time some stranger asks me to, whether he's a friend to Mr. Denton or not," the pilot said.

"I'm going to be back in five minutes with Theodore," said Solomon. "How much longer do you think it will take him to find a new pilot?" he asked as he turned to walk back towards the roof access door.

This seemed to decide the matter for the pilot, who threw his magazine back into the cab and pressed the engine starter button and throttled up the turbines. The rotor blades started spinning at great speeds. "Well, c'mon then," the pilot shouted over the increasing roar of the blades.

Solomon rounded the front of the helicopter with his head bowed low and then leaped into the passenger side.

"Where'd you say you were going again?" the pilot asked.

"Alhambra," Solomon answered. "As close to the giant outlet mall as you can land."

Lucy's emotions kept toggling between guilt and apprehension. One moment she was wondering what sort of trail, if any, they might find at the carnival site, and the next she was thinking about how far behind she'd fallen after taking the past few days to search for Fred. She'd missed her weekend class entirely, and was hopelessly behind on some major deadlines. Of course, thinking about her own problems while her son was missing only made her feel guilty for not being able to hold his safety above all else. And so it went, around and around —a loop as interminable as the highway they kept hurtling down.

"So, what's her sign?" asked Sheriff Marshal, pointing to Lucy, interrupting her thoughts.

"She's an Aries," said Renee.

Lucy rocked back in surprise. "How did you know that?" she asked.

"Because when someone says they're a fire sign, the next question is—which one?" said Renee. "And the only reason they ask that is because of y'all," she said, pointing at Lucy.

The sheriff chuckled.

"That boy Stan is an Aries, too," said Renee, "so I should have known he'd be trouble."

"I'm sure your sign is all fantastic," said Lucy.

Renee laughed. "Well, Libras are known for being cooperative and diplomatic," she said.

If Lucy had been drinking something, she would have spit it all over the car. "Diplomatic?" she said. "*Cooperative*?"

"Yep," said Renee, missing Lucy's incredulity completely. "But their weakness is they tend to avoid confrontation."

Now it was Lucy's turn to laugh out loud. She couldn't help it. She laughed until her side ached. "You've nailed it," she managed to say eventually.

"Well, my psychic and I have been working on it," said Renee.

"You need to give that man a raise then," said Lucy, still laughing.

"Aries," said Renee with a wave of her hand.

Lucy's phone buzzed, and she spotted the voicemail from Solomon. She quickly punched in the key code to access the message. She nearly dropped the phone when she heard what Solomon had recorded.

"Oh, my god," she said. "He found them! He found them! Solomon found them!"

Her shout startled Sheriff Marshal so much that he spilled his coffee. "Dagjum, what in samhill are you hollerin' about?" the sheriff asked, shaking hot coffee from his hands.

"Solomon thinks that the boys are in Algebra or Umbrella or— "

"Alhambra?" said the sheriff.

"That's it!" said Lucy

"Really?" said the sheriff. "Those boys traveled far, by grit and by gosh. But y'all won't believe that they've got a shop in that mall there that brews one of the tastiest cups of coffee I've ever tasted."

"Are they okay?" Renee asked Lucy. "Did he say anything about that?"

"His voicemail cut off," said Lucy. "His phone must have died. But we know where they are! How long will it take us to get there?"

"Well, I need to check in with my deputies about a few things, first," said the sheriff, "before I jet off so far south."

This time Lucy joined Renee in shooting the sheriff an icy glare.

"Uh, only about an hour if I push it," said the sheriff,

leaning forward in his seat to check the next road sign. "Yep, an hour should do it. This cruiser may not look like much, but she can move faster than a roadlizard on hot asphalt with a nasty case of jalapeño-induced diarrhea when I need her to."

"Gross," said Renee.

"Prove it," said Lucy.

"Next stop, Alhambra," said the sheriff, kicking the cruiser into high gear.

How long would it elude her? How far did she need to go to find it? It was hers. By all rights, it was hers! She deserved it. It was the world that had gone mad, not her. And she hated it, and everything in it, for they kept her from her ring, from her great, glistering, glowing ring. And she would have had it, would have ripped it from the scabby brat's little neck if only those hippies hadn't been there. If she detested one thing more than kids it was hippies, with their horrible fashion sense and ridiculous ideas. Not even the biggest junk shot of gold and diamonds in the world could stop the bleeding of their stupid little hearts. And what did they waste all their hare-brained ideas on? Just some dirty vermin and some filthy plants, nothing as beautiful as her ring. But if they had their way, no one would ever wear a diamond again.

She screamed in rage at the thought. She should have killed them when she had the chance, strangled them in their sleep with their tie-dyed bandanas. That would have been a fitting end for the likes of them. At least the tractors had turned their precious forest into mulch. She had so loved the sound. The chippers and grinders, bashers and mashers, slicers and dicers had made such wonderful music as they mowed the forest to rubble. Well, where else would the jewelry shops go? All the other girls had to go somewhere, didn't they? Because once they saw her ring all of them would want a diamond just like it. Well, not just like it, because hers was better than all the rest, but they could buy a cheaper version.

And now these fools were going into an outlet mall! If she were not so afraid of what they would do to the ring, she would have laughed at their stupidity. There was no place she knew better than a shopping mall (the sales team at Nordstroms had practically raised her), and she knew all of its secrets. It would be almost too easy for her to steal the ring back from them—she just had to wait for the right moment. She would stay to the shadows for now. The dark shadows of the abandoned Radio Shack. But soon, soon, her precious ring would be hers.

35

ASSAULT ON MORDOR

As the boys approached the dark doors to Mordor, some foul sorcery caused the gates to open automatically. The boys jumped back in surprise. Embarrassed, they all quickly composed themselves. Fred gave himself one last quick pep talk before he entered the enemy stronghold. This was it—the last, toughest leg of the journey. If he didn't tap in to every last bit of his concentration and courage, they'd all be lost.

He slowly stepped across the threshold. The Dark Lord's kingdom was even more terrifying than he had ever imagined, and he had to take a moment to steady his nerves. There were no stacks of corpses, huge spider webs, or gooey growths, but something far worse—racks upon racks of clothes for as far as the eye could see. The Dark Lord had disguised his den with a particularly wicked spell. A soft lullaby was coming from the speakers in the high ceiling. Fred guessed that the calming music was how the Dark Lord was controlling the orcs. A look of total disgust came over his face as he watched the servants of Mordor dig among the racks. He hoped that if he broke the spell, the poor, unwitting slaves could still be turned to the good side.

When he came to the first intersection Fred paused. White-tiled paths branched out in every direction. He stamped his feet in frustration. He had no idea where to go. He was too close to the seat of evil; the pull of the ring had become too strong for him to use it as a compass any longer.

"Well, which way, Dorothy?" Stan asked in a whisper.

"I don't know," Fred whispered back and then put on a fake smile and pretended to be looking at a pair of overalls as a squad of orcs passed by.

"Well, we better figure it out quickly," said Gemma. "Because even without ruby slippers, we do sort of stick out here."

"Like a sore thumb," said Stan.

"Like a wizard in a Wal-mart," said Gemma.

"Like a dwarf in a Dairy Queen," added Jimmy.

"Or like a hobbit in a hockey rink," said Alfred.

"Shh," said Fred, his eyes scanning the store. "You guys are hilarious, but be quiet unless you want to take a mace to the brain."

"Or an axe to the a—" started Stan, but Fred wrenched him along by the arm before he could finish.

"Follow me," he said as he walked briskly towards one of the cashier's desks. "I've got a plan."

A skinny, tired-looking orc was standing behind the desk. He was chewing on a white stick of some sort, which Fred guessed was the leg-bone of a small animal—leftovers from the last orc roast.

"Uh-huh-hum," Fred coughed as he reached the counter, trying to deepen his voice. "The boys upstairs told us to take up sentry duty around Mount Doom. You know how they can be." He was trying to sound like a regular working orc just having small-talk with the guys. "Anyways, Glugluk here," Fred pointed his thumb at Stan, "he said he knew the way, but of course we're just as lost as a bunch of burrahobbits in a dragon's den."

The orc stopped chewing his bone and stared open-mouthed at the fellowship.

"But, uh..." said Fred, his voice fading. The silence stretched on. Fred worried that he had given them away. He expected the minion was going to call out the alarm at any second. He mustered a nervous laugh and started slowly back-stepping away.

"Hey wait!" the orc called, spiking Fred's pulse. "Man, you nearly had me," he said. "They didn't tell me you were going to be filming a movie here. Where are the cameras?" The orc looked around, a big smile on his face. "What are you guys shooting? What is it, like *Granddaddy Day Care* or something? Is that Eddie Murphy in there?" The man came from around the counter to get a closer look at Alfred. "Hey, Eddie is that you? Eddie?" he asked, waving his hand in Alfred's face.

"Zounds, thou art a most obstreperous knave," Alfred said, retreating from the orc.

"Zounds," the man said laughing. "That's great. Hey, you still got it, Eddie, ya know that? That makeup is incredible. You can't even tell that it's you."

The servant of Mordor wasn't angry, but he was so excited Fred worried the orc would still draw attention to them. Swiveling his head around as casually as he could manage, Fred checked to see if anyone else was coming after them. He was ready to bolt and hide at the slightest sign that the enemy knew they were there.

Because he was on high alert, he was even more

surprised when someone snuck up directly behind him and whispered in his ear. "I can help you," the voice said, causing Fred to jump and wheel around.

The boy before him was dressed in the same clothes as the orc, but his eyes were different—intense but friendly. *Was he a guard, too, who had overheard Fred's question and decided to direct him to his post? Or something else? An ally?*

Before Fred could say anything, the stranger whispered again. "I'm a friend," he said.

It was more than Fred had hoped for—an ally working undercover in enemy territory! Then Fred remembered Alfred's spell. *Of course,* he thought. This guy had to be a friend, otherwise he wouldn't be able to see who they really were. *But what sort of friend was he?* The stranger spoke in an accent Fred did not quite recognize. It wasn't elvish, dwarfish, entish or orcish. It was closest to Australian, but it didn't exactly match that accent either. Fred put this question aside—the first orc was still there, and he needed an excuse to get away so that he could hear what this stranger had to say.

"Well, we have to be going," Fred said moving away from the guard. He tried to remember the name of the film the guard had mentioned. "Uh, *Grandpappy...Clay... Bear* isn't going to film itself."

The orc seemed confused by this, but after digging a finger into his ear and shaking his head, he said, "Oh, yeah, sure, don't let me keep you. Hey, if you need an extra, just let me know okay. Eddie Murphy, dang!"

The mysterious stranger led Fred and his companions away from the cashier counter and through the clothing racks. As he escorted them deeper into the villainous den, Fred started to grow more and more anxious. They'd been betrayed before. Their newfound "friend" could just as likely be leading them to an ambush, and there was no escaping an ambush in Mordor.

The stranger stopped in front of a large corridor and ducked behind the wall, pulling Fred down beside him. Now that they were relatively hidden, Fred was able to get a better look at the boy helping them. The kid was more than a little strange looking. His eyes were much too large for his face, and his glasses were even bigger, making him look slightly crazy. Fred imagined going undercover in Mordor for so long would do that to a person.

"This is it," said the stranger quietly. "This is what you're looking for." He pointed a thumb over his shoulder down the corridor. "They have two guards posted there all the time."

"Fred, who the heck is this guy?" Stan asked. "And where the duff is he from?"

"Sorry," the stranger said, pushing his glasses back up his nose. "I'm always forgetting to introduce myself. I'm Harry, Harry Gorman. JAFA."

"What?" asked Stan.

"Just another...uh...Aucklander. But my mom moved us here two years ago. Ever since I started working here, I suspected there was something more through those doors. I could just feel it. When you lot showed up, it confirmed my suspicions."

Harry switched places with Fred, giving him a better vantage to peek around the corner. In front of a door that read "Manufacturing Area: Keep Out," there were two heavyset orcs standing guard. One of them was slumped in a poker table chair, and the other was leaning against the wall, drumming on his thigh.

"Two guards should be no problem," Fred said, turning

back to his friends. "Jimmy could take them out in no time
with his arrows."

"Wrong, mate," Harry said, shaking his head.

"I beg to differ," Jimmy said, getting out his bow. "They
don't call me 'Deadeye' for no reason."

"They'll be calling you 'Dead Meat' if you try to shoot
those guards," Harry said. "There are twenty security
guards that monitor this mall. Some of them ride souped-
up golf carts and a few have segways, but they all have
tasers. And they love to use them any chance they get. Just
yesterday they shocked an eighty-year-old woman who
forgot she'd put a box of kitty litter on the bottom of her
cart."

"No doubt they thought she was a powerful witch,"
said Fred.

"Professor McGonagall was probably mighty pissed,"
added Stan.

"It certainly smelt that way," said Harry. "But my point
is, even if you take out two of them before they can sound
the alarm, anybody who sees you will be able to call for
help, and then the rest of the guards will be on you in no
time. You'd never make it. Trust me, this place is rigged to
prevent any kind of theft. They always boast that no one
has ever stolen a single thing."

"The funny thing is, all we want to do is return something," said Fred.

Stan gave a wry chuckle. "Maybe we should just go to
the exchange counter," he joked, but no one seemed much
in the mood for laughter.

"So, what do we do?" Fred asked.

Everyone went silent in thought.

"Maybe we create some sort of diversion," Stan
suggested after a moment. "We can have them chasing

alarms all over the mall. That way even if someone signals something down here, they won't have enough men to spare."

"Sounds good to me," said Fred. "But you know the mall better than we do, Harry. What do you think?"

"Well, it's no Mutara Nebula Maneuver, but it just might work," Harry said.

Stan silently mimed, "*Well, it's no Mutara Nebula Maneuver,*" and then glowered off into the youth clothing department.

"The only problem," Harry said, "and it's a big problem —you'd have to think of some way to avoid those tasers."

The boys went quiet again.

"I've got it!" Jimmy exclaimed after a minute. "Harry, does this mall have a sporting goods store?"

"Yeah, Scarborough Sports," answered Harry. "It's huge, so it will have everything you need, but it's on the complete other side of the courtyard."

"No problem, said Jimmy. "That means we'll get an idea of the course on our way. This is really important, though, Harry—do they have bikes at this sporting goods store?"

"Yeah, loads of 'em," Harry answered again. "And what do you mean by 'course'?"

Fred thought he had a pretty good idea.

"I'll explain when we get there," Jimmy said. "Just get us to that store as fast as you can."

Fred hadn't forgotten that the last time they had followed Jimmy's orders they ended up racing down some whitewater rapids, so he was a little nervous about Jimmy's plan this time. He especially didn't exactly love the idea of travelling all the way across enemy territory. But Jimmy was the only one with a plan, so Fred had no choice but to go with it.

Noticing that the covered walkway kept going on even after they left the store, Jimmy said, "How are we still inside? I thought this was an outlet mall?"

"It is," said Harry, taking them to a map. "It's basically a giant square, whose sides are just a string of outlet stores and whose corners are two-story regular indoor malls with one big department store in each. Mordor Wholesale Clothing is where we are, here," he pointed to the map, "and Scarborough Sports is over here." Their eyes followed his finger as it drifted diagonally all the way across the mall courtyard to another huge store.

"Morgoth's Mall is like the largest Destructicon ever built," said Stan.

"Yeah, it's enormous," said Harry, leaving the map behind.

They hurried to the end of the hall, skipped down a large flight of stairs and spilled through an entryway leading to a courtyard. Fenced in by the mall commons, the gigantic paved area was covered in picnic tables and kiosks. People were crossing in every direction. To Fred it looked like a giant futuristic city, or—better still—a giant metal and glass abbey of malls.

Fred took in as much as he could, trying to get a better idea of how the mall was laid out. Above him, a covered walkway ran parallel to the sides of the mall commons and connected to the middle of the opposite walkway. It was basically a large cross. Fred noticed that the four malls at the corners were also connected by covered walkways, which completed the sides of the square. A string of restaurants lay clustered beneath the central walkway that cut through the courtyard.

There wasn't a tree in sight.

This truly is the seat of doom, Fred thought. He stared

spellbound for a moment and then hurried to catch up to Harry, who was speeding across the courtyard, weaving in and out of shoppers. Reaching the large glass doors of another massive mall building, they pushed through the exiting crowd and raced up the stairs.

"Scarborough Sports is just down this hall," said Harry as he jogged along.

Fred kept searching for orcs. As he did, he couldn't help looking at all the shop windows. There were so many of them, and they were lit by such bright lights. He suddenly got an irresistible urge to buy something, anything. He fought against the desire, reminding himself of the importance of his quest and the danger all around him. But it was no use. The desire to possess something new was too strong. He dropped behind his companions and drifted towards a massive toy store. Something polished and bright, its smooth contours shining, caught his attention and drew him in like a tractor beam. It was Lion-O's legendary Claw Shield! A mystical buckler that could deflect any blow, even Mumm-Ra's energy bolts.

Fred was powerless to escape the pull. Before he knew it, he was no longer even resisting. He was welcoming it. The glow of the Claw Shield was like a warm bed calling to him. With the Claw Shield he'd be invincible, unstoppable! He didn't even need the ring; he could take on any foe with the shield alone. He picked his nose off the glass and started for the door.

A hand fell on his shoulder, stopping him.

"Let it go, man," said Stan.

"Let it go?" said Fred. "It's the Claw Shield! Think of the power."

"Let it go," said Stan.

"But it's a collector's item," said Fred. "No one else could compete with it."

"Are you listening to yourself?" asked Stan. "You're one raw fish away from moving to a black lake in the belly of a cave. Forget power, man, and forget collector's items. You need to be thinking about your family. You've come too far —we've come too far—to let the ring win now."

Stan's words shattered the trance that had taken control of Fred. Finally able to pry his eyes from the Claw Shield, he saw the rest of his companions looking back at him from down the corridor. He was delaying them, putting them in danger, but they weren't angry or impatient. In their eyes he saw only sympathy and love and courage. It nearly broke his heart. No plastic toy could make him feel that good.

"Do you know why I came back?" said Stan.

Fred shook his head.

"It wasn't the fire," said Stan. "I realized all of a sudden that we aren't the ones playing make believe. They are." Stan gestured towards all the people milling about the mall. "You're doing something real, Fred. Something that takes courage and creativity. Something that takes love. And we won't let you fail."

Fred gave Stan a huge hug.

"Okay, easy there, Crychelangelo," said Stan. Fred laughed and then stood back and wiped away his tears. "If you're done with the cheesy emotional bit, can we get to the final action sequence?"

"As long as you don't need a snack first," said Fred. Stan smiled at him and the two boys caught up with the rest of the group who patted Fred on the back in support.

"The bikes are on the top floor, I think," Harry said, reminding them they still had a quest to complete. He led them up the escalator and then directed them through the maze of helmets and soccer balls and basketball shoes until they reached the bikes. At this point, Jimmy sped ahead, scanning through the bikes, looking for something. He went down one aisle, up another and down a third, until he finally found what he had been searching for. The rest of the boys rushed to catch up with him.

"Isn't she a beaut?" Jimmy asked as he pulled a bike from the rack. Fred looked down upon a large recumbent tricycle just like the one he had seen in Jimmy's *GUTS* shop of horrors. Well, not exactly the same. This one actually looked like it could go. The lone wheel in front was connected by two black bars to the two rear tires, and the black seat was supported by a rounded arch of metal. A small metal platform jutted from the back of the seat, and another bar extended from the front tire, ending in a small steering wheel. "Road Warrior" was printed in grey block letters along the steering column.

"They're made by *Mearas Bikes*, the best brand in the business," Jimmy said as he ran his hand slowly over the bars. "This thing is speed incarnate, lighting in trike-form, thunder on three wheels." Jimmy seemed lost in his own world as he gazed on the 'Road Warrior.'

"Jimmy, maybe now would be a good time to explain your plan," said Fred, but Jimmy didn't take his eyes from the trike. "Jimmy!" Fred said again.

"Sorry," said Jimmy, forcing his eyes away from the vehicle. "Okay, so we need to have the guards confused, right?" he asked, and the boys nodded. "And we need them to think threats are coming from everywhere, right?" They nodded again. "And we have to move fast enough to stay out of the range of their tasers, right?"

"Just spit it out, Jimmy!" Stan said.

"Fine, but just remember you didn't come up with any ideas, okay?" said Jimmy. "So, here's what we do. We get them to chase us through the mall on these things. We cause massive mayhem, distract those guards, and then Fred slips away while the rest of us keep them busy. If we keep running them in circles, they'll think there are dozens of us, and they won't know where it is we're really trying to go or what it is we're really trying to do."

"Assuming that plan would work, there are only three trikes, Jimmy," said Gemma.

"You're not thinking fourth dimensionally, Gemma," said Jimmy.

"What the Hufflepuff does that mean?" asked Stan.

"Double-Dash!" Jimmy exclaimed with a smile. "There's enough room on the back platforms of these things for a passenger to sit and fire items at the guards. So, we go two to a trike. I'll take Fred, Gemma will go with—"

"No," said Stan. "Fred and I ride together."

Jimmy looked to Fred, who nodded. "Fine, Stan and Fred will ride together," said Jimmy. "Alfred and Gemma will go with each other, and Harry will ride with me."

"I appreciate the offer," Harry said. "But I think I can be more help to you in another capacity." He held up his pointer finger, and then he went running away, turning down an aisle about twenty yards away. The rest of the fellowship looked at each other, utterly confused.

A few tense seconds later, Harry popped out of the aisle and came sprinting towards them, carrying a few packages in his arms. He must have seen the uneasy expressions on their faces because Harry said, "Relax, mates, I'm not going to sell you out. I just thought of something that might help is all."

Fred figured it was finally safe to trust Harry. He would

never have helped them this far if he had only planned to betray them. "How will these help, Harry?" he asked.

"It'll take too long to explain," said Harry. "Just trust me on this. Take these walkie-talkies and tune them to channel four." He handed them the packages. "Then all you have to do is listen," he said.

"I guess we don't have any other choice," said Fred, taking the package and ripping it open. "Don't let us down."

"No way," Harry said, looking determined. Then he went jogging away from them again.

The walkie-talkies were pretty awesome, Fred had to admit. They came fully equipped with wireless headsets: a plastic extender brought the receiver closer to the mouth, and an extra transmitter button on the earpiece meant you only had to press a finger to your ear to speak over the radio. Alfred and the boys quickly put them on.

"Okay, Jim," Fred said. "What do we need to do to get ready?"

"I need you to go get some green and red kickballs and a yellow sports bra or two," said Jimmy.

Stan raised his eyebrows at the mention of the sports bras and looked at Fred. Slowly, both boys turned to look uncomfortably at Gemma.

"Seriously?" she said. "You can take on a Balrog but you can't deal with a bra?"

The boys shuffled their feet.

"Very rock and roll, boys," said Gemma. "And why does it have to be yellow?" she asked.

"Um...bananas?" said Jimmy.

Gemma threw up her hands. "Boys!" she said.

"So...Stan and I will grab the kickballs," said Fred. "Grandpa, you help Gemma get the...rest of the items."

"No wa— " Gemma started, but the boys had already sprinted away. Alfred smiled at her obliviously.

"Shall we?" he said, smiling.

"Um...sure," she said.

"Oh, and be careful you don't draw attention to yourselves," Jimmy added.

Gemma turned to glower at him, but he had already turned his attention back to the trikes.

Moving as stealthily as possible, Fred focused on finding the items Jimmy had requested. He walked quickly, but made sure not to run, his eyes daring down aisle after aisle. They passed shelves of golf equipment, lacrosse sticks, basketball hoops and scuba gear.

"There, I see them," said Stan, pointing to a container brimming with rubber balls of all colors and sizes.

The boys pretended to look at some baseball gloves as they slowly moved down the aisle towards the balls. Fred had to admit that their cover was pretty thin. Watching a little kid in a hobbit cloak looking at baseball gloves didn't seem all that convincing, even to him. *If only they sold Quidditch brooms here, we'd look right at home*, he thought. Somehow, they managed to reach the kickballs without being intercepted. They picked one green and one red ball each.

"Should we get a blue one, too?" Stan asked.

"C'mon, Stan, you don't want to win that way, do you?" Fred asked.

"No, I guess you're right," Stan agreed, grabbing an extra green ball.

Fred suggested they place the balls on the ground and dribble them with their feet, so that the guards could not see them. Before they'd gone half an aisle, they heard someone on the loudspeaker call for help in women's sportswear and groaned.

Fred and Stan quickly raced over to that section of the store only to find Gemma talking nervously to a female employee while Alfred stood there, huge and strange in his wizard's robes. Fred couldn't even imagine what kind of story Gemma was trying to weave in order to explain Alfred, and Fred knew he had to help her out. He advanced cautiously into the neon jungle of feminine undergarments, dodging and shying away from the delicates as if avoiding the venom-filled stinger of a giant spider.

"Hey therrrre, sis," Fred said, hoping this wouldn't ruin Gemma's story.

"Hiiii, bro," Gemma growled. "I was just talking with Becky here about how awkward it is trying to buy bras with your grandpa when he offered to show her a magic trick and pulled a string of bras he'd somehow grabbed and tied together from his sleeve."

Fred could see now that the employee was holding the multi-colored rope of sports bras and looking at it as if it had just turned into a live snake.

"Oh, well, oh geeze, haha," said Fred awkwardly. "That's old grandpa for you. Always trying to embarrass you, sis. We'll just grab him, and you know, let you get back to your thing here with Becky."

Grabbing Alfred and offering an awkward wave, Fred and Stan sidled away, feeling particularly suspicious. The woman did not follow but kept her eyes trained on them as they moved past. Fred turned down the first aisle that would take him out of the woman's line of sight, and then he started jogging on a return path back to Jimmy and the tricycles.

Jimmy was securing something to the back of one of the tricycles, biting off a piece of duct-tape and testing the

firmness of the adhesive with a jiggle, when Stan and Fred
arrived back at the bicycle section of the store.

"What's wrong?" Jimmy said. "Where's Gemma?"

Fred and Stan were so mesmerized by what Jimmy had
done with the bikes, all they could mutter was a collective
"Whoa."

Flanking Jimmy's *Road Warrior* were two other recumbent tricycles. On the right was a cherry red trike with the
name *Flash* printed in white, italic block letters. On the
other side, a silver-colored trike bore the name *Shadow* in
slate-grey paint, and smoke swirled around the name.

"I don't know what you troll turds are staring at," said
Gemma, who had just arrived. "But in case you didn't
realize it, Becky is officially onto us."

Jimmy looked over her shoulder. "Dang, I was hoping
for some more time, but I guess it's now or never," he said,
roping down his gym bag onto the platform behind his
trike. "Did you get the, um, items?" he asked Gemma.

"You mean the *bra*nanas?" said Stan, winking.

Gemma sighed heavily. "No thanks to Alfred the
Awkward," she said handing the brananas out to the boys.

"Awesome!" said Jimmy. Fred and Stan, you guys get
Flash, Gemma and Alfred take *Shadow*. You'll need these,"
he said, throwing them a long lighter and pointing to the
back of the trikes. There were three Roman candles stuck on
the bars behind each wheel. "You've got three boosts, so use
them wisely," Jimmy said.

"He-Man's hairy banana-hammock," Fred said in
amazement.

"Blue sparks!" Stan said.

They rubbed their hands along the painted metal, eager
to try out the trikes. "And take these, too." Jimmy threw
each of them a firework in the shape of a classic bomb. "My

bag is waterproof, so they didn't get damaged going down the river. Use your items well," Jimmy said.

"Jimmy, maybe Stan and I should use the masks again... you know, to hide our faces from the enemy," said Fred, hoping Jimmy wouldn't see right through him and realize that he just wanted to wear the mask because it was cool.

"You're right," Jimmy answered, smacking his forehead. "We can't let the forces of evil know that the ringbearer is here. You should have been wearing the masks the whole time." He handed the green Mandalorian helmet and Darth Vader's black helmet to Fred and Stan.

"I feel like we're about to take on the Death Star," Stan said to Fred as they put on their helmets and climbed onto *Flash*.

Fred had to agree. With the walkie-talkie headset set up inside his helmet, he really did feel like Boba Fett. He took the driver's seat, and Stan stepped on the back platform to "man the guns."

"You must have Jedi reflexes to drive the *Flash*," Stan joked.

"Just don't say you feel like you could take on the whole Empire by yourself," said Fred.

"Of course not, man," Stan replied. "Best friends together. Rough riders roll. To the end."

Fred smiled inside his helmet.

"Okay," Jimmy said, strapping on a regular bike helmet. "Be ready. This isn't Dr. Dodgeball, alright. There's no reviving your teammates here. If you get hit with a taser you're a goner."

Inside their helmets, the boys gritted their teeth. Alfred settled into the driver's seat of *The Shadow*, and he and Gemma both threw a thumb up to indicate that they were ready. They didn't have to wait long. Within seconds, two male Scarborough Sports employees turned the corner, Becky close behind them. The employees took one look at the fellowship and started directly for them.

"Hold," said Jimmy. "Wait for it."

Fred tensed with nervous excitement. One last great feat of bravery and then it was over, and he could go home to his mom and dad and share with them the great adventure he had just experienced. *Or it could all end in failure*, he thought suddenly. He could just as likely go home in shackles—tased and disgraced and sent to "juvie," proving all the Mrs. Bonnevilles of the world right.

He braced his feet against the pedals and tightened his grip on the steering wheel. The fact that he had put in some considerable amount of training time on Mario Kart gave him some confidence. And to think that parents were always saying how video games were a waste of time.

Fred was so deep in thought he hadn't noticed the subtle change that had come over the store. Everything seemed charged with a nervous tension. *The music has stopped,* he realized. The tune had been so bland that it had just drifted into the background, a dull buzzing—nothing more. But now that it wasn't playing anymore, the silence was conspicuous.

Harry's voice suddenly crackled through the walkie-talkie, breaking the silence. "I sure hope you Yanks know how to rock," he said.

Over the mall's speakers an acoustic guitar began to play some soft chords. Then a whispery voice came in. The song was relatively quiet, but Fred could tell the music was building towards something.

The sporting goods store's security team stopped in surprise, looking around as if they might find the source of the music over by the footballs or the golf clubs. The hesitation was just what Jimmy was waiting for. As the song reached the peak of its crescendo, Jimmy jerked his feet on the pedals, and the front wheel of his tricycle rose into the air. His back tires churned, sending him speeding forward in a wheelie. Alfred followed behind, laboring a bit at first until he got the trike moving. Fred pumped his own legs, and marveled at how fast the trike started to move.

The three of them barreled down the aisle, and Jimmy turned them straight towards the guards who had come to block their way. The Scarborough Sports workers had formed a hasty blockade. They held up their hands, ordering the boys to stop. But Jimmy shouted, "For the Lady!" and accelerated towards them. Fred and Alfred flanked him and zoomed ahead. The workers shuffled backwards clumsily and then eventually dove out of the way as the trikes tore past.

The boys practically flew out of the store. As the tires left the carpet of the sports shop and gripped the tile of the main hallway, they made an ear-shattering screech. Harry's music blared in the corridor, even louder than it had been in the store.

Just as they'd planned, the trikes split off in three different directions. Fred's heart pounded in his chest.

The chase was on.

36
HARRY AND THE HOBBITS

Harry was following all three trikes from the control terminal in the main mall surveillance room. The technician he had tricked into the hallway was banging on the locked door, demanding to be let inside. Harry had placed a chair under the knob to prevent even someone with a key from entering, so he wasn't worried that the technician would find a way in. Mall security was about to have bigger problems, anyway.

Playing air drums to Led Zeppelin's "Ramble On" as it screamed out over the mall's loudspeakers, Harry scanned the many glowing monitors before him. Except for the few stores that had their own separate p.a. systems, the whole mall was listening in. The customers on the screens were reacting to the music in a variety of ways. Some looked amused, others amazed, and a few even looked a little afraid. Harry didn't care—the herd needed to be shaken from their stupor every now and again. Besides, he knew the mall would only spin this incident into some kind of secret promotional event gone wrong and the people would forget anything happened at all.

From the control room, he could see into nearly every room in the mall commons. The mall had a few more of these surveillance rooms, and each one covered a different zone, but this room had video access to the whole mall. It just required a bit of navigating through the system to access cameras in other zones. For Harry, this was easier than picking off noobs in Fortnite. His fingers zoomed across the keyboard as he toggled between different cameras, continuing to track the tricycles.

As he expected, within seconds two mall cops got a transmission from Scarborough Sports and peeled away from their posts. They tilted all the way forward on their segways, moving fast towards Fred and his friends. The guards spotted one of the trikes almost immediately and began following it. Harry called out on the walkie-talkie.

"Breaker, breaker 1-9, this is the High King calling from the castle tower," he said. "Mad Max, you've got two marauders coming in fast on your tail."

"Copy, High King," Jimmy answered, "I see them." Jimmy kept pedaling fast as he picked up his NERF bow. Already notched on the bow was an arrow with a cherry bomb duct-taped securely to the tip. He used his mirror to see how far behind him the security guards were. The two portly men in matching blue uniforms were gaining ground on him fast, the crowd parting to let them through. They were yelling at him to stop, but he ignored them, lighting the fuse on the firework. Taking the steering wheel between his knees, he took careful aim with his bow and fired on the move. The arrow zipped through the air. It exploded as it hit the sprinkler and water showered down behind Jimmy as he raced past. Water cascaded down upon the guards in pursuit, whose segways lost their grip on the tile, slipping and sliding until they lost purchase completely. The guards were thrown to the ground in a flail of limbs and a series of large splashes. The men kept skidding on top of the water like skipping stones. Once they finally came to a stop, the guards struggled to rise and then collapsed on the ground.

"Alright, Max!" Harry shouted. "Both guards down!"

Unfortunately, this victory was short-lived. In a different hallway, Gemma and Alfred crossed in front of Jimmy, a pair of guards in a golf cart pursuing them, and Jimmy shouted out a warning before Harry could. "Mithrandir, this is Mad Max, you've got a marauder on your six," he yelled into his communicator.

"We copy, Max," Alfred called over the walkie-talkie. "Longbeard's got them in her sights."

"I told you that's NOT my call name," said Gemma.

"No time to debate, my dear," said Alfred. "The enemy is upon us!" He pedaled as fast as his wiry legs would churn.

Gemma called out instructions as they rolled. "A little to the left, Alfred," she yelled. "I can't get a clear shot."

Alfred responded, drifting to the left. Gemma grabbed a green kickball in her right hand, gripping the back of trike with her left. She prepared to throw, but the golf cart swung wide to avoid some shoppers, and she had to pull back, almost losing her grip on to the ball entirely. Getting a better grip, she cocked her arm again and waited for the golf-cart to drift back behind them. As soon as the cart came back into view, she let the ball fly. It nailed the driver squarely in the face before he could duck. The guard's hands slipped on the steering wheel, and the cart jerked straight into the wall, destroying the engine and tossing both guards clear of the wreckage. Gemma gave a shout of triumph.

"Smart shot," said Alfred.

Gemma turned around to say thanks and spotted something. "Detour through that music store!" she yelled.

"What?" Alfred asked. "We don't have time to window shop, my dear."

"Just do it!" Gemma shouted again. "I'm calling an audible on this play."

"Whatever you say, Longbeard," said Alfred, turning the tricycle with a sharp twist of the wheel. "This is Mithrandir," he said into the walkie-talkie. "Another two marauders down. We're rerouting through Mjolnir Music— looking for Thor's hammer. Mithrandir out," he said as they flew past a long-haired, tattooed greeter of Mjolnir Music.

"You guys need some help?" the attendant asked sleepily, as their passing tricycle blew his long hair back. "Whoa. Excellent," he said, watching them race away.

Mjolnir music was one of the biggest stores in McKellen Mall Commons. After spending a month polishing pianos and putting metal-tipped guitar picks in little cases made to look like engagement ring boxes, Harry knew this all too well. Guitars and every sort of musical instrument lined the walls from the floor to the ceiling and filled up aisles upon aisles of shelves.

Gemma scanned the store, finally spotting what she had been searching for on a large display at the back of the shop. She called out to Alfred who drove them towards the display. Alfred skidded to a halt, and Gemma jumped from the back of the trike. She climbed up a small mountain of amps and gazed on the object resting at the peak. Inside a glass case was an amp no bigger than a lunchbox.

Harry knew exactly what it was. It was the Shrieking Systems *SonicAmp*—the most powerful and the most portable amp ever made. The mall had a huge marketing campaign in the works, and Harry had been lugging huge cardboard posters of the amp around the basement. The amp itself was no bigger than a briefcase, yet it was louder than an amp ten times its size. The *SonicAmp* also came with a wireless transmitter, which let the guitarist rock out without worrying about tripping as she leapt and slid all over the stage. According to the posters, the device could transmit up to fifty feet away clear as a bell. The *SonicAmp* was so rare, that Gemma looked as if she had unearthed a new dinosaur bone, or discovered an alien race. Harry smiled.

"Longbeard, hurry," Alfred yelled up to her.

"If you call me that one more time," said Gemma as she pulled the guitar from her back and swung it at the glass case. The sharp edges of the guitar shattered the glass, and Gemma scooped up the *SonicAmp*. She leapt from the top of the pile of amps to land on the back of the *Mearas Shadow*. Alfred instantly kicked the silvery steed into high gear, leaving tire-marks on the floor as he started off. As they exited Mjolnir Music, a security guard on a segway spotted them and immediately jumped on their tail, calling to his comrades on his communicator.

Alfred masterfully steered the smoky trike around the shoppers, cutting and drifting the vehicle as he tried to find new paths through the crowd. "Longbeard, this knave persists," he hollered back over the walkie, beginning to breathe a little heavy. "And his taser is fully brandished. I would implement your plan post haste!"

"No, we've got to lure a few more guards in," Gemma replied, throwing another green kickball with little venom and missing wide.

Harry couldn't be sure, but he thought Gemma was missing her target on purpose, egging him on.

"Just stay ahead of them, my good wizard," said

Gemma. "At least far enough away to avoid those tasers," she added. "I'll do the rest."

Gemma lit the first two Roman candles. "You've got your speed burst, Alfred. Use it in the turn!" she yelled.

"Affirmative," Alfred said, gritting his teeth and bearing down, as if to will his legs to pump even faster. He jerked the trike to the left, and they drifted into the turn, candles firing yellow, then red. Alfred threw all of his weight to the left to prevent the trike from tipping over, and then the candles fired blue and shot the vehicle like a rocket into the straightaway.

Another golf cart nearly collided with them as it came hurtling from a side corridor and probably would have crushed them both had Gemma not used the fireworks when she had. Its driver nearly lost control as his vehicle narrowly missed the trike, but he quickly gathered himself and took up the pursuit again.

Harry had guessed at Gemma's plan and called out on the radio. "Longbeard, this is High King from the castle tower. You've got one more coming. If you can wait for ten seconds, you'll be able to take out all four guards. Do you read me, over?" Harry quickly switched the song on the loudspeakers to one with a better solo, and then returned his attention to the screens.

"Acknowledged, High King," Gemma responded. Sure enough, just as Harry had promised, another guard on a segway zipped through the doors of a computer store and began to pursue them.

"Okay, Alfred, get ready," said Gemma, lighting the fuses on the last four Roman candles and turning all the volume knobs on the amp up to eleven. "And plug your ears."

"Hug my peers?" Alfred asked. "What the jelly bean are you talking about?"

"Nevermind," Gemma said, "your ears have natural protection."

Gemma switched on the wireless transmitter and gently dropped the amp off the back of the trike. The amp began to make a slight electronic sizzle, shaking the air around it. As the guards neared the amp, Gemma took out a shiny metal pick and raised her sinewy arm high in the air. It must have taken all her patience, but Gemma waited. Only when the guards were right on top of the amp did she bring her arm down, striking the pick across the strings of her ax and carving out the most hair-raising, face-melting, brain-boiling solo Harry had ever heard. Two speakers in the control room burst into flames, and he had to put them out. The ax-woman's fingers were a blur as they hammered and slid all along the guitar neck. The fury of notes rocked the foundations of the mall and shattered the glass of every shop window within a hundred yards of the *SonicAmp*.

Nearby shoppers fell down like bowling pins.

At the sound of the first chord, the guards gripped their heads as if someone were drilling a hole through their temples. One of them dropped a taser and it fired as it struck the ground, sending a bolt of electricity directly into the golf cart's engine. Its circuits fried, the cart spun out, crashing into the segway and sending the man driving it through the air. He flew headfirst into a wall and was instantly knocked out. The driver of the golf cart frantically tried to gain control of the runaway vehicle, but it continued to jerk and wobble.

The guard on the other segway had taken his hands from the handlebars to cover his ears, which stopped the vehicle very suddenly, throwing him over the handlebars and onto the glass-covered hallway floor. The golf cart narrowly missed him as it snaked to the other side of the corridor and crashed into his segway. The cart flipped on its side and skidded into the wall. Its undercarriage sprayed the hall with sparks, frayed wires flapping.

"Yee-haw!" Harry yelled. "You just took out four birds with one great big rock. Keep it up, Longbeard!"

"Way to go!" Fred called out over the radio. "We heard and felt that way over here!"

"I think those mutants on Alpha Centauri's plasma moon heard that," Stan replied. "But we've got some bigger fish to fry, Fred." He paused. "Say that five times fast—fish to fry, Fred. Fish to fry, Fred."

"Stan, just tell me what's going on!" Fred demanded.

"Two carts coming up behind you fast, Underhill and Stoutheart," Harry warned him before Stan could. "They've got their tasers out, and they look trigger happy."

"Stoutheart's got them," said Fred.

"Alright, keep her steady, Fred," said Stan, fixing his aim on the driver of one of the carts. He balanced his body over his feet and hurled a green ball at the cart. The driver maneuvered to evade the ball, and it bounced off one of the support bars for the cart's roof

"Is it a hit?" Fred asked.

"Negative, negative," Stan said. "It just impacted on the surface."

"Try a red," Fred suggested, tossing a red ball over his shoulder to Stan.

Attempting a surprise attack, Stan caught and catapulted the ball in the same motion. The ball soared through the air with great speed. Harry thought that surely this ball would strike, but once again the driver dodged it at the last moment. This time Stan didn't get a chance to relay the miss to Fred. The passenger of the car immediately fired his taser at their cart. Stan raised a green kickball just in time to block the dart. The taser dart struck the ball, causing it to explode with a loud pop. Stan had to duck to protect himself from flying shards of rubber.

"What the heck was that?" Fred asked.

"A flippin' lightning bolt!" Stan answered, holding on to the back of the seat for dear life. "We almost got minimized. They've got some sort of Borg technology, man. They've adapted. The shells won't work."

"Okay, okay, we've got other options," said Fred, turning the pedals even faster.

"Underhill, mate," said Harry, "you've got another cart coming straight at you. You'll be boxed in unless you can make it to the next turn!"

"Stan, light the fires!" Fred yelled back.

Stan pulled the lighter from his belt and lit two of the Roman candles, one on each wheel. Peering over the back of the chair, he saw the third golf cart bearing down on them fast.

"Go, Fred, go!" he shouted, grabbing the trike tightly.

Fred jerked the trike to the left, narrowly skirting the front fender of the oncoming cart. The driver of the cart swerved crazily to make the sharp turn and to avoid the other two guards. His passenger, who had been ready to shoot his taser, had to hold his fire. The gunman brought the weapon up again, but Fred had pulled too far ahead, out of the taser's range.

Fred had turned down a hallway that led to the courtyard. The route before them offered them a choice: a steep, curling ramp or a sharp drop down some stairs.

"Drop a banana!" Fred shouted as the candles' sparks turned from red to blue and the trike shot forward. Stan flung one of the sports bras behind them. The center cart's driver saw it at the last moment and tried to avoid it, but his front right tire caught the bra and went into a skid. The driver jerked the wheel back the other way and lost control. Fred turned towards the ramp at the last second, while the out-of-control cart went bouncing and flipping down the stairs. It tumbled past them as Fred slid into a drift-turn. Stan had lit the next set of candles, and the yellow balls of fire were shooting out. Fred fought to keep the trike from tipping as they accelerated into the turn. The two other carts had missed the banana and were following them down the ramp, but Fred and Stan were gaining separation from them.

The candles threw out red fire and then blue. Fred and Stan hit the courtyard concrete at breakneck speed, coursing around picnic tables—the two golf carts close in pursuit.

"We need a plan!" shouted Stan.

"I'm working on it," growled Fred, whizzing by a restaurant. Up ahead there were two giant glass vats of soda pop. A little girl with pigtails was filling up her forty-four-ounce cup, which was almost as big as she was.

"Stan, fire a warning shot at that girl so that she gets out of the way, and throw me the lighter," Fred yelled.

Stan leaned up over the chair and hurled a green ball. It bounced off the vats, and the girl whirled around. Spotting them, she screamed and then dashed frightfully out of the way.

Fred lit the cherry bomb Jimmy had given them and held it for a moment like a grenade. "I'm a Freddio, and I'ma gonna ween," he said as he tossed it at the soda tanks just before it was going to explode. The bomb arced through the air, bursting in a brilliant shower of colors as it hit the vats. Fred and Stan zipped by the restaurant, watching large white cracks start to branch on the glass. At the last minute, the security guards behind them recognized what was happening. One of them broke off, taking the longer but safer route around a restaurant. The other sped on, trying to make it past the improvised booby trap.

The glass finally gave, and a wave of dark, syrupy soda came spewing from the tanks just as the security cart passed. The wave nearly toppled the cart, lifting it onto two wheels and soaking both guards. The driver tried to keep the cart from tipping, jerking the wheel back across. When the two tires landed on the pavement, the cart spun on the soda, throwing both guards clear.

"Awesome shot, Fred," Stan said, while Harry applauded in the control room. "But now all we've got is one red ball to take out the last cart."

"I know, and I've got a plan," said Fred. "But we've got to work quickly before that last cart makes it around the restaurant."

"What do we do?" Stan asked.

"Do you still have your Heelys?" Fred asked.

"Yeah," Stan answered.

"Okay here's what we do," said Fred before he silenced his walkie-talkie.

37
THE LAST LAP

Harry was worried. Fred and Stan had taken out one of the security carts with that sugar bomb, but Eric Heinze, the chief of security, was on their tail now. And Eric Heinze took his job way too seriously. He treated the mall like he was one of the stalkers on *The Running Man,* and it was his job to make sure the convicts (Heinze treated all customers like they were criminals) never saw the outside world again.

He was the last person you wanted tracking you, but Harry doubted that the security chief had seen anything quite like Fred and his friends in his ten years as a security specialist. Harry had seen Heinze stop everything from professional jewel thieves to small time crooks. No one had made away with anything since Eric had taken over, and the security chief was proud of it. He even kept a running tally on a big board out in front of the food court to frighten potential thieves. Harry hated having to scale the board to change the numbers, and he loved when Heinze went away for his public appearances. For several years now, the security chief had been touring the country, giving security seminars at other malls. His fame was on the rise in the mall cop community, and Harry knew Eric Heinze would do anything to make sure Fred and his friends didn't do anything to ruin that. One thing was for sure, no matter how this whole thing ended, Harry was glad he wouldn't be at the security meeting tomorrow.

Heinze's men had forced Fred into the courtyard. At first Harry had thought that might actually be the fastest way to get back to Mordor Clothing, but it was starting to look like the security chief was going to be able to box Fred and Stan in before they made it to the department store. Harry was getting ready to call over the radio that Fred should change his course, when Fred suddenly turned the trike and went around a cluster of teenage girls. The girls squealed as Fred zoomed by, and when he burst out on the other side of them, Stan was gone.

Harry rubbed his eyes. *Where had the gunner gone?* Harry was going to ask Fred, but he was worried Eric Heinze was listening in now. He didn't want to give away Fred's plan and lose the element of surprise. Against Heinze, they needed all the help they could get.

The courtyard was full of customers, and Fred was zipping around them as he angled for Mordor Clothing's front door. Although he was driving a larger, heavier security cart, Eric Heinze and his driver stayed right behind the cherry-colored trike as it dodged shoppers. Heinze was yelling, and the crowd parted suddenly. The security chief finally had a clear shot at Fred. Harry hoped Fred was ready to put his plan into action because he was out of time.

Eric Heinze raised his taser and trained it on Fred's trike.

That's when Harry spotted Stan. At least he thought it was Stan. The boy was a blur. He was zooming through the crowd too fast and too smoothly to be running. He was gliding and sliding in and out of groups of shoppers, so that even if Eric had thought to look behind him, he never would have been able to hit Stan.

But Eric was looking at Fred and nothing else. And the security guard's finger was hugging the trigger of his taser....

Stan timed his throw perfectly. Just before Eric fired the taser dart, a flash of red flew across the courtyard and struck the security chief's arm. His hand was knocked sideways, and the taser buried its dart in the leg of his own driver. The man's leg jerked, and his foot shoved the pedal straight to the floor. Eric tried to grab the wheel, but it was too late. The cart crashed into a picnic table with bone-jarring impact. For an instant the cart and the table were frozen in motion like two football players grappling at the line of scrimmage, and then they collapsed to the ground.

The engine buzzed frantically as it kept trying to push the cart forward, and then with a dull pop and a puff of white smoke it gave out. Eric dragged himself from the golf cart and reached out a hand towards the fleeing Stan. Then he passed out completely.

"Great shot, Stan!" Harry heard Fred say over the intercom. "That was one in a billion."

"Yeah, but it was all your plan," said Stan, skating up to the trike and hopping onto the back of it.

"Good teamwork, then," said Fred.

"What do we do now?" Stan asked. "We're out of items, and we still have Uruk-hai to face."

Fred shouted into the walkie-talkie. "Mad Max, this is Underhill, we need you!"

"Copy that, Underhill," Jimmy replied. "Mad Max is on his way. High King, map me out a route and fast."

"Copy, Max," answered Harry on the radio. "By my count, you've got four marauders still on the hunt. I'm checking the route now." There was radio silence as Harry scanned the screens. "Okay, Mad Max, the most direct route to Doom is to take a right at the next major corridor and then follow the main covered walkway straight across."

"Copy that, High King," Jimmy answered, turning his tricycle down the main hallway.

"Oh, no," said Harry.

"What is it?" Jimmy asked.

"I forgot that they're remodeling one of the outlet stores along that walkway," said Harry. "They've torn up the whole store—including the floor—and closed the walkway. It's a mess in there—you'll never make it. You'll have to go another way."

"There's no time!" said Jimmy. "I'll just have to find a way."

"You'll have to do it with some marauders on your tail, too," Harry said. "You've got two in pursuit. They're each driving some new kind of cart that I've never seen before. And they look fast, Max."

"Well, if they spent so much money on some new-fangled carts, it would be a shame not to see what they can do," said Jimmy.

"Just hurry, 'Deadeye!'" Fred screamed into the walkie-talkie.

"On my way," Jimmy said, pumping his legs even harder. The new carts rode up close behind him. "I hope you drank your Surge and brought your A-game boys, because this ain't gonna be no Peach Beach," he said. But the words were hardly out of his mouth when a loud bang, a blast of heat, and a shower of sparks forced him into an evasive maneuver. He looked back and saw, as Harry did, one of the drivers pull out another taser gun. Luckily for Jimmy the first dart had missed its target and hit the metal of a storefront, sending volts of electricity through the lights of the sign and shattering the bulbs.

"Whoa!" he said. "These guys take their job way too seriously. I guess the Imperial scout troopers had to do something when things went south, but who thought they'd end up working at the freaking mall."

"Max, watch yourself, mate!" said Harry.

Jimmy didn't respond. He was too busy maneuvering the trike around a giant display of women's perfume and make-up. The poster had two bright lights on it, and Jimmy had to put his hand up to shield his eyes. Blinded, he nearly bumped into the display. Then he skidded around a shelf of purses and into another straightaway.

Through the herd of shoppers and kiosks, Harry saw what awaited Jimmy at the end of the hall—bright orange barriers blocked off the entrance to the next mall. It was a most hazardous path.

"About time for a real challenge," Jimmy said. "These toaster jockeys are starting to become a nuisance."

He grabbed a green kickball and chucked it at one of the wooden barriers. The barrier toppled over, forming a bridge into the store, and Jimmy used it, racing into the chaos. Harry bit his fingernails. He hadn't gotten a good look at the renovations before and now he was realizing that they were even more extensive than he'd thought. Some chunks of the floor were missing entirely. Harry could see to the first floor through the gaping holes. The parts of the floor that were intact were so narrow, he couldn't believe Jimmy was managing to stay on the planks.

Harry watched in awe as Jimmy swerved and swooped along the course, dodging piles of rusty nails, stray two-by-fours, and panes of glass. Because they were able to follow Jimmy's lead, the guards had managed to stay on the course as well. They were firing taser darts left and right, barely missing Jimmy each time. *They must be new recruits*, thought Harry. *They're out to kill!*

But there was nothing Harry could say to help Jimmy now—he was moving way too fast. There was now so much smoke and so many sparks, Harry thought Jimmy must have been driving more on instinct than eyesight. And he was getting totally ridiculous with his moves, pulling off turns and jumps Harry thought were impossible. After an exceedingly sharp turn, the cart started to tilt, but Jimmy pulled hard on the wheel and righted himself before he careened off into oblivion.

For an instant the smoke cleared, and both Harry and Jimmy saw a little more of the shop. Up ahead, the entire floor had been pulled up, creating a large chasm. There was no way to cross! Jimmy was in deep trouble. Harry looked frantically for an alternate route, but there was nothing that could possibly help Jimmy except for several sheets of plywood that had been propped up against a tool bench. Maybe, just maybe, it could form a steep, rickety ramp, but Harry didn't think it would do the archer any good. With nowhere else to go, Jimmy pedaled for it as fast as he could.

"Mad Max, what are you doing?" said Harry. "You'll never be able to make that jump!"

"Probably not," said Jimmy.

"That's a huge drop, Max," said Harry. "You could get seriously injured. Don't do it."

Fred called in over the intercom. "Jimmy, it's okay. You don't have to—"

"Yes, I do," said Jimmy. There was a determination in Jimmy's voice that made Harry's hair stand on end. "I know what you're going through, Fred," Jimmy said quietly. "I've been bullied all my life, and I...I never had my parents around, and I never had the courage to do anything about it. Well, today that's all I have. And it makes me fast, and it makes me light. Like a leaf on the wind."

Something was spurring Jimmy forward at tremendous speed towards the ramp. Jimmy spun the steering wheel expertly, cutting across a narrow causeway and between two giant panes of glass. He slipped between them, getting rocked slightly as the edge of his back-tire scraped against the side of the pane. One of the guards wasn't so lucky. He hit the pane squarely, sending shards of glass spraying everywhere. Somehow the guard managed to stay on his cart.

Steering the trike with one hand, Jimmy lit another bomb-shaped firework. Rapidly approaching the gap, he lined up his cart with the ramp. Harry knew Jimmy's legs must have been burning with fatigue, but, somehow, he got the trike moving even faster. A few feet in front of the ramp and just before the fuse on the firework burned down, Jimmy tossed the bomb behind him. It blew up right before it hit the ground. The explosion shot him forward up the ramp and ignited the six candles on the back of the trike. He went airborne at terrific speed, his back pressed hard against the chair.

"Galadrielllllllllllll!" he shouted as he soared over the gap.

The exploding bomb blinded the guards behind him. One of them covered his eyes with both hands and missed the ramp altogether. He screamed as his cart toppled over the gap, bouncing against plank after plank as it fell to the ground floor in a heap of dust. The other driver managed to catch one tire on the ramp. He didn't get nearly as much air

as Jimmy and got caught in the wake of Jimmy's afterburn-
ers. The yellow and red fireballs from Jimmy's burners shot
straight into his cabin. His cart dipped while Jimmy's rose.
It crashed into a tower of paint cans on its way to the first
floor.

Even with the boost from the fireworks, Harry still
doubted that Jimmy was going to make the jump. It seemed
too great a distance to cover, even as he flew towards the
landing. He was going to miss it, Harry was sure, and then
the candles shot their blue fireworks, giving Jimmy the final
boost he needed. The front wheel touched down, and the
back two landed with a shudder. Jimmy let out a shout of
triumph as he pumped the brakes, trying to slow the trike
before he crashed into the far wall. He skidded to a full stop
mere inches from the wall.

"Harry, what happened!" Fred shouted.

"He...he made it!" Harry shouted. "I don't believe it, but
he made it!"

A shout went up over the channel.

"Get better, noobs," Jimmy said, taunting the fallen
guards. "Take notes, McLean, because that's how you do
'Wild Wheels.' 'Deadeye' has twelve-hundred points
heading into the final event. But anything can happen
there, folks—so stay tuned," he said as he sped off again.

"No time for a commercial break, 'Deadeye,'" Fred
yelled over the com. "We need you now!"

"On my way," Jimmy replied. "Be ready to jump on my
trike. Mithrandir and Longbeard rally at the gates!"

The fools had somehow managed to take out all the guards. How considerate of them. Now she had one less thing to worry about, and it would be even easier for her to take back her ring. She could almost feel its coolness around her finger. The thought made her shiver with delight, but she forced herself to focus. It had been difficult enough not to become distracted by all the amazing deals on dresses and purses and earrings going on at the mall. Everything would go so perfectly with the ring.

Oh, yes, a perfect pair of earrings would set off the engagement ring so nicely. But once you had the matching earrings, of course you needed the matching shoes, and then, of course, a handbag to go with the shoes, and then a tennis bracelet would complement the handbag so nicely, so then she'd need a necklace to go with the bracelet and the lipstick to bring it all together. Lipstick only reminded her that she'd need a new shade of nail polish to go with the diamond. How wonderful it would be to ask the attendants at the counter what shade went best with a flawless, ten carat diamond. How they would envy her! She shuddered again with pleasure. Once again, she forcibly brought her mind back to what she still needed to do. At least she had been able to snatch a gorgeous fur coat during the chaos and confusion, and she rubbed the soft sleeve slowly as she waited in the shadows.

From where she crouched, hidden under the stairwell, none of the factory workers could see her. They were only stupid peons, anyway—they could do nothing to stop her. The ring would be coming this way, right into her path. She didn't know how she knew, but she knew. It wanted her, wanted to rest on her fingers and be seen by very rich and very important people. She just had to wait for it come to her, wait just a little longer.

38
ALL IN THE FAMILY

The helicopter pilot put the aircraft into a hover above a small parking lot just across the street from McKellan Mall Commons. Solomon looked out from the cabin and saw that complete bedlam had broken out in front of the mall. People were streaming from the huge complex in a flood. There were even more people trying to get in.

"I'll never get anywhere if I try to go on foot," Solomon said to the pilot. "Do you think you could land me on top of Mordor Wholesale Clothing store, just over there?"

"No way," said the pilot. "I'd need clearance. A permit. Something."

"Alright, what if you didn't touch down?" said Solomon. "What if I just...jumped?"

"Like Stallone?" the pilot laughed. Solomon stared back at him desperately. "Hey, it's your funeral, buddy," the pilot answered, lifting the helicopter into the air once more.

Just then, another helicopter buzzed by them, startling the pilot and Solomon both. When Solomon saw "Richmond Industries" written on the side of the aircraft, his hands balled into fists. It was Leo.

"Get me to that roof as fast as you can," he said to the pilot.

The pilot banked sharply to the left and hovered a few feet over the roof. The roar of the helicopter blades was deafening. When Solomon leaned out onto the landing skids, he felt like he was in the middle of a tornado. The roof seemed a million miles away. Maybe the pilot had a point. *Stallone always makes jumping in and out of helicopters look easy*, he thought. If he survived the jump, he promised to write a strongly worded letter to Hollywood.

Taking a firm grip on the flimsy rope, he braced his feet on the skid. Once he was out far enough, he slid down to the end of the rope. This still left him five or six feet from the rooftop. He tried to relax as much as possible and then dropped. A shock rattled his ankles and his knees. Rolling clumsily onto his back and then lurching to his feet, he stumbled towards the roof access door. He was instantly out of breath. He was so embarrassed by his lack of fitness, he promised then and there to start exercising three times a week. After a couple failed tries, he finally kicked open the door, and stumbled down the stairs three steps at a time, breathing heavily.

When he reached the main floor he heard, and felt, an explosion. His heart pounded in terror, and he felt as if he might faint. He had to remind himself to breathe. Without even realizing it, he'd started running as fast as he could manage towards the noise. He just hoped he wasn't too late.

The crowd gathering around McKellan Mall Commons had grown so big that not even the sirens of Sheriff Marshal's cruiser could part it.

"Oh, Lord, please don't let one of these people carrying a gun decide to play cowboy," said Renee. "Can't you do something?" she asked the sheriff.

"Darling, I ain't Moses," he said. "And I can't arrest hundreds of people for running scared. I should be doing crowd control."

"These fools are full grown adults," said Renee. "My baby is in there somewhere."

Lucy jumped into action. "Sheriff, pull closer to those cars," she said.

"Ma'am, those cars ain't moving," said the sheriff. "You'd have better luck pushing a bee hive up a bear's backside."

"We don't need the cars to move!" said Lucy. "Just trust me."

The sheriff beat on the horn and leaned his out of the window. "Anyone still in my way after I count to three is going to get banned from the mall for life!" he yelled. Finally, the sea of humanity parted just enough for them to maneuver the car behind the string of log-jammed cars. Lucy threw open the door and pushed her way through a dense clump of people.

"Where are you going?" shouted Renee and the sheriff in unison.

"To get my son!" she shouted, jumping onto the back of the car. She slipped immediately, banging her knee against the car window. She gripped her knee in pain and then rose slowly and steadied herself before she started climbing over the backs of the cars. She'd somehow made it over three cars when she heard Renee call out behind her. "Since when did you become Spiderwoman?"

She turned around and saw Sheriff Marshal practically carrying Renee over the cars behind her.

"Shut up and speed up, Renee," said Lucy. "I'm done talking."

"I'm trying!" said Renee. "It's been a minute since I made like a monster truck."

Lucy scrambled over the SUV closest to the curb and screamed like a total madwoman at the crowd beneath. The terrified shoppers parted as she scrambled down the hood of the car. It still took her a long time to get to the mall entrance. She got hit by flying knees and elbows from every direction as she pushed through the crowd. She threw herself at the doorway but got pinned against the frame as people poured out. The metal pushed against the bruises on her spine, and she could barely breathe. She thought she was a goner herself until Sheriff Marshal appeared and pulled her free. This time it was Renee who went full crazy on the people frantically pouring out of the mall, and they gave the three of them enough space to squeeze past.

The inside of the mall was a little less chaotic, but there were still people streaming about every which way looking for an exit. Some people were trying to make off with loose merchandise. This scared Lucy more than anything. With all the commotion, it would be just as easy to kidnap a child as it would be to make off with a television set.

She started searching frantically. No one in the world probably knew less about shopping malls than she did, but she found a map and sprinted towards it.

"What are you looking for?" said Renee.

"I don't know," said Lucy breathlessly. "It's so big."

"Toy store?" said the sheriff, pointing to a store at the end of the corridor.

"Let's hope," said Lucy, as all three sprinted towards it.

An enormous explosion stopped them in their tracks. It rattled Lucy's teeth and caused her heart to skip a beat. Lucy couldn't move. She fell to her knees and started keening. The lid had been blown off all the emotions she'd been trying in vain to control. All her fear. All her worry.

"No, no, no," she cried. "Please, no."

Renee and the sheriff tried to get her up, but she was numb with fear. She sat there sobbing uncontrollably.

Suddenly, as if in a dream, Solomon was there. His hair mussed. His eyes exhausted but calm. He was saying her name and holding out his hand. He looked miraculous in the lights of the shops, but she felt a million miles away. It felt like swimming in a dream, but she reached out and took his hand and then they were moving, sprinting towards the explosion as fast as they could.

39

~~THE~~ **MOUNTAIN** ~~ROAD~~ ~~L~~**OOM** ~~COMPANY~~

Jimmy came blazing through the entrance to Mordor Wholesale Clothing Store. Fred and Stan hailed him from where they were crouching behind a rack of men's jeans. Jimmy slowed enough to let them grab on, and then he sped up as he turned down the hallway where the two security guards still stood in front of the "Manufacturing Area: Keep Out" sign. Fred cursed. The plan hadn't completely worked. Unfortunately, the two guards at the end of the hallway had not been lured away by the sounds of battle. It would make getting to Mount Doom more difficult, but after seeing Jimmy in action, Fred doubted he'd have any trouble with two more guards.

The guards already had their tasers out, but it looked like they were holding their fire until the boys got closer.

"How are we going to get past them?" yelled Stan.

"I've been saving one of Alfred's best fireworks for these two orcs," Jimmy said. "Load the arrow with the 'Apocalypse Rocket' and then get ready to run."

Fred reached into Jimmy's bag and grabbed the arrow with the rocket taped to it. The firework was so large Fred had trouble getting it out of the bag. It was shaped like a missile but it was so massive, Jimmy would have to fire it just as the fuse lit the powder or he wouldn't be able to aim it at all. The weight of the rocket would drag the arrow down if he fired too early, and if he fired too late, the rocket could carry the arrow off in any direction.

"It's loaded...and lit, Jimmy," Fred yelled. Jimmy stopped the trike abruptly, skidding to a halt sideways in the narrow hallway. He reached over his shoulder and grabbed the bow. He took aim and waited for the fuse to burn down. At the sight of the rocket, the guards finally decided to run towards the boys, but they were too late.

Jimmy's timing was perfect. He released the arrow just as the rocket fired. It screamed through the air in a twisting helix of smoke and red exhaust and exploded squarely in the center of the double doors. The two guards managed to duck fast enough to avoid the rocket, but the force of the explosion sent them sliding along the floor halfway down the hallway. Fred and Stan stared through the smoking hole in the door with amazement. The sign had been obliterated, and the rocket gave out a few last sparks before it fizzled and stopped for good. The guards did not rise.

"Go, guys, go!" Jimmy shouted. "I'll keep the orcs at bay until Alfred and Gemma arrive."

"Thanks, Jim," Fred said, jumping off the back of the 'Road Warrior.'

He and Stan raced down the hallway, hurdling over the unconscious guards. They stopped at the ruined door, taking off their helmets. They were so far behind enemy lines that nothing, not even Mandalorian armor, could protect them now. They sprinted to the end of the hallway, which forked sharply in two different directions. They took the left hallway and followed this until it branched again, giving them three options: left, right, or straight ahead.

"Where do we go?" Stan asked. "Mordor is a maze."

"Do NOT bring some Grievers down on us right now," Fred said through heavy breaths. But Stan was right—it was a maze. Fred bit his cheek as he anxiously studied each path. He had no clue which way to go either, and they didn't have much time to decide. Those guards wouldn't stay down forever. "Let's go straight," he said, hoping his instincts would lead them to Mount Doom.

They continued down the hallway. When he saw swing doors in the distance, Fred nearly jumped for joy. But he was so exhausted he probably wouldn't have been able to clear a toothpick if he'd actually jumped, so he just put his head down and ran as fast as he could for the end of the hall.

When he and Stan burst through the doors, they found themselves on a platform that overlooked an enormous factory floor. Below them hundreds of workers sat entranced before wicked-looking metal machines that clicked and chopped and coughed. The workers looked prisoners bound by invisible chains to their machines. They moved their limbs with a hopeless weariness as if they were but machines themselves. Dozens of sentries paced up and down the rows of tired servants.

As much as Fred pitied them, he couldn't stop his gaze from being drawn to the back of the room.

There, rising like a mountain from the factory floor, was a giant manufacturing machine. The top of the machine nearly scraped the ceiling. On the sides of the mountainous machine were several sets of ladders leading to different platforms and giant pipes that spewed smoke and hissed. Broad axles spun reels of fabric with a loud groaning sound, and every few seconds the whole thing rumbled ominously. On one jagged flank the name MOUNTAIN ROAD LOOM COMPANY had been covered by dirt and grime until only the letters M-O-U-N-T, D, and O-O-M could be seen.

"Great Eye of Thundera!" Fred exclaimed. "It's Mount Doom!"

"I'll be Splinter's fuzzy butthole," Stan said. "It actually exists. I don't believe it, but it actually exists."

"And the Dark Lord has strengthened its protection a dozen times over," Fred said despairingly, surveying the factory floor again. "But he should know that if we've made it this far, we won't be stopped now."

"Hey, you kids can't be down here," said a man in a hard-hat. He left the panel he had been working on and started walking towards the two boys, his work boots ringing on the metal walkway.

Fred and Stan looked at each other, not sure what to do.

"Hey, what's that up there?" Stan asked, pointing to a spot behind the man, who turned to look. By the time the man realized there was nothing there, Stan had landed a haymaker to his "family jewels." The man toppled like a hobbit who has had one too many pints of ale, his eyes bulging and his face growing as red as dragon-hide.

"Ooh, right in the groonies," Fred said as he and Stan ran around the man. It wasn't as difficult as winning a game of wizard's chess, but Fred was glad his friend was there to help him all the same.

They raced to the end of the walkway and sprinted down the stairs, dodging around the workers, some of whom were trying to grab them. *Don't they know I'm trying to help them?* Fred thought, seeing for the first time the brilliance of the Dark Lord's spell. The Dark Lord forced his servants to work for days on end with no rest, tiring them out so that they had no energy to fight him and no ability to recognize an ally come to help. Fred recoiled in horror from the crazed exhaustion in the orcs' zombie-like eyes.

Four servants of Mordor were trying to ring them in, so he and Stan jumped up on a long, white table and leapt to the next one. They kept bounding from table to table, avoiding the grasps of the factory workers. Jumping from the last table to the floor, they dashed across the concrete. Reaching the mountainous loom first, Fred grabbed hold of the metal rung of a ladder and began to climb. He pulled himself over the ledge and onto the first platform, turning around to help Stan. He was just about to grab Stan's hand when the most frightening creature either boy had ever seen—or imagined—grabbed Stan's leg.

"Give it to me!" the fiend yelled, lifting its face so that Fred could see that it was Joanne—or that it used to be. She looked like a dragon had swallowed her whole and deposited her out the other side. And as she had passed through the dragon's digestive tract, she must have gotten mixed up with the remains of a Warg. Her hair was greasy and had fallen out in clumps, the skin was hanging off her bones, and her eyes were even more glazed over than after she'd downed usual lunchtime martini. Her lips curling into a sneer, Joanne yelled again: "Give it to me now, you spoiled little brat! It's my DIAMOND!"

"Stan, c'mon, you can still make it!" Fred exclaimed. "Just grab my hand."

"Keep going, man," Stan yelled, struggling against Joanne's grip. "I'll try to hold her off."

"I can't do this without you!" Fred said. He couldn't believe this was happening now, when they were so close.

"Finish it!" Stan said, and there was steel in his voice that gave Fred fresh courage.

Fred waited for a second longer, not wanting to leave Stan behind, and then he pushed himself up from the platform and started running to the next ladder. He called to Jimmy on the walkie-talkie.

"'Deadeye,' we've got a problem!" he screamed. "Hurry!"

40
THE FINAL BATTLE

"On my way, Fred" Jimmy answered over the com. Alfred and Gemma were rolling towards him fast, some guards chasing behind them. Jimmy lobbed a smoke bomb over their heads to give them cover, and then he lobbed a cherry bomb to keep the guards in pursuit nervous about advancing.

"I've got to go," he said to Alfred and Gemma. "But take the rest of the fireworks and the kickballs. We shouldn't need that much time, so just do what you can."

"We'll do more than that," said Gemma, raising her ax.

"Fly, you fool!" said Alfred, grabbing a kickball and lobbing it to Gemma who smacked it towards the guards.

Jimmy turned and ran down the hallway towards the factory. He snatched a vest from his gym bag and buckled the snaps. Then he threw the bungee rope in a coil over one shoulder and his bow over the other. It was a lot to carry, but he was still zipping across the floor. He only had three arrows left, but each had one of the needles full of sedative.

He burst through the swing door into the factory. Unfortunately, the same worker Stan had knocked to the ground was still lying there. The edge of the door hit him in the very same spot he had just injured.

"Ooh, right in the Gonzo nose and Miss Piggies," said Jimmy as the man groaned in pain again. Jimmy apologized and then searched the cavernous room for Fred.

When he saw the manufacturing machine, his heart stopped. He couldn't believe it. Rising through the mist was the object he saw every night in his sleep, the obstacle he had been training for since the first episode of Nickelodeon *GUTS* hit the air. His magnum opus. His destiny.

The Aggro Crag.

He didn't realize how long he'd been staring at it until Fred called out again from across the factory floor. Jimmy jumped to action—he wasn't going to let his friend down, and he wasn't going to let the Crag beat him. He had been preparing his whole life for this moment. Now was the hour of his redemption.

He attached one end of the bungee cord to his vest and then swung the other end like a grappling hook before tossing into the rafters where it caught securely onto a metal beam. He tested it and then took a deep breath. Closing his eyes, he imagined standing atop the Aggro Crag and looking out upon all that he had conquered. He had tackled this obstacle a million times in his mind. He should have been nervous, but he wasn't. He was calm. He was ready.

Opening his eyes, he leapt over the side of the railing and plummeted towards the ground. Just as the bungee cord pulled taut, he planted his feet squarely on the concrete, pushing up with all his might. The cord yanked him into the air, up and away from the railing. Floating untethered in mid-air, he grabbed hold of a chain dangling from the warehouse ceiling, which was holding up a large cluster of lights. He cut his bungee with the sword and let the chain take him. His downward momentum turned to forward motion as the chain swung on its pulley. He would have crashed into a group of several workers who were ready to tackle him, if the catch on the pulley hadn't slipped. A huge panel of lights came crashing down, propelling Jimmy up into the air once more and out of the reach of the workers. Before the chain started to swing backwards, he managed to grab a hold of another chain and slide down to the floor beyond the reach of everyone.

As Jimmy's feet touched down, he heard Fred cry out yet again. He looked to the top of the Crag. Some foul creature with spindly arms and legs and a coat of fur had grabbed hold of Fred, and the two of them were struggling on the Aggro Crag's uppermost platform. Stan was at the base of the Crag, frantically climbing up the ladder towards his friend. But it was obvious to Jimmy that Stan would never make it in time.

The hideous creature suddenly jumped upon Fred, who was fighting mightily to prevent it from getting the ring. Dropping his shoulder, Fred managed to throw the creature from his back. He was free, but the effort of the heave caused him to lose his footing. He waved his arms, but he couldn't stop himself from tripping over the edge of the platform. He went sailing over the edge.

Jimmy gasped. For a second, he thought Fred was a goner. Then the creature's hand shot out and snagged Fred's arm at the last possible moment. It held him swinging like a pendulum over the ground many feet below. Stan had managed to climb up to the platform just below Fred and the creature, but he was still too far away to reach his friend to pull him to safety.

"Give me the ring and you live, brat," the creature

snarled at Fred. "If not, I let you fall and pick the diamond off your body."

"I'll throw it in the gears!" Fred shouted, ripping the ring from the necklace and opening his hand as if to drop it.

"NO!" the creature gasped. "Give it to me!"

"FRED!" Jimmy heard someone cry behind him. He looked up to the walkway. Fred's parents had arrived in a big group with Alfred and Gemma.

"Fire, Deadeye!" Fred shouted, drawing Jimmy's attention back to the Crag.

"You'll fall!" Jimmy shouted back, desperation in his voice.

"I've got him, Jimmy," Stan hollered over the roar of the loom. "Shoot her!"

Jimmy lifted the bow and loaded it in a flash. He pulled back the string and aimed carefully, his heart pounding in his chest. If this didn't work just right, Fred was toast. He waited as Stan shuffled back to the end of the platform. Jimmy slowed his breathing, using every last bit of concentration to master his nerves. Stan took a running start, and when he neared the edge of the platform Jimmy loosed the arrow with a loud twang that echoed through the factory. It flew across the room as if on an invisible rope and buried itself deep inside the creature's furry torso.

Joanne howled in pain and anger, dropping Fred and recoiling back, clutching at the arrow. Fred started to fall, and as he did, he tossed the ring into the bowels of the machine, where it was quickly swallowed up in a twisting maw of gears.

The ring of power was destroyed! But Fred was following it, dropping right towards the groaning, gnashing metal.

Jimmy's breath caught in his throat. For a brief

moment, he thought that he had fired too soon, and that they were going to be picking Fred up from the factory floor with a broom and a spatula, and then Stan took a mighty leap from the platform and tackled Fred in midair. He was moving fast enough to carry them both to the next metal walkway. The two of them hit hard and somersaulted as they tried to gain a grip on the grate. Once again, Fred slipped over the edge, his arms reaching up, searching for a handhold. Jimmy heard more cries from the parents behind him. Stan scrambled over and the two boys clasped hands just in time to prevent Fred from falling to a grisly demise.

But they weren't out of danger yet. This time it wasn't gears that threatened to kill Fred if Stan lost his grip. Just a few feet below Fred's dangling feet, what looked like two enormous steamrollers were flattening the sheets of fabric that passed between their crushing jaws. If Fred fell, he was going to be two-dimensional for the rest of his life.

"No!" a chorus of parents yelled from the walkway above.

"Jimmy, he's slipping!" said Stan.

"How do I shut it off?" Jimmy shouted to one of the employees, who were keeping their distance from him now, afraid of his arrows.

"Uh...you've got to push all the emergency shut-off buttons at each panel!" The man shouted back. "Those red ones."

Jimmy took off, sprinting towards the Aggro Crag. Without slowing, he jumped, planting his right foot on a rung halfway up the ladder, and then jumped again off this foot, grabbing the platform with his hands and heaving himself up. He was on his feet and running again in an instant, plunging through the gusts of steam issuing from the mountain of metal to the first emergency panel and shoving the giant red shut-off button with his palm. He continued along the metal grating, moving so fast his feet barely made a sound as they impacted. A wall of the Aggro Crag jutted out by the next ladder, and Jimmy ran straight at it, running up the flat surface and kicking off, turning in the air as he vaulted himself to the platform above. Once again, he pulled himself up onto the platform in a single, smooth motion and punched the next emergency shut-off button as he got to his feet. Another cry from Fred's mother caused Jimmy to look up. Fred had almost slipped out of Stan's grasp. Stan was straining hard trying to keep hold of him.

"Jimmy, hurry!" Stan shouted again.

Jimmy quickly calculated the quickest path to the last emergency shut-off button and Fred. The safest route would be to climb the ladder right next to him all the way up to the topmost platform and then run across, but climbing would take too long. If he wanted to save Fred, he would have to take the more dangerous, but more direct route.

He ran as fast as he could, leaping from the platform and sailing over a gap where dangerous loom machinery spun beneath him. Landing heavily on a smooth metal casing, he nearly slipped on the thin layer of dust which had collected on it. Once he regained his balance, he made his biggest gamble yet. He jumped onto the streaming fabric, riding it up at a forty-five-degree angle towards Fred as if he were a surfer catching a big wave. He had feared that the fabric would not be able to support his weight and that he would fall straight through the sheet into a pool of chemicals or a crushing press. Luckily for him, it held, and he rode it upwards until it lapped over a pulley. He slid down the sheet for a few moments, getting himself closer to the next landing, and then jumped from the fabric just as it was about to empty into a vat of lye. He was moving his feet as he flew, and landed on the platform already running. He slammed the last emergency shut-off button down as hard as he could.

The jaws of the presser beneath Fred began to slow. Jimmy heard everyone on the floor gasp with relief. But a fall from that height could still seriously injure Fred, so Jimmy kept moving. With a loud clang, he dropped down from the top of the Crag onto the platform where Stan was lying on his belly, his arms dangling over the edge, struggling mightily to hold Fred. Jimmy dove across the platform and grabbed Fred's hand just as Stan's strength gave out. With the last untapped bit of his energy, Jimmy heaved Fred up to safety on the platform.

Across the factory floor, Lucy and another woman Jimmy didn't recognize collapsed on the walkway, weeping into each other's arms. With the loom shut off, the factory was completely silent but for their cries.

And then the factory workers started applauding. Soon they were whistling and cheering so loudly Jimmy couldn't even hear himself panting for breath. It took him a second to realize they were cheering for him. In all his life, Jimmy Dingleman had never heard a sound so sweet.

"I'll go get them, Lucy," he heard Solomon yell as Alfred rushed to Lucy's side to console her. Solomon ran to the loom and started climbing the ladder.

Fred, Stan and Jimmy had rolled over onto their backs and were panting on the platform.

"Jimmy 'Deadeye' Dingleman sets a new record on the Aggro Crag and takes home the gold *GUTS* medal and a radioactive piece of the legendary mountain," Fred said between deep breaths.

"We've never seen a contestant quite like this, Moira," added Stan.

Though there were tears forming in his eyes, Jimmy beamed. It was easily the happiest he'd ever been in his entire life. Strangely, he found that he didn't really care that much that he'd finally conquered the Crag. He was so happy because for the first time in his life he knew he had some real friends.

41

AFTER THE BATTLE

Rolling onto his side, Stan groaned in pain and then gave an exhausted laugh. "You did it, Jimmy," he said. "You did it with style, too. You got more GUTS than a Gigantosaurus, man."

Fred was too tired to laugh. His ribs were sore from getting tackled, too. Through the grating above them, he saw that Joanne was even worse for wear. She was fast asleep, and her drool was dripping through the bars. Just in case her saliva could burn through metal like a xenomorph's, Fred pulled Stan and Jimmy aside.

"Eww, gross!" Stan said. "I guess Joanne showed her true colors today. And I guess her true color is 'Warg droppings.' I don't think there's any way your dad could ever marry that hot mess of crazy."

Before Fred could answer, Renee cried out from the factory floor. "Stanley Gardner," she screamed. "Get your narrow behind down from there before you break your neck."

"Uh-oh," said Fred. "That was a middle name drop."

Stan sighed. "Ah, I always knew this was coming."

Fred was suddenly ashamed at his selfishness. All along he'd been so worried about his problems, he hadn't really been thinking about how this whole thing would end for Stan. Stan had given everything to help Fred, and now Fred felt truly powerless to help his best friend. "I'm truly sorry, Stan," he said. "You've helped me so much, and I..."

"Don't be," said Stan. "At the start of this mess I was so angry with you because I knew that, lucky white kid that you are, somehow your family would be saved by this and mine would be, well just the same mess." He looked down at his mom and smiled. "But now I feel like I could talk to my mom for real." He held his hand out and Fred clasped it. "You did it, man," he said, and Fred hugged him.

"We did it," he said.

The machine suddenly shook and shuddered as if experiencing death throes, and Lucy and Renee cried out in worry again.

"Stay there, boys," Solomon shouted. "It's too dangerous. I'll come help you get down."

"Dad?" said Fred, amazed to hear his father's voice. He smiled as he watched his dad struggle to climb up the ladders and ledges of the giant loom. "You can do it!" he yelled when his dad had to stop and bend over to catch his breath.

When his dad finally reached the platform the boys were on, Fred sprinted towards him and hugged him hard.

"Be careful, Fred!" said Solomon as he scooped his son up in a hug. "Do you have any idea how scared your mother and I have been?" he said, growing tearful as he embraced his son. "How could you be so reckless? What in the world possessed you to do this?"

"Lots of things, Dad," Fred replied, still hugging his father with all his might. "But mostly, I just couldn't let you marry that terrible woman, and I knew you'd never listen to me."

"Oh, Fred," said Solomon, hugging Fred again. "I'm so sorry. I should have talked to you. I should have listened." Even though his dad was crying, Fred thought his father looked happier than he had in a long time. "I haven't been a good father lately, but that's going to change."

Solomon turned to Jimmy and Stan and grabbed them up in a hug, too. "I don't know how to thank you boys for saving Fred's life," he said.

"No, Mr. Oglesburg," replied Jimmy. "You should thank Fred. Because I think he saved all of ours."

"You know what, Jim," Solomon said, looking up at Joanne. "I think you may be right."

"SOLOMON!" Leo bellowed from the walkway. He and John Bonneville had both made their way to the factory floor, several police officers in tow. "You get my Jo-bear down from there now!"

"That nickname is a little on the nose, don't you think?" said Stan. Jimmy and Fred chuckled.

"And I want these vandals arrested," added Leo. "They've destroyed my property and assaulted, even attempted to murder, my daughter. Someone put those heathens in handcuffs now or else." Leo's jowls were turning as purple as a goblin tongue as he continued to scream.

"Yeah, put these heathens in handcuffs!" John Bonneville said, parroting Leo.

"And get back to work!" yelled Leo, gesturing to all the people on the factory floor. "I'm not paying you to stand around gawking."

"C'mon guys, let's get down from here," said Solomon. Even though the boys could all climb down more easily that

Solomon, they let him lead them to the factory floor. He and Jimmy would go down a ladder first and then help Fred and Stan climb down. Lucy and Renee were waiting at the bottom of the stairs, but before Fred and Stan could reach out to hug them, two police officers pushed Lucy and Renee out of the way and grabbed Fred and Stan roughly from the loom and threw them to the floor.

Fred's aching shoulder banged against the concrete, and then felt like it was going to be torn off completely as his arms got wrenched behind his back. His face was being pressed sideways into the floor, but he was facing Stan, so he saw a big man put a knee into his friend's back. He wanted to call out, but he'd lost his breath getting slammed to the floor. He heard Stan's mom call out hysterically, "No, please, no! He's just a boy, don't hurt him!"

But the weight of the officer on Fred's back didn't lift.

That's when Fred heard the gunshot.

The shot echoed through the factory and rang in Fred's ears. When it stopped, he thought he'd lost his hearing for a second because the factory was completely quiet.

"Get off them, now," said Sheriff Marshal, training his gun on the officer holding down Stan. "They're children, and you take orders from me, not the richest man in the room."

"You sure about that?" said Renee, running to shield Stan, as the officers slowly stood up, hands out. A look of realization came over the sheriff, but he kept his gun trained on the other officers.

"Easy, sheriff," one of them said. "He seems in his rights as owner of the store."

"He's not the owner yet," said Solomon. "Even if they completed the negotiations before I left, the final paper-work hasn't been processed."

The officers backed up some more after hearing this and Lucy rushed over, too, sweeping Fred up in a protective hug.

"How many times do I have to tell you?" Fred heard Renee sob as she clutched Stan.

"Now wait a minute," said Leo. "Soon enough I'll own this store and everything in it, and I want them punished to the full extent of the law. The full extent, you hear? That's still my daughter up there!"

"Mr. Oglesburg, will you please get the woman down?" the sheriff asked.

Solomon looked despairingly at the towering height of the loom, but took a deep breath and started his climb. Dripping with sweat now, he hoisted Joanne onto his shoulders and climbed down like a firefighter. It took him a few minutes, but he finally made his way to the floor. Sheriff Marshal ordered the other two cops to grab Joanne from Solomon's arms so that Solomon could get down himself.

"Finally," said Leo. "I want paramedics here instantly."

"Make sure they keep her knocked out," said Stan.

"Quiet," snarled Leo. "Or I'll make sure you get tried as an adult."

Renee put her hand over Stan's mouth and pulled him closer to her, glaring at Leo with anger and terror.

"They're already on their way, Mr. Richmond," said one of the officers.

"Then tell them to hurry it up!" yelled Leo. Suddenly his phone rang, and he snatched it off his belt in a flash. "What is it!" he yelled angrily into the phone. "I'm too busy right now, and I told you not to call me on this phone, Ricardo!" he screeched again before promptly hanging up.

Jimmy brought his bow up to his eye and fired an arrow

before Sheriff Marshal or the other two officers could even blink. His arrow buried itself deep in Leo's thick neck. Leo's face went white as a sheet, and then his knees buckled. He slumped to the floor.

"Thank you for that," Solomon said to the surprise of everyone.

John Bonneville muttered in terror as he watched Leo crumple into a heap.

"Everybody stay calm!" said Sheriff Marshal. "No weapons," he said to the officers, whose hands had flown to their pistols. They slowly lifted their hands away. "You, too," he said to Jimmy. "This ain't the OK Corral. You just can't go around shooting people like that."

"Understood, sheriff," said Jimmy, handing over his bow and holding up his hands. "And I wouldn't normally, but I just thought you should know that's the thief you're looking for." He pointed to Leo. Sheriff Marshal and the other two officers looked at him in disbelief. "I'm not joking," said Jimmy. "If you trace the call that just came in on that phone, you'll catch the accomplices."

"That's preposterous!" said John Bonneville. "This man is the new owner of this store and you should be worried about these hoodlums."

"How do you know, son?" the sheriff asked, ignoring John Bonneville. "That's a pretty big accusation."

"When we were in the trolls', err, thieves' capture, they said something I didn't get until just now," said Jimmy. "One of them asked how we could know about 'The Lion.' Leo is Latin for lion, and he just called the man on the other side of the phone, Ricardo. The leader of the gang that attacked us was called Ricky, and I'm guessing it was short for Ricardo."

"I'll have your job if you continue to listen to this

madness," said John Bonneville. "Those are paper thin allegations from a crazy kid who just shot two people!"

"It does seem like coincidence," said the sheriff to Jimmy.

"It could be, but I doubt it," said Jimmy. "I've read too many Encyclopedia Brown books to get this wrong. Have the officers check the source of the call."

The two officers looked questioningly at Sheriff Marshal. "Do it," said the sheriff.

John Bonneville looked like he might explode with anger. The officer grabbed Leo's fallen cell-phone, calling over the radio for someone to trace the number.

After a few tense moments a voice broke through the other side of the radio. "The call is coming from an abandoned factory in the heart of meth country, but it's not that far from the Chadarras station," it said.

"Send all cars to that address," the sheriff ordered.

"Wynnie's already on her way," replied the deputy.

The sheriff sighed. "Tell her not to blow the durn thing to kingdom come," he said. "I want those thieves to testify against this piece of trash in here. Cuff him," the sheriff ordered.

Suddenly realizing his allegiance to Leo was not in his best interest, John Bonneville took a step back.

"I guess it's time we faced the music, too," said Fred, stepping away from his mother and walking over to Sheriff Marshal. He held his hands out so that the sheriff could take them away.

"That's brave of you, son, but I don't think that's necessary," said Sheriff Marshal.

"What!" exclaimed John Bonneville. "Vandals just get set loose in California? No wonder your state is falling apart."

Sheriff Marshal bent down and patted Stan on the shoulder as well. "Well," he said, "considering these brave boys—nice to meet you, by the way," he said to Stan. "You're lucky to have that woman in your corner, son."

"I know, sir," said Stan, looking up at his mom.

"Well," said the sheriff, "considering these brave boys have helped with the apprehension of three criminals who are at the top of California's most wanted list and may have uncovered the identity of one of the biggest crime bosses in the West, the State of California is willing to overlook any minor transgressions they may have committed over the past week."

"Minor!" said John Bonneville. "What's major in this godforsaken state? Serial killing?"

"Yep," said the sheriff. "So are fraud and grand larceny among others."

"Is that a threat?" said John Bonneville.

"Just a reminder to make sure all of your finances are on the level," said the sheriff. "I'd hate to see 'The Lion' here bring you down with him."

John Bonneville huffed. He looked ready to retort, but backed away and snatched his cellphone out of his pocket instead.

"What I thought," said the sheriff.

"Are the boys really off the hook?" asked Renee.

"Yes, ma'am," said the sheriff. "Though I can't speak for Mr. Sowerbraun," he pointed to a tall skinny man striding towards them, "and the mall. There could be some damages."

Fred went over to Mr. Sowerbraun who was still checking his appearance in a mirror one of his attendants was holding up. "We're sorry for tearing up your mall, Mr.

Sowerbraun," said Fred. "But it was the only way to get to Mount Doom."

"Apologize?" said Mr. Sowerbraun, pushing his assistant out of the way. "No, son, I want to thank you!" he reached down to shake Fred's hand vigorously.

Fred looked at Stan, who could only shrug in surprise.

"Scarborough Sports has received nearly a hundred orders for those tricycles in the last half hour," said Mr. Sowerbraun. "Your exhilarating chase has instantly gone viral. All anyone can talk about is McKellen Mall Commons!" An assistant brought Mr. Sowerbraun a comb, and the man slicked his hair back and posed in the mirror again. "Now, if you'll excuse me, half of the news stations in Southern California are waiting to interview me. Need anything else from me, officer?"

"Not right now," said the sheriff.

Mr. Sowerbraun smiled and then turned to leave.

"Mr. Sowerbraun?" Fred asked.

"Yes?"

"I wanted to make sure Harry could keep his job," said Fred.

"So, is that who helped you pull this off?" said Mr. Sowerbraun. "Well, if he's that good, I think a promotion is in order. My security could obviously use some improvement. Maybe head of security should be a little more tech savvy, anyway. Consider it done."

"Wow—thanks!" said Fred. He couldn't believe his luck. He thought he was going to spend at least a year fending off Dementors in Azkaban or trying not to lose a finger in the spice mines of Kessel. He certainly didn't think he'd get off scot-free.

There were still his parents, of course. And they, at least, were sure to ground him for life. He turned to face them. "I guess you're gonna murder me for destroying your ring and drugging your girlfriend," Fred said to his dad.

"He better!" John Bonneville interjected, stowing his phone in his pocket. "That ring probably costs more than your life, boy. They should put you in military school. Send you to be exorcised by a priest. Lock you away and throw away the key. I told you that if you didn't discipline him this would happen, Solomon. Now you're out some forty grand. If that had been my engagement ring, I would have had the kid over my knee in a heartbeat."

"You know what?" Solomon said quietly. "I...it's the strangest thing, but I don't care about the ring."

Everyone turned away from the screaming John Bonneville to stare at Solomon, who looked sublimely happy.

"It's just a rock," he laughed. "Just another bit of carbon that's been pressed for a lot longer than most. And we value it because it's what? Because it's shiny?" He chuckled again. "It's all so silly when you really think about it."

"What are you talking about, Solomon?" John Bonneville asked. "You know that if you let the little brat get away with this, he'll never learn. They that are of a forward heart are an abomination to the Lord, and a fool's wrath is presently known, for the wicked shall be filled with mischief."

"Considering the circumstances, I think another quotation is more apt here," Solomon said. "All that is gold does not glitter, all those who wander are not lost." He put his hands on Fred's shoulders. "The old that is strong does not wither," he winked at Alfred, "and deep roots are not reached by the frost." He smiled at Lucy.

To Fred's complete surprise his mother grabbed his

father and kissed him fully on the mouth. They lingered long in the embrace. Alfred whistled.

"Get it, girl," said Renee.

When they finally pulled away from the kiss, the sheriff high-fived them both.

"Fine, eat the fruit of your own way, for all I care," said John Bonneville. "Your own devices will ruin you."

"Right back at you," said Renee.

"And if they don't do the trick, I've got one arrow left for the next bully that comes after my friends," said Jimmy.

John Bonneville's faced blanched and he raced fearfully up the stairs and through the double doors as if a Wookiee had just threatened him with dismemberment.

Jimmy shrugged. "Well, that's never worked like that before," he said, and everyone shared a laugh.

"Is it just me, or does anyone else want to get out of here before that thing wakes up," said Stan, pointing at Joanne.

"That sounds like a great idea," said Fred.

"We can go, sheriff?" Renee asked.

"Yeah, I know where to find you," he said, smiling.

"Yes, you do," she said, kissing him on the cheek before she led them all together up the stairs.

"Wait!" said Fred suddenly. "I almost forgot. Gemma, we still need to get you your audition!"

"Oh, I think I just had my audition," said Gemma, smiling as she patted her guitar. "Even the mammoths in the tar pits are thinking about investing in some earmuffs."

Fred laughed. "Well, do you want to stay at my place while you're waiting for a band to pick you up?"

"Thanks, man, but I'd like to stay close—just so I don't miss anything."

"She can stay with me," said Harry, who'd just arrived.

"Really?" said Gemma.

"Sure," said Harry. "Just to warn you, though, my mom likes to mop the floor in nothing but her mittens and a melon-cream mask."

"Oh," said Gemma, wrinkling her nose. "I guess I'll just take my boots off outside then."

"Maybe pick her up a *moo moo* before you leave the *mega mall*," said Solomon. Then, when no one laughed, and Lucy shook her head at him, he added: "Or not."

"Your dad tells the worst jokes," Stan said to Fred.

"I know," Fred answered, smiling at his father. "He'd be a good person to have in the Swamps of Sadness, don't you think?"

Stan laughed. "I guess he would."

"Y'all are certifiably insane, you know that?" said Renee.

"Well, technically, I'm the only one who is certifiable," said Alfred.

"The rest of us haven't received our certificates yet," Gemma joked. "I think we have to send in a few more proofs of purchase."

Laughing as he followed his parents up the factory stairs, the exhaustion of the journey finally caught up to Fred. He leg muscles twitched so much that eventually he asked his father for a piggy-back ride. He was glad they'd be able to drive back because he didn't think he'd be able to hike another ten feet. "What I wouldn't give for an eagle ride home," he said.

"You know, I think I can arrange that," said Solomon, leading them out an exit to the back parking lot, where the helicopter was waiting.

Fred looked at the helicopter and then back at Stan. Stan shook his head and beamed.

"Now, what do you say we all go home," said Lucy.

For the first time in a long while Fred knew then when his mother said they were going home, she meant *their* home, and that they'd all be going there together as a family once again. And that made Fred Oglesburg the happiest kid in the world.

EPILOGUE

Lucy Owen and Solomon Oglesburg were remarried on the summer solstice. It was an extravagant event, not in the manner of trappings or dressings, of course, but in joyous celebration. Friends and family brought their favorite picnic food to the banks of the Rogue River and tables bowed beneath the weight of pumpkin squares, lemon cakes, blackberry currants, turkey legs and casseroles.

Lucy and Solomon read their vows standing ankle deep in the water with their pant legs rolled up. They had fashioned their wedding bands themselves, carving them from the branches of a large oak tree that they had visited frequently when they were young and first in love. The wedding program informed the guests that wood from the oak tree was chosen because the oak is the symbol of marital fidelity and mutual fulfillment. Fred carried the rings to them on a garland of posies, wading into the water himself. The program listed him not as "the ring bearer," but as "The Lord of the Rings."

After the wedding, the guests flocked to the tables for

food and to the dance floor to hear music. The four-piece band played lilting tunes and everyone danced.

Alfred the Grand was in attendance, of course, and his guest to the wedding was the widow Thompson, whom he had very recently begun courting. Since returning home from California, Alfred had moved back in with his son and grandson, and he and Fred had been reading books at sunset every night on the porch.

Fred had suggested they read a book about birds and had invited the widow Thompson as a special guest. He and Alfred both loved having her around, and not just because she told him exciting stories about the birds—how they found their way home and how they discovered their mates and fell in love. The cookies and comics she always brought for him helped, too. Alfred had not yet managed to properly conjure a bouquet of flowers for her, but she didn't seem to mind, for she had plenty of her own.

Though Alfred was not scheduled to perform at the wedding, he had agreed to contract terms with the Kassir-bann Brothers and was set to begin performing his magic show on a regular basis very soon. He had not been back to visit Dr. White as of yet, but a mysterious and explosive display of fireworks had recently gone off in the Eisen Gardens' courtyard. Despite Dr. White's repeated claims that Alfred was to blame, the local police informed him that the magician was not a suspect.

Miroslav and his new foster family came to the wedding as well. The Farraguts were a wonderful young couple from Sacramento who were unable to have children of their own. Denny, Miroslav's new father, had brought a pair of base-ball gloves to the wedding, and he and Miroslav were enjoying a game of catch on the riverbank. Miroslav would be starting junior high in the fall and was thinking of trying out for the baseball team. His father had taken him to his first big league game a few weeks ago. The Giants lost to the Reds by a score of 5-3, but Miroslav told Fred he didn't care at all about the score. It was still the most fun he'd ever had in his entire life.

Harry Gorman had also traveled north for the wedding. Mr. Sowerbraun had generously granted him an extended vacation. He had not brought a date, but he had been dancing with a young woman named Sara, one of Jimmy's cousins, for most of the reception. Surprisingly, he proved to be an excellent dancer, gliding very regally across the wooden platform that they had set upon the grass. Most of the guests agreed that he and Sara would make a perfect match.

Elmer Marshal, no longer a sheriff, now a community organizer, had graced the Oglesburgs with his presence and was enjoying a fantastic cup of coffee along with much pleasant conversation. The topic of his new and fruitful work in the community frequently and *accidentally* arose during conversation, and his role in the apprehension of the four, now-famous thieves had greatly expanded in the telling. When she wasn't dragging him to the dance floor to embarrass himself, Renee was correcting the errors and omissions in his account. For the past few months, Elmer had made several trips up to Bithbon to visit with Renee "about the case," and they had developed a budding friend-ship, which was obvious watching them laugh on the dance floor. Each time Elmer nearly tripped over himself, he reached out for Renee's hand for support, and she patiently walked him through the different steps of the line dances. Stan and Fred joked that the former sheriff must have been trying to mess up because nobody was that bad on accident.

Gemma Lee, sadly, could not attend the festivities, as she was on tour with her new band—The Hammer Heads. The video of her solo on the SonicAmp had become an internet sensation, and she was quickly discovered and scooped up by a musical group in need of a true "ax-woman." Their entire North American tour was sold out, and a European tour was already being scheduled. Radical Hal, Phinney and Miller had joined the band as roadies. Gemma sent their love and a specialty cake in the shape of a guitar with a yellow sports bra dangling from the neck, which proved to be very delicious. Even the most persnickety guests agreed that it was a truly savory banana-flavored dessert.

As the dancing and eating continued, Fred, Stan and Jimmy sat apart from the crowd, talking beneath the over-hanging boughs of a cottonwood tree.

"It's a beautiful wedding," said Jimmy.

"I know," said Fred, whose face was hurting from smiling all day.

"You've gone full Han Solo now, have you?" said Stan.

Fred laughed. "And thanks, Jimmy," he added.

"Hey, Jim, what's up with the vest?" Stan asked.

"What do you mean?" Jimmy asked, adjusting the thin fabric.

"Oh, I'm sorry, *professor*," Stan joked. "For what purpose be thy tunic that covers only thou torso?"

"Well, if you must know, I'm going back to school in the fall," Jimmy answered. "I'm going to study to become a teacher, so I figured it was time I started wearing some-thing other than track suits. Plus, I think it looks cool."

"Cool?" Stan asked. "Name one person who wore a vest who wasn't a total fogey."

"Uhm, James Bond, Doc Holiday, Marty McFly—"

"Not fair, McFly's was a bubble vest," Stan objected.

Jimmy thought for a moment. "And none other than Han Solo himself!" he said.

"That's true, I never thought about it that way," said Stan. "Hey, do you think they make them in our size?" he asked Fred.

Fred just shrugged his shoulders and laughed. "Well, I hope someday we get you for a teacher," he said.

"Yeah, what are you going to teach?" asked Stan. "Potions or Defense against the Dark Arts?"

"Very funny," Jimmy smirked. "I'll probably teach history or philosophy or maybe both. And you two better hope you don't get me because I won't tolerate any funny business," he said in a mocking tone with an exaggerated shake of his finger. The boys laughed.

"I heard that *GUTS* is coming back on the air with brand new episodes," said Stan.

"Yeah, I heard that, too," said Jimmy rather casually, which Fred found rather odd, considering how much Jimmy loved the show.

"You're not going to tell us if they asked you to come on the show, are you?" said Stan.

"Oh, they definitely asked me to come," answered Jimmy, still not seeming as excited as Fred would have guessed.

"But that's great, Jim!" said Stan. "It's what you've always wanted."

"Eh, I told them no," said Jimmy.

"What?" Stan said, clearly taken aback. "Why?"

"I suppose because once you've done the real thing, going on a game show seems, well, kind of boring," said Jimmy. "Besides, I've moved on. I've got more exciting things coming up."

Fred had never been prouder of his neighbor—not even when he'd finally earned his black belt. Stan and Fred had attended Jimmy's belt test as promised, bringing signs that read "Betty Sue for President." With his friends there for support, Jimmy had finally broken all the boards and taken home his belt. He had been more than delighted to buy the pizza afterwards.

"I never thought I'd see the day," said Stan, still shaking his head in surprise.

"Here's your bowl of fruit, Stan," said Katie Greene, returning from the tables of food and handing Stan a bowl brimming with all types of fruit.

"Thanks, Katie," said Stan as she sat down right next to him, her eyes trained wistfully on his face.

"Umm, err, do you want some?" Stan asked.

Katie nodded, opened her mouth and closed her eyes, clearly begging Stan to spoon her some fruit himself. Stan gave Fred a look of hopeless bewilderment. Fred bit his lip to hold in a laugh. Stan cautiously fed Katie a spoonful, and she giggled happily.

"Well, I'm off," said Jimmy, standing up and brushing grass from his trousers. "I've got some applications to finish, and I teach archery tomorrow at the Y."

"Seeya, Jim," said Stan, and Katie gave a little wave.

"Goodbye, 'Deadeye,'" said Fred.

"Until next time, my dear hobbits." Jimmy gave a bow and went walking through the trees, whistling some elvish tune of yore.

"Hey, Katie," said Stan. "Why don't you find a spot by the river to stick your feet in, and I'll be there in a second."

"Okay, Stanny-poo," she cooed. "Don't keep me waiting for too long."

"Uhm, I won't," Stan said, shaking his head. Katie stood up and skipped away.

"She seems smitten there, Stanny-poo," said Fred.

"Yeah, I think it was the video of *me* saving *your* butt that got plastered all over the news that won her over," Stan gibed.

"Really, I thought it was your charm and winning smile," Fred jabbed back. "I'm sure the fact that you're the new star linebacker on the football team didn't hurt."

"No, I don't suppose it did," said Stan.

The boys smiled. They grew silent for a moment as they both looked at the wedding guests, who were attempting to do the electric slide but failing miserably.

"Well, I guess you did it, Fred," said Stan. "I'm not sure if I still believe how you did it, but you got your parents back together."

"*We* did it," corrected Fred.

"Yeah," said Stan. "And the whole world saw it."

"Which is more than I could have hoped for," said Fred. "And yet, I don't think we made much of a difference. That *Real Millionaire Momsters* show is the most popular show in the world, I guess."

"Joanne make any special guest appearances?" asked Stan.

"Not yet," said Fred. "She's still in rehab at Eisen Gardens, I think."

"Then we're still safe," said Stan, winking. "Well, we have to believe that some people saw what you, I mean, *we* did, and it made them at least think about things," said Stan. "Did I tell you that my dad saw us?"

"Really?" said Fred. "That's great. So how was it? Seeing your father, I mean?"

"Not so bad," said Stan. "Actually, I was scared out of

my mind." He laughed. "But, you know, I knew I could do it. It's just like everything else now—I just kind of know I can do it. Once you've braved Mordor, visiting prison is like a day at the beach, right?" Fred laughed with him. "My dad was happy to see me. And it was good for me to see him. He's my dad, and he messed up, but he doesn't have that greed anymore. He said he was proud of me and that what we did inspired him to be a better man."

"Sounds like it went well then," said Fred, smiling.

"Yeah," said Stan. "He also told me that Leo is not exactly having a good time inside."

"I'm sure prison isn't as comfortable as what he's used to," said Fred. "But I bet he's still better off than Joanne. I hear the interior decorating over at Eisen Gardens just isn't to her liking."

Stan laughed. "No, I doubt that she's going to like anything over at Eisen Gardens. I couldn't think of a more fitting punishment for both Dr. White and Joanne than to have to spend time with each other."

"No, I guess I couldn't either," laughed Fred.

"Did you see that they posted the class lists already for next year?" Stan asked.

"No," said Fred excitedly. "Are we in the same class?"

"Of course," said Stan. "The streak continues."

"Who do we have?" Fred asked.

"Uhm, a Mrs. Gorf, I think," Stan answered.

"Yikes, she sounds terrible," said Fred.

"Well, anybody is better than Mrs. Bonneville," said Stan.

"You've got that right," agreed Fred.

"Well, I better get to Katie," said Stan, "Or else she'll have a hissy-fit. I'll see you at the tree house later?" he asked.

"Of course," answered Fred. "I owe you a beat down in Smash Bros."

"Yeah, *that's* likely," said Stan and then moved away towards the river.

Fred leaned his back against the tree, closed his eyes and listened to the music. Everything was perfect—he couldn't have imagined a better ending. His only worry was that it wouldn't last. With his eyes closed it felt too much like a dream, and he grew scared that the laughing people and the tables of good food would all suddenly disappear when he woke, so he opened them quickly. Luckily his parents were still spinning and laughing on the dance floor, and their guests were heaping their plates full with food.

Fred felt a wave of relief and joy pass over him. It was all very real. He had succeeded on his quest, and he had brought his parents back together. Another huge smile came to his face. His parents saw him watching them, and Solomon whispered something to Lucy and then the two of them came walking towards Fred.

"Hey, Fred-O," Solomon said, sitting down by his son and tousling the hair on the top of his head. "You having a good time?"

"Yeah, Dad," Fred answered. "The best."

"That was an unbelievable cake that Gemma sent," said Lucy. "And it looks like Alfred and Stan are both sick in love. And Harry and Renee aren't far behind."

"Don't let her hear you say that," said Lucy.

Fred laughed.

After a short pause, Solomon said, "So, Fred-O, we were wondering if you were ready for another adventure."

"So soon?" Fred asked. "I don't know. We just got finished with the last one."

"Well...it's not that kind of adventure," said Lucy.

"What do you mean?" Fred asked.

Solomon and Lucy looked at each other and smiled.

"Your mother's pregnant," said Solomon. "You're going to have a baby sister."

Fred's jaw dropped, and his eyes grew as wide as saucers.

ACKNOWLEDGMENTS

First and foremost, I want to thank my parents, whose love and generosity have always helped enable my storytelling journey. Thank you for reading to me, for making up tall tales, and for sharing countless books, none of which I plan to return any time soon.

I also want to thank my hilarious, dynamic, loving, and lovely wife, Camrynn, and her fabulous family. This book wouldn't be what it is without their influence and support.

To everyone who put up with me at the Penn State creative writing program, thank you, too, for your patience and guidance. Special thanks to the wonderful writers and teachers Toni Jensen and Bill Cobb for their earnest engagement with my work and for their continuing counsel.

Finally, I want to thank Craig Randall and the team at Switchboard Publishing LLC for seeing the promise in this book and making it a reality. I'm really grateful to be counted among their authors.

Made in USA - North Chelmsford, MA
1341999_9781959510901
11.22.2022 1550